"Dragons,"

No one had

her face.

"Dragons,"

rose to her feet

"Look!" she cried. "Silver dragons!"

Like quicksilver arrows just loosed from a bow, three silver dragons shot up from the valley. Two from the left, one from the right, they rose unerringly to the receding form of Pyrothraxus. At the last moment, Pyrothraxus saw them and swerved. They crossed just beneath him, screaming, long plumes of white frost arcing from their mouths to strike and freeze his wings. A gout of flame from his nostrils responded to the attack, but too late and much too slowly. The smaller, quicker silver dragons rose above him and met, hanging in the air for a moment, as though conferring, while Pyrothraxus laboriously increased the beat of his wings.

Bridges of Time Series

Spirit of the Wind
Chris Pierson

Legacy of Steel
Mary H. Herbert

The Silver Stair
Jean Rabe

The Rose and the Skull
Jeff Crook

DragonLance®

The Rose and the Skull

BRIDGES OF TIME SERIES

JEFF CROOK

For Jessie, who, for some odd reason, married me.

Cover art by Larry Elmore

First Printing: March 1999

Library of Congress Catalog Card Number: 98-85784

9 8 7 6 5 4 3 2 1

ISBN: 0-7869-1336-3

21336XXX1501

U.S., CANADA,
ASIA, PACIFIC, & LATIN AMERICA
Wizards of the Coast, Inc.
P.O. Box 707
Renton, WA 98057-0707
800-324-6496

EUROPEAN HEADQUARTERS
Wizards of the Coast, Belgium
P.B. 2031
2600 Berchem
Belgium
+32-70-23-32-77

Visit our website at www.tsr.com

Chapter One

"The old order changeth, yielding place to the new."
Idylls of the King - Alfred, Lord Tennyson

The smaller, nimbler Ergothian pirate ship steadily drew away from *Donkaren*, much to the chagrin of the slower ship's captain. Sir Wayhollan Farstar stood on the forecastle of his war galleon and pounded her skull-carved rail with his mailed fist, watching in disgust as the black-sailed sloop receded toward the shore of the Isle of Cristyne. He'd hunted the black sloop across the Sirrion Sea and down the coasts of Northern Ergoth for many a week now, and just when it seemed she was in his grasp, she'd escaped, aided by a fair wind, slipping past his sentry ships in the night and sailing south. If ever she reached the harbors of Cristyne, there was little even he could do. Cristyne was officially neutral territory, but the people there cared little for the authority of the Knights of Takhisis, even going so far as to harbor wanted pirates—"privateers" they called them. Everyone knew the citizens of Cristyne were allied with the Knights of Solamnia, and Captain Farstar suspected the black sloop was but a front for Solamnic operations. From Palanthas to the Bay of Balifor, she had harried the Knights of Takhisis's shipping for many a month, knocking off supply ships and avoiding every war galleon

1

sent to capture her. *Donkaren* was a fast warship and her captain experienced, but as he watched the sloop grow smaller and smaller, Captain Farstar knew she'd escaped once again. That knowledge ate at him like a cancer.

"More sail!" he shouted.

"Captain, we've run up every yard of cloth we have on board," said the first mate behind him. "We can do nothing against this unfavorable wind."

"Where can we find more wind?" the captain wondered aloud.

"In the olden days, a cleric might have served, praying to our Dark Queen for a wind to aid us," the mate answered, "but of course, nowadays . . ."

"Nowadays Takhisis doesn't answer our prayers, I know," the captain finished for him.

"You haven't got a rabbit's foot, have you? I'd settle for a little luck."

"Nay sir," the mate chuckled. "I haven't. A kender's foot is luckier, they say."

"You haven't got one of those, have you?" the captain asked.

"Nay sir. I lost mine in a game of dice before we set sail," the first mate said solemnly. "We might toss salt over our shoulders."

"That's only if you spill it, to ward off bad luck," the captain said.

"Aye, that's right. I had forgotten, sir," he sighed. "Me old mother used to have a store of knowledge about such matters, the gaining and losing of luck. Let me see if I can remember any of it, though I fear it was all poppycock." He snapped his fingers and slapped the palm of his hand against his forehead, as though trying to knock loose the memories from his brain.

Captain Farstar checked the progress of the black sloop. It was but a tiny dot in the distance, almost lost against the rising bulk of the Isle of Cristyne.

The captain swore under his breath, but the mate was still stuck on the subject of good luck. "There was something about a broom and a chair," he said absently while tapping his teeth with his finger. "Perhaps you are supposed to swallow something. Now what was it?"

Captain Farstar was just about to lift the mate by his belt and throw him into the sea when the lookout above called, "She's turning, sir!"

"What's that you say?" the captain shouted.

"The black sloop, she's tacking east, sir," the lookout answered.

"Are you certain?" he asked as he ran to the bowrail and peered as best he could over the waves.

"Perhaps it was bread," the mate muttered.

"Yes sir, she's turning hard to port. It looks as though she's got into some reefs and is trying to avoid them," the lookout said.

"There are no reefs on the north side of the island," Farstar remembered aloud. He barely made out the profile of the ship against the dark shore of the island, and he wished he had some kind of farseeing glass like the kind the gnomes made.

"She's running, sir. She's putting on full sail and running!" the lookout shouted with joy.

"Takhisis be praised. Maybe she does still hear our prayers," Captain Farstar said.

"Prepare to come about!"

The first mate was jolted into action. The ship began to creak and groan as the sailors hurried to their tasks. He shouted up to the lookout, "What's she running from?"

"Can't tell, sir," the lookout answered.

"Come about. Helm, steer for the head of the island. We'll catch her there." *Donkaren* heeled over as the helmsman steered to port and the stronger wind took her sails.

Salt spray began to burst from her bow as she cleft the waves, gaining speed.

"There's a true lucky sign," the first mate shouted into the rising wind. "A dragon-shaped cloud, blowing in from the west."

"I see it," the captain shouted in answer.

He looked up. The lookout was shouting and pointing at something, but he couldn't hear what the man said. He walked back along the starboard rail to get out of the spray so he could see. Following the line of the lookout's arm, he saw the man pointing to the same cloud the first mate had spotted.

The cloud was indeed dragon-shaped. It had even grown a little in the last few minutes.

Suddenly, the cloud dipped lower, closing on the fleeing black sloop. Captain Farstar felt a lump rise in his throat and watched in growing terror as the cloud slipped in above the mast of the Ergothian ship. Rooted to the deck, he could not turn away or shout orders; he could only watch in horror. Fire boiled out from the cloud and descended on the tiny pirate ship, flames leaped along her deck, swallowed her sails. Little globules of fire began to leap into the water all along her sides, and Captain Farstar knew they were the shapes of men, the ship's crew, now living torches desperately seeking the water.

The dragon banked, rising, and turned for another pass at the pirate ship. At that moment, Captain Farstar found his feet and his voice.

He turned and raced toward the helm, shouting, "Bring her round, bring her round! Put the wind at her back!" So riveted by the sight was the helmsman that the captain reached the helm before he responded. Captain Farstar threw his weight against the wheel and swung her around himself.

As the ship turned, the wind rippled out her sails and filled them with a boom. They strained taut, and the masts creaked; the ship lurched forward. The crew had not moved; they all watched the spectacle in silent fascination. Captain Farstar glanced back over his shoulder.

The black sloop was a pillar of fire and billowing black smoke. The dragon glided over her bow, headfirst into the flames, and it settled on her, beating its wings to hold itself aloft. The monster was so enormous, the pirate ship looked like a toy beneath it, and she sank almost immediately under the dragon's weight. The sea closed over her in a rush of steam, mercifully dousing her flames. The dragon rose off her, pounding the air with its huge wings, and aided by the thermals rising from the steam, it soon soared high above the wreck. Only the ship's mast still stood above the water—charred and licked by flames. Captain Farstar turned back to the helm.

His crew erupted in yells of delight, cheering the dragon. "Captain, why are we turning?" the first mate asked. "He's a red dragon, for sure. You can tell by his fiery breath. The reds are our allies."

"Open the weapons locker," the captain responded. "Distribute crossbows to all hands!"

"Why, what for?" the mate asked.

"Do it, man!" the captain ordered.

With a puzzled expression, the first mate turned to obey. As he walked slowly along the poop deck, he returned the questioning gazes of the crew with baffled shrugs while he fiddled with his keys, searching for the one that opened the weapons locker. Spray from the leaping bow drenched the deck and the sailors on it.

One of the men pointed and said, "Here he comes."

"Coming to check us out, to see why we're running, I'm sure," the first mate responded lowly, so his voice wouldn't carry.

"He'll not attack, once he sees our flag, will he?" a man asked, brushing salt spray from his eye.

"Of course not. Once he sees our lily and skull design, he'll leave us be. No red would dare attack one of the Dark Queen's ships," the mate said. "Ah ha! there you are." He slid the correct key into the massive lock sealing the weapons locker and turned it. The lock popped open.

"By the gods, he's a big one," the crewman said with undisguised awe.

"Nay, he only looked big in the distance, on account of . . ." The first mate's voice trailed off as he glanced up and saw the dragon approaching on the wind. He stepped back and shouted up to the captain, "Sir, what kind of dragon is that? He looks awful big!"

"He's not one of ours," the captain answered.

His eyes still locked on the dragon, the first mate opened the locker with a sharp jerk on the handle. He stepped inside and began handing out crossbows and boxes of heavy quarrels.

The captain maintained his stand at the helm while sending the helmsman below to assist the first mate. He stood alone, the sharp sea spray dousing his hair, and muttered unheard curses into the wind, occasionally glancing back to check the progress of the dragon. As it drew closer, the dragon's wings seemed to spread out across all the sky, from horizon to horizon. Never before had Captain Farstar seen such a dragon, and he'd served in the Dark Queen's navy since before the Chaos War. He had heard of such dragons, new dragons from across the sea. Larger and more powerful than any dragons ever before encountered, they cared little whom they attacked or whom they destroyed.

The first mate ordered the sailors and soldiers of *Donkaren* to their posts. The captain, watching his crew moving as though in a daze, their eyes ever on the dragon, already knew his ship was lost. Still, he held to the wheel, hoping against hope. He drew his saber and glanced once more over his shoulder.

The dragon came in at mast-height. The scales of its underbelly were the color of desert rock—a dull burnt orange that seemed to radiate heat. Its bulk filled all the sky, its great shadow blocking out the sun, so that it seemed the ship had sailed into the Abyss. The dragon's wings robbed *Donkaren* of her wind, and her sails began to droop. She slowed. The sailors and soldiers along her rail stared up in fascinated horror, like nestlings hypnotized by the serpent approaching their nest. The dragon's great head, almost as large as the ship itself, snaked down to gaze at them in return. The dragon seemed almost to hover above them, to hang impossibly in the air, its wing tips dipping hissingly in the sea. The heat emanating from its body beat down on the crew's upturned faces like an unseen sun, drawing the moisture from their mouths and their eyes, drying ropes and rigging, stiffening salt-encrusted sails. Steam began to rise from the decks.

"Fire your weapons!" the captain shouted, but it seemed as though the sound of his voice was also sucked up by the intense heat of the dragon's body. "Damn your hides," he croaked. "Attack!"

The dragon's great head snapped around to stare at the captain at the sound of his voice. Captain Farstar stiffened, then staggered back as if from an unseen blow. The dragon's jaws parted.

The first mate had dragged his crossbow to his shoulder. His muscles felt numbed, paralyzed, like in a nightmare, every movement an agony. He sighted at the dragon's eye and pulled the trigger.

At that moment, the dragon breathed. A pillar of white hot liquid fire descended upon Captain Farstar and burst through the deck to the cabins below. Wood, canvas, rope, flesh, all erupted in flames or turned instantly to ash from the heat. The first mate watched his bolt rise toward the dragon's eye, trailing smoke. The fletching turned to ash without ever catching fire, and it veered off course, striking the dragon's neck and bouncing off its scales. As it fell, it burst into flame and was consumed before ever it reached water.

And then it was gone. The dragon vanished from overhead with a roar of wind. Fire leaped along the rigging. The ship's pitch seams began to bubble as flames raced below deck. Men dashed about, screaming, some of them alive with flame, others wild-eyed, crying, tears streaking their soot-stained faces. They abandoned the ship in droves, and those who could swam for the distant shore of the Isle of Cristyne. The dragon swooped over them and doused them in flame. The sea exploded in steam.

The first mate stood at the rail, an intense heat, burning through to the soles of his feet. He knew any moment the deck would collapse, but his only thought was to remain with the ship. "She's my ship now, my duty. I'm her captain, if only for a moment," he said aloud, to no one. A flaming yardarm crashed through the deck behind him, and roaring flames shot up through the hole. As the rigging burned through, the wind lifted the sails out to sea. Ghostly flaming sheets rising on the breeze, they shredded into tatters and wisps and fell with a hiss into the water. *Donkaren* began to settle as she burst her seams and let in the sea.

Then, the dragon came again, like a whirlwind, its huge wings thumping the air as it descended on the ship from above. As it dropped, it stretched out its claws and took the ship by the bow, staving in her sides with its massive talons. The dragon was much too large to settle on the ship, so it kept its wings moving, but still its massive weight dragged her down by the bow. Her stern rose into the air.

The first mate held to the door of the weapons locker to keep from sliding down the ship's sloping deck. The sea rushed up, dousing the flames but sending up a scalding steam. With a groaning hiss, she slipped below the waves, and the first mate, holding tight, went with her. The blue closed over his head. He released his hold and rolled in the sudden quiet of the sea, feeling her cool hands ease his burns.

As he slowly sank into the dark, the first mate saw the ship rising above him. He watched in awe as her blackened sides slid by him, massive, like the passing of a great whale. She rose to the silver surface overhead and burst free of the water, leaving it and taking to the air. Her passing pulled him up with her, and finally, he too breathed free air again.

He bobbed on the surface for a moment, then found a bit of wreckage and climbed wearily atop it. He noticed with some surprise that it was the door to the weapons locker. Exhausted, he rolled over and looked up at the darkening sky. There he saw the dragon, rising, *Donkaren* gripped firmly by the bow and streaming water out all her holes. Like some great bird of prey with a fish in its claws, the dragon flew slowly away to the west.

Chapter Two

Lord Gunthar leaned forward in his chair and tapped a spoon against the silver cup set before his plate. He cleared his throat and smoothed his long gray mustaches, the symbol of his Solamnic heritage. The cup was engraved with kingfishers and roses, and the handle of the spoon was gilded with roses and stamped with a golden crown. These symbols matched the decorations on his antique armor, on his breastplate, the greaves on his legs, and the broad silver filigree binding his flowing silver locks. Rose, kingfisher, and crown were repeated in all the things around him—the back of the wooden chair in which he sat, the hilt of the ancient longsword hanging at his side, even the tapestry displayed behind him, with its scenes of knights astride dragons of silver thread and gold embroidery. One rode at the forefront of the battle, a great silver lance in his hand, his mustaches rippling in the wind of his speed. The knight on the tapestry looked like a younger version of Gunthar, for Lord Gunthar uth Wistan, Grand Master of the Knights of Solamnia, was old, his mustaches gray, the lines of care etched deeply in his weatherworn face. The hand that held the spoon and tapped the cup, the same hand that had once wielded a sword in battle, now shook slightly with the first signs of palsy.

He set the spoon beside his plate and cleared his throat. He rose slowly, carefully shifting his weight onto his feet before standing. He cleared his throat again, then wet his lips with some wine.

"Thank you, Knights, ladies, and gentlemen, for attending this banquet on such short notice," Gunthar said. "I am sure you are curious as to why I have called you all here this evening. This will be explained shortly. I hope that in the meantime you will enjoy the fare of the kitchen of Castle uth Wistan. There is plenty of meat, wine, and ale if you like it."

He smiled and stroked his mustaches, his eyes wandering to the smoky raftered ceiling. "Speaking of ale, I am reminded of a time during the War of the Lance, when two most unexpected visitors showed up at my door. At the time, I didn't appreciate the importance of this happenstance, if that is what it was, for I was weary from the road, having just returned from seeing the fleet on its way to Palanthas. That was during the War of the Lance, just before the battle at the High Clerist's Tower."

Lord Gunthar continued to unfold his tale, though few heard him. Most had not even noticed that he had risen from his chair, so intent were they on devouring the roast meats set before them, guzzling the wine slopped generously into cups whenever they wanted it, or wagering on fights between gully dwarves and hounds over the scraps and bones thrown to them. Gunthar stood before them like a man standing before the sea, and his words were lost in the tide of their noise.

His table stood upon a raised dais at the front of the hall, beneath the great tapestry. To his right and left sat Knights of some renown, those who had attained the highest rank—the Order of the Rose, and the leaders of the orders of the Crown and Sword. To the left and right of this main table were two other tables, both very long. The table to the right was occupied by Knights of the Order of the Crown, while at the table to the left sat the Knights of the Order of the Sword. Opposite Gunthar's table stood a fourth table. It was unoccupied, though places had been set for twelve. The four tables formed a great square, and the floor in the middle seethed and boiled with gully dwarves and large gray hounds of the kind used to hunt boar and deer.

"And so the old man said," Gunthar continued, chuckling to himself, " 'Bring me the good ale, from the barrel beneath the cellar stairs.' Well, you can imagine my surprise! I mean, how on Krynn could he have known about the barrel beneath the stairs? Of course, you've probably all heard that Fizban was really Paladine, so it is perfectly obvious now how he knew about the barrel beneath the stairs, but at the time I was very much taken aback. And of course, he had a kender with him. . . ."

Gunthar laughed at the memory for a long time. His eyes seemed to get lost in the smoky shadows of the ceiling. He didn't finish his tale, at least not out loud, although it appeared from the smiles that occasionally danced across his thin lips that he was telling it to himself.

But no one of any real importance was listening. While the Knights caroused and the hounds cracked bones, gully dwarves licked spilled wine from the flagstones and Gunthar silently reminisced, a lone gully dwarf stood on the floor before Gunthar's table, apparently enraptured. It was almost as though he really understood what the old man had been saying. Gully dwarves were the lowest of all creation, despised by nearly every race upon Krynn. As a people, they were universally filthy, stupid, greedy, and malicious—traits they themselves took pride in and cultivated. Most people, in fact, would rather their homes be infested with plague-carrying rats than gully dwarves. But Gunthar seemed to tolerate them well enough, and they did provide a few moments of diversion for the Knights gathered to feast in Gunthar's hall.

It was highly unlikely that this particular gully dwarf had the slightest conception of what Gunthar was saying. More likely, he had eaten something that didn't agree with him (another rare occurrence in gully dwarf annals!) and was simply waiting for it to pass, and the smile on his face was like the smile of a human baby under similar distress. It just so happened that he was facing Lord Gunthar when the attack overtook him, and thus the source of confusion. Or if he did understand a word or two, his attention was probably caught by the mention of ale and food, and he was only waiting to hear these words again.

In any case, as the old man resumed his seat, like his image reflected in a carnival mirror the gully dwarf sank to the floor in front of him. His baggy clothes collapsed around him, until he looked like a half-empty sack of potatoes topped by a small dirty face with a bulbous nose and big, watery, and rather mousy eyes. Atop his head, he wore a ragged fur cap of rat hides loosely stitched. His own hair stuck out through the holes in the cap, which gave him the look of someone who has just woken up.

As Gunthar finished, a cloud of quiet sadness darkened his eyes. His gaze strayed to the window that overlooked the courtyard to the east, and he sighed deeply, shaking his head.

"I agree, milord," said the Knight to Gunthar's right, mistaking the cause of the old man's sudden sadness. "These young Knights have no respect for the old tales or the old ways."

Gunthar started from his reverie. "What's that, Liam?" he asked.

"I was mentioning the lack of respect of the younger generation for the tales of the old days," the Knight said, his face stern as he eyed the other Knights.

"They'd like to be making their own tales, my friend," Gunthar said, "not listening to the rehashing of all our old adventures."

"But don't we pull lessons from the past and apply their wisdom to the future?" Liam asked his elderly master. "How can they expect to triumph on the battlefield if they don't listen to and learn from those who fought before them?"

"The old orders are passing away, Liam. Things aren't as they were when I was young, or even when you were young. The old lessons no longer apply. As Sturm taught us, rules and measures are fleeting. They must change with time or become useless and burdensome. For the Knight, the only thing that remains constant through all that change is his honor." Gunthar smiled. "Or her honor," he amended as he glanced around the room. Of those Knights gathered at this feast, almost half their number were women. A few sat at Gunthar's own table.

"Yes, milord," Liam acquiesced as he lifted a cup of wine to his lips.

"And who knows, perhaps one day even these ragged creatures," Gunthar continued, indicating with a wave of his hand the score or more gully dwarves moiling on the floor with the dogs, "perhaps even they will take their place at this table."

Liam choked and set down his cup.

"Or even kender. Paladine forgive us if we do." Gunthar laughed.

Liam's face grew pale. "Milord?" he gasped.

Gunthar laughed and placed his hand on the shoulder of his friend and fellow Knight. "Oh, don't worry Liam. Such changes are not in my destiny to make. Perhaps, when I am gone and you take my seat at this table, circumstances will dictate that you implement such a drastic change to our ancient order. Or perhaps the one who succeeds you will do it. Who knows? I merely speculate. Stranger things have happened."

"Yes, milord Gunthar," Liam said.

"Now, mark that little one there on the floor." Gunthar said good-naturedly as he speared a hunk of roast with his fork and used it to point at the gully dwarf sitting on the floor before their table. "He's not like the others of his kind. If ever there was Knightly material among the Aghar, he is it. Watch how he follows my every word."

"I think he is more interested in your food, milord," Liam said, noticing how the gully dwarf's mouth had dropped open at the sight of a piece of meat being waved at him. A long string of drool dribbled down his chin and rolled off the thistley mass of his beard and onto his shirt, joining the stains of a thousand others there.

"Nonsense. He understands every word I say. Don't you, my boy?" Gunthar finished by shouting.

The gully dwarf nodded vigorously, upsetting his rat-skin cap. It dropped down over his eyes. With a snarl, he grabbed it and bit it, rolling over backwards, tumbling a large dog, which then fell on top of him. A second gully dwarf, thinking the first had caught something tasty, leaped in for a bite. Both vanished in a swirl of gray-furred bodies and filthy, baggy clothes. Gunthar roared with laughter.

"As you say, milord," Liam said.

"Why so formal this eventide, Liam? Whatever is the matter with you?" Gunthar asked.

"May I be frank?" Liam asked.

"Be whoever you like. This is supposed to be a festive occasion," Gunthar joked.

Liam returned his master's attempt at jocularity with a hard stare. The old man's smile faded. Liam then said, "Milord is too lenient with these younger Knights. Listen how they carouse, like common adventurers in some seedy wilderness alehouse. One can hardly hear oneself think in here. They have no respect for your lordship or your house, and milord does nothing when they trample his hospitality. They assault the servants in word and deed, and milord does nothing. We gather here to feast for the slightest of reasons, while the Knighthood deteriorates."

"Well, I just thought . . ." Gunthar began, but Liam continued.

"Our numbers dwindle, and we replace our losses, out of necessity, under less strict guidelines. This *rabble* is the result. And rather than using the old Measure to enforce some sort of discipline, milord allows them a free rein," he said.

Gunthar rose from his seat, and though old, his stature was nonetheless dominating. Some parts of the room grew quiet, sensing the sudden tension. The small gully dwarf crawled from beneath a pile of dogs and other gully dwarfs, his rat-skin cap intact but sporting a few new holes. He resumed his seat on the floor before the table, his little black eyes fixed expectantly upon his master.

Gunthar turned to the others at his own table. "Is this true? Do others feel that I am too lenient?" he asked, not in a loud voice, so the others would not hear.

No one responded. Most seemed absorbed in fiddling with the food on their plates. Only two seemed confident enough to return their master's gaze—a female Knight with fiery locks sitting at the left end of the table, and a balding male Knight sitting to Liam's right.

"Lady Meredith, is this how you feel?" Gunthar asked the first.

She opened her mouth to respond but then shut it and merely nodded, turning her attention to the servant refilling her cup.

"Quintayne?" Gunthar then said, turning.

The balding Knight nervously smoothed the wisps of hair still covering his pate. "Out of respect for your lordship . . ." he began. "Well, we thought it best to . . . um . . . well, we thought we could . . . um . . ."

"We did not feel it was our place to tell your lordship how to maintain the affairs of his own house," Liam finished.

"Until now," Gunthar said. He slowly resumed his seat.

"I am sorry, milord," Liam said in a low voice.

"Yes, yes, I know Liam. No need to apologize," Gunthar sighed. "Perhaps I am a bit too lenient, but it is only because they are so young. Unlike most of us, who knew from the day we were born that we would become Knights, most of these young people never dreamed that they could one day join our ranks. While we were born and bred with discipline every moment of our lives, they are the children of war and know only the civilian's code of survival. I think if we treat them too harshly, many would leave us.

"A time will come, soon I think, when they shall be forced to learn the hard measures of discipline. We live in relative peace now, but as you all know, in war the only thing that sets us above the rest is the discipline among our ranks on the battlefield. We fight not as a body of individual soldiers but as a single unit, and only our unquestioning devotion to our duty, as defined by the Rule and the Measure, makes this possible."

"This is what we fear most, milord," Liam said fervently, his dark eyes flashing. "When the time comes that they must submit to discipline and direction, they will be unable to do so. Better to teach them now, in peace, than in the fires of war, where one mistake can mean disaster."

"They shall learn their lessons hard or not at all," Gunthar patiently argued. "That is the way of the younger generation. But they'll learn the Measure and the reason for it in practice, not in books or lectures from boring old men. Those who survive will be the better for it."

"But how many will die, how many battles will be lost before they learn?" Liam protested.

"You only have to win one battle to win the war, Liam," Gunthar said, "the last one."

Liam looked away lest his anger get the better of him. None of the other Knights turned his way; most picked at their food or pretended to sip at their wine. A few of the Knights at the other tables had grown quiet and were trying to listen to the dispute between their elders. The tension at the head table had even been noticed by the gully dwarves and hounds, who pricked up their ears and waited for something to happen.

For the moment they waited in vain. While Liam collected himself, the female Knight at the end of Gunthar's table said, "Milord Gunthar, we have feasted here three times this month, each time under the nominal excuse of discussing some aspect of your revisions to the Measure of Knightly Conduct. If we only knew why you have called us here tonight, perhaps it would set some hearts at ease."

"At ease, Lady Meredith? What do you fear?" Gunthar asked.

"Milord, we waste away with luxury and feasting," Quintayne responded before she could answer. "We want fighting and adventure, not more meat and wine." From those younger Knights listening there came many an "Aye!" and an occasional "More meat and wine!"

Meredith scowled at her fellow Knight, but she said, "Sir Quintayne is right. There are many Knights here still in need of their quests. We wonder when these will be assigned."

"Yes, yes, I know. We will get around to that when time allows," Gunthar said.

"When time allows!" Liam whispered incredulously.

"There is still much to do here. We can't be sending our forces all over creation fulfilling quests, not while danger lurks at our back door," Gunthar said.

"Danger?" Liam asked.

"Have you forgotten Pyrothraxus? The dragon who holds all the northern half of our island, including the homeland of the gnomes? As the wise man said, it is never good to leave a live dragon out of your calculations."

"If you are so worried about the gnomes, we should send some knights to try and rescue them," Meredith suggested.

"Or we could send someone to rescue the dragon from the gnomes," Quintayne said. Gunthar snorted, and there were chuckles all around.

"We shouldn't stir up the anger of the dragon," Liam chided the others. "He's left us alone for the most part, and we are not yet strong enough to challenge him. No need to bring his anger down upon us now."

"Liam is right. For the moment, we watch and defend, and spend our time fortifying and garrisoning our northern castles," Gunthar said.

"Garrisoning? With whom?" Meredith asked. "Our numbers are slow to rebuild, even with the relaxation of our admission standards."

"That is why I have called you all here tonight, to discuss revisions to the Measure concerning the admission of Knights into our order," Gunthar said. Liam groaned, as did many of the others.

Twice already this month, Gunthar had summoned them from their castles all across the Isle of Sancrist to feast and discuss this very same topic. Nothing had been settled then, and most doubted anything would be settled now. In truth, the majority of Knights in attendance this evening didn't care. The reputation of Gunthar's table was known throughout Krynn. No one turned down an invitation to dine there. So what if it meant listening to the old man babble for a while? They received a hearty meal in the bargain, not to mention all the wine and ale they could drink. It had been this way for going on two years now, and the younger Knights hoped it would go on for quite a few more. The older Knights were a different story altogether. They began to whisper to one another, pausing occasionally to turn worried glances upon their Grand Master.

"Now, before you start complaining, let me say that what I shall propose tonight is not without precedent. I am but building upon what has gone before us. I'll not say any more about it until after supper, when the Grand Chapter is convened. So enjoy your meat, and there is plenty of wine to go round."

A cheer went up from the tables of the younger Knights. "Well, at least they heard me say that," Gunthar said in Liam's ear. Liam chuckled, despite himself.

"Don't be angry with me, my old friend," Gunthar continued privately to Liam. "I need you beside me. I need your strength of will and purpose to help me muddle through. My revisions to the Measure of Knightly Conduct will be my parting gift to the order, but it consumes so much of my time and energy. Without your help in the mundane affairs of the Knighthood, I simply could not manage. I could not have chosen a better protégé, student, or friend."

Liam's face softened at these words. Gunthar studied his friend's face, seeing with fatherly eyes the young Knight of twenty years before, though of late strands of gray frosted his temples. Proud chin, stern brow, dark and brooding eyes, Liam was ever, from then to now, the picture of seriousness. Some of the younger Knights called him "Old Stone Face," for even when angry, his features remained like carved marble. Only the flaring of his nostrils and the quivering of his long, black Solamnic mustaches betrayed his feelings, whether of mirth or of rage. Gunthar knew that Liam's cold manner, considered aloof by most, was but his way of showing his great love for the Knighthood. Still, he hoped that someday Liam would learn compassion, that he'd learn to see things from both sides and not see the world always in black and white.

"You are stubborn, my friend, stubborn and rigid as an elven prince," Gunthar continued. "You love the Knighthood so much you don't want to see it change. But without change, a living thing stagnates and dies. The Knighthood is a living thing, like an ancient tree of the forest, greater than both of us, older, grander. As long as we let it live and breath and grow, it will go on when we are gone. We each have the power to destroy it, by strangling it with our love for it. That is what happened in the past, in the days before the War of the Lance. Great men with the best of intentions tried to strengthen the order by making it more and more rigid. It took a lowly Knight, Sturm Brightblade, and his sacrifice at the High Clerist's Tower, to show us that without the Oath, *Est Solarus oth Mithas*—my honor is my life—the Measure is meaningless."

"I've heard all this before, milord," Liam said, smiling patiently.

"Well, hear it again, and understand it better, Liam. If I teach you nothing else, I hope I teach you this. An honorable Knight does the right thing, even without the Measure. The Measure is this," he said as he snapped his fingers. "It is nothing, without honor.

"These young Knights were admitted based upon their innate sense of honor. For most of them, it wasn't something they were taught, like we were. They learned it on their own, much as Sturm did. Granted, they are undisciplined, but they are not a rabble. When the time comes, their honor will stand them in good stead. You must learn to trust the younger generation and have hope in them, for they are not entirely hopeless."

Liam's eyebrows raised at these words. He turned to look at the carousing horde filling Gunthar's tables, their chins dripping with gravy and their cups more often raised for refilling than in toast. They shouted, laughed, jostled each other in friendly roughhousing, tossed bones and scraps to the gully dwarves and hounds, and laid wagers on who would get which bone and how long he would keep it. Many were Solamnic by birth, once a concrete requirement for entrance into the Knighthood, but now no longer; a growing number of non-Solamnics were filling the ranks, from Abanasinia, Northern Ergoth, the lands around Balifor, Kalaman, Tarsis, even in one case, a barbarian of Estwilde. Many had fled the coming of the great dragons and the destruction these powerful new dragons were causing to the lands of Krynn. Most had been children during the Chaos War, and they were marked by it, having been forced to grow up too soon. One noticed it most in their eyes; at one moment joyful, filled with mirth and good humor, the next quiet and resigned. They lived for the moment, knowing the moments could be few.

"And besides," Gunthar continued, "I call them here on such frequent occasions to keep an eye on them." He smiled. "I'm not so big a fool as you think I am."

"My lord!" Liam exclaimed.

"No, no you don't have to pretend. I know you think I've grown soft in my old age. You may even think I'm a few sticks shy of a cord," Gunthar said.

"Lord Gunthar!" Liam protested. "I never doubted . . ."

"Yes, you have, as have many others. They will doubt me still more after tonight. Look there! My friend has got his cap back," Gunthar said, abruptly changing the subject and pointing to the rat-skin capped gully dwarf.

Gunthar raised his cup in silent toast to the small filthy creature on the floor before him. The gully dwarf's nest-like beard parted in a wide grin, and he blushed to the tips of his ears.

Chapter Three

The feast continued well into the evening. Many Knights ate to the point of near-paralysis, having their fill of beef, pork, mutton, and chicken, as well as ducks, geese, capons, and woodcock. There were also pies galore, in which had been baked all manner of meats and vegetables, potatoes and carrots, leeks from Solamnia, onions, and garlic from the Abanasian plains. There was sheep's stomach stuffed with meat and barley, lamb boiled in butter and poured over a shield-sized platter of rice from Northern Ergoth. It fairly rained bread and sweet butter.

Lord Gunthar ate sparingly, as was his habit. While the meal continued, minstrels played from the alcoves around the hall while skalds sang of battles, Knights, and quests of long ago, of the coming of dragons, of the fall of Istar, of the sacrifices of Huma Dragonbane and of Sturm Brightblade. Some of the gathered Knights told of their most recent adventures or of news from across the sea. Many discussed the devastation of the Dragon Purge. More argued about what was to be done. Few agreed about anything, except for the need for more wine. More wine was served.

Wagers were laid on the game of tossing bones and gristle to Lord Gunthar's hounds and the gully dwarves, but as the gully dwarves were, in general, the more devious and resourceful, they most often obtained the best scraps, with the exception of one small, nimble-footed female hound whose speed and agility won her an unusual share of the spoils. As the evening wore on, she again and again robbed unwitting gully dwarves of their prizes. Once she was caught, and a tug of war ensued between the hound and two gully dwarves over a large and meaty beef bone. The hound had the larger end firmly gripped in her jaws, while the gully dwarves, one male and one female, wrestled over the small end.

Finally with a howl of frustration, the female gully dwarf loosed her hold on the bone and made a leap for the dog, her yellow teeth flashing as she prepared to make use of the gully dwarf's primary mode of attack. She grabbed the hound by the paw and raised it to her mouth. The hound, sensing danger, released the bone and scampered away, her nails scratching at the slick stone floor.

Before the female gully dwarf could enjoy her triumph, a low brown blur dashed in and tossed the gully dwarf free of the bone. The female gully dwarf climbed to her feet and snarling, faced her attacker.

"Gulpfunger spawn," she spat. She shook the nap of hair from her eyes.

She cringed when she saw her opponent. "Uh oh," she said. Her face grew pale, and she quickly glanced around for an escape route.

"That right, Gerde!" shouted the rat-skin-capped gully dwarf who had earlier drawn the attention of Lord Gunthar and Sir Liam Ehrling. "How many times I tell you, no bite my friends the dogs?"

"Don't know," squeaked Gerde. "Two?"

"Two and two and two!" he answered.

Without warning, a silver cup whistled by the rat-skin capped one, splashing him with wine. He ducked, too late to do any good as he'd already been missed, but Gerde took that opportunity to escape. Meanwhile, the male gully dwarf, forgotten in the commotion, slunk away with the bone.

A Knight directly opposite him stood, his face red with anger, his auburn Solamnic mustaches trembling. "You miserable little rat!" the Knight shouted. "You cost me a small fortune just now! I'll teach you to break up a contest on which I've wagered." The Knight reached across the table for a heavy silver meat platter. The gully dwarf curled into a ball on the floor.

"Sir Limpole!" Gunthar roared as he leaped to his feet. The Knight stopped with the tray poised above his head. He eyed the elderly Grand Master. "Put down that tray this instant," Gunthar growled.

"Put it down, I say!" Gunthar shouted when the Knight did not immediately obey. Slowly now, Sir Limpole returned the tray to the table. Gunthar glared across the room at the young Knight of the Sword.

"Consider yourself under sanction, young man, until we can convene a general chapter to review your actions," Gunthar said. A gasp escaped most of the Knights gathered at the feast.

"My lord, I must protest!" the young Knight shrieked in his surprise. "He's . . . he's only a gully dwarf!"

Liam leaned closer to Gunthar and said in a low voice, "My lord, you can't mean . . ."

But Gunthar did not hear him. "Only a gully dwarf! Only a gully dwarf!" he cried, he jaw muscles quivering. He pushed back his chair and strode around the end of the table, down the steps of dais, and over to the cringing gully dwarf. Though elderly, Gunthar's steps were still sure and confident, energetic, not faltering or hesitant. Only the shaking of his hands and the slight nodding of his graying head betrayed his advanced age. He stepped between the gully dwarf and Sir Limpole.

"This gully dwarf is the master of my hounds," Gunthar said.

"My lord, I do apologize," Limpole began, but Gunthar cut him off.

"Servant of this household or not, it matters not. He is weaker than you, and you are bound by honor, Sir Knight, to protect him, never to attack him," Gunthar said. "I have been lenient to a fault with the lot of you, as Sir Liam will testify." He turned slowly to gaze at all the gathered Knights as he continued. Few met his eyes, and those who did quickly looked away.

"Many times, I have let slide your lack of respect for your elders and your betters. When others would have you punished for your insolence, I have argued for leniency. But what Sir Limpole has done here tonight betrays a marked deficiency. Such matters must come before a general chapter for discussion and judgment. These are not my rules. They are the rules of the order to which you all belong."

He turned then to look down at the gully dwarf cringing on the floor. "This little fellow displayed great honor and courage by confronting one of his own kind to protect his charge—the hound. I wonder how many of you would have done the same," he said. At these words, a low mutter circled the room. Sir Quintayne rose from his chair.

"Lord Gunthar, these are strong words. What Sir Limpole did is unconscionable, but to compare a blooded Knight with a gully dwarf . . . why it's . . . it's simply preposterous," Quintayne said.

"Is that so, Sir Knight?"

"There is no comparison. Gully dwarves are notorious cowards. They are weak, cruel, and selfish. They'll sell out their own people if they think it will save their own miserable hides, not to mention the treachery they display when it comes to other races. Only their staggering stupidity keeps them from being a danger to us all. Even a brave man must fear a coward," Quintayne argued.

"Who here can honestly say the same despicable traits are not present in much of the human race? They are present in abundance, even within the Knighthood. There are some of you here tonight who would sell out all your fellows just to preserve your own lives, some who would do anything to revenge an imagined wrong. Some might even kill their own brothers if it increased their power," Gunthar said.

He turned to the gully dwarf. "Stand up, my boy. Don't be afraid." Slowly, the terrified gully dwarf rose to his feet, but he shrank as best he could behind Gunthar's legs, clinging to the old man's knees and not daring to face the stern looks of the gathered Knights.

Gathering his courage, Sir Limpole said, "There are some here who would say you care more for these vermin than you do your own Knights, Lord Gunthar."

"I do care for my gully dwarves a great deal, especially this one. They are weak and deserve our protection. If you doubt the honor of this one, I will tell you more about him and let you judge for yourselves," Gunthar said.

"Lord Gunthar, consider what you are saying," Liam said. More and more, angry looks were turned upon the elderly Grand Master as he stood beside the gully dwarf.

"I have considered it, Liam." He turned to face the others and said in a loud voice, "Knights, I present to you Uhoh Ragnap, esquire, of the race of Aghar dwarves. Uhoh is master of my hounds, with all the duties and responsibilities attendant to that position. On this day, when one of my hounds was come under threat of physical harm, Squire Uhoh defended the hound against one of his own kind, another gully dwarf. What say you? Were the actions of Squire Uhoh honorable and commendable as is fitting for a squire to a Knight?"

A roar of outrage answered the Grand Master. Quintayne pounded the table and shouted, "Lord Gunthar, be reasonable. Surely you aren't suggesting a gully dwarf be admitted as squire into the Knights of Solamnia?" Liam Ehrling merely placed his face in his hands and sighed. Arguments broke out all around the room and continued unabated for many minutes.

Slowly, Gunthar's head drooped. He seemed to wilt with age before their very eyes. He heard some calling for his resignation, some saying he had surely lost his mind and was no longer fit to lead the Knights. But amidst the tumult, he heard one voice calling, "Yea, yea!" He searched the crowd until he found the lone dissenter. It was a young man from Tarsis, a Knight of the Sword. For the most part ignored by those around him, this one Knight stood and repeated his answer to Gunthar's question. Gunthar's spirits rose.

"Sir Ellinghad," Gunthar shouted until the din subsided. "Sir Ellinghad. What say you?"

"I say yea, the gully dwarf's actions were honorable," Ellinghad affirmed.

"There you have it!" Gunthar shouted, but before anyone could answer, he turned to another. "Lady Meredith, Lord High Clerist, what say you?"

"The gully dwarf's actions were . . . yes, they were honorable," she began. Again, shouts of disapproval arose, but she pounded the table with her fist until they quieted. "Yes, the gully dwarf performed honorably, but I must agree with my peers in this matter, Lord Gunthar. You cannot mean to admit a gully dwarf into our ranks."

"That is not what I intended," Gunthar said. He reached down and patted the gully dwarf on the top of his rat-skin cap. "Uhoh is brave and honorable for a gully dwarf, but he is not, nor could he ever be, a Knight."

"Then why, in heaven's name, why did you . . ." Liam

cried, only to end in stammering dismay.

"To prove a point," Gunthar answered.

"Milord, with all this talk about our rules of admission, what exactly are you proposing?" Meredith asked. "Why did you bring us here?"

Before Gunthar could answer, a horn sounded from the tower battlements outside. Another followed from the courtyard below the window. Strident it blared, silencing all arguments, resounding with a note of fear. Before its last echoes died away, the door to the chamber burst open, and a Knight entered, breathing heavily and sweating from his run.

"Lord Gunthar," he panted. "Dragons approaching from the east."

Chapter Four

"What kind?" Liam shouted, rising to his feet. "What color?"

"Blue dragons, milord," the Knight answered.

"The Knights of Takhisis have broken the peace!" Liam roared. "I knew they would."

"Send for the silver dragons! Break out the dragonlances. To arms! To arms!" Sir Quintayne shouted as he leaped atop a table, sending plates and bowls crashing to the floor.

Gully dwarves, momentarily distracted by the horns and the sudden commotion, forgot their fears and rushed in to clean up the mess. Soon they were growling and snarling as though nothing had happened, happily licking spilled soup from the flagstones.

"Wait a moment!" Gunthar shouted into the din as the gathered Knights rushed to prepare for battle. Adding to all the noise, the hounds began to bark excitedly. Gunthar fought his way through the throng, trying to reach the door before anyone could get out.

"Wait!" he shouted. "Sir Ellinghad, hold the door!" The young Knight of the Sword was the first to reach the door and was about to tear from the room when he heard Gunthar call his name. He stopped and did as he was told, preventing anyone else from leaving.

31

"There is no cause for alarm. I invited them!"

The room grew suddenly quiet at these words. Liam slowly turned to face Lord Gunthar. Through clenched teeth, he growled to the messenger, "How many blue dragons have been spotted?"

"Twelve, sir," the Knight answered. "Four flights of three each."

"Has the shore watch spotted any ships?"

"None so far."

Liam's mustaches began to quiver, and his dark eyes smoldered beneath his brow. "Lord Gunthar," he said with obvious restraint, "How do you know this isn't the precursor of a larger attack?"

"I know, as I said, because I invited them," Gunthar said, then tripped over Uhoh, who had not left his side and was, in fact, still clinging to his legs. Sir Quintayne caught and steadied the elderly Grand Master. "Uhoh, my boy, you'll have to let me go so I can go greet our guests," Gunthar said.

"No, Papa. No go, Papa," the gully dwarf whimpered.

Angry at the interruption, Liam said loudly, "You should have warned us, milord."

"And what would you have said, had I told you I sent overtures to the leadership of the Knights of Takhisis, inviting a discussion of the merger of our two great orders?" Gunthar asked as he pried the gully dwarf's fingers loose from his thigh. A gasp escaped the gathered Knights. The tension between the Grand Master of the order, and his protégé and handpicked successor, electrified the air.

"You didn't!" Liam whispered.

"I did. And what would you have said if I had told you that they accepted, enthusiastically? That we both agreed that if any Knighthood at all is to survive upon Krynn, it must be a united Knighthood."

"Lord Gunthar, how could you have done this on your own, without consulting us?" Lady Meredith asked. She stepped before Liam Ehrling, breaking the tension between the two powerful Knights. Continuing, she said, "It goes against everything we stand for. It is a direct violation of the procedures called for in the Measure."

"I know that, Meredith. Aren't I rewriting and revising that very Measure?" Gunthar said as he finally freed himself from the grasp of the gully dwarf. "Houndmaster Uhoh, take the hounds to their quarters and see that they have water," he ordered. Reluctantly, Uhoh stepped back and nodded.

Satisfied, Gunthar turned to the door. For a moment, he and Liam faced each other in silence. Liam, a head taller than the elderly Knight, seemed on the verge of challenging his master or preventing him from leaving the room. Gunthar, seeming to sense this, straightened his back and stepped toward the door. Liam's eyes dropped, and he stepped aside.

"Open the door, Ellinghad, and attend me," he said.

The young Knight obeyed, swinging wide the door and falling in beside the Grand Master as he passed. The other Knights filed out of the room behind them.

Liam Ehrling gave one last look around the wrecked banquet hall, its floor still crowded with dogs and gully dwarves, the tables littered with food and dripping with spilled wine. His eyes lighted on Gunthar's houndmaster. Strangely, the little creature snapped to attention and saluted in perfect imitation of a Knight. Liam snorted, turned, and stalked out.

Gunthar led the way from the banquet hall to the courtyard. All along the way, servants and men at arms rushed about, frantically making ready for the unexpected visitors. Some seemed preparing for war, while others acted as though a visiting dignitary had arrived unannounced.

As he walked calmly through the chaos, Gunthar explained his actions.

"Desperate times call for desperate measures. There often comes a moment when one man, or one woman for that matter, must make a decision and take upon his shoulders, or her shoulders, the responsibility of that decision. If I had brought this before a Grand Chapter, you would have argued for centuries before making a decision, and by then it would be too late." He turned a corner and descended a wide staircase, Knights trooping behind him.

"When Pyrothraxus discovers how weak we really are, he won't long remain content to enslave the gnomes of Mount Nevermind. He has already learned that he can attack with impunity the shipping around this island. A few months ago, he sank an Ergothian privateer and the ship the Knights of Takhisis sent to capture her. They then sent an expedition to find their lost ship, and that expedition vanished without a trace."

Gunthar paused in an archway at the foot of the stairs and turned to the Knights above him. "It won't be long before Pyrothraxus tests our northern defenses and finds them nonexistent. Our castles there are virtually empty, the lands around them lying fallow, growing wild. We need Knights to man the towers and the walls and dragons to defend them. I'm no magician, able to conjure up armies from the rocks and stones, just like that," he said with a snap of his fingers. He turned and continued down a corridor lined with torches in silver sconces.

"We need experienced fighting men," Gunthar said. Someone behind him cleared her throat. "And women," he amended over his shoulder.

"But Lord Gunthar, surely we can find Knights somewhere else," Sir Quintayne said.

"Where, Quintayne? Recruiting hasn't been this low

since the days following the Cataclysm," Gunthar said.

"I've always thought we should open the order to dwarves and elves," Lady Meredith said. "There are examples from the past—the dwarf Kharas and the elven princess Laurana."

"They were only honorary members," Quintayne said.

"You forget, we were led to victory by Laurana during the War of the Lance," Meredith snapped.

"And Tanis Half-Elven, more recently," young Elling-had added. Quintayne scowled at the interruption. "Nevertheless—" he said, but never got to finish his thought.

As they approached the door to the courtyard, guards poured out of barracks rooms lining the corridor before them, hastily strapping on armor as they rushed outside.

Gunthar stopped at the door and hushed their arguments, saying to Lady Meredith, "The elves and dwarves have their own problems. How do I look?" He nervously smoothed his mustaches.

Lady Meredith stepped up to him and adjusted the hang of his sword, her cobalt blue eyes twinkling. She took the moment to whisper to him, "Milord, are you absolutely certain this is the right thing?"

"No," he returned with a smile.

"Lord Gunthar, before you proceed," Liam Ehrling said from the back. "I wish it known that I am utterly opposed to this. The Knights of Takhisis cannot be trusted."

"I am sure, Sir Liam," Gunthar returned, "that they feel the same way about us."

The captain of the guards of Castle uth Wistan stepped in from the courtyard and bowed to Lord Gunthar. "Milord, we are ready."

Chapter Five

"*Do you feel them?*" *Alya shouted into the wind.*

"Feel what?" Tohr asked in return, twisting in the dragonsaddle to better hear his lieutenant.

"Eyes, in the forest below, watching us," she shouted as she leaned forward in the large, three-man saddle.

"What did you say?" asked the Knight riding behind her. She ignored him.

"I hadn't noticed," Tohr answered her.

For a moment, their dragon ceased the slow beat of his wings and glided through the night air above the Forest of Gunthar. He twisted its great cerulean-scaled head around to gaze at the riders on his back.

"I feel them," he said in a voice which boomed like a great bass drum. "And I've seen them, too, silver dragons, lurking about down there in the dark. They don't want us here," he said, then returned to his flying. The riders lurched back in their seats as the dragon's great wings resumed their slow rhythm, and the creature rose to fly over a tall tree-covered hill rising from the dark ahead.

As they turned, Alya Starblade glanced behind them. In the dark sky, she picked out eleven other blue dragons, all similarly accoutered with the large, three-man dragonsaddles. They flew in perfect formation, four groups of three each. Occasionally, starlight glinted off a buckle here or a spur there, the only sign that each dragon also carried riders. She shifted again in the seat, trying to ease her aching back. The saddles were almost unbearably uncomfortable, having been originally designed for the transport of draconian troops, and the heavy dragonscale armor she wore didn't make things any better.

At least, she thought, there aren't any silvers following us, upsetting our blues.

"How much longer before we get there?" shouted the Knight behind her. Alya ignored him, but she was wondering the same thing herself. The flight from Qualinost was the most grueling dragon flight she'd ever undertaken in her brief but eventful career as a Knight of Her Dark Majesty, Takhisis. Silently, she cursed the short supply of blue dragons of late. Even only a few years ago, all thirty-six Knights sent on this expedition could have ridden their own dragons, in battle harnesses that were a luxury compared to these blasted draconian contraptions. But the coming of the new dragons from across the sea had changed all that. Blues and reds were vanishing, the black dragons had retreated to their murky swamps and meres, the greens had gone the-gods-only-knew where, and the whites were useless, restricted as they were to the arctic regions.

As much as she hated boats, Alya almost wished they had taken a ship, but then she remembered how unsafe it was to sail to Sancrist these days. Her youngest sister had gone down with *Donkaren*, a war galleon in the Knights of Takhisis's navy, when it was attacked by the red dragon Pyrothraxus off the coast of the Isle of Cristyne. That was only a few months ago, at the beginning of summer, but already the leaves of the trees were turning to gold and auburn. The pain of that loss was still fresh to her.

A growl from their dragon started Alya from her thoughts. Below them, gray stone battlements shone dully in the starlight. The tops of the towers of a Solamnic castle rose from the trees crowning a hill. The dragon's flight took it within spear-throwing distance of the castle's towers, and as they flew over it, Alya was delighted to see the startled faces of a group of sleepy guards staring up at them in surprise and horror. She laughed into the wind.

"This land would be so easy to take," she said. The dragon agreed with a laughing rumble, which attested its willingness to join such an endeavor.

"What?" asked the Knight behind her.

Without turning, her commander and the leader of this expedition, Sir Tohr Malen said, "Yes, but you couldn't keep it. Look behind you."

Alya turned. A huge bonfire, built in an iron rack atop one of the castles towers, flared and burst into flame as she watched. In its light, she saw the figures of armed men running frantically about, pointing at the sky. One by one, the other dragons also passed over the castle, their blue-scaled bellies sharply underlit by the fire.

"Now look there," Sir Tohr said.

In the darkness a few miles ahead of them, atop another hill, a glimmer of fire sparkled. Soon, it too was a raging bonfire. At Tohr's command, the dragon banked to avoid flying too near it. Before long, as far as they could see, hilltops blazed with signal fires. Some seemed to blink, as Alya saw men waving blankets before them.

"What are they doing?" she asked.

"They have a code," Tohr answered. "They are not only signaling that danger is approaching but also what kind of danger. It is really quite ingenious."

"I could stop them," the dragon offered.

"There is no need. We are expected," Tohr said.

"Are you sure? Those people seem quite surprised to see us," Alya said of a tiny village carved from the forest below them. In the clearing, she saw villagers dashing about with torches and staring fearfully over their shoulders at the sky.

"But we aren't being attacked by silver dragons," Tohr answered her. "Don't imagine for a moment we could have gotten this far if Gunthar hadn't forewarned the silvers of our arrival."

"Steer clear of the signal fires and villages," Tohr ordered the dragon. "We want to avoid any possibility of an incident."

"Yes, Lord Tohr," the dragon growled.

"And when you leave us, fly straight back to Neraka where our supreme commander Mistress Mirielle Abrena awaits your return. As long as you are over Sancrist, the silvers will be watching you, so no looting along the way, or you'll ruin everything."

"Yes, Lord Tohr."

Alya leaned well forward in the saddle and placed her hand on Tohr's arm. At her touch, he started but did not turn. "And no fraternizing with your superiors, soldier," he said out of the corner of his mouth.

"Yes, Lord Tohr," she answered in a low voice.

"What?" asked the Knight behind her.

Finally, Alya answered him. "No one was speaking to you, Trevalyn," she snapped at him over her shoulder.

For perhaps the hundredth time, he tugged his cloak closer around his body. "I hope this doesn't take much longer," Trevalyn snarled. "I must have rest and time to study my spells."

"Why? You can't cast them!" Alya laughed.

"It is the curse of the mage that he must nightly renew his spells," the Knight said, repeating it like a mantra.

"Magic is dead. It vanished with the moons," Alya taunted. "You are here as a representative of the Order of the Thorn, nothing more. Don't try your tricks and mysteries on me. You have no power." She turned, saying

39

under her breath, "And I don't know why the Thorns are still part of the Knighthood anyway. They're useless."

* * * * *

It is well that she couldn't see Trevalyn's face at that moment. He imagined spouts of flame erupting from her eye sockets, finally contenting himself with watching the panorama of Sancrist Isle at night, spread below him like a velvet ebon blanket sprinkled with shining jewels.

Swiftly, their dragon led the winding way among the low forested hills of southern Sancrist, flying just above the treetops, because it was well known that Lord Tohr Malen did not care for heights. Trevalyn eyed the rich forest lands below with something akin to contempt. He was of a desert-loving race; he cared little for forests and farmlands, except to destroy them with his magic. Now his magic was gone, as Alya had said. At the end of the Chaos War, when the gods fled Krynn, they took magic with them, leaving the mages of the world powerless, as empty and hopeless as princes robbed of their birthright. Still, some inkling of magic was left to Trevalyn. His senses were still attuned to things. The wind brought to his keen nostrils the sweet heathery smell of cattle and cattle barns, the toothy aroma of wood smoke and roasting meat, but it also roused the wet, rotted-wood stink of silver dragons, reminding him that this land was guarded ceaselessly by those cursed shining foes. There, in an undercurrent of the breeze, floated the sulfurous but utterly alien fume of the strange new dragon who lorded over the northern half of this island. Trevalyn knew of Pyrothraxus—what mage didn't know of the new dragons from across the sea, what mage didn't see them in their dreams and long for the magic they seemed to possess?

The Knights of the Thorn were a dying breed. Once a

mighty wing of the Knights of Takhisis's attack, they wielded powerful magic, taking their honored place among the Knights of the Lily and the Skull. They wore robes of gray, breaking with the long tradition of magic upon Krynn, declaring themselves a separate order from the Black, Red, and White-robed mages. The battle to establish their independence was hard-fought, but won.

Now, however, the Thorn Knights were little more than functionaries, relics of a passed age. Not even their fellow Knights respected them. Even though Takhisis had fled Krynn along with all the other gods during the Chaos War, her paladins and clerics still commanded a measure of respect even among dragonkind. The Knights of the Skull, as they were known, were a fearful lot; absolutely fanatical and absolutely confident in their ultimate place at the side of their Dark Queen, they were virtually fearless in battle and ruthless in all their affairs. The Knights of the Lily were the consummate warriors, as pure as the fire from the world forge, and just as unforgiving. The Knights of the Thorn . . . well, their glory had passed, it seemed. Those who remained were generally venomous old men and women, hating themselves and what they had become but unable to let it all go and seek a new life.

For now, Trevalyn's main concern was for the mission to Castle uth Wistan, somewhere near the center of the southern forest of the Isle of Sancrist. He'd never been here, nor had any evil creature, not at any time within living memory, for this was the land of the Whitestone Glade, the heart and soul of Solamnic Knights, where Vinus Solamnus received the vision that led to the founding of the Knights, many centuries ago. The very thought of such a good and holy place filled Trevalyn with loathing. Everything about this mission bothered him. He and the Knights of his talon were coming not to make war, but peace. They were forbidden to attack anyone, even if provoked. Nothing about this seemed right. He was filled with foreboding and unease. To make matters worse, the crisp autumn air made his joints ache. Not for the first time since they began this journey across the chill Sirrion Sea, the Knight of the Thorn longed for his warmer northern home.

Trevalyn's musings were interrupted by a movement from Lord Tohr, the leader of their little expedition. He saw Lord Tohr pointing to the left. There, still some distance ahead, the white-stone battlements of a large and ancient castle rose above the treetops, sharply illuminated by the pale moon overhead. All its windows and casings glowed with yellow light, while the trees surrounding it were starkly silhouetted by several large bonfires burning in the castle's courtyard.

"Castle uth Wistan," Lord Tohr shouted into the wind. The dragon nodded his great head and began to descend.

As they dropped to treetop level, their passing stirred the leaves of the tallest trees. At this height, they were able to hear the woods ringing with horns and saw lines of torches winding along the trails towards the castle. Looking down, Trevalyn and Alya were amazed at the speed with which the citizens of this land answered the call to arms. It seemed little less than half an hour had passed since the first signal fire was lit, announcing their approach, and already the people were rushing to take up positions of defense. Torchlight glinted from polished helms and gleaming spears, sparkling below them like stars in the surface of a vast lake.

Suddenly, a clearing opened before them, and Castle uth Wistan loomed ahead, brightly lit by numerous bonfires both outside its walls and within the courtyard beyond. A great throng of armed warriors stood in ranks before the gate, with captains astride armored horses flanking their lines. Here and there, a long silver dragonlance protruded from their ranks, glinting dangerously in the firelight. The dragon growled and increased his speed.

Alya was pleased to see that as their dragon cleared the trees and burst into view in the sky above the castle, the ranks of the gate guards wavered, while their captains struggled to regain control of their frightened mounts. The dragon flew straight toward them, huge and menacing, his dragonfear surging before it like a tide, spreading panic among the guards. As he neared the castle walls, he banked and pulled up sharply, skimming the battlements with his long rudder-like tail as he shot high into the sky above the castle. Alya looked behind her as they rose almost vertically and saw the hated Knights of Solamnia pouring from the castle into the courtyard below. As the pressure of the steep climb pressed her back in the dragonsaddle, she thrilled in the dragon's fancy flying, but she knew Lord Tohr was probably furious, if not a little frightened. He hated flying and especially heights.

The dragon continued to rise showily into the night sky, slowing, until he finally stalled high above Castle uth Wistan. He seemed to hang there for a moment, and in the stillness Alya heard cries of fear as the other dragons glided over the castle below them. Then the dragon began to fall, performing a backwards pike like a diver, until his nose was pointed once more at the ground below. He fell like a spear, his wings tucked close to its body, the wind of his speed becoming a deafening roar. The ground rushed up toward them. Lord Tohr began to pound the dragon on the neck with his fist, and slowly the creature unfolded his wings and slowed their descent, his massive joints and wing tendons creaking.

As they dropped past the walls of the castle, the dragon's wings fanned the flames of the bonfires and sent swarms of sparks and clouds of hot ash billowing throughout the courtyard. At last, the dragon folded back his wings, dropping the last few feet to the ground. His claws scrabbled at the cobblestones paving the courtyard as he settled to earth.

Lord Tohr remained seated while the other dragons descended around them, one by one, the wind from their wings filling the air with smoke and ash from the bonfires. Slowly they filled all the courtyard with their massive blue-scaled bodies, standing shoulder to shoulder, wings brushing against one another as they shifted uncomfortably. The courtyard grew strangely quiet. No one dismounted as yet. The Knights of Takhisis waited for a signal from their leader, and meanwhile they silently studied their old enemies, the Knights of Solamnia.

Across from them, standing before the huge wooden doors that opened into the main part of the castle, several dozen Knights of Solamnia maintained their ranks despite their fear of the blue dragons. Outwardly they showed no emotion, but Alya was pleased to see many sweating nervously. Several seemed almost incapable of standing still, shifting constantly from foot to foot as though ready to flee at any moment. Alya laughed under her breath.

Still Lord Tohr did not move from his seat just behind the dragon's neck. Perhaps he was allowing the tension between the two groups of Knights to build, perhaps he was unwilling to make the first move, as it might show weakness on his part, or perhaps he was still recovering from their wild ride. In any case, the dragons plainly showed they were becoming uneasy. The great blue ridden by Tohr and Alya rumbled deep in his chest.

Nor did any of the Knights of Solamnia make a gesture to break the standoff. They stood quietly, their features aloof, even disdainful. Alya searched the group for their leader, Lord Gunthar uth Wistan, finally spotting him in center of the group. Though one of the oldest living men on Krynn, the Grand Master of the Knights of Solamnia still stood tall and proud, like a Knight from a greater age, but one now long passed. He stood perfectly still, his back erect, one hand resting on the pommel of the great sword hanging at his side as he surveyed the dragons and their riders.

A little to the left and just behind the Grand Master lurked another man, a Knight who had been described in detail to Alya. He stood a head taller than Lord Gunthar, and his locks and long Solamnic mustaches were still dark, despite the fact that he was one of the oldest of the active members of the Knighthood. Not so old as Gunthar, but still, he'd been among the Knights at the High Clerist's Tower when the armies of Takhisis attacked the city of Palanthas. Unmarried, with no children and no familial ties to distract him, Sir Liam Ehrling, Lord High Justice, was utterly dedicated to the Knighthood. He was the protégé of Lord Gunthar and was universally expected to succeed as Lord of Knights when the ancient Grand Master finally died. Though his face remained as expressionless as stone, his dark eyes smoldered beneath his brows, and he glanced more often, Alya noted with some interest, at Lord Gunthar than at the dragons and Knights of Takhisis gathered in all their glory and terror before him.

"I don't think they trust us," she whispered to Tohr.

"And I don't trust them," Tohr answered. "This still might be a trap."

"Well, we'd better do something, or we'll end up sitting here all night," she said.

"Gunthar invited us. Let him make the first move," Tohr growled.

As though in response, Gunthar stepped forward. A handsome young Knight stepped out with him, but the old Grand Master shooed him back with a wave of his hand. He stepped out into the courtyard and approached the dragons.

"Stay here," Lord Tohr commanded. He rose in the saddle and then climbed down from atop the dragon, using the saddle's straps and decorations to assist his decent. Once on the ground, he walked forward, pausing briefly by the lowered head of the blue as though to confer for a moment.

The dragon whispered, as best as a dragon can whisper, "If he makes one wrong move, I'll blast him."

Without turning or even showing a hint of emotion, Lord Tohr responded. "You'll do nothing. If you pull one more stunt with me, I'll see you spend the rest of your days nursing hatchlings. Do you understand me?"

"Yes, Lord Tohr," the dragon rumbled.

With that settled, Lord Tohr Malen continued across the courtyard. Though his back obviously ached from the chill hours spent in the cramped dragonsaddle, he bore himself with rigid dignity, his left hand resting on the great black mace strapped to his waist, his right hand swinging sharply at his side, marking time in a swift military step.

Gunthar, though no less dignified, approached more slowly. The hand that rested on the pommel of his great sword trembled slightly, but not with fear. His spurs rang as he walked, piercing the near-quiet of the courtyard. A gust of wind stirred the bonfires, making them crackle and sending sparks floating high over the courtyard.

The two great Knights stopped a few yards apart and eyed each other. By the sharpness of Gunthar's glance, Tohr, a quick judge of men, decided the Grand Master was neither deceitful nor deranged, as some had suggested when the unexpected offer to join the two orders was first presented to the Knights of Takhisis. Since Gunthar had made the first move by crossing the courtyard to meet him, now Tohr returned the gesture by speaking first. "Tohr Malen, Knight of the Skull, at your service," he said, bowing slightly at the waist.

"Gunthar uth Wistan, Knight of the Rose, at your service," Gunthar responded, bowing in kind. "Welcome to

Sancrist Isle." He stepped forward and extended his hand.

Tohr advanced and met him. Their two hands clasped before them, between them. They stood for a moment facing each other, each lightly gripping the other's hand in a firm handshake. Then they turned so that both parties of Knights could see their joined hands.

Tohr made a sweep of his free hand to indicate the dragonmounted Knights behind him. "I present to you the delegation of the Knights of Takhisis. We beg leave to reside in this land, and look forward to the merging of our two great orders," he said.

"Welcome!" Gunthar shouted, his voice booming across the courtyard. "Welcome to Castle uth Wistan!"

He was answered with a cheer as the Knights of Takhisis began to dismount.

Chapter Six

Lady Jessica Destianstone's stomach writhed as she watched Gunthar stride across the courtyard to meet the leader of the Knights of Takhisis dismounting from his dragon. Not because she had just devoured enough meat from Gunthar's banquet table to satisfy three ravenous dwarves, or because the tense scene between the other Knights and Lord Gunthar had just been interrupted by the arrival of the Knights of Solamnia's most hated foe; she simply never imagined she'd be this close to a blue dragon, much less twelve of them. Their aura of magical fear had started cold icy sweat rolling down her cheeks, and her stomach felt as if she'd swallowed a cold stone the size of a dragon orb. Nervously she slapped the pommel of her sword as the leader of the Knights of Takhisis stopped beside his dragon's head and muttered something from the corner of his mouth. Jessica tensed, expecting some treachery.

But nothing violent occurred, as yet. The leader of the Knights of Takhisis strode forward, meeting Lord Gunthar in the center of the courtyard. The two great Knights clasped hands, but it was hard to tell whether the handshake was one of friendship or rather more like that of two men wrestling. The muscles of the Dark Knight's arm bulged as he squeezed Gunthar's hand, and Gunthar fought back gamely. They turned, and Gunthar shouted something. The Knights of Takhisis responded with a roar and began to dismount from their dragons. For a moment, Lady Jessica thought they were attacking.

"Sheath that sword, Lady Knight," muttered the older warrior standing at her shoulder.

Looking up, she noted for the first time that Sir Liam Ehrling had moved in beside her. She quailed at the thought that he'd been at her side the entire time and hoped she hadn't been thinking out loud, a habit brought about by her almost constant solitude. Jessica spent most of her time in lonely watch upon the northern frontier of the Knights' lands, in a drafty old tumbledown castle, with only an ancient dwarven squire to attend her horse and arms. She'd come at the summons of Lord Gunthar, though she hardly knew why she'd been summoned. Never once since becoming a Knight of the Crown had she attended a banquet at Castle uth Wistan, and now here she stood, at what was apparently a momentous event in the Knighthood's history. Why she'd been commanded to attend was completely beyond her, and she wished she were back in her comfortable old chilly castle, curled up with a book and a candle by the fire.

Relieved that the Knights of Takhisis were not attacking after all, Jessica allowed her sword to drop back into its sheath. The Dark Knights were gathering around their leader and Lord Gunthar. Gunthar shook hands with a handsome female Knight of Takhisis who'd ridden on the same dragon as their leader. She was head and shoulders shorter than the leader of the Dark Knights, but they bore similar features, from raven curls damp with sweat from wearing the massive dragonhelms, to their thin, somewhat arrogant aquiline noses; the two might have been brother and sister. Next, a man cowled and robed all in

gray stepped forward, nodding to the Solamnic Grand
Master before retreating to the rear of the gathering crowd
of Dark Knights. Finally, a Knight of some importance
strode up from the back and was introduced to Gunthar.
As he bowed, he removed his dragonhelm, allowing long
white locks to spill down upon his shoulders. As he
turned his head to say something to another Knight, Jessica noticed his delicately pointed ears, and her breath
caught in her throat.

"A dark elf," she whispered.

"That won't be the last unusual thing you'll see this
night," Liam muttered, and Jessica realized she'd given
voice to her thoughts. Dark elves were those elves who'd
been "cast from the light" by their own people. Lonely,
hunted, they most often found acceptance in evil alliances,
whether it was with the black-robed mages or the clerics
of Takhisis. Jessica hadn't heard of the Knights of Takhisis
accepting dark elves into their order, but such a move was
not unexpected. Evil has no prejudices, her old master had
told her. It accepts all equally. When the old magical arts
began to fail, and when all the gods left Krynn, the dark
elves were sure to find some other path. The Knights of
Takhisis seemed the perfect place for them. Though she'd
never met a dark elf, the mere thought of such a creature
filled her with loathing. The elves in general were a noble
people, dedicated to the beauty and glorification of all that
is good, so when an elf fell into the clutches of evil his fall
was all the more tragic and horrible.

With the introductions completed, Gunthar led the way
across the courtyard, all the Knights of Takhisis in his
train. Behind them, the dragons fanned their wings impatiently, eager to be off. As he walked, the old Grand Master
talked animatedly to the leader of the Dark Knights.

As they neared, the Knights of Takhisis spread out and
stopped to face their counterparts across a few yards of

cobblestone. Because she stood beside Sir Liam, Jessica found herself in the center of things.

Gunthar and the leader of the Knights of Takhisis walked to the end of the line of Solamnic Knights, where Gunthar began to introduce everyone. He stopped at each Knight and drew him or her forward to shake hands with the leader of the Dark Knights and his two apparent lieutenants, the petite but strikingly handsome woman and the dark elf. The gray-robed Knight, obviously a mage of some sort, had slipped to the end of the line, where he stood aloofly, greeting no one and avoided by all. Slowly Gunthar made his way toward Liam and Jessica, and Lady Jessica noticed that Liam seemed as if he wished he were somewhere else. Constantly muttering under his breath, occasionally a curse or oath escaped his lips loudly enough to be heard by those nearest him. Some nodded in agreement, though no one said anything out loud.

Meanwhile, Gunthar had already introduced most of the Knights of the Sword and was nearing the first of the Knights of the Rose, those who'd shared his table at the banquet. Jessica leaned out from her line to watch and listen.

"Sir Ellinghad Beauseant, Knight of the Sword," Gunthar said, introducing the young Knight who'd supported him in the matter of the gully dwarf. Ellinghad stepped forward and eagerly shook the hand presented to him. "Lord Tohr Malen, Knight of the Skull," Gunthar said.

"Milord, it is an honor," Ellinghad responded.

"Lady Alya Starblade, Knight of the Lily."

Ellinghad bowed from the hips and took her hand.

"Sir Valian Escu of Silvanost, Knight of the Lily."

"*Quenta solari nen heth y mori,*" Ellinghad said to the dark elf. "May the stars shine upon thy road." Gunthar's face beamed at the show of honor displayed by the young Knight, greeting the elf in his own language.

51

"And upon thine," the dark elf answered in some surprise, glancing at his leader. Lord Tohr nodded in approval.

The line moved. "Lady Meredith Turningdale, Lord High Clerist . . . "

"Sir Quintayne Fogorner, Lord High Warrior," Gunthar said, much nearer now to Jessica. She closed her eyes and tried to quiet her breathing. Nervously, she fingered the hilt of her sword, caressing the tiny golden crowns decorating its pommel.

"They are only people," Liam whispered, as though to assure her.

"Sir Liam Ehrling, Knight of the Rose and Lord High Justice," Gunthar said.

"Sir Liam, I have so looked forward to our finally meeting," Tohr said, extending his hand.

"While I have not," Liam answered shortly. Gunthar cleared his throat and shot a pleading glance at his Knight. Tohr shifted uncomfortably, his hand still raised in friendship.

"For Lord Gunthar did not give us the luxury of anticipating your arrival. Please forgive us. You were a bit of a surprise," Liam finished with a small smile. He accepted Lord Tohr's hand and shook it heartily. Gunthar sighed in relief and introduced the others.

"I hope, Lord Ehrling," Alya said after she'd been introduced, "that we might soon come to earn your trust. It is not easy for us to forget our old prejudices."

"Neither should they be forgotten," Liam said diplomatically, "but I am sure, in time we can come to understand one another." Alya smiled and removed her hand.

"Lady Jessica Vestianstone of Isherwood, Knight of the Crown," Lord Gunthar said at last. Automatically, she extended her hand. Lord Tohr took it and shook it strongly. Jessica felt her tiny hand swallowed up in the huge grip of the leader of the Dark Knights.

"Lady Jessica occupies Castle Isherwood, on our northern frontier," Gunthar said.

"Is that so?" Tohr asked with some interest. "Have you seen the dragon Pyrothraxus during your watches upon the border?"

"No, milord," Jessica answered, "though once I believe I heard him."

"Isherwood is one of the castles to be granted to your Knights," Gunthar said. Jessica started at these words, and looked around confusedly.

"I believe this is news to Lady Jessica," Alya said as she stepped forward and took her by the hand.

"Yes, milady," Jessica said.

"I'm sorry, but I've promised those lands to Lord Tohr. You'll be reassigned, of course," Gunthar explained.

"But milord . . ." she stuttered.

"You are fond of this castle?" Alya asked.

"Yes, milady. I . . . love the old place. It is like home to me."

"Then perhaps Lord Gunthar can be convinced to allow you to stay with us there, as a show of solidarity between our two orders," Alya said.

"I agree," said Lord Tohr. "It won't do much good to merge our Knighthoods, yet keep the Knights separate. They should begin to work together, to share quarters and meals and duties, so as to get to know one another more quickly. I believe that once we come to realize that we are all Knights of honor, our prejudices will begin to slip away."

"Perhaps," was all Gunthar said. "We'll discuss it later, Lady Jessica."

"Thank you, milord," Jessica sighed.

The leaders of the Knights of Takhisis moved on. The dark elf stood quite near, waiting to shake hands with one of the Knights of the Crown. Jessica studied him, trying to guess at his nature by his physical features, the way the writers of old books often did. He bore the fine, delicate features of his elven heritage, from his thin nose and sharp cheekbones to his high forehead and slightly slanted, almond-shaped eyes. His shoulder-length hair, which Jessica had first thought was solid white, proved to have a few strands of auburn around his pointed ears. He carried himself with nobility and looked people in the eye as he spoke to them, apparently unashamed of his elven features.

The armor he wore was dull and black, unpolished so as to not reflect light. Its most prominent ornamentation was of black lilies. Lilies were repeated on the breastplate, greaves, bracers, helm, and gauntlets, as well as his sword and its scabbard. Twined with the symbols of the lily were leering skulls and knotted thorny vines. Lily, skull, and thorn were the three symbols of the Knights of Takhisis, just as the crown, sword, and rose were the symbols of the Solamnics. After examining his spurs, which were also black and apparently made of iron, Jessica's eyes returned to his face, and she found him staring at her. She started with surprise and looked away. Realizing how guilty she must look, she forced herself to return his gaze.

But he had already turned away and was involved with more of the formal introductions. Jessica's faced burned as she silently cursed herself. Angrily, she slapped the hilt of her sword.

At last, Gunthar's introductions were complete, and he led his guests toward the main entrance into the castle. There he stopped and turned to face the Knights of Takhisis. Gunthar said in a loud voice, "Honored guests, future brothers and sisters in arms, the banquet to celebrate this momentous event has already begun. However, to further celebrate the union of our two great Knighthoods, seven days hence a great hunt will be held. Let Knight join Knight in pursuit of a common foe—the great boar Mannjaeger."

A great cheer went up, both from the Knights of Takhisis and the Solamnics. Mannjaeger was a semimythical creature rumored to haunt the great forest covering the southern half of the Isle of Sancrist. A bane to farmer and traveler alike, he'd often been hunted but more often was the hunter himself. Few had bloodied him; more were bloodied by him. Many folk had been killed over the years. Some bards claimed Mannjaeger was immortal, for certainly tales of a great and dangerous boar of the forest of Sancrist had been around since the days of Vinus Solamnus. Most of the gathered Knights were thrilled to have the chance to test their lances against such a foe.

They cheered for many minutes, many already discussing hunts of the past and tactics for the future. Finally, they grew quiet again, and Gunthar continued,"Now, join us within."

At his bidding, the line of Solamnic Knights parted to allow the Dark Knights to pass within, but Tohr stopped just within the entrance and turned. He made a quick sharp gesture at the dragons, and Jessica felt Sir Liam tense beside her.

First one dragon, then another, then two more crouched and leaped into the air, unfolding their wings at the same time and pounding the air with huge, powerful strokes. Slowly they rose, fighting to clear the castle walls. The wind from their wings swirled round the courtyard in madly spinning vortices, sucking up sparks and ash and dust into whirling columns. Jessica coughed and blinked and covered her face. When the winds died down and the smoke and dust finally cleared, the courtyard was once again empty, as though no dragon had ever been there. Only a lone defiant angry roar sounded from the sky above.

"I thought your dragons were to remain with you," Gunthar said to Lord Tohr.

"Lady Mirielle felt it wisest that they return to Neraka," Tohr answered smoothly, "until such a time as this arrangement shows evidence of some permanence."

"I see," Gunthar said, leading the way into the castle. Lord Tohr fell in beside him, and the other Knights of Takhisis followed.

"You understand, Lord Gunthar, that it is difficult for us to overcome decades of mistrust. For dragons, the mistrust goes back centuries and ages. Having silver dragons and blues in such close proximity only invites disaster, until we can prove our efforts at peace and unity are sincere," Tohr explained. "It would be a shame to allow our efforts to be destroyed by a couple of hot-headed young dragons."

"That is true," Gunthar said, though his voice didn't sound very enthusiastic. However, his face immediately brightened. "In any case, you will find the banquet in your honor has already begun. Some of us have already eaten our fill . . . ." At these words, several nearby Knights groaned in satisfaction, but a few made comments to the effect that they could be persuaded to dine a second time, for the sake of their guests, of course. Gunthar continued, "But we'd be honored to share a table with you and your noble Knights. You must be hungry after your long dragonback ride."

"Famished!" Lady Alya laughed. "And frostbitten. Though I' m sure you have something to take the edge off, Lord Gunthar, if half the tales of your cellar are true."

"As a matter of fact, I was just relating a story about a particular barrel of ale and two unexpected visitors . . . " Gunthar smiled.

As the last of the Knights of Takhisis filed into the castle, the Knights of the Rose stepped in behind them, followed by the Knights of the Crown. Jessica found herself just behind Sir Liam. Gunthar's and Tohr's voices echoed in the hall ahead, but the footsteps of so many heavily booted Knights, the jangle and creak of armor, and the murmuring of dozens of conversations, made it impossible to understand what the two leaders were discussing.

As they made their way back to the banquet hall, Jessica noticed Sir Quintayne drifting back until he reached the side of Sir Liam. The two then continued side-by-side, their heads close in whispered conversation. As the body of Knights slowed to turn the corner and ascend the stairs, Jessica heard Quintayne hiss, "Thirty-six Knights! Without the dragons, I fail to see the point of their coming at all."

"I'm rather glad the blues have gone. At least now, if they try something, they won't have their dragons to assist them," Liam answered.

"But the entire reason for all this is that we join our forces to face the threat of Pyrothraxus. What good are thirty-six Knights? We need ten times as many," Quintayne whispered.

"Not many more Knights of Solamnia held the High Clerist's Tower against an army of thousands," Liam said as they shuffled onto the staircase.

"Yes, but we don't have a dragon orb," Quintayne argued.

"Thirty-six Knights of Takhisis could turn the tide of a close battle," Liam countered. As Jessica mounted the stairs, she leaned forward to better hear them.

Liam continued in a low voice, almost to himself, "Or turn us against each other."

Chapter Seven

The door boomed shut, resounding in the empty hall. Gunthar sighed and pushed aside a plate, then carefully laid his head on the table. The only other occupant of the banquet hall, a female boar hound, rose from her place by the dying fire and strode daintily on her long legs across the room, her nails clicking on the flagstones. She stopped once to sniff at a meaty bone lying on the floor, then continued around the table, approaching Gunthar's chair from behind. When she reached him, she shoved her muzzle under his elbow, begging for a pat on the head. When he failed to respond, she tossed her head, jerking Gunthar awake. He laughed and sat up, wearily running his hands through his thin gray hair. The hound scratched at his thigh with one of her huge paws.

"Yes, Millisant, it's time for bed," Gunthar yawned. "Were you left behind?" He pushed his chair back and stood. "Let's get you to your kennel and me to mine."

Gunthar crossed the banquet hall to a large window overlooking the courtyard, Millisant following at his heel. He opened the window and stepped out onto the battlements. Below, the bonfires burned low, shedding a pale red glow over the courtyard. A few guards stood at their posts or walked their watches, but otherwise the autumn night was quiet. Here and there, a window in some other part of the castle glowed with a dim yellow light. Gunthar breathed deeply of the rich autumn odors, of the wood fires and the smells of the forest. He reached down and tousled the hound's ears.

"Do you smell that?" he asked her. "It makes the old heart leap."

Together, they strode along the battlements toward the kennels. Around towers and angles they walked, taking the grand tour as Gunthar called it, to enjoy a last sniff of air before bed. Millisant trotted obediently at heel, matching her pace to her master's. Along the way, they met a few guards standing watch, men and women who snapped to attention at their approach. Gunthar nodded to them as he passed, and Millisant sniffed them curiously.

Where the forest drew closest to the castle walls, there was a stair that led down from the battlements to a small inner courtyard. Here were the kennels and the stables, and the smokehouse where meats and cheeses were preserved. Near this area, there was an angle where part of the castle jutted out to take advantage of a bluff of rock. As Gunthar approached this place, Millisant suddenly moved ahead of him, her head dropped low, her hackles bristling. Gunthar slowed, his hand straying to the sword at his side. The torches along this section of wall had burned out, but he saw a lone figure blocking the way. Millisant growled dangerously. The figure snapped around, surprised.

"Who goes there?" Gunthar asked.

"Oh, Lord Gunthar, it's you," the figure answered in apparent relief. It stepped forward where the light was better, but Millisant's snarls brought him to a stop. "It's Tohr," he said from the half-shadows.

"Lord Tohr, what brings you out here? I thought you had retired for the evening," Gunthar said.

"Am I not free to go where I please, Lord Gunthar?" Tohr asked.

"Yes, yes, of course you are," Gunthar apologized. "Millisant, heel." Slowly, the hound retreated to his side, and he scratched her behind the ears to calm her.

Tohr stepped into the light but stood with one hand still behind his back. "It's a fine night," he commented as he looked up at the stars. "We don't often see such clear nights in Neraka."

"It's the forest," Gunthar said. "It filters out all the bad, leaving everything clean and new." He sighed. "I have often wondered what it is like in Neraka. I always imagine it to be a dark place, the sky heavy with reeking smoke, dragons gliding watchfully overhead. . . ."

"It's only a city now," Tohr said. "Not really that different than any other city. But we don't often see the stars there. It is so quiet here, so peaceful," Tohr sighed. "In Neraka, our supreme leader, Lady Mirielle Abrena, requires constant vigilance, constant training. The streets tremble from the boots of marching feet."

"What is she like?" Gunthar asked.

"Lady Mirielle? She is much like you, my lord Gunthar. Her heart and soul is the Knighthood. It is her life," Tohr said. He smiled. "She was very surprised to receive your letter offering to join our two orders. She was considering sending you just such a proposal herself."

"Really!" Gunthar said with some surprise. "Then why did she wait two years to respond?"

"Like yourself, she had many prejudices to overcome before making such a move. I must admit, when first she told me of her plans, I had my doubts," Tohr said.

"It is difficult for either side to trust the other," Gunthar commented.

"Very difficult," Tohr said.

He turned and leaned against the crenellated wall, looking out over the dark forest. As he did so, he moved his hand to his side.

"What have you got there?" Gunthar asked, no longer able to control his curiosity and his feeling that he'd caught Tohr doing something.

"Where?" Tohr asked.

"In your hand there."

"Oh, this?" he produced the folded scrap of paper. "This . . . this is nothing. A note someone sent me."

"You'll forgive me, Lord Tohr, but I must ask to see it," Gunthar said.

Reluctantly, Tohr handed over the scrap. Gunthar took it and stepped closer to one of the still-burning torches. With a quick glance at the leader of the Knights of Takhisis, he opened it and quickly read:

Abandon this foolish notion and leave this land, or you and all your Knights will suffer the consequences.

The unsigned note seemed hastily scrawled on a blank page torn from the back of a book. He held the paper up to the light and saw the watermark of a publisher in Kalaman. He examined the handwriting, but it bore no unusual qualities or identifying style. It could have been written by anyone. Angrily, Gunthar crushed the paper in his fist.

"Where did this come from?" he asked.

"I found it . . . affixed to my pillow with a dagger, when I retired to my room," Tohr said. "Here is the dagger." He produced a small stiletto from his belt.

Gunthar took the weapon in his trembling hand. "This is one of my daggers. I thought I'd lost it." Gunthar's head sank wearily, and he sighed deeply, as though the weight of all Krynn lay upon his shoulders.

"Lord Tohr, I must apologize for mistrusting you," he said. "Truly, you have shown yourself an honorable man by trying to conceal this from me."

"Really, Lord Gunthar, it is nothing; probably the idle threat of some young Knight who'd had too much wine tonight," Tohr said. "Their prejudices will change with time and understanding."

"This is the act of a coward, and I won't allow it. The culprit must be found and punished," Gunthar swore as he tucked the note under his belt.

"Our Knights are young, Lord Gunthar, like fiery young stallions. We must give them loose reins or risk breaking their spirits. There is no need to let one idle voice stir up more suspicion and mistrust than already exists," Tohr urged.

Gunthar smiled. "I see we think alike," he said. "But still, I've been too lenient with them of late. This note is proof of that. Something must be done."

"Only, I beg you, wait a while. Allow time for our Knights to get to know each other, for the barriers of prejudice to lower a bit," Tohr asked.

Gunthar stiffened his back and jutted out his chin. "Very well, then. I will take your advice. I won't mention this until after the hunt." He grinned broadly and grasped Lord Tohr's shoulder. "Come, my friend. I was just returning this young lady to her kennels. Would you like to see my other hounds?"

"Of course," Tohr said, bowing. "Truly, they are the finest of their kind that I've ever seen."

Tohr and Gunthar continued along the battlements, followed closely by Millisant. "They are my pride and joy," Gunthar beamed as he turned onto the narrow stair leading down into the stable yard. "You shall meet the greatest of my hounds, a hero among boar hounds, the great Garr. Always in the past, we've never been able to properly hunt Mannjaeger because we never had the proper dog. But Garr is the one. He shall bring Mannjaeger to bay!"

In his excitement, Gunthar tried to turn to see his

guest's reaction and missed a step. He slipped, teetering over a forty foot drop to the stone courtyard below. Tohr's arm shot out and caught the Grand Master by the sword-belt, dragging him to safety. Together, they leaned against the inner wall, and Gunthar clasped the younger, stronger Knight to his breast, his old heart beating wildly.

"Thank you, my friend," he gasped.

"Lord Gunthar, if this was a test of my good intentions, you could have waited until we reached the lower steps," Tohr joked as he helped Gunthar regain his balance. "I am . . . uncomfortable with heights."

After catching his breath, Gunthar continued down the stairs, more carefully this time and without turning as he talked. Behind them, Millisant awkwardly negotiated the steps. Gunthar explained in some detail the pedigree of Garr, of the bear and boar and deer he had run, and his hopes for the hound's success in the next hunt. They crossed the stable yard, nodding to a couple of retainers they found playing a game of dice outside the door to the kennels.

"We found a stray in the banquet hall," Gunthar said to them in greeting. "She wants back with her fellows."

"Yes, milord," the retainers said as they rose and opened the door. A fetid odor of warm dog and gully dwarf wafted out. One of the retainers took a torch from a sconce and stepped inside, leading the way.

"Did you two get plenty to eat tonight, Fawkes?" Gunthar asked the elder retainer.

"Most certainly, milord," he answered, contentedly patting his belly. "Come on in here, Millisant my lass." The hound trotted inside.

The kennels was a close, dark, low-roofed room that seemed to stretch catacomb-like into the shadows. But unlike a catacomb, the air was warm and dry, if exceedingly ripe with the strong seedy odors of hounds and gully dwarves. The stone floor was strewn with straw, rinds, and well-chewed bones. Most of the hounds slept in a great pile in the center of the chamber, with here and there a small, thick-toed foot or stubby-fingered hand sticking out, twitching in some gully dwarf dream, but off to the side, near the wall, lay curled a hound of enormous size. As Gunthar, Lord Tohr, and the retainer entered, he raised his great head from the floor and blinked at them sleepily with his brown eyes. Millisant trotted over to him, her whole body wagging, and rolled over on her back before him, exposing the lighter gray fur of her underbelly. She licked Garr's face, washing his chin whiskers, and he accepted the attentions of the packling with noble patience.

"That is Garr," Gunthar said proudly.

"Truly, a splendid animal," Tohr said in undisguised awe.

Garr closed his eyes as though regally accepting the compliment. He lowered his head and sniffed Millisant's ears, accepting a friendly ear-chewing from her in return. That finished, Garr settled his chin on his paws and seemed to drop off to sleep.

"There will never be another like him," Gunthar whispered.

"Millisant, bad girl!" said a voice behind them.

A small, rat-skin-capped gully dwarf pushed his way past the Knights' legs and entered the room. At the sound of his voice, the female hound rose, but remained where she stood, her tail drooping between her legs.

"I look all over," the gully dwarf said. "I look two places. Two places, many times." He walked over and patted her on the head with his grubby hand. Millisant fawned before him, though she was twice his size.

"Lord Tohr, may I introduce to you the master of my hounds—Uhoh Ragnap, esquire," Gunthar said.

"Oh, hello, Papa," Uhoh said. "I not see you when I come in. I find Millisant. Sleep now." He flopped down beside Garr and seemed ready to do just that.

"Lord Gunthar, why must you allow these gully dwarves to sleep in here? With their stink, they'll ruin the hounds' noses for sure," Fawkes complained.

"Master Uhoh knows the rules," Gunthar said. "Regular bathing for everyone, every day, for three days before the hunt," Gunthar added. "Uhoh, I'd like you to meet Lord Tohr Malen. Lord Tohr is a Knight who'll be staying with us for a while."

Uhoh remained seated on the floor, staring up at Lord Tohr. He seemed most intent on Tohr's armor, with its skull and thorn and lily symbols, and the symbol of the five-headed dragon of Takhisis. He scratched his head through his rat-skin cap, as though trying to remember something. Slowly, he stood and settled his baggy clothes around his body.

"Very pleased meeting you," he said, extending his hand to Lord Tohr.

"He is remarkable, for a gully dwarf," Tohr said from the corner of his mouth as he gingerly shook Uhoh's small, filthy hand. "That's a very interesting name you have there, Uhoh. How did you come by it."

"Ragnap very old and pres . . . pres . . . pres-something name. It go back two generations," Uhoh said proudly.

"I meant your first name. How did you get the name 'Uhoh?' "

"All Aghar get name when born. I get name. Brother get name. Momma get name. Everybody get name. Why you get name?"

"But why were you called 'Uhoh?' Tohr asked slowly.

"Momma got to call me something. Can't call me 'Hey you!'" the gully dwarf said a little angrily.

"I see, but what I meant was . . ."

"That my brother's name," Uhoh said.

Tohr stopped. "What is?" he asked.

"Heyoo. Heyoo Ragnap," Uhoh said.

Lord Tohr turned an exasperated glance upon Gunthar and found him suppressing a smile. "Perhaps I can help," Gunthar said, stepping forward and laying a calming hand on Tohr's shoulder. "Uhoh, tell us the story of when your mother named you."

"Good story, Papa. My favorite," Uhoh said with a smile. He flopped to the floor and leaned back against Garr's chest. "Now, long time, two summers ago, I born. Momma hold me when Aunt Oopsie say, 'What you name pretty boy?' Momma don't know, so she shrug, and drop me plop! on head. She look down and say, 'Uhoh.' "

Scattered applause sounded from the pile of dogs in the center of the room. During the discussion, several of the gully dwarves sleeping there had wakened. Apparently the story was also one of their favorites, for they continued to clap, though few had moved. Uhoh nodded his head and smiled at them.

"Well, enough with tales," Gunthar said with a yawn. "Time for bed. Good night, Uhoh."

"G'night, Papa," the gully dwarf answered as he stretched and yawned, then curled up beside Garr. The hound laid his head on Uhoh's thigh.

"And remember, baths for everyone three days before the hunt," Gunthar said.

"Yes, Papa. Two days," Uhoh mumbled sleepily.

Gunthar walked with Lord Tohr, discussing matters of lands and castles to be garrisoned by various Knights, and of formalities needed to be performed before the joining of their two orders. Finally, they reached the guests' chambers, and Gunthar stopped before the door to Tohr's rooms.

"I'm still worried about that note," he commented as he

prepared to leave. "Perhaps I should post a guard before your door," Gunthar said. "Someone I can trust."

"There is no need, Lord Gunthar," Tohr said. "I don't believe there is any real danger, and if there is, well . . ." he patted the mace which hung at his belt. "I'm not too old to swing old Belle."

"Your mace is named Belle?" Gunthar asked. "How interesting. My wife's name was Belle."

"Yes, I know. My condolences on your loss, Lord Gunthar," Tohr said, bowing.

"Thank you, sir," Gunthar said. "She lived a full life. Do you know, this bedroom was our bedroom before she passed. When she died, I hadn't the heart to stay here, so I moved to a smaller, cozier room in another part of the castle."

"I do not blame you. Surely, the memories associated with this chamber are still too fresh in your mind," Tohr sympathized.

"Yes, well, good night again,"' Gunthar said. "Come along, Millisant. Now where did she go?"

"We already returned her to the kennels, if you remember," Tohr said.

"Did we?" Gunthar asked in genuine surprise. "Ah, yes of course. How stupid of me. Well, good night again." He turned and strolled down the hall. Lord Tohr shook his head and slowly closed the door.

Chapter Eight

Liam eased the door shut, then glanced up and down the dark castle hall. From the opposite wall, a pale beam of light spread from beneath a door, while the other dozen or so doorways lining this hall showed no such light. Liam stood quietly in the darkness, listening, noting a muffled snore coming from somewhere down the hall, but otherwise this section of the castle was silent. The light under the opposite door wavered, as though a shadow had passed before it. Liam tensed and quietly stepped over to the door, pressing his ear against the wood, but he heard no sound.

He rapped lightly on the door, whispering, "Lord Gunthar?"

There was no answer, but again the light shifted. He heard a rustling noise, as of papers being shuffled.

He rapped again, louder. "Lord Gunthar?" he queried.

Still, no answer. Liam tensed and drew the dagger from his belt. He tried the handle of the door. It was unlocked.

He opened it and stepped quickly inside, closing the door behind him and pressing his back against it. Quickly, he scanned the room—Lord Gunthar's private study. A huge wooden desk dominated one corner of the room, while behind it stood a great window, its sashes thrown wide and its long filmy drapes billowing in the night breeze from the courtyard. The other walls were lined with shelves of books and scrolls, battle maps, and atlases of Krynn. A few small tables stood in comfortable nooks, bearing the prizes and honored awards of Gunthar's long and distinguished career. Atop the desk, a tall red candle burned in a bronze dish. The breeze from the open window caused the candle's flame to dance, sending drips of wax running down its length to add to the pool of hardened wax already nearly filling the dish. The floor before the desk was littered with loose papers obviously blown from the desktop by the wind.

With a sigh, Liam sheathed his dagger and began to clean up the papers from the floor. In his distraction, he failed to notice at first the nature of the documents in his hand, but as he straightened them into a proper stack on the desktop, he glanced at the contents of the top page. He read;

While an enemy still occupies the field, the Knight of the Crown may not exit the battle unless he has been relieved to find him safely home and well by his superior forces are needed when assaulting a fortified position. The standard rule is 3-to-1, although a 2-to-1 advantage has been relieved by his superior, or is unable to locate another brother or sister Knight still occupying the field, the standard of his unit, or is otherwise incapacitated and unable to maintain the Knight's horses and arms, in general, one man-at-arms and one retainer shall be granted the Knight as servants.

Liam sank into the chair behind the desk and read the next page, finding it much the same as the first: confused, scrawling, in different hands, as though each break in the train of thought was written by a different person. Neither page was numbered or otherwise gave an indication as to their order. The text of the following page was interspersed with doodles of dragonsaddle designs and dragonlance mountings. The next sheet was covered with Gunthar's own name written again and again, each version in a bolder or more elaborate script than the last. One sheet was an unfinished letter to Gunthar's lady wife. "My dearest Belle," it began, and described events of only three days before, although she had passed away four years ago.

Liam let the papers slide from his hands. "Four years ago today!" he whispered, stunned at this realization. He found it hard to believe that Gunthar's choice of this day, of all days, to invite the Knights of Takhisis to Sancrist was anything other than a deliberate choice. Still, perhaps the old man truly didn't remember. Liam hoped so. He looked again at the papers, noting here and there in the rambling text broken fragments of the Revised Measure of Knightly Conduct.

Over the centuries, the original Measure written by Vinas Solamnus, the founder of the Knights of Solamnia, had been amended so often that it now filled dozens of volumes. It covered every possible aspect of the life of a Knight and how he should react in almost any given situation. It was huge, unwieldy, and rigid, and had nearly led to the destruction of the Knights in the years preceding the War of the Lance. At that time, the Knighthood had grown so dependent upon the Measure for the direction of their lives, they had forgotten the Rule that accompanied it and was the foundation for their concept of honor. *Est Solarus oth Mithas.* My Honor is My Life.

In the afterdays, taking the lesson of Sturm Brightblade to heart, Gunthar began to revise the Measure, to make it more fluid, less demanding. What Sturm had taught them was that a man can be a great Knight without the strict guides of the Measure to direct his actions and define his responsibilities, that true and noble honor teaches the Knight his duty of its own accord. Brightblade had learned much of honor simply by listening to the old tales of Huma and the other great Knights as told him by his mother, and by taking them to heart and trying to emulate those heroes, he had rediscovered the true essence of Knighthood—*Est Solarus oth Mithas*—at a time when it was most needed. In those dark days before the War of the Lance, with enemies all around them, the Knights of Solamnia had seemed more concerned with fighting among themselves over points of honor. Political intrigue had become the order of the day, with various factions vying for the overall power of the Knighthood. Gunthar himself had not been exempt from this, as his position as leader was very much in doubt. But in the darkest hour, when it seemed the Knighthood might truly split, hope arrived in the form of Sturm Brightblade bearing a mysterious dragon orb, a hope not readily apparent to all, because the division in the Knighthood was most immediately defined by support for or against Squire Brightblade. Sturm's arrival seemed likely to deal a final blow to the order.

In the end, however, the arrival of the young Knight brought about a cascade of events which led to the consolidation of Gunthar's power, a turn in the fortunes of those arrayed against the forces of Takhisis, and an eventual end to the war. Sturm's ultimate sacrifice at the High Clerist's Tower helped to heal the cancer threatening to choke the Knighthood, teaching them by its example the true meaning of honor.

Liam Ehrling had been one of the Knights there that eventful day at the High Clerist's Tower, when the dragonarmies of Takhisis attacked. As a Knight of the Crown, he had served under Sturm's command and had taken part in the trap set for the blue dragons attacking them. He never forgot his pain at the realization that their victory had been purchased with the life of a man he'd admired since the first day they met. On a personal level, Sturm's example had helped make Liam the man he was today. Where before he'd been less than serious about his training and his duty, after that fateful day when the tide of the war turned, Liam devoted himself to becoming the best Knight he could possibly be. Once frivolous and given to jollity, he became serious and focused, almost single-minded in his pursuit of excellence, and absolutely devoted to the protection and preservation of the Knighthood Sturm Brightblade had given his life to save.

And now it seemed the deterioration of Gunthar's mental capacity threatened to undermine everything. Was it not enough that he had set the Knighthood on its ear by proposing and moving forward with the merging with the Knights of Takhisis, but the very document meant to help lay the foundation for the future Knighthood seemed no nearer completion than if it had never been written. Gunthar had promised its delivery by the end of the year, and Yule was swiftly approaching, only three short months away! If the state of the entire work was like that of the few sheets scattered across Gunthar's desk, the future of the Revised Measure looked bleak indeed. Liam tore at his mustaches in his frustration, glancing around the room for some sign of a more complete manuscript. The stack of papers on the desk must be Lord Gunthar's early notes, he surmised optimistically.

He heard a voice outside the door and·recognized it as Lord Gunthar's, mumbling as usual. He heard him say, "Mulled wine?" as though to someone he was inviting to join him within.

"Damn, he has company," Liam softly swore. "Probably Lord Tohr." He rose from behind the desk and slipped swiftly to the window as the door opened. Liam stepped outside onto the battlements, but rather than return to his own room, he remained a moment, hidden by the curtain. He'd hoped to have a private word with his master, but now he considered the opportunity to listen to what the leaders of the two orders were planning.

The door shut, and he heard Gunthar cross the room to his bedchamber. In a few moments, he returned. There was a creaking noise, as of someone settling into one of the large comfortable leather chairs in the study.

"Risk! Nonsense, my boy!" Gunthar said, apparently in response to some comment Liam had failed to hear. He stepped closer to the window, careful so the curtain wouldn't reveal him if it blew aside.

"Many were the times your father threw his shield in front of me and stood over me, protecting me when I was down," Gunthar said.

So that's it! Liam thought. Tohr Malen's father was a Knight of Solamnia! No wonder Gunthar trusts him!

"Have you failed in the past, Sturm?" Gunthar asked his guest.

Liam's breath caught, and he wondered if he had heard right. Did Gunthar just call Tohr Malen 'Sturm?' He shuddered at such a show of mental weakness before their enemy.

"Then I have no fear for the future," Gunthar said.

Throughout all of this, Liam had not heard a single response. Tohr Malen had not struck him as being a soft-spoken man. Liam began to wonder just exactly to whom Gunthar was speaking.

Almost in answer to this unspoken question, Gunthar quickly followed with, "I pledge your good fortune in battle, Sturm Brightblade."

"Brightblade?" Liam gasped. He stepped into the room and found Gunthar standing alone before an empty chair, a mug raised in toast.

At Liam's sudden entrance, Gunthar turned. Without any apparent change or surprise, he said, "Ah, Liam. I was just having a little warm milk before bed. Care to join me?"

"Milord, I was . . . passing on the battlements and heard your voice. To whom were you speaking?" Liam asked. He walked over to the chair and examined it, finding it entirely empty.

"Speaking? Speaking?" Gunthar asked, confused. "Oh, I suppose I must have been talking to myself. Somehow, I've got into that habit. Sometimes I don't even know I am doing it."

"That must have been the case," Liam answered reservedly.

"Well, a cup of milk, then?" he asked.

"Thank you, no. I'm off to bed," Liam said. Slowly, he moved toward the door.

"Didn't come to try to change my mind, then?" Gunthar teased.

"It's too late for that, isn't it, my lord?" Liam said. "We cannot send them away honorably, now that you have brought them here, not unless they do something to betray your trust."

"Ah, Liam," Gunthar said warmly, "that is why I chose you to succeed me when I die. Your sense of honor is beyond compare."

"You chose me, my lord?" Liam asked.

"Of course, the Measure prescribes that a vote be taken to determine the next Grand Master, but as my wishes have been explicitly stated in my will, I doubt anyone will challenge you," Gunthar said.

"You do me too much honor, my lord," Liam said as he bowed. He opened the door, then turned to face Gunthar. "Speaking of the Measure, how is your work progressing?"

"Almost finished," Gunthar said, smiling hugely. "Just need to tighten things up a bit, a snip here, a cut there, for clarity's sake."

Liam sighed, his mind wracked with doubt, but he said, "Very good, my lord. Well, good night."

"Good night, Liam," Gunthar answered. "Pleasant dreams."

With a frown, Liam closed the door and leaned his head against the wooden frame, his emotions torn between loyalty to his lord and duty to the Knighthood.

From beyond the door, he heard Gunthar close the window, then ease himself into one of the chairs.

The Measure doesn't provide for his removal from office, and he won't listen to reason. But if something isn't done soon, he'll lead the Knighthood into ruin, Liam thought.

"Fizban!" Gunthar shouted inside the room.

Chapter Nine

During the week between their arrival and the day of the hunt, the Knights of Takhisis spent the time gingerly getting to know their Solamnic counterparts. They shared quarters and messes and turns about the watch. On the third day, a contingent of both Knights rode out to inspect several nearby castles, including Castle Kalstan, where Sir Liam Ehrling made his home when not attending Lord Gunthar. Gunthar could not help but notice Liam's scowl as his one time enemies tramped the grounds of his beloved castle, inspecting it approvingly.

Two Knights of Takhisis were sent to Xenos to invest the castle there and to prepare for Lord Tohr's eventual arrival. Xenos was to be handed over to Tohr as the base of his operations.

Nevertheless, aloofness remained between the once-opposing orders. Gunthar and Tohr were always close by, defusing short tempers. The boar hunt would be the first true test of the Knights' unity.

The morning of the hunt rose gray and cold with the first breath of winter. A deep icy mist lay over Castle uth Wistan, shrouding its topmost towers and transforming the great trees of the surrounding forest into shadowy wraiths of giants. Water dripping from the eaves of the castle formed pools in the cobblestone stable yard where squires and horses waited, stamping their feet in the cold. The smoke of their breath wreathed the horses' heads, their harnesses jingling in the still air whenever they moved. The hounds, crowded in the door of the kennels, sat shivering with their gully dwarves, licking their wet noses, and yawning sleepily. Garr stood aloof from them all, a simple leash of well-chewed leather dangling from his great neck, his iron-gray chin whiskers sparkling with condensed mist. Uhoh scratched his cap and chewed the tip of his beard. A rooster crowed halfheartedly.

All the outer courtyard had already filled with people from the surrounding countryside—peasants, craftsmen, farmers, and merchants. Visitors had arrived from outlying cities and villages, from Garnet and Knas, Markennan and Gavin. They came in carriages, on horseback, and by foot, and they quickly filled the courtyard, spilling over into the open spaces between the castle and the forest. Some erected multicolored tents to shelter the wares they hoped to sell. Many came to watch the hunt, to see the Knights ride out with their hounds and their spears in all their pomp and glory, but most came to get a glimpse of the mysterious Knights of Takhisis so recently come to their island stronghold. Although it was a festive occasion, with jugglers and performers and street magicians entertaining the crowds atop hastily built stages, and merchants in their stalls hawking everything from buttons to barrels of wine, the cold and misty morning dampened all sound, while the chill fog subdued the mood of many a fair-goer. Jugglers dropped their batons and pins, troubadours forgot entire verses of even the best-known ballads, while the hawkers' cries were less than enthusiastic. Most people shook their heads in dismay, or made surreptitious signs to ward away evil.

No one really expected the infamous boar, Mannjaeger, to be killed this day. Mannjaeger wasn't flesh and blood. Weapons of iron, wood, or steel couldn't harm him. Most people native to Sancrist firmly believed the boar was an evil spirit left over from the Age of Dreams. Certainly, tales of his destructive ways stretched back into legend. Just as the hills had always been here, so had Mannjaeger. Huge he was, a giant among boars, the evil ruler of all lesser boars, the stories said, standing fully as tall as the tallest horse, his great black, razor-haired back humped like the hump of a whale, his hairless haunches crawling with ticks and bearing the scars of enough spear thrusts to fell a dragon. His ivory tusks, it was said, were each fully a yard in length, dusky twin scimitars able to shear through even the mountain-forged links of dwarven mail. Some stories said his hot breath turned flesh to stone, while others held that it was the hate-filled glare of his baleful red eyes that froze men's blood and turned the bravest boar hound into a whimpering cur. Arrows turned to smoking ash upon striking him, and his hooves struck sparks wherever he stepped, lighting the fires that set fire to farmers' fields and barns.

Many were they who'd tried their luck and their courage against the terror of Mannjaeger. It was even said that Vinus Solamnus had hunted him in his time, without success. But perhaps Mannjaeger's most famous victim was Lord Gunthar uth Wistan's grandfather, old Seigfreid uth Wistan. One warm summer's day, whilst berry picking with his grandchildren, the elder lord of Castle uth Wistan surprised the boar in a thicket of whortleberry. Unarmed, he fought gamely to save the lives of his grandchildren, and paid with his life while they escaped.

Lord Gunthar was remembering his ancestor as he made his way to the stable yard, last in a long orderly procession of strangely subdued Knights of Takhisis and Solamnia. Like those already outside, the chill and foggy weather had affected the spirits of the Knights as well. They seemed introspective as they remembered the legends and myths surrounding the creature they were about to hunt. Not that they were afraid, for most of them had faced monsters equally fearsome. No, more than anything else the timing of the hunt felt wrong. It seemed hurried and ill-planned, and the bad weather only helped to strengthen their feelings that the hunt should be postponed. Gunthar's greatest worry was that the icy weather would prevent his hounds from scenting the boar's trail, but he was determined to go ahead with the hunt. His Knights needed saddle time with their new comrades in arms.

As they neared the door to the stable yard, a trumpet blared from a tower overhead. As if in answer to the fanfare of horns, the mist began to lift, unveiling banners with kingfishers, swords, and roses on fields of argent and blue hanging majestically from the towers. But for the first time, as a sign of the change, pennons of black and red also hung between those of blue, with images of skulls and lilies and wreathes of thorns emblazoned in gold upon them. At the sound of the trumpet, the Knights of both orders exited the castle, filing into the stable yard where their horses waited.

As Lord Gunthar stepped out into the gray dawn, the other Knights were mounting their horses and awaiting his arrival. Lord Tohr Malen sat astride a magnificent black stallion given him by his host for the occasion, while Gunthar's trusted retainer, Fawkes, held the bridle of Gunthar's own steed, Traveler—a dapple gray. Sir Liam clambered into the saddle of his great horse—a bay gelding—and sat hunched with a dark cloak gripped tightly around his body and the hood pulled low over his face against the cold. His breath, floating in smoky clouds from the hood, gave him a sorcerous appearance. Gunthar felt more than saw Liam's eyes staring out from that cowl. The past week had not been easy for Gunthar, watching his favorite student and chosen successor sulk and mope about the halls of the castle, a veritable harbinger of gloom. Well, Liam was just going to have to accept that this was the way things had to be, that was all. Gunthar slapped his heavy leather gauntlets against his thigh and descended the short stair to the cobblestones below.

As Fawkes held the stallion's bridle, Gunthar mounted into the saddle. Traveler sidestepped and danced a circle as he took the reins, until Gunthar brought him under control. With a wave of his hand, he sent Fawkes scurrying into the stable.

"Knights! Ladies! Gentlemen!" Gunthar shouted in a voice that seemed overloud in the lifting mist. "I pledge you all good hunting! Let us drink the stirrup cup of hot mead, as our fathers did of old."

At these words, Fawkes reappeared carrying a large steaming pewter horn. The vessel was carved with images of leaping stags, while wild, satyrlike creatures chased them with drawn bows. He handed it up to Lord Gunthar, who raised it in toast to his fellow Knights. When he had drunk, the horn passed among the others.

In all, both orders of Knighthood were equally represented, with six members from each. For the Solamnics, Lord Gunthar was their leader, with Liam Ehrling, Quintayne Fogorner, and Meredith Turningdale. Ellinghad Beauseant was present for the Knights of the Sword, and Lady Jessica of Isherwood represented the Crown Knights. Lord Tohr Malen led the Knights of Takhisis, with his seconds Alya Starblade and Valian Escu. The other Knights of Takhisis were ladies Cecelia and Delia Waering, sisters both by blood and by their vows of obedience to Takhisis. The lone Thorn Knight was the gray-robed Trevalyn Kesper, who sat in his short-stirruped saddle like a frost-bitten scribe on a stool, his knees up around his chest and his arms wrapped around them for warmth.

Each pair of Knights would be accompanied by a squire, who would carry spears and provide another pair of eyes during the hunt. Since the Knights of Takhisis had brought no servants with them, squires were chosen from the available men-at-arms at the castle. Also, much to the Knights' dismay, gully dwarves were to trail along, to attend to the hounds. Most considered the gully dwarves more a hindrance than a help, but they consoled themselves with the fact that all would quickly be left in the dust once the chase began.

Gunthar chose Uhoh to attend him. While the others waited their turns with the cup, he introduced the gully dwarf to Trevalyn. Already discomfited by having to participate in such a vigorous event as a hunt and miserable in the cold, wet weather, Trevalyn withdrew deeper into his gray robes and said not a word in response. Gunthar shrugged and raised his hand to get everyone's attention.

"When the first hound strikes a trail, the nearest squire will blow his horn," Gunthar directed. "When you hear it, break off your hunt and converge with the sound of the horn. The forest is crisscrossed with game trails, so it is rather easy to become lost if you do not know the way. If you do get lost and cannot find your way back to the castle before dark, we will blow the great horn from the tower gate every turning of the glass, until all have returned safely, or until darkwatch. You should find blankets and provisions in your saddlebags, should you not make it back to the castle by that time."

Lord Gunthar rode now to the gate, the others turning their horses to follow him. The people in the courtyard stopped whatever they were doing to watch. Gunthar halted his horse and stood in the stirrups, turning to face the Knights. "The gods grant you grace and good hunting.

Knights! Forward!" Trumpeters on the battlements blew a fanfare as Gunthar and his Knights rode out.

The people cheered and crowded close to gawk and stare, while the gully dwarves and hounds surged forward, running around and between the horses' legs to get to the front. The large gray hounds cavorted and capered about on their long legs, barking as though laughing with joy. The squires with their bundles of tall spears flanked the group of Knights, some riding well wide of the procession to catch the attention of a group of fur-cloaked ladies gathered near one of the stages. As the Knights crossed the courtyard to the blare of trumpets, pandemonium erupted among the merchants' stalls. Cages tumbled and tables toppled, with chickens and small children cackling and flying every which direction, pursued by hungry gully dwarves. Gunthar rode in front, with the pairs of Knights in ranks following him. Trevalyn Kesper brought up the rear, while a string of whispering children followed at a short distance, daring each other to throw a stone at the gray-robed Knight. He made it a point to ignore them, until a panicked chicken crashed into his head with an explosion of white feathers. His audience rolled on the wet ground, giggling hysterically, but he soon left them behind, his dignity as ruffled as the feathers he picked out of his beard.

Uhoh Ragnap scurried hither and thither, thwacking gully dwarves on the head with a discarded riding crop he'd picked up somewhere, and rousting hounds with the toe of his boot, until he managed to get all his charges outside the castle walls. One or two of his fellow Aghar burped feathers and hid their guilty smiles behind grubby hands. The Knights rode out behind the last hound, followed by the squires, who had to duck their spears to get them under the postern. Once free of the confines of the courtyard, they loosened their reins and galloped about the green. Uhoh sighed and leaned against the wall, and the great hound Garr paced over and stood beside him, staring sleepily at nothing in particular, as if to say, "When you are ready to be serious about this, let me know."

Uhoh was not allowed a long rest, for soon the hounds and gully dwarves had found the merchant stalls outside the walls of the castle. A stampede of sheep nearly toppled the stage where an acrobat was demonstrating his balancing skill atop a ladder. He fell with a shriek into a cart laden with apples. "Fungduggers!" Uhoh cursed as he stomped off, the riding crop held menacingly in his small fist. He turned back to the great hound. "Garr! Find. Gather," he shouted.

With a yawn, Garr trotted into the crowd. Soon, canine yelps of pain sounded over the noise of the fair, as hounds pelted by the merchants, singly or in small groups, emerged to gather near the edge of the forest. Alongside them trotted gully dwarves sporting fresh new red welts.

Finally, everyone collected near the forest: Knights, squires, hounds, and gully dwarves. The crowds pushed along, trying to get a glimpse, wishing to be near when the hounds were loosed. All the while the mist continued to lift until, as though Paladine himself, gone now from Krynn but not forgotten, gave his divine approval to the proceedings, the sun broke free from the mist and bathed the field in scarlet and gold light. The colors of the tents and banners and flags leaped out from the mist, seeming to burn it away like a bad dream.

The Knights began to talk excitedly of hunts remembered and forgotten, hounds yelped and barked, horses stomped and blew in their eagerness to run, filling the air with military noises and smells of cavalry. Gunthar smiled hugely, seeing his Knights and the Knights of Takhisis forgetting their differences in their excitement about the day.

Gunthar rose in the stirrups and gestured to a nearby

squire. "Release the hounds!" he shouted. The squire lifted a silver trumpet to his lips and blew a long wild quavering air. The pack erupted with howls and boiled into the forest. Uhoh, clinging to Garr's leash, was dragged, laughing hysterically, into the underbrush by the massive hound. He soon vanished in the gloom. The crowd roared with delight.

Next, knights and squires put spurs to their mounts and leaped in pursuit. Lord Tohr's black warhorse led the charge down the main road to Gavin, while others veered onto smaller trails along the way. Soon, most of the Knights were out of sight, strung out along miles of dark winding forest paths, while all around them in the impenetrable wood they heard hounds yelping and barking uncertainly as they searched for a scent of the boar. They quickly left behind all but the sturdiest of the gully dwarves, most of whom were only too glad to return to the fair.

Within a hundred yards of entering the forest, Trevalyn Kesper was bounced from his saddle and landed with a thud in the middle of the road. This was not unexpected, as the Thorn Knights were mages and not used to the rigors of the saddle. His horse continued along its merry way, apparently intending to continue the hunt despite the loss of his rider. He rose and stalked back to the castle.

As the morning progressed, the hunt spread farther and wider throughout the forest. Lord Gunthar found himself alone, having lost his squire at the crossing of a thinly iced stream. Soon he came upon Uhoh trotting back down the trail, a bit of broken leash still in his fist. A nest of leaves and twigs stuck out from his rat-skin cap. "Hello, Papa!" the gully dwarf grinned with dirt-caked teeth. "This some hunt!"

As if in answer, a horn blew wildly somewhere to their left. "There he is!" Gunthar exclaimed. He stopped his mount and allowed Uhoh to clamber up behind him. They heard hounds baying and howling, the sound dwindling in the distance. With Uhoh finally settled in, Gunthar touched spurs to Traveler's sides and charged off down the forest path. The trail was well known to him, for he'd rode it many a time, even at night, so Gunthar was not afraid to allow Traveler his full head. The forest raced by in a blur of speed, wind whistling in their ears.

After a while, Gunthar reined in his mount to listen. Uhoh clung tightly to his waist, almost squeezing the breath from the old man. As they stood on the trail beneath a huge elm tree, Uhoh pointed off to their right. At first Gunthar didn't hear, but then perhaps the hounds drew closer, for he caught, at the edge of hearing, a squire's horn blowing.

"Aha!" he growled.

He was about to give Traveler a spur when Uhoh tugged at his elbow. "No, Papa! No, Papa!" he shouted. "Listen."

Now behind them, another horn was blowing. Then another to their right, and then ahead. All around them hounds bayed, hot on a trail, some moving away, one toward them, one across their path.

"Some mischief is afoot, my boy," Gunthar said to Uhoh. "There can't be this many boars in the forest today."

"Mischief, Papa. Very bad mischief," Uhoh agreed as he renewed his grip on his master.

Gunthar struggled to breathe. Somehow, the forest seemed close and hot, the air too thin, or perhaps it was Uhoh's vicelike hold around his belly. He felt the blood pounding in the veins of his neck, flushing his cheeks. Beads of sweat appeared on his brow.

"Uhoh, loosen up a bit, my boy," he gasped. "Let me catch my breath."

Struggling to breathe, Gunthar urged Traveler ahead, but the horse only took a few hesitant steps. The air seemed to grow thinner by the moment. Gunthar heard Uhoh gasping frantically behind him. It was as though all the air of the forest was being sucked up, devoured, even from their lungs. The sounds of the horns and hounds dwindled and faded, until all they could hear was their own wheezing.

Then they heard it—a woofing and chugging sound, like a gnomish engine broken loose and running berserk through the forest. Twigs cracked and branches snapped, the ground thudded as something hugely dark and menacing bulled through the forest immediately to the left of the path. Gunthar felt it more than he saw it, like a great shadow of evil moving at the edge of sight. A hot fetid air carried a smell wholly wild and untamed to his nostrils. This was a smell he remembered; it rose up, ghostlike, from his childhood memories. He'd smelled it the day his grandfather was slain.

Uhoh whimpered and buried his face in Gunthar's back, while Traveler pranced and whinnied hysterically. Gunthar fought to control his mount, while at the same time fighting to control his own terror. He hadn't really expected to see Mannjaeger this day. The hunt was just an exercise of knightly skills, with the possibility of getting meat for the table. Even to Gunthar, who'd seen his own grandfather slain by the beast, Mannjaeger had always seemed the stuff of legends, a dark figure prowling through the nightmares of his childhood.

The monster passed them by without even turning its head to look at them. It was like some boulder, freed from a mountain side and rolling along, oblivious, elemental, almost ethereal. When it had gone out of sight, Gunthar found his voice, as did Uhoh.

"Hell's bells," the elderly Knight swore.

Uhoh cried, "Oh, bad mischief. Very bad mischief two times!"

Gunthar tightened his grip on his spear and urged his mount down the trail. The forest seemed to close in around them, sending questing roots into the path to trip Gunthar's horse and dangling branches to slap his eye. Before long, their progress brought them back within the spell of thin air surrounding the beast. They heard it chuffing through the undergrowth ahead of them, and the air grew charged with tension and fear, as though they had caught up to a slow moving thunderstorm. It was all Gunthar could do to keep Traveler forging ahead; trained warhorse that he was, he balked at every breaking twig.

The trail turned suddenly and unexpectedly, in a way unfamiliar to Gunthar's experience. He wondered if he hadn't taken a wrong turn somewhere along the way. In any case, he now noticed in the distance ahead an arch of golden light marking the end of the trail. Traveler stepped up when he saw it and began to trot. Gunthar tried to rein him back, but to no avail; the horse seemed desperate to reach the light. Gunthar swore and shouted, tugged and tore at the reins, but Traveler galloped onward, tossing his mane and snorting.

Suddenly, a loop of leafy vine seemed to materialize before them. It hung over the path as perfectly as a trap intentionally set. Traveler easily ducked his head under it, but Gunthar, atop the saddle and encased as he was in stiff armor, could not bend so low. Desperately, he tried to fend off the vine with the shaft of his spear, but his aim was awry from the palsy in his hands. The vine looped under his arm. Gunthar dropped the reins and grabbed the saddle horn, hoping to hold himself in the saddle. The vine stretched taught, creaked, branches snapped overhead, but the great dappled war horse plunged against its pull. It was more than the old man could take. His fingers slipped from the sweaty leather horn. The vine catapulted him from the saddle.

It was very strange, those brief few airborne moments. Gunthar had flown dragonback during the War of the Lance, but even riding a dragon wasn't that much different than riding a horse—if you didn't look down. But this was different. For one thing, he had a gully dwarf crawling over his shoulder. Secondly, he no longer claimed a saddle between his legs, even though his legs retained the saddle shape in mid-air. Thirdly, the moment he realized he was airborne, he could only think of how he might land.

But the flight lasted a few heartbeats at most, hardly enough time to think of a landing. As the ground rushed up at him, Gunthar realized he still had hold of his spear, so he threw it away to keep from landing on it. Uhoh continued to claw and scratch until he was on top of Gunthar's chest. The old man landed flat on his back, and small as the gully dwarf was, Uhoh's weight crushed the air from Gunthar's lungs.

Uhoh screamed. Even after they hit the ground, and even after they'd been on the ground for a while, he continued to scream. He screamed until Gunthar summoned enough strength to push him from his chest, where Uhoh still clung in terror. Slowly, Gunthar sat up, feeling twinges race up and down his spine.

"I'm going to pay for that in the morning," he moaned.

"Very bad mischief," Uhoh whimpered.

"Very bad indeed. Why did you have to land on poor old Papa?" Gunthar asked.

"Uhoh on bottom, very bad," he answered. "Papa two times as big as Uhoh."

"I feel like I've just lost a dragon joust," Gunthar said. He looked around, wincing at the pain of turning his head. "Now where did that crazy horse get to? I thought surely he'd stop when he felt us fall. It isn't like him to run away."

"Horse go that way," Uhoh said, pointing to where the path ended under the shimmering arch.

Gunthar rose painfully to his feet, assisted with a feeble shove from behind by the gully dwarf. "I'm not as young as once I was," he said. "Do you know how old I am, my boy?"

"Two and two and two?"

"That's right. Two and two and two, and many more two." He put his fists in the small of his back and straightened up, groaning.

"That many," Uhoh said with awe. "You older than Great Highbulp."

"I am older than these very hills. When I was born, this place was flat. No trees, no mountains. Just me. The hills came later," Gunthar moaned as he finally reached his full height.

"Come. We go now," Uhoh said.

"No, no. That's the wrong way," Gunthar said as Uhoh retreated up the path.

"This way to castle," Uhoh said, pointing hopefully.

"But we have to find Traveler, my boy. We have to finish the hunt. A true Knight never breaks off contact with the enemy so easily," Gunthar said.

Reluctantly, kicking leaves and angrily swinging his arms, Uhoh returned to Gunthar's side.

"That's better. Chin up, my boy. You are already on your way to becoming a true Knight. Let's see where this path leads," Gunthar said.

"Probably very bad place," Uhoh mumbled as he stumbled behind his master.

They followed the unfamiliar trail for another hundred yards or so, before it finally opened into a large glade filled with golden light. Gunthar squinted in the brightness, but the hazy air prevented him from judging the position of the sun, and thus the time of day. The air hummed with unseen wings. As Gunthar and Uhoh entered the glade, their feet kicked up swarms of grasshoppers and tiny lace-winged midges. The grass was tall and golden-green, as were the leaves of the strange bushes growing in natural hedges along the banks of a silver stream; their leaves were golden on one side, forest-green on the other, and they bore berries of silver and red. The air was warm and humid, more like a summer's day in Palanthas than an autumn morning on the Isle of Sancrist.

"This is altogether uncanny," Gunthar said. "I've lived here all my life, but I've never seen this place before. Or have I?" He stroked his mustaches and looked around. Something seemed very familiar about this place.

"That a long time," Uhoh said as he scratched his rat-skin cap.

"I can't seem to focus my eyes in this light," Gunthar commented.

Uhoh squinted and peered, but being a gully dwarf, he relied more on his sense of smell. "Smells like faeries," he said.

"It does look rather elvish, doesn't it," Gunthar said. "Is that a whortleberry patch I see?"

"Definitely fairies," Uhoh said, sniffing again. "Lots of faeries. Two and two and two."

"It certainly seems peaceful. I can't remember being more at peace. This is very strange. I feel so sleepy," Gunthar said with a gaping yawn.

"Fairies very bad. We go now. Back to castle," Uhoh said as he tugged at his master's hand.

Gunthar leaned against his spear. "How did I get here?" he mumbled. "I was looking for something. What was it?"

"Nothing. Come go," Uhoh said insistently.

"My Measure!" Gunthar exclaimed. "Where did I put it?" He patted the pouches at his belt, then stared down at

Uhoh. "Tasslehoff Burrfoot, did you take my Measure?"

"What? No! Me not know," Uhoh said, his voice trembling with fear.

"Tell Lord Derek this is no time for political squabbles. We need every able-bodied Knight for the defense of Palanthas!" Gunthar shouted. He spun on his heel and stalked deeper into the glade. Uhoh followed him at a distance.

As he neared the stream, Gunthar froze in mid-stride. Suddenly, the glade was still, silent. A cloud moved in front of the sun, darkening the air. Gunthar blinked, then stepped back in confusion. He raised his spear in defense, threatening the empty air.

And then he saw it—a great shaggy shape under the eaves of the forest on the opposite side of the glade. It looked like a piece of a mountain come to life and descended from the highlands. Its back rose in a spiked hump fully as high as a grown man's head, while its head was as big around as a pickle barrel. It stared at Gunthar and seemed to yawn, baring its long, glistening ivory tusks, self-whetting weapons as sharp as the blade of an elven dagger. Its piggy red eyes seemed almost to glow in the shadow of its tremendous bulk. When still, it looked as inanimate as stone—when moving, as unstoppable as an avalanche. The tall grass, and even small trees and bushes, bent before its onrushing mass. Quickly, almost before thoughts of danger could form in Gunthar's charm-befuddled mind, the boar crossed the glade and vanished into the gloom of the forest.

Gunthar took another startled step back, almost dropping his spear as he stumbled into Uhoh. Slowly, the normal sounds of the magical summer glade returned.

"Papa go," Uhoh whispered, but Gunthar didn't answer.

Instead, he watched another shaggy shape appear from

the forest, almost at the same spot where he'd seen the first one. This one was smaller and ran with its nose to the ground. For a moment, Gunthar was confused, but then the shape lifted its head and bayed long and mournfully.

"Garr!" Uhoh shouted.

The great hound tucked back his ears and dashed across the meadow, hot on the trail of the boar. "He's got the scent," Gunthar said. "By the gods, he's got him now! Come on, my boy, follow me!"

Gunthar seemed to draw youth and vigor from the excitement of the hunt. Once his quarry was spotted and his hound bayed the scent, he seemed to forget his aches and pains. Gunthar loped across the meadow and splashed through the stream, the weight of his armor seeming hardly any encumbrance at all. He felt almost as though he were flying with winged feet, as if he might leave the ground and take to the upper winds. The heavy boar spear, with its crossbar of iron just below the steel head, plowed a wake through the grass before him.

Chapter Ten

"There, there, my boy," Gunthar said with a sigh, trying to comfort the gully dwarf. "There, there."

Uhoh wept as he lifted the heavy, deadweight of Garr's head and placed it in his lap. The hound's black tongue, clenched between his fangs, oozed a little blood, but his barrel chest no longer swelled with breath, and his eyes, though still deep and brown and not yet glazed with death, were dull, unseeing. Uhoh wet Garr's muzzle with his tears as he kissed the dog again and again.

"No, Garr. Very bad. Come home, Garr," he cried as he rocked back and forth.

"Don't cry, my boy," Gunthar said. "He died as he would have wished—in . . ." his voice cracked, and he was forced to look away. "In battle," he finished, staring up at the sky and blinking in the sunlight.

"Garr no die," Uhoh sobbed. "Garr no die now."

"He died like a true Knight, in single combat with his sworn enemy," Gunthar said to the sky.

Uhoh stroked the dog's fur over and over, his tears rolling in tracks through the grime on his face. "Poor Garr," he moaned. "Maybe Uhoh take you home, patch ouch, and Garr not dead no more."

He had done it before. He'd taken care of Gunthar's

hounds for many months now, and more than once he'd tended their wounds and helped them to heal. With his small fingers, Uhoh tenderly searched the hound's body for an injury, but he found no indication of blood or torn flesh or broken bones of any kind. The only blood came from the hound's bitten-through tongue.

"Why Garr die?" he asked.

"That is the way of things, my boy," Gunthar explained. "We grow old, we get hurt, or we get sick. It is how nature moves."

Uhoh rolled the dog over and examined the other side. Again, he found almost nothing. Other than a small cut on the dog's flank, he bore no readily apparent injuries. "Why Garr die?" he asked again.

"Ours is not to reason why, my boy," Gunthar said. "We just have to accept it."

"But him not hurt," Uhoh said.

"What?"

"Him not hurt."

"Let me see. Are you sure?" Gunthar asked as he kneeled beside the hound. Together, they examined Garr from nose to tail. Gunthar paid particular attention to the tiny wound on the hound's flank, finding it well-crusted with dried blood. "This must have happened earlier in the hunt. It looks like a tusk wound, but I suppose it could have happened anywhere. Certainly not in this fight. Poor Garr breathed his last as I found him."

He stood and examined the ground around the boulder. "Yes, there was a desperate battle here. Look how the ground is torn up by the beast's hooves, where he charged and turned and charged again. I wonder that I never heard it. The ridge must have hidden the sound. And what's this?" He stooped and picked something from the litter of leaves. "It looks like a scale. What do you make of this, my boy?" he asked as he handed the object to Uhoh.

The gully dwarf looked at the queer find as it lay glistening on the palm of his hand. The thing did indeed appear to be a scale, but not like the scale of any fish Uhoh had ever eaten. It looked more like a lizard's scale, but he'd never seen a bronze-colored lizard before. Or had he?

"Oh, very bad mischief. Very bad!" Uhoh shouted.

"What's wrong?" Gunthar demanded.

"Very bad veryveryveryverybad!" Uhoh jumped to his feet.

Gunthar turned and faced the dark eaves of the forest. "Be quiet," he whispered. "I hear it now." He cupped his hand over the gully dwarf's mouth. Uhoh fell silent. They listened together.

There was a grunt.

"Go home now Papa," Uhoh mumbled into Gunthar's palm.

He began to run in place. Gunthar fumbled for his spear and dragged it to his side. Without ever allowing his eyes to leave the forest, he managed to lift it before him, the butt of the spear lodged under his foot. He stared into the wood, seeing only the lighter gray of the trunks standing in serried ranks, until spots began to burst before his eyes. Boar-shaped spots, he thought them. He blinked.

A gut-wrenching squeal shook the trees. The ground rocked, and loose soil spilled down the slope. Like a piece of a mountain brought magically to life, Mannjaeger appeared from the shadow of the wood into the full light of day, red eyes burning with hatred. For some reason, Gunthar fixated on the pink tongue lolling between twin scimitars of yellow ivory. He almost seemed hypnotized by it. It curled and rolled, the black spots on its underside sliding like the pattern on the back of a snake. A droplet of blood rolled down the length of the tongue and splattered on a leaf, joining the small puddle forming below his mangled throat. Garr had struck a mighty blow after all.

Raw flesh gaped from a horrific bite, one that would have felled a lesser beast.

Only at the last moment, when he felt the living thing struggling in his hands, did Gunthar come back to his senses. He flung the writhing gully dwarf aside, then tried to bring his spear to bear, but it was too late. Mannjaeger plowed into him. Gunthar felt the world heave beneath him as a force like that of a battering ram exploded against his breastplate.

His ancient Solamnic armor, crafted a century ago by the best Solamnic smiths, served him well. The boar's tusks screeched against his steel greaves and clattered uselessly on his breastplate. Nevertheless he felt the hammer force of each blow and the crushing power of each bite. In a matter of moments, he was bleeding from a dozen wounds, more from the tumbling he received than the boar's tusks. He never was quite able to regain his feet. Every time he seemed about to get his balance, Mannjaeger struck him again. He felt like the survivor of a shipwreck who finds his greatest danger is of being drowned in the shore surf. He soon began to grow weary, as each new wave struck him down and dragged him back out to sea.

Then the boar was gone. He no longer felt its weight, no longer smelled its rancid breath. He lay still in the leaves, suddenly at peace. He didn't dare open his eyes, for he felt the ground beneath him shake as the monster prowled around his body, sniffing, grunting.

"Gulpfunger spawn!" There was a loud meaty thwack, and a squeal like the rusty gates of the Abyss being pushed open by hell's own legions. Gunthar dreaded to open his eyes. He only wanted to lie there and let himself fall asleep. "Glickenspogger!"

Slowly, Gunthar sat up and clenched his teeth, waiting for the inevitable blow of a renewed attack. He clenched shut his eyes and hoped it was all a bad dream, and that he'd be waking in his own warm bed beside his lovely wife Belle, and that everything, everything he'd ever seen and done and suffered had all been one long spicy gnome-cuisine-induced nightmare. No Council of Whitestone. No War of the Lance. No Sturm Brightblade to die at the High Clerist's Tower. No attack of Palanthas by the Dark Lady's army to claim his eldest son's life. No Chaos War to take his last son. No heartbreak to slowly rob his Belle first of her wits and then of her life. Paladine, I pray, give me a life quietly average. I never wished to lead the Knights. I'd trade it all for a little castle on the coast and my family at my side again. My boys, my poor poor boys. I miss them so.

"Get away from Papa, you . . . you . . . you Chugsnorter!" Thwack. Squeal!

Gunthar sighed and opened his eyes.

Uhoh crouched beside a boulder, a small round stone poised behind his ear, ready for throwing. For some reason, Mannjaeger hesitated. Perhaps he had never before smelled a gully dwarf and was trying to figure out if they were too noxious to eat. He restlessly plowed the earth with his hooves and snorted the air. Thick strings of bloody drool poured from his champing jowls.

Gunthar was surprised to find his spear undamaged and near at hand. In fact, he thought it lucky he hadn't been speared by it himself. He used it to help himself to his feet, while the boar was distracted with the gully dwarf. Not until then did he notice he had not passed through the meat grinder unscathed. One particularly vicious slash had rent the chain mail protecting his thigh and sliced a finger-long wound as cleanly as if it had been done with a razor. But for some reason, the wound burned like dragon fire, robbing that leg of all strength. He leaned heavily on the spear just to keep from falling, and despite his best efforts, a groan escaped his lips.

Mannjaeger spun at the noise. Finding the more immediate threat of the man, he charged. With black spots swimming before his eyes, Gunthar balanced himself on one foot and lowered his spear to receive the charge. Uhoh shouted something unpronounceable and hurled his stone. It struck the boar in the eye, causing him to swerve slightly and impale himself on Gunthar's poorly aimed thrust.

Mannjaeger screamed as he lunged away, blowing blood from his mouth and tearing the spear from Gunthar's grasp. Gunthar collapsed, but the boar charged into the forest, dragging the well-lodged weapon behind him. He continued to thrash and bellow, hidden by the shadow of the wood, until finally all sound died away.

Gunthar groaned and rolled onto his side. With the danger gone, the pain in his leg grew to blinding intensity. He clawed at his wound, trying to see the cause of the burning. Strangely, the wound had already crusted over with dried black blood. Gunthar fell back in the blood-spattered leaves beside Garr's body. For a moment, he grew quiet as he looked into the dog's empty eyes. Then he began to thrash and moan in pain.

Uhoh was by his side. "What wrong, Papa? What wrong?" he asked.

"The dagger! Betrayed!" Gunthar cried. "Fool! Planned . . . they led us . . . apart. Only Garr able to follow the true trail, and he knew I'd follow Garr. I should have known. But how? I chose him. I trusted him." The pain engulfed his hips and abdomen. He felt as if he was slowly being lowered into a pot of boiling oil.

"Who, Papa? What?" Uhoh whimpered confusedly as he tried to calm his master's throes.

"I chose him. I trusted him," was all Gunthar seemed able to say. Spittle flew from his lips and bloody foam poured down his chin as his words became lost in horrible convulsions. He seemed to twist upon himself like a wounded snake. His lips drew back in a fearful grimace, and the woods echoed with his screams. In terror, Uhoh scrambled out of the way and hid behind the boulder. He pressed his face against the cool stone and bit his lip.

Finally, his master grew quiet. Uhoh peered around the boulder and saw Gunthar lying flat on his back, as still as stone. Even the palsy was gone from his hands. Uhoh crept to his side, fearful of what he might find, but as he drew near, Gunthar's bloodshot eyes swiveled in his head. He blinked, then a weak smile stirred his Solamnic mustaches.

"Ah, very good, my boy. I was afraid I was going to die alone," he said faintly. "I'm sorry, I can't seem to move my hands. Come closer and hold mine, won't you, my boy?"

Reluctantly, Uhoh touched his master's hand. He found it cold and hard, like marble. Though his body was rigid, the muscles of the old man's face continued to twist and writhe. "What wrong, Papa?" Uhoh whispered.

"You must do something for me, Uhoh," Gunthar said.

"What, Papa?"

He groaned as a fresh spasm wracked his face. "He thought I was a fool. I was. Now I know. Now I understand. This was the plan from the very beginning. How else . . ." Gunthar's voice trailed off, and his eyes grew dim.

"What me do, Papa?" Uhoh asked again.

"What's that, my boy?" Gunthar started. "Where was I?"

"You with Uhoh," the gully dwarf cried.

"Uhoh, you must do something for me," the old man whispered weakly. "Come closer."

Uhoh leaned over his master, his mud-caked ear nearly touching the old man's lips. The old man whispered something almost inaudible, then sighed heavily. Then, convulsing, Gunthar shoved Uhoh away. "The Knights!" he screamed, long, quavering, dying away. This final effort seemed to drain the last spark of life from his body.

"Knights bad?" Uhoh cried in confusion.

"They've killed me," Gunthar whispered, his eyes closing.

"Knights very bad!" Uhoh growled.

The old man roused at these words. He strained, trying to grasp the gully's dwarf's hand. "No, not all the Knights. You must run home and warn the others. Do you understand?"

"No," Uhoh cried in frustration.

"Good, I knew I could count on you," Gunthar said, smiling weakly as he relaxed.

"Me run away home?" Uhoh asked.

"Yes. Go now," Gunthar said, then his face grew still. His eyes lost their focus and seemed to stare beyond the clouds. A last cloud of steamy breath floated from his lips and dissipated in the cool autumn air.

Uhoh shook his master's body. "Papa, what me do now?" he asked. "What me do now? Papa? Papa!"

He stood and placed his hands on his hips, scolding the still form of his master. "Papa stay. Papa not leave Uhoh."

Gunthar's face seemed to relax. The lines of age and worry fell away, replaced by almost a glow of peace. Uhoh fell to his knees beside Gunthar and stroked the old man's hair with his small, grubby hand. "Uhoh no go. Uhoh stay with Papa," he whispered as tears began to stream down his cheeks, cutting new tracks through the grime. He laid his face against his master's chest and closed his eyes.

"Uhoh never leave Papa," he cried as sobs wracked his little body. He wept until exhaustion claimed him and the peace of sleep stole over his eyes.

Chapter Eleven

"Make sure you get this right," the bozak said to his coppery subordinates as they stooped over Gunthar's body. "It's got to look like he died here in fierce combat." One of them began sprinkling blood from a vial all over the area surrounding the slain hound.

While all this was going on, three more of the copper-scaled draconians appeared from the forest, dragging a large heavy object behind them. As they cleared the wood, they stopped and leaned back against their load, panting heavily with their long, forked tongues lolling and short wings fanning the air. "This is good enough," one of them gasped. The others sighed in relief and staggered away to other tasks, leaving the body lying just off the trail opposite the Grand Master.

Even dead, Mannjaeger was an awesome sight. Although lying on his side, his great bulk loomed like a mountainside, dark and brooding. His head could have served as the battering ram of a minotaur pirate galley, while the look in his eyes, even in death, might turn a medusa to stone. His flesh crawled with lice and parasites sent scurrying for new pastures, now that Mannjaeger had met his demise.

One of the draconians dragged Gunthar's spear from

the forest. He walked over and stabbed it into the body of the boar at least a dozen times, finally fixing the weapon deep in the boar's lifeless chest. Then he removed a bottle from some secret pocket in his uniform and poured fresh blood into the dead wounds. That done, he broke the shaft of the spear over his copper-scaled knee and carefully laid it in Gunthar's outstretched hand. Meanwhile, the bronze-scaled draconian paced the area muttering to himself and sprinkling dust in some kind of mystical pattern. Wherever the dust fell, leaves and twigs that had been disturbed by the movements of the draconians returned to their original places, footprints in the soft soil vanished, while even the air seemed cleansed by its passing, removed of its hot metallic odor—the stench of draconians. The draconian completed his magical work and folded his clawed hands into the sleeves of his robe. The others finished their tasks and darted into the woods, leaving only the bronze draconian and one copper-scaled kapak overlooking the site of Gunthar's death.

"What now, oh great one?" the kapak asked.

"Our work here is complete," the bronze pronounced from the cowl of his robe. "Soon now, my illusions and the illusions of the others will disappear, and those hunting phantom boars will give up their chase and return to the castle. When they do, they'll find Gunthar has not returned, and they'll search for him. That will give us enough time to collect our fee and be gone from this place."

"And then?" the coppery draconian asked with a sly look in his red eye.

"And then nothing, my kapak friend," the bronze snarled. "You return to your sneaking, while we bozaks return to our cleaning up your mistakes with our magic."

"Mistakes! What mistakes? This has gone off perfectly, according to our plan. We didn't even need your help," the kapak snarled. " The Old Man says 'take the bozaks' so we take the bozaks."

"And a good thing, too. If not for me, you would have completely forgotten our gully dwarf friend over there," the bozak laughed derisively. "Go now and make sure his wounds are sufficient to have killed him, even without your poison. We can't have anyone getting suspicious."

With a murderous glance at his companion, the kapak drew an odd dagger from his belt. The dagger's blade was made from a boar's tusk, polished and razor sharp. He started across the trail, but the bozak yanked him back with an excited snarl.

"Idiot!" the bozak screeched. "You'll ruin my spells of concealment. Go around! And be careful."

Glaring at his companion, the kapak stalked around the bodies, stepping carefully with his clawed feet to avoid disturbing a single twig or leaf. Despite his awkward appearance, with large reptilian wings and long snaking tail held aloft for balance, he moved as gracefully and noiselessly as a Palanthian cutpurse. As he neared the body of Lord Gunthar and the gully dwarf lying still as a stone beside him, his long tongue slithered out in anticipation of the mutilation to come. Draconians were cruel, malicious creatures, artificially created when darkest magics were used to twist and defile the eggs of good dragons. A little wanton destruction and mutilation is not so lowly an entertainment as to not excite their appetite for evil. The kapak laughed under its breath as it grasped the gully dwarf by the wrist and rolled him over.

Uhoh awoke with a heart-stopping scream of terror. Its volume momentarily stunned the kapak so that he nearly let go. Still half blind with sleep, Uhoh shouted, "I tell no one, Papa! I not tell!" He kicked and fought to escape, his small but dangerous yellow teeth flashing as he snapped at the claw that held him.

Recovering from his surprise at finding the gully dwarf alive, the kapak struggled to maintain his grip, all the while trying to avoid those clashing yellow teeth. Gully dwarf bites aren't usually poisonous, but they hurt. With a deft move, he flipped Uhoh over and lifted him by one foot. Like the special holds used by minotaur alligator wrestlers, this seemed to have some mystical calming effect on the gully dwarf. Now upside-down, he fell still and quiet, blinking at the draconians fearfully.

"I'll bleed him out," the kapak said as he lowered his tusk-dagger to Uhoh's throat.

"Wait!" the bozak snarled. "Idiot. Don't kill him yet."

"Why not?" the kapak shouted angrily. "Make up your mind, boz!"

"Find out what he knows. Didn't you hear him? 'I tell no one, Papa,' he said. Tell no one what? What did Gunthar tell him before he died?" the bozak asked in hurried and excited whispers.

"Speak up, little rat," the kapak demanded. "What did Gunthar say to you?"

"Papa say lots of things," Uhoh squeaked.

The kapak shook him violently by his leg. "You know what I mean. What are you not supposed to tell? Speak up, before I cut you."

"Kill me, you never find out," Uhoh whispered.

The kapak started at these words, his fanged, reptilian jaw dropping open in surprise. Unable to hear, the bozak demanded, "What did he say?"

"This is no ordinary gully dwarf!" the kapak growled as he shook Uhoh even more violently than before. Uhoh's teeth clacked together like steam-driven gnomish castanets.

"What did he say?" the bozak demanded.

"He won't talk," the kapak said, still shaking Uhoh.

"Bind him, then. We'll take him back to the mountain

for . . . deeper questioning," the bozak ordered. "If Gunthar suspected anything and spoke of it to the gully dwarf, we'll need to know what it was so we can warn the others. Destroy all paths that lead back to the mountain—that is the fourth law of Iulus. There can't be a single clue tying us, or he who hired us. No traces, no witnesses."

Reluctantly, the kapak sheathed his tusk-dagger and loosened a coil of thin rope from his belt, all the while holding Uhoh aloft. Meanwhile, the bozak made a last few magical adjustments to the surrounding area, just to make doubly sure no draconian tracks remained in the soft forest soil. Uhoh whimpered softly, a bit dazed from his shaking. Then he blinked, suddenly alert, and quiet. A few leaves rustled, as though stirred by some unseen breeze. The kapak halted, sniffing, testing the air with his tongue.

From the concealing undergrowth just off the path, a large gray blur streaked out. The kapak screamed in agony, dropping Uhoh on his head. The gully dwarf rolled to his feet, wincingly gripping his bruised pate, and shouting excitedly, "Millisant!"

The boar hound had a firm toothy grip on the kapak's tail and was shaking it like a snake, growling low in her throat. It was a testament to her strength and anger that the screaming draconian was tossed about like a gnome with his suspenders caught in his own machine. Yanked from his feet, he kicked and clawed at the forest floor, trying to regain his footing and ruining all the bozak's careful work of concealment.

With a snarl of rage, the bozak leaped into the fray, then leaped out, painfully shaking his well-chewed hand. With a leaping cavort and a high baritone bark of victory, Millisant dashed away, followed quickly by the gully dwarf. The draconians stared in stunned silence at the woods, then angrily began to blame each other.

Chapter Twelve

A horn continued to blow mournfully throughout the night. As the first snow of the year began to fall, outriders were sent along the better-known trails, calling for Lord Gunthar in case he was lost in the dark. Uhoh slipped past them without being seen, but as he neared the castle, he wondered how he was going to get around the guards at the gate. He sat in the bushes with Millisant at his side and waited. There was nothing else to be done, but he simply had to find a way into the castle without being seen. Soon the snow lay thick across his shoulders and stood in a comical white pile on Millisant's snout. She whuffled and settled onto her haunches, blinking her long lashes at him. Uhoh nodded, as though he understood her perfectly.

As Uhoh sat there, growing sleepy with the cold, a commotion erupted near the gate. Lord Gunthar's horse, Traveler, had appeared from the wood, lame with a tusk wound. As Uhoh watched, Liam Ehrling and Tohr Malen came out from the castle and examined the shivering, exhausted horse, while more riders were quickly mounted and sent out in search of Lord Gunthar. From the castle poured a great many of the other Knights, while a crowd of lingering fair-goers gathered close by to try to get a glimpse of the horse. Uhoh slipped in beside them and inched his way toward the gate, Millisant at his heel. He glanced around and saw the guards busy watching the spectacle, so he dashed beneath the postern and into the courtyard of the castle. As he entered, grooms from the stables hurried out to see to Traveler's wounds, while villagers and Knights alike speculated upon Gunthar's fate.

More than once as they made their furtive way to the stable yard and the kennels, Uhoh and Millisant were forced to detour around Knights and guards nervously patrolling the castle. Luckily, there were still quite a number of peasants and merchants who had not yet gone home from the fair. Besides, what was one more gully dwarf or dog?

Sheep, cattle, and goats wandered the night-darkened grounds searching for some nibble of food, or huddled in small pens sleepily eyeing all the commotion. One old heifer waited alone by her owner's stall, lowing pitifully for a milking, but no one paid her any mind. Every so often, a trumpeter atop the tallest tower of the castle blew his mournful dirge over the forest, a noisy beacon to those lost in the night.

After what seemed liked hours, Uhoh finally reached the stable yard. He found it empty and dark. Inside the stables, horses from the hunt slept in their stalls, while the grooms and retainers were out searching the grounds for any sign of the castle's lost master. Uhoh crept to the door of the kennels and silently opened it. A low dangerous growl answered him.

"Shhhhh!" he hissed.

The growling stopped. "Who there?" someone asked.

"It me. Uhoh Ragnap, esquire," Uhoh answered.

"Uhoh dead. You his ghost?" A note of fear had crept into the speaker's voice.

"I not dead!" Uhoh said. "See. No spook. Me real." He proudly slapped his chest.

Slowly, a pair of gully dwarves appeared from the darkness. Uhoh stepped back so they could see him more clearly in the dim light from the courtyard. One of them was small even for a gully dwarf; she hardly came up to Uhoh's elbow. The second gully dwarf, though much larger than his companion, kept fearfully to the shadows. He was taller than Uhoh by a head, not counting the nest of hair standing straight up from the crown of his head.

"We hear they blow horn for you," the taller Aghar said from the shadows.

"Me no lost," Uhoh said. "Uhoh never get lost."

"What about time when . . ." the taller one began, before the shorter gully dwarf interrupted him.

"They blow horn 'cause you dead," she said as she stepped forward and gave Uhoh a vicious poke to the ribs. "But you not dead. You 'live!" She stepped back in awe.

"Me almost killed by slagd," Uhoh said. "But Uhoh 'scape. Very clever."

"Slagd!" the tall one cried as he vanished again.

But the short one was not so credulous. "Where you see slagd?" she asked suspiciously.

"Uhoh not see. Uhoh picked up, dropped on head by slagd, almost killed!" Uhoh said.

"If you not see slagd, how you know they slagd?" she asked.

"Shut up, Glabella," Uhoh said to her. "You not understand 'cause you not there."

"Psh. You lie," she answered him.

"Me not lie. Papa dead!" Uhoh shouted impatiently. His voice echoing around the stable yard sent him cringing into the shadows of the kennel. He lowered his voice. "Papa dead," he whispered. "Me there. He tell me Knights bad. He tell me secret nobody knows, me run away home. He tell me tell nobody."

"Papa dead?" Glabella asked. "What secret?" she added

with a greedy hiss, her little black eyes flashing.

"Me tell you, it not a secret no more. Very imp . . . very imp . . . very big secret. And slagd want to kill me."

"Why they try kill you?" Glabella asked.

Uhoh scratched his cap and thought for a moment. "Don't know," he said finally. "Maybe they mad 'cause I kill their pig."

"What pig?"

"Big pig what we hunt," Uhoh said.

"Psh. You lie. You not kill pig. Nobody ever kill pig."

"You not know nothing," Uhoh snarled. "Pig dead. Papa dead. Slagd try to make Uhoh dead. Me run away now."

"How many slagd?" the tall gully dwarf asked from the darkness.

"Two!" Uhoh said importantly.

"That many!" the tall one screeched.

"Shhhh!" came a hiss from the darkness. Someone yawned loudly, but Uhoh couldn't tell if it was another Aghar, or just one of the hounds.

"Be quiet, Lumpo. You scream like someone step on toe," he reprimanded the tall gully dwarf. "I sneak back to get things. Now I go home." He entered the kennel and felt his way to the far wall. There he found a small, well-chewed leather bag with a long strap. He slung this over one shoulder and turned to leave, stumbling over the bag because it hung almost to his feet. "Millisant, come!" he whispered. By the time he reached the door, the female hound was at his side, her long tail wagging excitedly.

"Why you run away, Uhoh?" Glabella asked in sudden concern. "You no lie?"

Uhoh stopped and placed one hand ceremoniously over his protruding belly. "Uhoh swear," he said.

"Slagd really try to kill you?" she asked.

"That right. Me know secret. They try to make me talk,

but me get away. Millisant come, bite slagd on tail, he drop me on head. Me run away." He patted Millisant on the head, ruffling her ears. She licked his filthy face.

"And Papa say Knights bad?" Glabella asked, catching Uhoh by the sleeve as he started past her.

"Not all, he say. He say warn the rest. You warned now. Me go home."

"Home!" They were awed by the magnitude of his decision.

Glabella sniffled. "Me go home, too," she said. She dashed off into a corner to gather her things. Uhoh sighed and scratched Millisant behind the ears while he waited.

Suddenly, Lumpo turned and vanished into the utter darkness of the kennel. "You not leave me alone with these gullduggers," he cried. "Me go home, too."

Soon Uhoh's companions were ready. Each one wore a leather bag similar to Uhoh's slung low to the ground. Glabella's dragged behind her wherever she walked. With a sigh and a shake of his head, Uhoh stumbled out into the stable yard with Millisant close at heel. Glabella followed, and Lumpo brought up the rear.

"Where home?" Lumpo asked.

"Town," Uhoh answered.

"Oh. How far?"

"Two days. Not more than two," Glabella said.

Chapter Thirteen

Three days had passed since Dalian Escu stumbled upon Gunthar's body lying in the snow. At his feet had lain his broken spear, by his side the noble hound who'd fought Mannjaeger to the death. Master and hound, together they rested, with a soft coverlet of frosty white solemnly veiling their still forms, as it should have been. Nearby loomed the massive elemental bulk of the great boar, his body pierced a dozen times by Gunthar's spear before the final fatal blow lodged in his heart. Unlucky thirteen, some noted.

In the cold dawn, they brought the Grand Master out from the castle to the courtyard, where fresh snow was falling on the bowed heads and slumped shoulders of those gathered for the funeral. Most were simple villagers and townsfolk from all over the Isle of Sancrist, but others had crossed seas to be here. Word of Gunthar's death went out with dragonback messengers to Northern and Southern Ergoth, to the Isle of Cristyne, to Qualinost and to Palanthas, and dignitaries from the nearest lands of Krynn had come at the summons. Silver dragons were seen circling in the gray, snow-laden clouds overhead, and also, someone claimed, a lone gold dragon had passed over the battlements in the night. The day before, blue dragons had come bearing more Knights of Takhisis, as well as condolences from their supreme leader, Lady Mirielle Abrena. Sir Liam Ehrling, distraught by the death of his master, had kept to his room until the morning of the funeral.

As the doors opened and the pallbearers appeared, a hush fell over the crowd. Freshly fallen snow muted the footsteps of those who bore Lord Gunthar. He rested not in a casket. Instead, he lay upon a wooden stretcher, and four Knights carried him—Knights of Solamnia Quintayne Fogorner and Ellinghad Beauseant, and Knights of Takhisis Tohr Malen and Valian Escu. Behind them strode Meredith Turningdale, bearing Gunthar's shield, and lastly Liam Ehrling, bearing his sword. Lord Gunthar was covered with a white linen shroud strewn with red roses and tiny golden crowns. At his feet lay the ivory tusks of Mannjaeger, trophies of his last battle.

In silence, they laid him on the snow-covered ground, and in silence the mourners passed, leaving roses and other tokens at his side. Flakes falling from the sky alighted softly on his face but did not melt, until he looked like some ancient god of winter, asleep in his snowy bower with his offerings heaped about him. Liam stood at his head, Lady Meredith at his feet, and they quietly greeted each person as he or she stopped beside Gunthar's form. Though he struggled to maintain his composure, many a choked tear streaked Liam chiseled face, while Meredith let her grief flow like quiet rain.

When all had paid their respects, the bearers once again lifted Gunthar and returned him to the castle. Never again would he leave it.

The gathered Knights and delegates of towns, villages, lands, and nations filed into the old chapel behind the pallbearers and took their seats in the pews lining the aisle. They laid Gunthar on the altar beneath an ancient symbol of the platinum dragon, then stepped back and made their way to their seats. When all were finally seated, the chapel grew quiet, so quiet that ice crystals were heard striking the glazed windows of the chapel. Outside, the snow had changed to sleet, as the townspeople, villagers and foresters of Sancrist began to make their way home, returning to the farms and fields, homesteads and mills they'd left to pay their last respects to the master of Castle uth Wistan. Many did not know what the morrow would bring, whether the Knights of Solamnia would die with the Grand Master, or be reborn in the merging of the two orders. Many of those gathered in the chapel wondered the same thing.

So profound was the silence of the chapel that several people started when, with a loud click, a door behind the altar opened. From it emerged a man bowed with the weight of many years. Thin wisps of gray hair hung in streamers around his wrinkled brown face, and he leaned heavily upon a stick as he hobbled through the door. He was helped along by a younger woman dressed in long robes of pristine but unadorned white. From a single, simple comb, long raven tresses streaked with gray spilled loosely over her shoulders. Hers was a face of classical beauty, with its proud chin and cheekbones that some might have called haughty, were they not softened by wisdom and age. But her dark eyes held no light. She stared blankly ahead, so that even those at the back of the chapel knew at a glance that she was blind. Still, she somehow led the elderly man down the steps and to the front pew, where he took his seat beside Liam Ehrling.

As she turned, he held her hand a moment longer, and croaked in a voice weary with grief, "Thank you, Crysania."

"You are welcome, dear Wills," she answered.

As if by magic, the music of her voice cleansed the room

of the brooding silence that had gripped it since Gunthar
was brought in. The people seemed suddenly to relax in
their pews; there was a noise of shuffling and adjusting,
the creaking of armor and the rustling of fabric. Someone
coughed, and there were even a few whispers.

"Who is he?" Jessica Vestianstone quietly asked the
person sitting beside her—a wealthy merchant from the
town of Gavin.

"Wills, Gunthar's old retainer. He must be over a hundred. I didn't know he was still alive," the man whispered.
"That's Lady Crysania. I can't believe she's here. Someone
told me she is living some place on the island, though I
don't know where."

"Lady Crysania!" Jessica whispered excitedly to herself.

She didn't need anyone to point out her hero. As a child,
Jessica had listened enraptured to the tales and songs of
Crysania and her love for the dark mage, Raistlin Majere.
She had indulged in many a romantic dream of one day
meeting someone for whom she too would risk the Abyss.
To Jessica, Crysania's bravery and loving sacrifice were
like a beacon towards which she strove, across the barren
sands of her own life's drudgery.

Lady Crysania moved slowly up beside the altar where
Gunthar lay, feeling the air with her hands, until she
touched the hem of his shroud. Gently, she placed her own
hands on his and bowed her head in silent prayer. The
chapel grew quiet again, but this was a quiet of peace,
broken occasionally by a sob. Crysania lifted her head and
smiled.

"Good morning," she said softly to the congregation.

A scattered few answered. Jessica held her breath. She
never dreamed such a day would come, that she might
actually hear the voice of Lady Crysania. Despite the
solemnity of the occasion, her face almost glowed with joy.

"They tell me Lord Gunthar died in battle against the

beast known as Mannjaeger. They say that Lord Gunthar was a warrior, and that he would have preferred to die in battle," Crysania said. There was a general grunt of approval from the congregation. Jessica saw Liam nod his head appreciatively.

"I'll not try to comfort you with such notions, for I do not believe them," Crysania said. A hush fell over the chapel.

"Gunthar was not a warrior," she continued. "True, he led the Knights of Solamnia through two devastating wars, and probably no leader since Vinus Solamnus himself has done more to keep this noble order together in the face of adversity. But as you all know, rarely did Lord Gunthar take his place in the forefront of battle. He was not a great warrior.

"He was a great leader. He left it to other, more capable hands, to strike the blows in the cause of good.

"I am here today because Gunthar uth Wistan was a man of peace. It has been said that to lead men in battle is simple. To lead men in peace takes courage and strength, and above all, honor. When the wars are over, the old warriors fade away. Lord Gunthar led you through more days of peace than he did of war, yet he did not fade away. The Knighthood is alive today because of him.

"Many of you honor and revere Huma, who fought and died to save Krynn from the armies of Takhisis. Many of you revere Sturm Brightblade, who fought and died as an example of honor. Some of you honor his son Steel Brightblade, who chose personal honor over loyalty to his Dark Queen, and fought and died to save Krynn from Chaos. How many of you, I wonder, truly honor this man here..." Crysania's voice broke, but her blinded eyes never wavered.

"... this man who fought, and fought, and fought," she continued, emotion choking her voice, "... who never stopped fighting to hold together your order, amidst the pride and arrogance and foolishness of people too numerous to name. He fought battles without swords, without honors, without victors. Often he fought alone, against the better judgment of his peers. Until the end he fought alone to try to preserve that which he held most dear, even above his own personal honor.

"When we lay to rest this great man, let us not pretend that he fought great battles. He did not save the world. He preserved it, so that those who survived the great battles might have a place to come home to. Lord Gunthar was a man of peace, and in peace, not war, he achieved his greatest deeds. And like the deaths of those great Knights who went before him—Huma Dragonbane, and Sturm and Steel Brightblade—let his death bind you together in a purpose greater than yourselves. Do not allow him to die in vain."

Crysania bowed her head. As one, with the rattling of swords and creaking of armor, the pallbearers rose from their seats.

"So ends the line of Gunthar uth Wistan," Crysania chanted in invocation. "He goes now to join his longfathers of old, his sons, and his wife. Unto Paladine we commit his soul, but unto the earth we consign his flesh. Never shall we see his kind again."

Slowly, reverently, the pallbearers ascended to the altar and took their places beside Lord Gunthar's body. Crysania descended to the front pew and helped Wills to rise. Together, the old retainer and the former priestess of Paladine climbed to a great iron door to the right of the altar. As they passed, the pallbearers lifted Gunthar from the altar. The Knights sitting in the congregation rose and began to file into the chapel's aisles, while those not of either Knighthood remained in their seats.

Crysania opened the iron door, where servants waited

with lighted torches. Arm in arm with Wills, she descended a staircase cut into the living rock beneath the castle, torchbearers leading the way. The pallbearers followed, then came the Knights of Solamnia. Last of all, the Knights of Takhisis entered, closing the door behind them. Those remaining in the chapel rose quietly and began to disperse, the villagers and townspeople to their waiting carriages and horses, the dignitaries from the elven lands, Ergoth, and Palanthas to their guest quarters in the castle. The chapel was left empty and silent once again, while outside the sleet turned to rain.

The stair wound down and down, but gently, not like a dungeon stair. The walls were wide and the steps broad, for it was made to be traversed by those carrying a heavy burden. Two torchbearers descended before the Lady Crysania, and two followed behind the last Knight of Takhisis, but those Knights near the middle of the group walked in near darkness. Jessica was among these. She paced in solemn procession, with one hand lightly touching the Knight before her, and she felt a hand on her shoulder as well. No one spoke. All seemed lost in their own private musings, with only the shuffling of feet and jangle of armor to break the silence.

Finally, the stair ended in a long dark hall. Over the heads of those before her, Jessica saw the torchbearers; the flickering light of their torches went before them in a great arch on the walls and ceiling of the passage. They entered a low stone crypt, where they busied themselves lighting torches hanging in sconces on the walls. The Knights before her filed into the crypt, some moving to the left, others to the right. As Jessica entered, she moved to the right, where other Knights from her own Order of the Crown waited with bowed heads. She moved in beside them and took her place. The others followed behind her, until it seemed all the small burial chamber was filled with

Knights. The air began to smell of hot steel and leather, so that Jessica found it more and more difficult to breath.

They deposited Gunthar's body on a stone bier near the center of the chamber. All around him, in the shadows and in niches in the walls, lay the sarcophagi of his ancestors, his grandfathers and their grandfathers. Castle uth Wistan was ancient beyond reckoning. Cracks in the walls showed evidence of the Cataclysm that wracked Krynn over three hundred years before, raising mountains and draining seas, and destroying the city of Istar where the kingpriest, in his arrogance, called down the gods' righteous anger upon himself.

Some people said the uth Wistan name dated back to the Age of Dreams. But it had found its inevitable end here, with the man who lay now in the center of the chamber, for his good ladywife and his sons laying round him, their spirits gone before him to prepare a place. He was the last of his line.

The Knights crowded all the remaining spaces of the crypt, many straining to see their late Grand Master's body, others only too glad to let the shadows hide their tears. Lady Crysania stood beside Lord Gunthar's body, while the guard of honor took their places at her side: to her right, the leaders of the Knights of Solamnia, and to her left those of the Knights of Takhisis. Lady Meredith Turningdale laid Gunthar's shield across his knees, then Liam Ehrling placed his sword on his breast. He stepped back, his face a mask of stone. Crysania lifted her hand; it shook visibly.

"Return this man to Huma's breast," she said.

Ellinghad Beauseant stepped forward and turned to face the gathered Knights. He began to chant, and others soon took up his song. Jessica found she knew the words as well, though she didn't remember ever learning them.

Return this man to Huma's breast:
Let him be lost in sunlight,
In the chorus of air where breath is translated;
At the sky's border receive him.

Beyond the wild, impartial skies
Have you set your lodgings,
In cantonments of stars, where the sword aspires
in an arc of yearning, where we join in singing.

Grant to him a warrior's rest.
Above our singing, above song itself,
may the ages of peace converge in a day,
May he dwell in the heart of Paladine.

And set the last spark of his eyes
In a fixed and holy place
Above words and the borrowed land too loved
As we recount the ages.

Free from the smothering clouds of war
As he once rose in infancy,
The long world possible and bright before him,
Lord Huma, deliver him . . .

As the last notes of the chant died away in the stone corridors of the vault, Ellinghad bowed his head and stepped
back.

With tears in her eyes, Crysania lifted her hands and
cried, "Return this man to Huma's breast beyond the wild,
impartial skies; grant to him a warrior's rest, and set the
last spark of his eyes free from the smothering clouds of
wars, upon the torches of the stars."

Her hands dropped to her sides, and her long black hair
hung down around her face as she bowed her head.

Slowly, one by one, the Knights filed past Gunthar's body. Each Knight paid his or her respects in their own way, some bowing to one knee in humble prayer, some leaving some small gift or token of remembrance. Jessica was surprised by the seeming honest grief of many of the Knights of Takhisis, for most had known Gunthar only as their enemy. One by one, they filed out and returned up the winding stair to the chapel, before making their way to whatever post or duty called them.

Jessica was one of the last to kneel beside the Grand Master's tomb, but she was unsure what she was supposed to do. She felt like praying, but she didn't know to which gods she should pray. All had left Krynn during the Chaos War. Her heart, like the tomb, felt empty and cold, but she knew others were watching her. Finally, she whispered, "Peace be with you, my lord," and rose to her feet. As she turned to leave, Crysania lifted her head and smiled sadly. Blushing, Jessica hurried up the stair.

When she reached the chapel, Jessica stopped. Compared to the tomb, the air here seemed fresh and alive. A cool gray light filtered through the tall, narrow, glazed windows lining the walls while a steady rain beat upon the roof. She felt suddenly thankful that she was warm and dry and above all alive. The cold dead air of the tomb had filled her with a horror she realized only when she was free of it. She thought of Lord Gunthar down in the cold of the grave, alone for all eternity, and she began to weep for him. Long sobs wracked her body. She crept back to the darkest corner of the chapel, to a place where she could be alone with her sorrow. Where a column rose between two pews she crouched and let the sobs take her.

Jessica Vestianstone had joined the Knighthood only two years ago. She came from a wealthy merchant family from the city of Gavin, here on the isle of Sancrist, the second-youngest child of eleven. She'd joined the Knights of Solamnia because there was no place for her at home. She had no desire to marry and have eleven children of her own. She longed to do something greater, to serve in a noble cause, to take part in a great endeavor. Had the gods not abandoned Krynn, most likely she'd have ended up a priestess of one god or another.

By the time she reached her teens, her two oldest sisters were captains of successful merchant ships in their father's business. Between voyages, they began to teach Jessica the martial skills of swordplay and archery. She proved talented, and her natural humility and sense of honor brought her to the attention of some local Knights of Solamnia, Sir Quintayne in particular. He'd encouraged her to join and sponsored her application. Jessica had no doubt that in the old days she'd never have been accepted, as she wasn't aggressive by nature, but in the post-Chaos world, the Knighthood needed bodies to fill the gaps in their lines.

Almost immediately after she was accepted, they'd placed her at Isherwood. Alone in the middle of a wilderness, and almost never called to attend Grand Chapters, Jessica never really got to know any of her fellow Knights. But at Isherwood she was mistress of her own life at last. She delighted in exploring the wild hills surrounding the castle, while the ancient building itself charmed her with its simplicity and nobility. It was the sort of castle she'd always imagined princesses of stories being exiled to by their cruel fathers, lonely princesses awaiting the arrival of a noble Knight to rescue them. Only now, she was the noble Knight. She felt weary and alone. Gunthar's funeral made her realize how many of her hopes and dreams lay unfulfilled, without hope of ever coming to pass as long as she remained isolated at Isherwood, or now that the Knights of Takhisis were taking it, at some other musty, dank, unimportant post.

* * * * *

When she heard the iron door close, Jessica paid it no mind. She thought no one could see her where she hid, but the one who saw her needed no eyes to see. Jessica felt a light touch on her shoulder, and turning quickly, she found herself staring up at the one person in all the world she least wanted to find her weak, weeping like a child.

"Lady Crysania!" she gasped. "I was . . . I am . . ."

"You were weeping," Crysania said. "As a dear friend was fond of saying, a deaf gully dwarf could have heard you."

"I'm sorry," Jessica sighed.

"Why? Your tears do you honor, if they are shed honorably," Crysania said.

"But . . ." Jessica began. She sank to her knees as new tears welled from her eyes. "I wept for myself," she cried. "I wept for Lord Gunthar, for the loneliness of the grave he must feel, but only because I am already there. When I joined the Knights, I dreamed that I would make a difference. I dreamed of glory. But since joining, I have labored the long days in a desolate castle, alone but for an old dwarf to care for my horse."

"Many were the times I felt as you," Crysania said. "On the long march to the dwarven plains, I was alone in the midst of many. Though I loved, I loved alone, and though I strove to bring light to the darkness, I strove alone and still the darkness triumphed. The time was not yet come, as I learned, and as you must also learn." She stooped to help Jessica rise.

Jessica brushed back her tears and tried to compose herself. "I am sorry, Lady Crysania. It was selfish of me to weep for myself. My tears were better shed for Lord Gunthar."

"But why? When we weep for the dead, truly we weep for ourselves, for our loss, not theirs, and for our own fear of the grave, not theirs. The tears you shed do you no dishonor, lady Knight," Crysania said. "We all weep in darkness."

Suddenly, Jessica clasped Crysania's hands and bowed to one knee. "My Lady, please allow me to serve you," she cried.

"You have duties and responsibilities here," Crysania said.

"I am to be reassigned," Jessica said excitedly. "They are giving my post to the Knights of Takhisis. I have no other duties as yet. If you were to request . . ."

"Patience, patience, dear girl," Crysania said softly but firmly. "There is much yet for you to do here."

"What do you mean?" Jessica asked.

"Come, take my arm and walk with me," Crysania said.

Together, they strolled from the chapel, passing along a hall lined with windows that looked onto the courtyard. The rain came down like a gray curtain, almost obscuring the outer wall from view. A few hazy shadows walked their posts atop the battlements.

As they passed throughout the castle, Jessica waited for Crysania to say something more, to finish her thought begun in the chapel, but instead the former high priestess of Paladine made small talk, asking about Jessica's name and her family, and about the castle where she lived. Jessica told Crysania how much she loved the crumbling old place. Lonely as she was, she enjoyed the solitude and peace she found there.

Finally, they reached the guest quarters of the castle. Crysania stopped beside one of the doors and felt unfamiliarly for the latch. Until that moment, Jessica had almost forgotten the Lady Crysania was blind. Gently, she guided her hero's fingers to the knob. Crysania smiled.

"Thank you. It was very good to meet you, Jessica Vestianstone," she said. "I hope we will talk again before I leave."

"As do I, milady," Jessica answered with a bow.

Crysania smiled and opened the door. As she passed within, Jessica caught a glimpse inside the room. Directly across from the door there stood a large bed, where a profusion of blankets spilled onto the floor. As the door swung shut, the head of a huge white tiger lifted from behind the blankets and blinked sleepily at Jessica. Her breath caught at the suddenness of his appearance, and she almost cried out before she noticed that he was not a tiger after all, but a man. He rose as Crysania entered, but then the door closed, cutting off Jessica's view.

Jessica's head dropped. Dejected, she shuffled away, finding her way eventually to her own quarters just as the call to mess was being sounded. But she had no appetite. Instead, she entered her small room and sat on the bed in the dark, while in the passage outside her door Knights rushed to the dining hall. They talked, laughed, joked, and bickered, just as they had always done. Already, the life of the castle was returning to normal, even before the echoes of the crypt had faded away.

Chapter Fourteen

Giles Gorstead stumbled sleepily to the front door of his small cottage. His nightshirt was still twisted and wrinkled from bed, and his disheveled brown hair looked like a bird had been nesting in it. Without even thinking, only angry at the disturbance of his sleep, he yanked open the door and stared out into the night. What confronted him brought him sharply awake. Quickly, he swung the door almost shut and peered out through the crack.

"What do you want?" he asked sharply. "This ain't no inn, if that's what you're looking for. Inn's up the road."

"I am ssssearching for gully dwarvessss," answered the heavily robed figure standing on his porch. Black robes covered every inch of the stranger's body, and his face was lost in the shadow of an enormous cowl.

Giles shuddered, but he said angrily, albeit with a slightly higher pitch to his voice, "We've got no gully dwarves here. Good night." He slammed the door and shot home the bolt.

"There are three of them," the voice hissed from behind the door. "I tracked them to this place, but I've lost their footprints in the fresh snow."

"Well, they're not here!" Giles shouted. "Good night."

"They sssstole ssssomething from me, an item of great

value," the stranger continued. "I would pay dearly to have it, and the thievessss, returned to me."

"Well, if I see any, I'll be sure and let you know. Good night!" he shouted as he dashed across the room and snatched the poker from the fireplace.

He returned to the door and listened but heard no other sound. Slowly, he eased to the window and peered from behind the curtain. Krynn's new white moon shed a ghastly pallor over the new-fallen snow, illuminating the night as though it were day. The front yard and the porch were empty. No footprints marred the snow. Giles shuddered and made a sign to ward away evil.

He spent the remainder of the night beside the window, watching for any sign of the stranger, but the porch, the yard, and the road beyond remained empty, as desolate as a ghost town. He dragged a quilt from the bed and huddled by the window, awaiting the sun, while he grasped the iron poker so tightly his knuckles turned white.

When the late autumn sun finally arose behind a thick blanket of snowy clouds, the light found him asleep, his cheek pressed against the sill. He blinked, then winced as he withdrew his face from the hard, cold wooden frame of the window. A deep red indentation creased his face. He found his fingers so stiff from gripping the poker, he almost couldn't open them.

The fire on the hearth had burned low during the night, so by the time he woke, the room was freezing. He tossed a few chips on the fire and stirred the coals to get the fire going, then took a kettle from the mantle, and breaking the crust of ice on the bucket beside the door, filled it with water. He then hung it from a rack over the fire.

While he waited for the water to boil, he pulled on a pair of heavy boots and slung a thick woolen cloak over his shoulders. From a barrel in the corner he filled a basket with corn, then stepped outside into the snow. Looking up, he noticed the sky was darkening, and he guessed that before the day was done, the snow would change to rain. Elsewhere on the island, in the courtyard of Castle uth Wistan, the citizens of Sancrist and all Krynn were paying their respects to Gunthar.

Shivering with the cold, Giles Gorstead hurried across the porch and down the steps. He made his way around the cottage to the back, noticing as he passed that the snow on the windward side of the building had drifted almost to the lower windows, but the snow in the back was not as deep because of the protection afforded by a number of tall oak trees. Their spreading branches shaded and sheltered almost the entire ground between the cottage and the barn. His boots crunched in the snow as he walked, sounding unusually loud in the silence of the forest.

As he neared the chicken coop, Giles began to cluck his tongue and toss handfuls of corn on the snow-covered ground. He spread the corn evenly, with a practiced swing of his arm, all the time calling, "Here chick-chick-chick-chick." Usually, the hens came rushing out at the first sound of his voice, but this morning they seemed slow. Perhaps it was the cold which made them sluggish, for he heard only a few rustling noises from the henhouse.

Then, something fell from the sky, grazing his forehead. It landed like a brick in the snow. Giles crouched warily, staring all about, ready to dodge the next missile. "Come out, you coward!" he shouted, sure that his assailant was the mysterious visitor from the night before.

When no one answered, and no other missiles followed, he glanced down at the thing that had nearly brained him. It was a very dead, very frozen chicken—one of his own. He picked it up and examined it for a moment before another thump caught his attention. About a stone's throw away, another frozen chicken lay in the snow.

Mightily puzzled, Giles glanced up, and to his horror saw dozens and dozens of his chickens lining the lower branches of the trees. Every single one seemed frozen solid to its perch. Giles couldn't imagine why they'd taken to the trees, when he had seen them safely in their coop only yesterday evening. He wondered how many, if any, were still in the coop. He crossed the yard and ducked through the low doorway, dropping his egg-and-feed basket outside as he entered.

It took a few moments for his eyes to adjust to the darkness. Dim light filtered through cracks in the wooden walls, poorly illuminating the confines of the low-roofed building, but even in that near-darkness, he saw that the roosts were empty. Near the door, shelves with dozens of round nests of hay lined the walls, but these too were empty. A few feathers littered the floor, but otherwise the place seemed deserted.

Even more baffled than before, Giles turned to leave, but at that moment, a ripping snore sounded from a dark corner of the coop.

"Who's there?" he shouted.

A startled snort answered him, then a burst of hurried whispers. "Speak up! Who's there?" he demanded.

"Nobody," someone answered.

Another voice added, "Nope, nobody here."

"Somebody's there!" he shouted. "Come out into the light so I can see you."

Slowly, three squat figures emerged from the shadows. One wore a ragged flat cap, which seemed made of rat-skins poorly sewn together. White flecks littered his scraggly beard, probably pieces of eggshell, Giles noticed with growing rage. The shortest of the three stumbled over some kind of sack dangling from her shoulder; a chicken foot protruded from the loose flap of the bag. The third and tallest of the three had a mass of chicken feathers stuck to his chin, like some kind of ridiculous white beard.

"Gully dwarves!" Giles screeched. Millisant stuck her nose out from under Glabella's skirt and yawned. "And a big dog!" Giles exclaimed. "You . . . you . . . you . . ." His face deepened to scarlet, and the veins of his neck stood out like cords.

"Nobody here," the tall one said sleepily.

"Who's going to pay for my flock? All my chickens, lost!" he cried as he tore at his hair.

"We only eat two," Uhoh said, "and two eggs."

"Not more than two," Glabella added as she patted her round belly. Lumpo belched, smiling through his feathery beard.

Giles looked round for some kind of weapon, anything, a bucket, a hoe handle, just something to beat the three gully dwarves to death. Finding no suitable bludgeon, he decided to strangle them instead, and he even took a couple of steps toward them before realizing that here were three gully dwarves nicely trapped inside his chicken coop. Like a bolt out of the blue, a plan to recover his losses struck him, stunning him with its brilliance.

He stopped, and seeing his hands extended threateningly toward the gully dwarves, as though he were already wringing their miserable necks, he quickly tucked them into his pockets. He attempted a pleasant, nonthreatening smile, but it looked more like the grin of the cat who ate the bird. Uhoh had already taken a step back, and seeing that smile, he took another.

"It's all right," Giles said. "What's a couple of chickens?"

"Dinner," Lumpo commented.

Giles Gorstead ground his teeth, but he continued as he backed towards the door, "It'll be raining before long. Why don't you three stay here for the day, where it's nice and warm and dry. You can have all the chickens you want."

Uhoh frowned, but Glabella smiled and said, "You nice man. We stay."

"That's right," Giles said. "I'm a nice man." He ducked through he door, then poked his head back inside. "Don't go anywhere. I'm just going to get your breakfast. Breakfast in bed." He vanished.

"See there. I told you this good inn," Glabella said to Uhoh.

Outside, Giles hurried across the yard to the barn. As the day began to warm, and the snow changed to sleet, more chickens in the trees started to thaw and drop to the ground, like some horrible harvest of fruit grown ripe. Giles almost screamed in rage as he saw them littering the snow, but he continued on his way. In the barn, he grabbed a hammer, some nails, and a couple of boards from the scrap lumber pile. Wanting to be milked, his cows mooed sadly at him from their stalls, but for the moment he ignored them. He shuffled back across the yard to the chicken coop, the load held tightly in his arms, until he reached the door. He dropped the things in the slushy snow and poked his head back inside. Again, the darkness was blinding. He couldn't see the gully dwarves, but he said, "Only a moment longer."

Quickly, he shut the door and slid a wooden bar into place. Then, just to be sure, he nailed two boards, one at the top of the door and one at the bottom, to prevent his captives from slipping through the cracks.

As he worked, he shouted, "This is to make sure no foxes or wolves get in while I'm away. Have to run to market to get bacon. Back in a jiffy!" He tossed aside the hammer and dashed away. Once on the road, he ran through the falling sleet toward town.

Before long, the road became icy and slick. Giles was still wearing his pajamas, with only his heavy boots and woolen cloak to protect him against the cold. More than once, he slipped and fell before finally reaching the Oxen

Yoke, the town's only inn. Despite the early hour, wood smoke rose from its single chimney, and a wan yellow light glowed in the window, proclaiming the tap and common room open for business. Giles crashed through the door, wind and sleet blowing in with him. The barkeep glared at him with raised eyebrows.

"Have you seen a certain stranger, robed all in black?" Giles panted without even saying hello.

He wasn't concerned with formalities at the moment, and in truth he didn't care much for the barkeep anyway. He suspected the man watered the beer. With a shaky finger, the barkeep pointed at a dark corner beside the fireplace.

Pushing aside the long sausages which dangled like Yuletide ornaments from the low rafters, Giles made his way across the common room, until he stood before the table indicated by the barkeep. At his approach, a shadow detached itself from the deeper shadows of the corner and leaned forward into the light glowing from the hearth.

"I've got them," Giles said, still gasping for air.

The robed figure stiffened. "Where?"

"At my place," he said.

The stranger leaped to his feet. "Ssssshow me," he whispered excitedly.

"First, the reward you promised," Giles demanded. He didn't trust strangers, least of all those who took such care to hide their features.

An angry hiss answered him. The stranger seemed to hesitate. "When I have them, you will be paid, but I must ssssee them firssst," he said at last.

"And if they don't have your property?" Giles asked.

"What?"

"The thing they stole from you?"

"Oh, that. Do not worry. They cannot have ssssold it yet. But if they have, you will ssssstill get your reward," the stranger said.

"Very well then." Hesitating a moment, Giles said, "Follow me."

Together, they exited the inn and made their way through the increasingly wet weather to the farm. Along the way, Giles was disconcerted by the fact that no matter how slowly he walked, the stranger seemed always to struggle behind him. It was as though the fellow wished never to have his back to Giles. Only the promise of a handsome reward kept him from confronting the mysterious man. With the complete loss of his flock of chickens, he needed every silver piece and steel coin he could scrape together just to survive the winter.

They reached the cottage just as the sleet gave over to rain. As they crossed the yard to the coop, the stranger seemed very much amused by the sight of dozens of frozen chickens carpeting the ground. He hissed and giggled inside his cowl. When he saw the door to the coop nailed shut, he laughed even harder. "Sssso that issss why you ssssought me out," he said. "If you'll pardon my expresssssion, you wissshh to 'recoup' your lossssessss."

"Yes, yes, very funny," Giles snarled as he used the hammer to pry the boards loose from the door. "You'd just better be ready with that reward. Don't you try to cheat me, or I'll nail you up in there with them." He knocked the wooden bar free and snatched open the door.

"Breakfast is served!" he shouted as he motioned the stranger inside. Slowly, with seeming trepidation, the stranger approached the low door, his feet squelching in the slushy snow on the ground. Without removing his cowl, he ducked inside.

The rain beat down on Giles's unprotected head as he waited outside the coop. Some forgotten motherly part of his mind told him that he would catch his death out here, but he only ground his teeth and glanced at his dead chickens to remind himself of his purpose. Somebody had to pay, that's all he was sure of.

All of a sudden, the stranger stepped out of the coop. He turned to face Giles, his features still hidden by the cowl, his hands wrapped in the fold of his voluminous sleeves.

"There issss no one in there," he hissed angrily.

"What? Impossible!" Giles shrieked as he threw down his hammer and ducked into the coop. Again, it took a few moments for his eyes to adjust to the darkness. Meanwhile, he shouted, "Where are you, you miserable little rats?" Silence answered him.

He thrashed about the interior of the coop, tossing aside nests and shelves and bales of hay in his fury. "They can't have escaped!" he cried. "It's impossible. There is no way out. This coop is as tight as a ship. Not even a weasel can get in here when it is shut up!"

Exhausted by emotion and exposure, Giles shuffled wearily back to the open doorway. Outside, the stranger stood impassively in the rain. "I don't understand," Giles complained as he sank to the floor, his face in his hands. "I just don't understand."

A strange pattern of ice on the floor caught his attention. It was a footprint, a slushy footprint. A slushy three-toed, reptilian footprint. Giles jerked and fell over backwards, as though struck a blow by some invisible weapon.

"Draconian!" he gasped.

"Ah, now that issssss unfortunate. And after all the care I took to conccccceal my identity," the stranger lamented as he pushed back his cowl. A long reptilian snout emerged, surmounted by a wide, heavy brow overshadowing dark, beetling eyes. Long bronze horns swept back from his low, crested forehead. A narrow forked tongue as red as blood slithered out from between two long fangish teeth and flickered in the air.

"What do you want with three gully dwarves?" Giles asked.

"Three? I only want the one. The otherssss, they are nothing, but the one, I would have paid handsssomely for the one. Now, you musssst pay," the draconian said.

"Wait!" Giles shrieked.

The draconian took a few steps back, then planted his feet in the mud. "Ssssssomebody mussssst pay," he hissed as he drew a wand from his robes. He pointed it at the coop.

"No, wait!" Giles screamed.

The draconian spoke a single word, and a tiny ball of light streaked from the wand and into the coop, where it struck Giles squarely in the chest and exploded with flame. The roof of the coop sailed high into the air as the walls burst outward. For a few moments, a living ball of fire writhed on the floor, screaming hideously, before it grew still.

Satisfied, the draconian pulled his hood back over his head, turned, and stalked away. Moments after he vanished around the corner of the cottage, the barn door opened and Lumpo appeared, a metal pail dangling from his hand.

"Look. The inn is on fire!" he said. He lifted the pail to his lips and drank deeply. When he finally lowered it, creamy milk flowed in runnels to the tip of his scraggly beard. He smacked his lips and sighed contentedly. Millisant trotted out, and seeing the lowered bucket, stuck her head into it and lapped greedily. Lumpo seemed not to notice.

Uhoh stepped out from behind him and gazed at the roaring flames that was once the chicken coop. "It a good thing we get out before he nail door shut," he commented as he squeezed milk from his beard. "That two times we nearly killed already. We not listen to Glabella no more."

"What I do?" Glabella shouted from inside the barn.

"You no have luck picking inn. Slagd find us in Pig Mud

Inn yesterday, nearly catch me. Lucky I got lots of nice pig mud on me, slip away like worm," he laughed, wriggling in imitation of his narrow escape the day before. "Now Chicken Inn burn down. Lucky I decide to milk nice cow for breakfast, before it go bang!"

"I say we milk cow!" Lumpo argued. "Me got lots of luck that way."

He sniffed the air. "I be glad when nice man get back with bacon," he commented.

"You eat too much," Uhoh said.

"Do not!" Lumpo protested.

"You eat two chickens last night. Now you hungry again," Uhoh accused as he turned and entered the barn.

"Do not! I only eat two chickens," Lumpo said as he followed Uhoh.

"Ha! I see you eat two chickens. You not deny it."

"Two chickens? I only eat two, not more than two."

Slowly, the barn door closed as the burning ruin of the chicken coop spit and hissed in the rain.

Chapter Fifteen

As Seamus Gavin skidded to a stop outside the door to the library, a sheaf of papers spilled from his large leather portfolio and fluttered in all directions. He stooped and hurriedly gathered them, only to have the pair of heavy books that he held precariously under one arm slip and tumble noisily to the floor. All the while, he muttered "Sorry, so sorry," even though he was quite alone in the hall.

While he fumbled on the floor for his things, the door to the library opened, spilling a warm light into the hall. Seamus peered up and puffed at the loose gray hairs dangling in his eyes.

"Seamus Gavin! I thought I heard you out here. We'd almost given up on you," Lady Meredith Turningdale chuckled as she helped the elderly merchant from Palanthas to rise.

He patted her arm and sighed. "There never is enough time in the day, Lady Meredith. If it's not one thing, it's another. I don't know how I manage. Thank you. You are so very kind," he said as she gathered his papers and books and carried them in a stack into the library. "Just set that anywhere. I'll sort it out after I catch my breath."

As he entered, some of the other Knights in the library

greeted him cordially, and he smiled and nodded to each in turn. Quintayne Fogorner poured him a glass of brandy, while Liam Ehrling offered him the largest and most comfortable chair nearest the fire. Meanwhile, Lady Meredith introduced him to the other Knights, the ones he didn't know. These men and women were not Knights of Solamnia. They wore the dreaded symbols of the Knights of Takhisis. He shook hands with Lord Tohr Malen and Alya Starblade, and with the queer-looking dark elven Knight, Sir Valian Escu. Last of all, he met a Knight robed all in gray; Trevalyn Kesper was his name, but this man declined to offer his hand in greeting. Instead, he shot Seamus a look of appalled indignation and returned his attention to the book in his lap. With an icy glare at the Knight, Meredith pulled Seamus away and settled him into a chair by the fire.

"We were just discussing what the Knighthood should be called, now that our two grand orders are to be joined," Lady Meredith said to Seamus.

"Is that so?" Seamus said pleasantly. "And what have you decided?"

"Nothing as yet. Sir Quintayne and many others believe it should remain the Knights of Solamnia, but Lord Tohr is against this. He believes Gunthar's intention was that the two orders of Knighthood should merge, not that one should absorb the other," Meredith said.

"Yes, but as the new Knights of Solamnia. Greater, stronger, more powerful than before," Quintayne said.

"Then why not call it the Knights of Takhisis?" Alya asked as she smiled over the rim of her wine glass. "What difference would it make?"

"For one thing, Takhisis abandoned Krynn, along with all the other gods, during the Chaos War," Quintayne answered. "For another, she is anathema to our order."

This was followed by tense silence.

"How can we be called the Knights of Solamnia if we represent all the peoples of Krynn?" Alya argued smoothly.

"We were named not after a land, but after the founder of our order, Vinus Solamnus," Quintayne said.

"Our founder was Lord Ariakan. Perhaps we should call ourselves the Knights of Ariakan," she countered.

"Perhaps Lord Gunthar had some ideas about what we should call ourselves," Lord Tohr said.

"Sir Liam would know," Meredith said.

Liam sat in his chair and stared into the fire, looking very tired. The others had noticed the dark circles under his eyes; they hadn't been there before Lord Gunthar's death. It seemed some terrible burden was wearing him down. In the days since the hunt, he had hardly touched his food. No one had even seen him until the day of the funeral, and since then his every attempt to be sociable ended in weary sighs. His voice seemed strained, when he bothered to speak at all.

"I . . ." he began, then sighed.

"Sir Liam will know shortly," Seamus interrupted. "Lord Gunthar left a scroll with me, which he directed be given to Sir Liam, should the unexpected occur. Well, as we all know, and to our everlasting sorrow, the unexpected has occurred, and that is why I have called you together this evening. Thank you all for coming."

He stood and moved behind the table where Meredith had laid his papers and books. "Lord Gunthar left his will and other important documents with me, the executor of his estate," he said as he shuffled through the papers. "He was not survived by any blood relatives, so he directed that you all be present at the reading of his will. Ah, here it is! Now what did I do with that—ah, there. Now then. Where was I? Oh yes! The scroll for Liam." He shuffled through all the papers again, then searched his portfolio. With a worried look, he patted his pockets, then with a triumphant smile he produced the scroll and handed it to Liam. Liam unrolled it and scanned its contents while Seamus moved on.

Seamus returned to his chair and from a case at his belt removed a quill and a small bottle of ink. He spread a sheet of parchment across his knee, dipped the quill in the ink bottle, and said, "Now then, so everything is nice and legal, let's see . . ." He squinted and began to write, slowly voicing each word he penned. "Gunthar uth Wistan, Knight of Solamnia, Grand Master. Of Sancrist Isle, Castle uth Wistan." Satisfied, he leaned back and dipped his quill in the ink.

"We must write it all down for the ages. Cause of death?"

"Wounds suffered in battle with a wild boar, exposure, and old age in general," Meredith answered wearily. "He shouldn't have been out there in the first place, at his age," she mumbled.

"Yes, but could you have stopped him?" Quintayne asked.

"Death by misadventure," Seamus wrote aloud. "Now then, I assume the body was examined in the usual manner—by a cleric recognized and acknowledged by the Order of the Sword?"

"As Lord High Clerist, I speak for them," Meredith said. "There were no clerics available, other than the Lady Crysania, and she could hardly be expected to pronounce the cause of death."

"There were witnesses to the tragedy then?" Seamus asked.

"There were no witnesses," Meredith answered.

"Then who . . . ?" Seamus asked.

"I determined the cause of death!" came the answer from the corner. Trevalyn Kesper rose from his seat and crossed to the fireplace.

"You?" Seamus exclaimed. He turned an incredulous glance upon Lady Meredith. She shrugged.

"Sir Trevalyn was a cleric of Takhisis before he joined the Order of the Thorn. His investiture is still recognized by the Knights of the Skull," Tohr said.

"But this . . . this is irregular," Seamus stammered. "There is no precedent."

"There is no precedent for any of this, Seamus," Meredith said. "We live in unprecedented times. But the Knights of the Sword have agreed to recognize Sir Trevalyn's authority in this matter."

Seamus scratched his head. "Well, I suppose it will have to do," he muttered, "if Sir Trevalyn will sign his name here."

With indifference, the gray-robed Thorn Knight placed his mark on Seamus's document. "And Lady Meredith, sign here to signify your acceptance of his judgment." She signed where he indicated.

"Now two witnesses," he said.

With a heavy heart, Liam also signed his name at the bottom of the paper. Seamus sprinkled sand on the ink, then turned to await the final witness. No one seemed willing to volunteer. It was as though by not signing the death certificate, they might prolong the day when they must finally accept the reality of Gunthar's death. When no one else seemed ready to step forward, Valian Escu rose from his seat.

"I'll witness it," he said.

Seamus did not at first seem willing to hand over the quill. Then Meredith whispered, "We are all one Knighthood now, Seamus." With obvious reluctance, he finally allowed Valian to sign. That accomplished, Valian returned to his seat and drank deeply of a glass of pale white wine. Seamus spread the document on a side table to allow the ink to dry thoroughly.

"Well, now we can begin with the will," he said as he shuffled more papers and set them aside, holding out one and spreading it on his lap. "Are we ready?"

"Yes," Meredith answered.

"I, Gunthar uth Wistan, being of sound mind and body, do hereby acknowledge and authorize Seamus Gavin of Palanthas to execute my wishes in regards to my estate and properties, as described below.

'To the Knights of Solamnia, all properties and treasures in my holding shall be returned according to those amounts set forth in the Measure, except for the following as noted below.

"To Uhoh Ragnap, esquire, my 'adopted' son, I leave the estate and property known as Castle Kalstan, to be his own, and to be master thereof. An amount of money already set aside in trust shall be used to maintain and keep the estate in a condition worthy of its status and lineage, and to provide for the well-being of the master of the castle."

Liam leaped to his feet. "What!" he screeched. Trevalyn Kesper began to laugh hysterically, despite the dark looks given him by Lord Tohr.

"That was his wish, Lord Ehrling," Seamus said.

"Seamus, really! Did you know of this beforehand?" Meredith scolded.

"I did. I drew up the documents, including the papers that make Uhoh his ward. It is all perfectly legal," the old man said.

"That crazy old fool, he speaks of a gully dwarf as if he were his son! Seamus, you have been a friend of the family for more years than I can count. How could you have let him do this?" Quintayne asked.

"I advised against it, but Lord Gunthar had made up his mind. As you know only too well, when Gunthar set his mind to something, neither you nor I nor Paladine himself could sway him from it," Seamus said. Wracked by sobs of laughter, Trevalyn had to find a seat to keep from falling over.

"Sir Kesper, if you cannot control yourself, you may be excused," Tohr whispered. "Speak not a word of this to anyone, I warn you."

"Lord Tohr, who would believe me if I did?" Trevalyn said as he wiped tears from his cheeks and made his way to the door. He shook his head and giggled, "Gave it to a gully dwarf. Oh, this is too rich!" He closed the door. They heard him laughing all the way down the hall.

"My apologies," Tohr said.

Liam spun back to face Seamus. "You don't honestly intend to honor this will, do you?" he said.

"It's a legal will," Seamus said.

"But that is one of the most important castles on the entire isle. It's my castle. It's where I live, by the gods! Gunthar gave it to me first. We can't possibly give it to a gully dwarf," Liam argued.

"You can challenge the will, if that is your desire," Seamus said.

"Of course I challenge it!" Liam shouted. "Seamus, I can't believe you actually intend to honor it. Couldn't you see that his mind was not sound?"

"He seemed perfectly sane to me, no different than his usual stubborn self," Seamus said. "In any case, if you intend to challenge the will, that is your right. In the meanwhile, I must meet with the gully dwarf, Uhoh Ragnap, to inform him of his rights."

"I'll send someone to fetch him from the kennels. That's where he lives," Meredith offered. She opened the library door and stepped out into the hall. A moment later, she returned. "He'll be here in a few moments."

"He's a gully dwarf. He won't understand a word of what's going on!" Liam said in amazement. "I myself can't believe what I am hearing."

"Nevertheless, he is Gunthar's legal heir, and as executor of the estate, it is my duty to represent his rights, even if he doesn't understand them himself," Seamus said to Liam. "And don't be in such a hurry to contest the will, Sir Liam. There may be other parts of it that you won't find so foolish."

"What do you mean?" Liam asked narrowing his eyes.

"Allow me to finish reading the document, and you will see," Seamus said coldly. He cleared his throat and resumed his reading.

"I, Gunthar uth Wistan, also hereby make my wishes known concerning the succession of leadership of the Knighthood. Therefore, those who would honor my memory, honor my wishes and elect Lord Liam Ehrling to the Grand Mastership of the Knights according to the rules provided in the revised Measure.

"The undersigned, on this day, et cetera, et cetera," Seamus finished. He folded the will and returned it to his portfolio. "There are many minor provisions included also such as measures for providing a seneschal for Castle Kalstan. However, if you choose to challenge the will . . ."

"I am not concerned about the succession," Liam said. "I am the leader of the Knights of the Rose, the Lord High Justice. I am the natural choice."

Quintayne nervously cleared his throat. "Ummm, my Lord Ehrling, not to be disrespectful, but I believe there are those who would challenge that assumption."

"Who?" Liam asked suspiciously. Quintayne pointed at Tohr.

"He's right, Liam. The Knights of Takhisis have every right to put forward and elect their own leader," Meredith said. "It is foolish to assume that just because you are the Lord High Justice of the Knights of Solamnia that you should be elected Grand Master of whatever Knighthood emerges from this."

Tohr shifted uncomfortably in his chair. "I did not want to say anything with the pain of Gunthar's death still so fresh in our hearts, but Lady Meredith is correct. I honor your loyalty, Lord Ehrling, but if I correctly understand Lord Gunthar's intentions, that our two Knighthoods truly be merged, then an obvious candidate for the Grand Mastership is our current leader, Lady Mirielle Abrena. She has led us successfully for five years now, refounding our headquarters in Neraka, and piecing together the remnants of our forces that survived the Chaos War. Under her leadership, the Knighthood has been reforged into the strong body it is today."

"He has a point, Liam," Quintayne said.

"Surely you aren't serious," Liam laughed. "Do you mean to tell me that we are going to sit here and allow the Knights of Takhisis to accomplish through happenstance that which they were unable to win in battle?"

"What are you insinuating, Lord Ehrling?" Valian Escu demanded. His deep, angry voice charged the air with tension.

"I am insinuating nothing, elf," Liam answered. He turned to face his fellow Knights of Solamnia. "I am merely saying that we shouldn't let them defeat us using our own Measure."

"We are not at war, Liam," Meredith said. "No one is winning or losing here."

"If you must blame someone," Alya said, "blame Lord Gunthar. He is the one who made all this possible."

"But he chose me!" Liam shouted.

"Yes, and as you have asserted, he may not have been in his right mind when he did it!" she returned, undaunted by the older Knight.

Liam turned away, shaking his head in frustration.

"What is the nature of the document Lord Gunthar left for you, Sir Liam?" Meredith asked. "Perhaps it will shed light on this issue."

Liam sat heavily in his chair and reached for his wine glass, but his hands shook so he nearly dropped it. He sighed and returned it to the table. "It gives directions for the naming and ordering of the new Knighthood," he said.

"Really? Then read it to us directly," she said with forced enthusiasm.

A soft knock on the door interrupted them. Meredith rose and answered it. Jessica Vestianstone entered, followed by a squat, filthy little gully dwarf dragging an empty sack and a doll with no eyes.

"Is this Uhoh?" Seamus asked.

"No sir. I could not find Uhoh," Jessica said. "He is nowhere to be found. This gully dwarf is called Gerde. She claims that Uhoh has run away."

"That right," Gerde proudly proclaimed. "I see Uhoh go way."

"And when did he leave?" Seamus asked as he covered his mouth and nose with a handkerchief. The others in the room reacted similarly to Gerde's profound body odor.

"Two days," she answered.

"That would be the day of the funeral," Seamus remarked.

"No, before that," Gerde said. "Two days."

"I see. Tell me, do you know where he was going?" he asked.

"Yes," was her answer.

After waiting a few moments and seeing that was the extent of her response, Seamus asked, "Where was Uhoh going?"

"Home."

"Where is home?"

"Town."

"Which town?" he asked,

"Only one Town," she said.

"There are many towns on Sancrist. Which one is home?" Seamus asked.

"Town," she said.

"Where is this town?" Meredith asked, trying to help.

"Town is home," Gerde said.

"Town is home, home is town. What can you expect from a gully dwarf?" Liam groaned.

"Excuse me," Jessica interrupted, "I think I know where she means. Occasionally, I find gully dwarves rooting around my castle at Isherwood. They tell me they are from someplace called simply Town. I believe it is somewhere near the castle."

"Excellent!" Seamus exclaimed. "Of course, someone should be sent to find Master Ragnap and bring him back here as soon as possible."

"Sir Valian and I are leaving for Isherwood in a fortnight," Alya said. "I was hoping Jessica could accompany us, if not to stay, at least to show us the way and familiarize us with the castle and surrounding lands. Afterwards, Valian will continue onward to inspect the other border castles, while I oversee repairs to Isherwood's defenses."

"To my knowledge, Lady Jessica has no pressing duties," Quintayne said. "She can go if she likes. In any case, she probably needs to return to the castle to collect her personal belongings."

"Lady Jessica, will you ride with us?" Alya asked.

"I am honored," she answered, bowing.

"We can search for Uhoh along the way," Alya said. "By all accounts, gully dwarves are notoriously slow travelers. They tend to stay wherever there is food, until it runs out. We should find him within a few days, then we can send him back with a squire and continue on our way."

"Most excellent indeed," Seamus exclaimed. "Well, if you don't mind, I'll skip the reading of the scroll, and I bid you all good night. I have many other duties to attend to before I find my pillow."

After gathering his books and papers, he managed to find his way out the door. Meredith saw him out, then returned to her seat.

"I think we can also send our . . . guest on her way," Tohr said, holding his nose.

Jessica steered the gully dwarf to the door. "I'd better take her back myself, so she doesn't get lost," she said.

"Good idea," Alya laughed. "See you in the morning."

When they had gone, Lady Meredith said, "I think, ladies and gentlemen, that it would be a good idea that none of tonight's discussion find its way outside this room. Until we determine how the succession is to be decided, the others do not need to know that a dispute even exists."

"Agreed," Tohr said, "but the question remains, how is this to be decided?"

"I think that answer lies with Lord Ehrling. Liam, you were about to read Lord Gunthar's directions."

"Yes, well, it rambles a bit. You can all read it, but basically it does name the new order. Gunthar wished that it be called the Honorable Knights of Sancrist Isle," Liam said.

"Why, that's perfect," Meredith remarked. "I think it's wonderful, don't you?"

"It does seem . . . perfect to me," Tohr said. "It doesn't favor either of the old orders, yet at the same time echoes the names of both."

"It emphasizes honor," Valian said. "For it is honor that shall bind us together, not loyalty to a particular cause or god."

"What of the individual orders of Knighthood?" Quintayne asked.

"There are none," Liam said. "No Knights of the Rose or the Skull, or anything else. Gunthar says, 'Each Knight shall choose the path best suited to his needs, without regard to rank or station. All Knights shall be known simply as Knights of Sancrist Isle, or Knights of Sancrist.' It goes on to say that the new white moon shall be our sole symbol, for as the moon is a symbol of the new world, so it shall be the symbol of the Knighthood."

"What of the Thorn Knights?" Tohr asked.

"Of those Thorn Knights who wish to remain, Lord Gunthar asked that they be given positions as clerics within the Knighthood," Liam said.

"No Orders of the Rose, Sword, or Crown?" Quintayne asked. "How will we maintain the command structure or know how to position our troops in lines of battle?"

"It doesn't say," Liam answered. "One of the many ways in which it is maddeningly vague. Here, see for yourself." He handed it over to Meredith.

"There's not much else," she exclaimed, handing it to Tohr.

"Yes," Liam sighed. He wearily rubbed his eyes and sank deeper into the chair.

"The remainder must be detailed in his Revised Measure," Quintayne said. "He was supposed to reveal it to us this Yuletide."

"I have it now," Liam groaned.

"Ah, what kind of shape is it in?" he asked.

"It's not ready," he mumbled into his hands. "Not ready."

"Not ready? What's left to be done?" Quintayne asked.

"Oh, you are all welcome to look at it, but we don't dare reveal it to the others. It is in terrible shape, a hodgepodge of quotes and repetitions and nonsense. It will take weeks, months perhaps, to pick through and glean the relevant material. Since Gunthar's death, I've been trying . . ." He broke down, his voice quavering with exhaustion. ". . . trying to make some sense of it."

"Liam, you should have come to us," Meredith chastised him.

"Yes, divide it up, give each of us a part, and let us work together," Quintayne said.

"I have made an extensive study of the original Measure," Tolu said. "We have a few copies in Neraka and other places," he explained offhandedly. "In any case, I am only too happy to offer any assistance you might need."

"No," Liam protested, rising wearily to his feet. "No. This is my task and mine alone. I knew Gunthar better than anyone; I knew his mind, the way it worked. I must finish this alone."

"As you wish, my lord," Meredith acquiesced. "Until then, we must not let anyone know of this. Are we all agreed?"

Everyone nodded. "We will maintain the original schedule. The Measure will be revealed at Yuletide, just as planned," she said.

The group rose from their seats. Lord Tohr lifted his glass. "To the Honorable Knights of Sancrist Isle," he offered.

"To the Knights of Sancrist Isle," they toasted in unison. As one, they drained their glasses, then filed out, leaving Liam alone in the library. He sank into his seat.

"Gods, what have I done?" he whispered.

Chapter Sixteen

A fine breeze blew up from the valley, stirring the leaves of the trees of Nalvarre's orchard. Actually, it wasn't his orchard, but he called it his orchard even though he hadn't planted a single one of the pecan or walnut or hickory trees that grew in such profusion here. Nalvarre settled back in a pile of leaves and closed his eyes, letting the breeze cool his tired and aching feet. The wind in the trees and the bubbling of the spring were like a magic lullaby sung by Nature herself. However, it certainly failed to work its drowsy spell on the hundreds of squirrels busily gathering nuts for the winter. They chattered and scurried through the leaves as though winter might descend any moment and catch them unprepared.

Despite last week's early snow, Nalvarre knew that winter was still weeks away, so he allowed himself a few moments' rest from his work. Like the squirrels, he was gathering nuts to store for winter. Two heavy baskets lay nearby, one brimming with pecans, the other with black walnuts. He left the tougher hickory nuts to the squirrels and other animals. Indeed, there was more than enough for everyone. Nalvarre never dreamed of keeping all the nuts to himself, not like the farmers of the lowland forests, who set traps and poisons or kept dogs to protect their orchards from the woodland creatures. He lived in harmony with the land according to the teachings of Chislev, once a goddess of forests and woods. Like the other gods, Chislev had abandoned Krynn during the Chaos War, but Nalvarre still lived by the rhythms of nature. He watched the animals, watched over them, and learned from them how to live without the crutch of civilization.

In autumn he also harvested wild grains from meadows, and apples and persimmons from fruit trees in the valley. On the lower slopes, wild grapes grew, and from them Nalvarre made his own wine. He gathered honey and stored it in jars he made himself, from clay he dug, shaped, and then fired in a primitive stone kiln. His house was made of stones from the stream and thatched with reeds from the lake in the valley. Everything he needed he found around him, and what he didn't use he returned to the land.

The one thing that wasn't in the valley or on the mountain was other people. Nalvarre lived alone, and he liked it that way. By far, he preferred the company of meerkats to merchants, squirrels to squires. Nobody bothered him. No one even knew he was living there.

He lazed away the afternoon under the trees by the brook, watching the squirrels and laughing at their antics. There was no hurry. Really, he didn't even need the nuts. He had plenty of food already stored away, and he only wanted the nuts to make pies for Yule. He still liked to keep the holy days by cooking traditional foods, the sorts of things his mother used to make. He lay in the leaves and thought of all the wonderful things he liked to eat, until his stomach began to growl, and he thought of the barley cakes he'd baked that morning. Quickly, he gathered his laden baskets and hurried down the mountain, leaving the orchard to the squirrels.

The setting sun found him nearing his door. His house was built in the shade of a great beech tree, beside a bank where a mountain stream purled. The chimney stood out against the reddening sky, a tendril of smoke rising in the still autumn air. As he crossed the shallow stream, stepping with familiar ease from stone to stone, he noticed that his door stood ajar, though he remembered closing it. He'd had a problem in the past with trespassing bears, so he always made sure to close it when he went out.

Nalvarre quietly approached the house and set his baskets on the ground beside the woodpile before prying loose a wood axe from a log. He eased up beside the door and glanced quickly inside. The darkened room held no intruders, but a queer smell wafted from the open doorway. It was a wild, musky smell, but not like that of a bear. Some new creature had found its way to the mountain, something beyond Nalvarre's experience. He nervously gripped his axe.

"Hello?" he softly called. Nothing answered him. He slipped inside and peered warily about.

The room seemed empty, but the evidence of intruders was obvious. His favorite chair, the one in which he spent many a winter evening by the fire, lay in shambles on the floor. It was as though some giant had sat in it and collapsed it under his weight. Next, Nalvarre noticed that both the barley cakes he'd baked that morning were gone. A few crumbles on the table marked where he'd left them to cool. The lid of the apple barrel lay on the floor, and about half the apples were missing. He noted in passing that there wasn't a sign of an apple core anywhere, not even a seed. His butter churn was dismantled and lay in pieces under the table, and all the butter had been eaten. Even the bones from the fish he'd had for dinner last night were missing from the refuse jar beside the door. The only thing the marauder hadn't touched were the honey pots lining the mantle.

Nalvarre spun around as something trotted through the still-open door. It was a dog, a very big dog, which skidded to a stop at the sight of him. Not a wild animal, for despite the twigs and leaves snarled in her nappy gray fur, the dog had obviously been well cared for at some time. And not vicious, for the dog seemed more startled by Nalvarre's presence than anything else. Still, he held his axe at the ready. They faced each other across the kitchen table.

"How did you get here, girl?" Nalvarre asked in a calm but forced tone.

At the sound of his voice, her head dropped and her tail began to wag. She waggled over and nuzzled his extended hand. He leaned the axe against the table and stooped to pet her. She licked his face and thumped her tail against the floor.

"Are you lost? Where is your master?" Nalvarre asked as he examined her. She seemed in good condition, certainly well fed. "You've been eating well, I see," he said. "Probably from my larder." He petted and stroked her, picking leaves and other debris from her fur.

"You're a hunting dog," he said as he rose. He took a log from the bin beside the hearth and used it to stoke up the coals of his fire, then added wood chips and sticks until he had a small, merry blaze.

"Did you lose the trail? You've done a remarkable job of getting lost. There isn't a castle or village within miles of here," Nalvarre said. "I imagine you are hungry, aren't you? I was going to have barley cakes for my supper, but since you ate them, we'll have to find something else. How about fish? Do you like fish?"

The dog edged closer to the fire and wagged her tail.

"Fish it is, then. I'll just go out and see if there are any in my traps." He walked to the door and turned, expecting the dog to follow him, but she remained near the warmth of the hearth. "Why don't you stay here," he laughed. "I won't be long."

Nalvarre walked downstream about a hundred yards to

a place where the current widened after spilling over a small fall. He waded out into the stream and reached under the surface, then pulled up a large, funnel-shaped basket woven of wooden sticks. In it wriggled five shiny brown trout. He nearly dropped the basket in his surprise. Never before had he caught so many at once. In the summer months, he would have returned to the stream those he couldn't eat himself, but tonight he had a guest, and since his winter store had been unexpectedly depleted, he decided he'd dry whatever fish he and the dog didn't eat. He waded ashore and sat on a rock to clean the fish while the last light remained in the sky.

As he returned to his cabin, Nalvarre heard voices inside, and through the open doorway, he saw shadows dancing on the walls. It sounded and looked like two or three or maybe fifty people arguing. There was a loud scream and a crash. He rushed inside.

He found in the middle of the floor a heap of broken sticks and thrashing blankets that had once been his bed. Somehow, it had fallen from the loft. In the midst of the disaster, several small creatures were fighting and spitting, punching and gouging, all the while cursing like drunken sailors. Nalvarre waded into this and grabbed one of them by the scruff of its neck, yanking it free of the wreckage. "A gully dwarf!" he exclaimed when he finally saw what he'd caught. The other two continued their battle.

"What's this all about?" he demanded, shaking the suddenly docile gully dwarf.

"Lumpo keep taking all of blanket," Uhoh explained.

"Not!" Lumpo shouted as he angrily swung his elbow and clocked Glabella under the chin. She went sprawling across the floor, a very surprised look on her face. Nalvarre angrily snatched her to her feet while Lumpo, victorious, settled down in the wreckage of the bed and pulled all the blankets around him. He didn't seem to mind the sticks and splinters.

"See," Glabella muttered drunkenly. "Him take all of blanket."

"Yes, I see," Nalvarre said. He reached in and pulled Lumpo from the bed and set him roughly on his feet. "I also see that you've wrecked my bed! Just look at it!"

The three gully dwarves gathered close to look at the bed. "It not a very good bed," Glabella commented.

"Stick poke me in back," Lumpo said as he rubbed his kidney. "How you sleep in bed like that?"

"It didn't used to look like that," Nalvarre said. "It used to be a good bed, until you three destroyed it. Just look at what you've done." He lifted the broken pieces of the bed, trying to see if any of it was salvageable. In frustration, he threw the pieces to the floor.

"And just look at my chair!" he shouted as he walked over to the fireplace. "You broke this, too, didn't you?"

"No. Millisant broke chair," Uhoh said with assurance.

Nalvarre turned to Glabella. "Why did you break my chair?" he asked.

"I not break chair. Millisant break chair," she said.

"Well, which one is Millisant?"

Uhoh pointed at the dog curled up by the hearth, watching them with her chin on her paws. At the sound of her name, she wagged her tail.

"Lumpo stand on chair to reach pots on shelf, but he too short," Uhoh explained. "So I climb on Lumpo's shoulders. Then Glabella climb on me. We do good. Glabella reach pot. Then Millisant jump on chair, chair break. Millisant break chair."

Nalvarre sighed and shook his head. "You ate all my food. You ate my barley cakes. You even ate the garbage. Why?"

"We very hungry," Uhoh said.

Lumpo nodded in agreement. "Bad fish. Too many bones," he said.

"Did you ask if you could come in my house and eat my food and break my chair and destroy my bed?" Nalvarre asked.

"No," Uhoh said.

"No, you didn't!"

"Of course, you not here when we get here," Uhoh amended.

"Well, I'm here now! What do you have to say?" Nalvarre shouted.

"I tired and hungry. I stay two days," Glabella answered. Uhoh and Lumpo concurred.

Nalvarre was stunned to silence. He'd heard about gully dwarves, he had seen them at a distance but had never encountered one before. These seemed to be prime examples. Well, he didn't mind the occasional visitor—that went for raccoons raiding his fish traps or bears devouring his picked berries. Looking them over Nalvarre laughed.

"Oh, I see," he said. "Only two days?"

"Not more than two," Uhoh said.

"Well, supper will be ready in a bit," Nalvarre said. "Do sit down." The gully dwarves eagerly settled themselves on the floor around the fireplace.

"You can sit at the table. There is a bench," Nalvarre said. "I'll be back. Lucky for me, you didn't find my root cellar." He stepped outside.

"Uhoh, you think he gonna nail door shut like the last innkeeper?" Glabella wondered aloud. "I not want this inn to burn down with us in it."

"You do bad job picking inns," Uhoh said. "One burn down, one hit by lightning, one we wake up everybody gone poof, one they chase us out with sticks." He rubbed his head with pained remembrance.

"At least I pick inns. Way you go, there no inns nowhere. Just trees and rocks and nothing to eat forever," Glabella said. "I starve. I disappear poof if I not get supper."

Uhoh countered. "I pick this inn. This good inn!"

"Bed break. Chair break. Lumpo get bone stuck in throat. I eat two apples and my belly hurt," she said.

"You eat two and two and two apples. You not fool me," Uhoh said.

Nalvarre bustled back in the room, his arms loaded with various edible roots. He tossed them directly into the fire. Lumpo began to sniff the air and eye them hungrily.

"You're still sitting on the floor!" Nalvarre said. "Please, do try the benches." With obvious reluctance, the three rose from the floor and settled onto the bench beside the table—Lumpo at one end, Glabella at the other, and Uhoh in the middle.

Nalvarre lifted a skillet from the nail where it hung and set it on the coals of the fire. He looked around, then snapped his fingers.

"No butter," he said. "Well, we must make do. A little wine, perhaps."

From a gourd, he sent a stream of red liquid hissing into the heating pan. He tossed the fish in after it, then while shielding his face against the heat with the palm of one hand, he sprinkled herbs over the lot and flipped the trout with a wooden fork. A fine aroma filled the air, and Lumpo's stomach growled like a bear. Millisant pricked up her ears.

In no time at all, Nalvarre had a hearty meal prepared and set on the table for all. Millisant had already begun her supper; she lay on the packed earth floor and gingerly picked out fish bones with her teeth. The gully dwarves would have begun as well, but Nalvarre thwacked their knuckles with his fork enough times that they finally agreed to wait until everything was ready. He produced a loaf of bread from somewhere (how the gully dwarves had missed it was a mystery, but he was glad they had), and though there was no butter, there was plenty of fresh, sweet honey. He set candles of beeswax on the table and the mantle, and he filled a large stone bowl with wine into which everyone dipped their cups. Neither Glabella nor Lumpo had ever before tasted wine, but Uhoh had sometimes been allowed to lick clean Lord Gunthar's glass at the end of meals. Nalvarre's heady upland vintage was more potent than anything Uhoh had tasted, and it certainly delivered a stouter wallop than the beers and ales familiar to the gully dwarves' palates.

"This one good inn!" Glabella proclaimed after her third cup. "Best inn." She slapped Uhoh on the back in congratulations of his choice, causing him to spill his drink. He eyed her angrily and dipped his cup into the bowl again.

"Inn?" Nalvarre asked, puzzled. "Oh, I see. You think this is an inn."

"That right. I always pick inn, but Uhoh pick this inn. He pick good," Glabella said a little loudly as she took a yam from Uhoh's plate and stuffed it into her mouth.

"So you three are travelers," Nalvarre said.

"No, we Aghar," Lumpo said from the end of the table. "That mean we gully dwarves. Traveler is Papa's horse."

"Yes, of course. What I meant to say was, you three gully dwarves are on a journey," Nalvarre amended.

"I thought you say this a bench," Lumpo said as he eyed the bench suspiciously.

Nalvarre laughed. "It is still a bench," he said. Lumpo relaxed. "What brings you to my . . . hmmm . . . inn?"

"Nobody bring us. We come alone," Glabella said as she swallowed the last of the yam. "We walk two days and two and two days, hunted by slagd. We hungry, we cold, but we brave. We not scared of slagd."

"I scared of slagd," Lumpo said.

"I not. I bite slagd on nose. That show 'em!" Glabella boasted.

Uhoh snorted. Glabella slapped him.

"Slagd scary," Lumpo agreed.

"Excuse me, but what are slagd?" Nalvarre asked.

"Dragonmen," Uhoh said with great solemnity.

"Draconians?" Nalvarre asked in astonishment.

"That right!" Glabella said."He's smart."

"Draconians are chasing you?"

"Uhoh see them kill Papa," Glabella said.

"That big secret!" Uhoh shouted as he slapped Glabella. He turned to Nalvarre and said fiercely, "You not supposed to hear that."

"Draconians killed your father?" Nalvarre asked mystified. "I don't understand. Why would they kill a gully dwarf?

"They not kill gully dwarf, they kill Papa," Glabella said.

"You not supposed to say!" Uhoh shouted.

"When did this killing happen?" Nalvarre asked with genuine curiosity.

Draconians were even more rare in his experience than gully dwarves. Of course he had heard of the evil dragon-bred creatures, but to have gully dwarves and draconians both cross his threshold—mixed up together somehow—was hard to credit.

"Papa not killed two days ago," Lumpo said. Uhoh turned on him again, and seemed ready to strangle him. "I not tell him!" he whined as he backed to the end of the bench.

"Why we not tell?" Glabella asked Uhoh. "You say Papa tell you warn others. He others."

"He not others. You others. He maybe a bad Knight," Uhoh said.

"I'm not a Knight," Nalvarre said, a little miffed.

"You human," Uhoh said.

"That's right, but not all humans are Knights. I was a priest of Chislev once, the goddess of nature," Nalvarre said.

"You talk to gods?" Uhoh said in awe.

"I did, once upon a time," he explained hesitantly. "I still do sometimes, when I feel alone. I don't know if she listens, or if she can even hear me. But I protect and care for the land and the creatures that live on it. If draconians are really hunting you, though I can't imagine why, and you are in danger, perhaps I can help. I'd like to know more."

Uhoh gave him a long hard look, as though weighing his decision with all the mental powers at his disposal. Gunthar had been right when he said Uhoh was unusual for a gully dwarf, for he was unusually self-aware. Perhaps this was a result of his mother dropping him on his head when he was a baby, no one knew. The gully dwarf had spent the last few years living with Knights (or at least in their stables and kennels), so to him, being human had come to mean being a Knight. But this human was obviously quite different than every Knight he'd ever met. For one thing, Nalvarre wore a truly attractive beard, one enviable even by gully dwarf standards. No Knight of Solamnia wore a beard like that. His clothes weren't in much better condition than Uhoh's, while Knights tended to dress meticulously when not encased in armor.

Then, too, Nalvarre smiled at Uhoh and his companions just as Gunthar had always done, and he had gray hair like Gunthar, though not as gray nor so well groomed as the Grand Master's. Nalvarre spoke to Uhoh, not at him, very much unlike most Knights, except for Gunthar.

Still, Uhoh didn't know whether to trust Nalvarre. Already on this trip they'd nearly been captured twice by their dreaded slagd pursuers.

Throughout their journey, the shadowy creatures had dogged their trail, filling the gully dwarves with terror. They were allowed no rest, no time to stop and feed to their satisfaction. At night in the lonely places of the wild, they heard whispers and stealthy footsteps stalking around their hiding places, and only their gully dwarf instincts for self-preservation kept them still and quiet, and thus alive.

Uhoh was weary, weary down to his very bones. He nodded and sighed.

"Tell me what happened," Nalvarre softly said.

"It all happened when me and Papa and Garr hunt big ugly pig, Man-something-or-other," Uhoh said.

"Mannjaeger?" Nalvarre exclaimed.

"That him," Uhoh said.

"You were hunting Mannjaeger, you and your father and Garr?" Nalvarre asked.

"Yes."

Nalvarre's eyes widened. "You are a remarkable fellow," he said.

Uhoh stared at him without comprehension.

"Go ahead with your story," Nalvarre said.

"First Garr die, but he got only a little scratch," Uhoh continued.

"Was Garr your brother?" Nalvarre asked.

Glabella burst out laughing. "Garr a dog, like Millisant," she giggled.

"I'm sorry. So the boar killed Garr. Do continue," Nalvarre said.

"Then pig attack Papa and knock Papa down, so I throw rocks at pig and pig let Papa go. Then Papa stick pig with pig sticker. Pig run away," Uhoh said.

"Your father stabbed Mannjaeger with a knife?" Nalvarre asked in disbelief.

"No, it long stick with knife on end. Very heavy," Uhoh explained.

"I see," Nalvarre said.

The longer this story went on, the less he felt like believing it. To think, the gully dwarf was not only hunting Mannjaeger, but actually wounding him, and with a spear! It was common knowledge that an armed gully dwarf is more a danger to himself than to his enemies.

"Then Papa die, like this," Uhoh said as he performed a remarkable imitation of the convulsions which twisted Gunthar's body.

"Papa get scratch here," Uhoh continued, indicating his thigh. "He say, 'Come close' and he tell me big secret nobody supposed to know. Then Papa say," Uhoh croaked in a remarkable imitation of a dying man's whispered last words. " 'The book . . . Kalaman . . . Liam . . . in bell room . . . tell him . . . tell no one.' Then slagd come, and I run away home," he finished in his normal voice.

"We go home too," Glabella said.

Lumpo's head hit the table and he began to snore.

"But what does this big secret mean?" Nalvarre asked, scratching his thick, tangled beard.

"You not suppose to know secret," Uhoh said, pounding the table. "I tell you, that before."

"I'm sorry, but let's get back to the draconians. I thought you said the draconians killed Papa. Why?"

"I come to that!" Uhoh frowned. "You tell story, or me?"

"Do continue," Nalvarre apologized.

"Before hunt, slagd do this and that. They make hoobajooba with hands so dogs don't go right way, but me and Papa we go right way," Uhoh said.

"And Garr," Glabella added.

"What?" Nalvarre asked in bewilderment.

"That easy spell," Glabella interrupted. "I learn do that when I only two."

"A spell?" Nalvarre asked. "Do you mean they performed magic?"

"Big magic. That hoobajooba spell easy. All you need is chicken foot," she said. "I got chicken foot. You wanna see?" She began to dig in her bag.

"Some other time," Nalvarre said to her. He turned to Uhoh. "So the draconians cast a spell to confuse the hunters? But somehow allowing you, and your father, and Garr to find the boar. It sounds feasible . . ."

"That what I say," Uhoh said. "Feasible!"

"Remarkable!" The very strangeness of the story did lend credence to it. "So after Papa died, then what happened?" he asked.

"I fall asleep. I wake up with draconians all around. Two, at least two. So I fight and get away."

"Really?" Nalvarre asked in surprise.

"No!" Glabella shouted. "Millisant bite slagd on tail and he drop Uhoh on head, just like when he a baby."

"Then I run," Uhoh said a little sheepishly. "They chase. I run away home."

"Where is home?"

"Town," Uhoh said.

Town. Nalvarre had heard rumors of this place. It was a fairly recent colony of gully dwarves. Almost no one knew of its precise whereabouts. There were a few other people, like Nalvarre, who lived in the wild hills alone: rangers, druids, hermits, and the like. Occasionally they met to exchange news or to trade. Recently, there had been talk of this burgeoning gully dwarf Town with everyone wondering how so large a population of the miserable creatures had sprung into being, virtually overnight.

Town was said to lie several days journey to the north, well into the acknowledged realm of the red dragon Pyrothraxus. The only human habitation in the area was an old castle of the Solamnic Knights, built to guard a pass that had fallen out of use ages ago. Over the nine years since Nalvarre had lived in this region, the castle had only been garrisoned twice; the rest of that time it stood empty, a home to rooks and lizards.

"That is quite some tale," Nalvarre said at last. "I don't quite understand all the details, but I trust they'll emerge in the light of day. In the meanwhile, you three are welcome to stay here as long as you like."

Uhoh was nodding sleepily, as Glabella blinked. She reached across the table for another yam and tried to stuff it in her mouth, but somewhere along the way she drifted off. Her head fell on the table with a thud, though her fingers remained firmly locked on the yam. She snuggled it to her cheek like a doll.

Uhoh yawned, his jaws cracking. "We stay two days," he said. "Not more than two." He stretched and rose from his seat, stumbled over and curled up with Millisant by the fire.

"Poor little buggers," Nalvarre whispered as he looked at them.

He quietly cleaned up the supper dishes, extracted his blankets from the wreck of the bed, and climbed into the loft to find a place to stretch out. As he drifted off, he gazed down on his visitors and wondered. He thought about them as sleep stole over him, and in the night he dreamed the trees were full of thousands of squirrels with gully dwarf faces, all jabbering ceaselessly, while black wolves stalked the ground below.

Chapter Seventeen

Four draconians, their clawed feet bruised and bleeding, scrambled among the rocks and boulders of one of the most barren and forlorn regions any of them had ever seen. Every broken stone and pebble seemed sharper than the obsidian blades and arrowheads of Abanasinian warriors, every bush was a thorn bush, every vine a tangleroot, every stunted tree spiked with needles or prickly with splinters.

The one in the lead was the smallest of the four. A baaz draconian, his scales had a brassy golden hue, and he bore two ram-like horns curling from his sinister reptilian head. He wore a dirty green cloak thrown over his folded wings, as though he were a ranger or scout. The next two had scales of a coppery tint and wore tight-fitting outfits of blackened leather designed to allow full range of motion both to their limbs and to the batlike wings sprouting from their backs. These kapaks, as they were called, were larger than their baaz companion, and they pushed him relentlessly with their taunts and venomous comments. The fourth of the group was the largest. His reptilian scales glimmered with a silvery sheen, glaringly reflecting the light of the midday sun. He wore armor of chain and plate specifically designed to fit his draconic body. A long, heavy sword was slung across his back between his wings. He was a sivak, one of the most powerful of all draconian races.

They were following a trail that seemed little more than an ancient wash in the grim and waterless mountains surrounding them. Perhaps it was a goat path, though no goats were to be seen. They had not seen another living creature since the sun rose over this accursed land. They stumbled wearily along, stones turning under their feet, slippery shale sliding away beneath them and bringing them to their knees again and again, snarling at each other, spitting curses with each breath.

"There's nothing here!" one of the kapaks growled.

"This is the way," the sivak answered in an even tone. "Krass has been here many times in the two years since we arrived on this island. Isn't that right, Krass?"

The baaz wearily nodded his head.

"I think Krass is lost," the kapak said. "Why would his lordship live out here in this barren waste, when he has all of Mount Nevermind to do with as he pleases?"

"You have answered your own question, Dreg," the sivak said. "The gnomes of Mount Nevermind give him no peace."

"Rebels?" the kapak, Dreg, asked.

"No, tinkers. They're always poking and prodding at him, trying to find out how he works. He can't kill them all. He's tried. They're worse than gully dwarves," the sivak said.

As they topped a small, razorback ridge, the baaz scout stopped and pointed into the valley on the other side. Clambering up next to him, the other draconians saw a wide, low-roofed cave yawning blackly from the opposite hillside. A tendril of oily smoke streamed from the upper lip of the opening.

"There it is," the sivak gasped while pressing a fist into his cramping side. "Pyrothraxus's lair."

They scrambled down the side of the ridge and up the opposite hillside, finally reaching the mouth of the cave just before dark. From this point, by looking south down a long valley, they could see the summit of Mount Nevermind blushed with pink from the setting sun. The long shadows of the hills had followed them down the ridge, until now they stood in a peculiar half-light, where every boulder and stone stood out in stark relief, as though cut from paper, while the entrance to the cave was a dark and misty hole, without depth.

The gleaming yellow bones of dozens upon dozens of creatures—men, beasts, gnomes, and dwarves—lay strewn about the mouth of the cave, relics of the insatiable appetite of the dragon of Mount Nevermind. Three years ago he'd come in a storm. He'd conquered the ancient mountain city of the gnomes in a single day—much to his own chagrin. Those who should have trembled in his presence instead prodded him with questions or worse. They slipped into his lair while he was sleeping and stuck him with stovepipe-sized needles attached to steam-driven syringes. They begged him to breathe fire on them so they could test their newest flame-retardant fabrics. Where was the joy in destroying creatures who cared so little for their own destruction? They, in fact, measured and recorded the manner and level of their own destruction! Such were the circumstances which drove Pyrothraxus to seek safety in a cave unworthy of his tremendous importance, a cave barely large enough to hold his beloved bed of treasure, much less his gargantuan self.

Still, the entrance to the cave was large enough to sail a ship through. As the draconians entered the cathedral-sized chamber, they were awed by its size and more so by the huge gouges in the solid rock of the floor, evidence of the dragon's passing. There was little among dragonkind which could impress a draconian, but the ungodly size of

Pyrothraxus, as well as that of the other new dragons from across the sea, filled them with wonder and just a little fear. They walked cautiously, reverently, holding their collective breaths, drawn by the thought of what awaited them within the cave. They stepped inside.

The dim light from the twilight outside was enough to illuminate the mountain of gold and steel that rose before them. Never in all their lives had they dreamed of such wealth. The sight of it was almost a religious experience, stirring them to the very core of their draconic souls. It rose like a great ocean wave, bearing upon its crest two entire ships! Gems gleamed like stars, in color, in light, and in countless multitudes. The wealth of half a world lay before them . . . unguarded!

"His lordship doesn't appear to be home," Dreg whispered with a hiss.

Before anyone could answer, there was a bone-crunching thud. Droplets spattered them. A second crunch sounded hollowly from above. Staring up, they saw a reptilian head as large as a two-masted galleon gulping down the remnants of Dreg. The three remaining draconians cowered in terror.

"Lord Pyrothraxus, we come bearing tidings from Master Iulus," the sivak hurriedly explained.

The huge head turned to gaze down upon them, its red eyes glowing like two dwarven forges. A gout of flame shot from one barrel-sized nostril, illuminating their upturned faces. The sivak, glancing around, spotted a niche in the passage, which might offer some protection.

"A kapak!" the huge dragon boomed, his voice shaking stones loose from the walls. "Kapaks give me indigestion."

One massive claw splashed ringingly in the coins nearby, followed by another. The dragon pulled itself off its ledge above the entrance to the cave and slithered down to the bed of treasure. The underbelly, passing so near and hugely round, radiated heat that dried the moisture from their mouths and eyes. Last of all came the great serpentine tail, as long again as its entire body, head, and neck. It settled onto the coins and began to bubble and purr, stoking the fires in its belly and filling the chamber with a sourceless red glow.

"What have you brought?" the dragon asked, bored.

"Tidings, O most puissant lord. Gunthar uth Wistan is dead," the sivak declared.

"Brilliant, General Zen!" Pyrothraxus roared. "Most excellent news indeed." He lifted his head and shot a victorious gout of flame splashing against the roof. Gobbets of molten rock rained down. "So the plan is proceeding?"

"He knows you, my general?" the baaz asked the sivak.

"I first negotiated with his lordship for permission to build our castle in his territory," General Zen answered. "In exchange for protecting us from the prying eyes of the south, we promised to give him the Solamnics' lands when they are won." Then to the dragon, he shouted, "Everything is ready, Your Eminence."

"It is all working out exactly as you promised, General Zen," Pyrothraxus laughed. The volume of his voice set ripples flowing through the sea of coins.

"Indeed it is, my lord Pyrothraxus. In fact—" the sivak began, but his thoughts, and the attention of the dragon, were interrupted by the chiming of a small silver bell.

"What is that noise?" Pyrothraxus asked.

The sivak cursed under his breath. "A magical device, my lord, for communicating over long distances. One of our agents in the south—"

"Answer it," Pyrothraxus demanded, the fires in his eyes flaring.

After one final moment of hesitation, Zen reached into a pouch at his belt and removed a large silver hand mirror. As he did so, it rang again, more loudly this time. He waved one clawed hand over its surface three times while fingering the strange designs carved on its handle. The reflective surface of the mirror dulled, then went black. A face appeared, hazy, almost indistinguishable.

"What do you want?" Zen hissed.

"The gully dwarf hassss essscaped," came a tiny, metallic voice from the mirror.

"Very well. Continue your search. Report when you find something," Zen hurriedly ordered.

"What gully dwarf?" Pyrothraxus asked.

"The one who witnessssssed Gunthar'sssss death," answered the voice from the mirror.

"Shaeder!" Zen shouted as he ducked into the niche he'd spotted earlier.

"What!" Pyrothraxus roared. An explosion slammed Zen into the wall of the niche, and flames licked at his ankle spurs and wing tips. It continued unabated, unbearable heat scorching every inch of his flesh. The stone around him began to steam and then to flake away. He felt a scream escaping his mouth, but no sound of it reached his ears. The dragon fire consumed everything—breath, flesh, the very will to live. Only the stone of the living mountain protected him, barely.

Finally, the fire and deafening noise ended. His hoarse scream echoed in the suddenly silent chamber. Collecting himself, Zen grew quiet. The voice from the mirror whined, "I'm getting some interference on my end."

He listened, but dared not leave the protective niche.

"You can come out now, Zen," the dragon purred. "I promise not to kill you, for now."

Warily, Zen stepped out. Pyrothraxus eyed him sleepily, but the fires glinting behind his lowered lids showed that his anger remained. On the floor where the baaz and the other kapak had stood, not an ash, not a mote of dust remained to show that they'd even been there. Steam rose from the rocks. As the mountain began to cool, it cracked and groaned as though in pain.

"Find this gully dwarf," Pyrothraxus said. The calmness of his voice only made it seem all the more sinister. "If your plans are discovered, I won't protect you or the Knights who recruited you to do their dirty work. If you fail, rest assured, someone will pay!"

* * * * *

Uhoh and his companions did indeed stay with Nalvarre two days. They stayed two and two and two, until it seemed the food might run out after all.

After the first day, he learned not to leave the gully dwarves unsupervised in the house while he was gone in search of food. They would attack nearly everything that was even marginally chewable, even the leather hinges on the cupboard doors. They were worse than goats. Nalvarre had never approved of locks, but for the time being, he rigged a simple bolt to the door to keep everyone out. Uhoh, Lumpo, and Glabella were free to wander where they liked (Nalvarre pointed out more than once the nearness of the stream and its usefulness as a bathing facility) and to eat anything they found, just so long as they stayed out of the house and the root cellar.

Millisant hunted rabbits and rollicked in the meadows like a filly in clover, while Glabella became quite adept at snatching trout from the stream without net or hook. She sat on the bank as still as a cat and scooped them out when they swam by, flinging them onto the bank where Uhoh and Lumpo waited. Most were eaten long before they found their way to a skillet.

Meanwhile, no shadowy figures lurked in the trees, no stealthy footsteps haunted their dreams. Uhoh was content and happy in a way he had not been since before

Gunthar's death. At night, they slept as only happy gully dwarves can sleep—like stones. Millisant chased rabbits in her dreams.

At night, they sat by the fire and Nalvarre told them tales of the gods of long ago and of the ways of the forest creatures, and for the most part Lumpo slept through his stories and Glabella half-listened while she nibbled and snacked almost without stop. Only Uhoh seemed truly interested.

The gully dwarves also told tales, but these were quickly unfolded and quickly resolved in the usual gully dwarf fashion, without point or purpose. The standard model sounded something like this: "You remember that time when . . ." followed by much laughter, and a few lingering comments along the lines of "That funny story. Tell it again." Sometimes the story was told wrong, which led to rip-roaring fights on the floor, which didn't do the furniture much good. Nalvarre's carpentry skills improved.

When things got quiet, someone was sure to break into "Ninety-nine Bottles of Beer." That usually lasted them until they dropped with exhaustion, hoarse and croaking, as they never had got the idea that you were supposed to count backward in the song. Every verse told of the endless supply of ninety-nine bottles of beer.

A disquiet crept over the wood as autumn deepened into winter. Nalvarre felt it, though he was at a loss to name its source. The gully dwarves, it seemed, felt it as well, for Lumpo's dreams had turned and he often woke screaming, and Uhoh spent more and more time standing in the door after supper watching the quiet woods. Glabella's appetite increased; she seemed like a bear putting on fat for the lean times ahead.

More than once, as he returned home through the darkling woods, Nalvarre turned at some half-glimpsed shadow, only to find nothing there. He found himself listening for stealthy footsteps on the path or wondering at the sudden quiet and whispering of the trees. It left him feeling unsettled. He took to carrying an axe everywhere he went. Images of red dragons hovering in the sky came unbidden to his mind. He began to wonder if Pyrothraxus were not extending his influence from his northern lair at Mount Nevermind.

One morning, as Nalvarre was preparing breakfast, he said to the gully dwarves, "If I don't lock the door today, will you promise not to mess things up here? I may not be home by nightfall, in which case you three may need to stay here alone. Can you do that, and can I trust you not to wreck the place?"

"You trust us," Glabella assured him as she patted his leg. "We good."

"I'll leave plenty of food out, so you won't need to go rooting around for more. You'll have to trust me that I'll be back tomorrow," Nalvarre continued.

"We trust you," Uhoh said. "We promise. I watch these gulpfungers. Uhoh boss!"

So it was that after breakfast, and with many grave misgivings, Nalvarre left the three waving good-bye in the doorway of his house. He took his staff and started down the mountainside. He planned to travel to the valley floor, to an ancient well hidden deep in the forest there. It was the meeting place for rangers and druids, a place to leave trade goods and to find useful items in the unique barter system used by the denizens of the forest. Only rarely did two traders meet face to face. One might leave a basket of apples. The next person might take the apples but leave an elven knife. The third might take the knife but leave a sack of flour. Then the first might return and take the sack of flour.

This time Nalvarre wasn't going there to trade. He felt the need for news of what was passing in the outside world, and he hoped to run into someone at the well who might shed light on his recent forebodings.

It took him most of the day to make his way to the valley forest. He followed the stream that ran by his door, traveling a path he knew well, for he had made it himself. Wherever the path crossed the stream, he'd built simple bridges—of logs on the heights and of rushes nearer to the valley. As it meandered down the mountainside, the stream gathered to itself other smaller streams, rivulets, and trickles, until as it neared the valley floor, it became a torrent, rolling and tumbling over many a noisy fall and rapid. Finally, it reached the lower meadows and slowed to a cold crawl, wandering through bogs and fens until it reached the lake, where it spread its waters beneath the sun to warm. Reeds grew there in abundance in the shallows, providing shelter for multitudes of small water birds, while trout thrived in its cold depths.

The air was considerably warmer in the valley. While on the heights winter was fast approaching, in the valley autumn lingered in a profusion of harvest golds and brilliant scarlets. The forest rustled with a soft breeze, and sunlight dappled the path in a shifting dancing pattern of golden patches of light. It seemed so pleasant here that it was hard to believe anything was wrong, and Nalvarre began to doubt himself. He stopped and through a gap in the trees gazed back up at the mountain. He wondered what the gully dwarves were doing, and visions of them devouring every stick of furniture in the house brought a chuckle.

As the day waned and Nalvarre penetrated the heart of the forest, the sun found fewer and fewer holes in the canopy through which to shine. A deep and abiding gloom embraced the very center of the forest, for here the trees were ancient beyond reckoning, mighty and tall. Like pillars in a dark and silent temple, their gray trunks marched in serried ranks in every direction, blending in a dark haze at the very edge of vision. Only the path, barely visible in the gloom, marked the way. No water flowed here, no stream crossed the path, for the rain that fell here rarely found its way through the thick canopy to the ground below. It was intolerably dusty and dry, almost like a desert.

The gloom only deepened as night fell, but Nalvarre did not stop for the evening, and neither did he light a torch. He knew the path by heart, so he continued well into the night. Soon, a cool wet breeze rose before him, freshening his pace with its promise of water, and before long he stepped out of the wood as though passing through a door in a wall. A wide ring of oaks towered above a forest meadow fully a hundred paces across. In the center of the clearing stood a ruin of wide marble columns, glowing like a vision from an enchanted dream. High above, the unfamiliar stars of Krynn, newly formed after the Chaos War when the Greystone of Gargath shattered, wheeled in a crystalline black sky. Dew glimmered on the thigh-high grasses, wetting Nalvarre's robes as he passed through on his way to the well beside the ruin. A small fire burned there, promising warmth as well as news and company.

Still, Nalvarre approached warily. It was best not to appear unexpectedly from the darkness, for the forest people were wary. He might find an arrow in his throat before given a chance to explain himself. As he drew nearer, he slowed his pace. A heavily robed figure huddled beside the fire, warming his hands. "Hello in camp," Nalvarre called out. The figure looked up, but made no other move.

"May I approach?" Nalvarre asked, first in the common tongue, then in Solamnic. The figure nodded and waved, and Nalvarre stepped into the light of the fire. "Greetings," he said.

The robed stranger answered him in Solamnic, "Hail, brother of the wood. Please sit and enjoy the warmth of my fire."

Nalvarre gladly accepted the invitation, for although the forest had been stuffy, the meadow of the well was cool with the breath of autumn. As he settled himself near the fire, he caught a glimpse of the stranger's face beneath his hood.

"Laif? Laif Lorbaird?" he asked.

The stranger started, as though surprised by the sound of his name, then smiled and pushed back his hood, revealing a tangle of oil-black hair. He nodded in acknowledgment.

"I thought that was you, Laif," Nalvarre said. "By the gods, it's been a long time."

"Hasn't it, though, my friend," Laif answered. "What brings you here?"

"I was troubled by a strange feeling of uneasiness you might say, which has descended on the wood where I live," Nalvarre said. "What passes in the world?"

"Many things, many changes," Laif said in thick Solamnic. "The Knights of Solamnia and the Knights of Takhisis have joined to form one order."

"No!" Nalvarre gasped.

"It is true. Knights of Takhisis are even now garrisoning Sancrist castles long abandoned," Laif said.

Nalvarre shook his head in disbelief.

"Lord Gunthar is dead," Laif continued.

Nalvarre nodded sadly. "Well, that at least is not unexpected. He was very old. How did he die?"

"He was killed during a boar hunt," Laif said.

"A boar?" said Nalvarre in some surprise.

"He was old," Laif said. "They say the excitement probably killed him, not the boar."

"I see," Nalvarre said, unsettled by the coincidence between this news and the story of the death of Uhoh's Papa.

"What brings you here, my friend?"

176

Laif leaned forward as though to relate a great secret. The firelight set his dark eyes smoldering. "I hunt a great evil. It has come from the south and passed through all the woods, spreading discord and fear. Probably that is what you felt. I have tracked it this far, but I lost its trail."

"You, a ranger of the wild wood, lost the trail?" Nalvarre laughed. "I find that very hard to believe."

Laif's eyes burned all the more fiercely. "This evil is very clever," he said. "It travels in the shape of a gully dwarf and in the company of other gully dwarves. I don't suppose you have seen any of these creatures?"

Nalvarre suddenly felt very cold inside. Perhaps it was the way Laif's eyes glimmered in the firelight, like glowing coals, when he asked about the gully dwarves. Some instinct warned Nalvarre to say nothing of his guests.

"Not for many a season," he lied.

"Ah!" Laif sighed as he pulled his hood back over his head. "That is unfortunate."

"I must be going now," Nalvarre said rather suddenly.

"Are you sure you won't stay?" Laif asked pleasantly.

"Quite," Nalvarre said. "I really must go. Thank you. Good luck to you."

"Fare thee well," said Laif in formal Solamnic. He leaned back and rolled himself in his robe, as though settling in for the night.

Nalvarre hurried away without seeming to hurry. He was glad to be away from the fire and into the concealing darkness of the meadow. This meeting, which he had hoped might relieve his disquiet, only alarmed him all the more. He hurriedly crossed the meadow, glancing often over his shoulder.

Just at the edge of the meadow, as he glanced yet another time to check for dark pursuers, he tripped and fell flat on his face. He lay in the tall grass for a few moments, listening, before crawling back to pick up his staff. He found it lying across the carcass of some dead animal. Obviously, this was what he had stumbled over. He picked up his staff and prepared to leave, but at that moment the moon raised its ghastly white face above the tops of the trees, flooding the meadow with a pale glow. The white columns of the ruin stood out like cardboard cutouts illumined with faerie fire against the dark of the forest. At Nalvarre's feet lay the body of man. With a growing sense of horror, he rolled the corpse onto its back. He gasped and stepped back, then glanced in alarm at the fire. It burned merrily alone, with no one in sight. Nalvarre turned and fled into the forest.

Laif Lorbaird lay in the grass and stared with milky eyes at the wheeling stars, a dagger protruding from his heart.

Chapter Eighteen

The fire on the hearth had nearly burned itself out. In the dark of the night, Millisant rose from her place by the fireplace and padded softly to the open doorway. The three gully dwarves lay in a tangled knot on the floor, snoring peacefully for the moment, though earlier they'd been fighting each other over the one blanket. Something woke Millisant from her dreams, some almost unheard noise that alerted all her canine instincts. She sat in the doorway and looked out into the night, breathing the chill mountain air in clouds of steam, which hung about her like thunderheads. She looked grim and sorcerous, like the guardian of a wizard's lair. Outside, the stream bubbled and purled, sparkling like quicksilver in the pale moonlight.

Occasionally, she sniffed the air, lifted her nose high to catch the slight breeze off the mountain. She smelled the usual smells of rock and stone, water and snow, leaf and tree and root. She smelled the mouse's nest in the thatch of the roof, the rabbit skins tacked to dry on the south wall, the rock snake's den under the house, and of course, she smelled her gully dwarves.

However, there was a new smell, one that filled her with unease. It smelled like the copper pans the cooks at the castle used to catch the blood of the animals they

DRAGONLANCE

slaughtered. It smelled like metal and blood, like slaughter, like death. She sat in the door and felt a desire to howl grow ever stronger as the moon climbed the sky. The primal needs were awakening in her. She wanted to howl to call together the wolf pack to protect her and her pups from whatever lurked out there in the forest.

It came like a shadow, slinking from the trees on the opposite bank of the stream. Millisant's hackles bristled, and she backed away from the door, into the shadows of the room. On it came, crossing the stream now. Shrouded in robes of ebony, it crept toward the house. It crouched outside the door, its head cocked to one side, and it snuffled at the air. Millisant hid in the shadows, as silent as the intruder himself, her lips pulled back from her teeth. She gathered her paws under her body, her muscles tensed like iron springs. She dug her claws into the packed earthen floor.

The intruder rose and crept to the door, stopping beneath the lintel. It gazed into the room, and seeing the gully dwarves huddled asleep on the floor, it hissed in what might have been glee. It turned, and Millisant saw its face. For a moment, all courage left her.

It wasn't a human face. From beneath its voluminous hood there protruded a long reptilian snout. Twin horns like those of a ram curled to either side of its head, while the back of its robes stirred as its wings rose. A long serpentine tail thrashed free of the robes and thudded excitedly on the ground. It took one step into the room, drawing a dagger from the folds of its robes as it entered.

With but one thought—the protection of her charges—Millisant silently launched herself at the draconian. By some sixth sense, he turned just in time to see an bear trap of yellow teeth rising to his throat. Millisant was a boar hound, a huge dog, nearly as tall as the draconian when standing on her hind legs, so when she struck, her weight

180

lifted and carried them both through the door and outside the house. With a choking scream, the draconian beat his heelspurs upon the ground, his throat locked in Millisant's powerful jaws. In his death throes, he slashed her legs with his dagger, but she didn't let go until he grew still. She released him, and only just in time. Before his head hit the ground, his flesh turned to stone. She yelped and dashed away, her tail tucked between her legs.

The gully dwarves had awakened at the sounds of the battle. Glabella was the first to the door. She rushed outside and found Millisant cowering at the edge of the stream, and a draconian lying on the ground before the door. She nearly bowled over Uhoh on her way back into the house. She scrambled into the loft and hid.

Hurling a curse over his shoulder, Uhoh stepped outside and nearly tripped over the prone draconian. A scream from the house spun him around in time to see Lumpo standing in the doorway with his eyes rolling back in his head. He sank like an empty sack on the doorstep.

Uhoh shoved his fists on his hips and stomped one foot. "Why you scared? This slagd dead!" he shouted.

"Shhhhhh! Maybe only sleeping!" Glabella hissed from the loft.

"Look, dead like stone!" Uhoh said as he kicked the draconian. He regretted that demonstration as he hopped around holding his stubbed toe. He fell to the ground and pulled off his shoe, fully expecting to see his toe swollen as big as a peach. He stuck it in his mouth and sucked it like a thumb.

Meanwhile, Millisant limped to Uhoh's side. While he sucked his toe, he stroked and petted her. She fawned and wagged her tail, all the while favoring her injured leg. Noticing this, Uhoh spit out his toe and examined her forelegs. His hands came away red with blood.

"Me scared!" Glabella wailed to the heavens.

"Shut up and come here!" Uhoh shouted. "Millisant hurt! Bring medicine."

By holding Millisant's injured leg, Uhoh helped her limp into the cottage. As he passed Lumpo's still form, he kicked the unconscious gully dwarf. "Get up! Put wood on fire!" he ordered.

"Wha . . . what?" Lumpo mumbled.

"Put wood on fire!" Uhoh shouted in anger.

"I not know how," Lumpo said.

"Take one stick, put on fire, blow," Uhoh said as he helped the injured hound lay by the fireplace. Glabella scurried down the ladder from the loft and went in search of her bag.

"I not know how," Lumpo whined.

"Do it!" Uhoh screamed.

To his everlasting surprise, Lumpo actually managed to stoke up the fire. Soon, a warm blaze filled the room with light. Carefully, tenderly, Uhoh cleansed Millisant's wounds. Glabella busied herself with various charms, feathers, and small dead mummified animals reputed to have magical powers in gully dwarf lore. She waved these in the air and uttered innocuous phrases, only stopping occasionally to assure Millisant of her imminent recovery.

Uhoh bound Millisant's wounds with strips torn from Nalvarre's blanket, then helped settle her comfortably by the fire. Millisant thumped the floor with her tail and gobbled down the scraps from last night's supper as Uhoh fed them to her. Lumpo stood in the corner with his mouth hanging open, eyeing each bite as it passed from the plate to the dog's waiting mouth. Suddenly, Glabella shouted and shook a chicken foot in Millisant's face, then stepped back proudly with her hands on her hips.

"There, that do it. Chicken foot cure work every time," she said.

With Millisant taken care of, Uhoh remember his shoe and stepped outside to get it. His foot was cold, especially his toe. So it was with complete surprise that he found the stone dead draconian gone. Only a pile of dust marked where it had lain. He sidestepped to where his shoe lay, and without ever turning his back on the dust, stumbled quickly though the door. He slammed it shut and pushed the table up against it.

"Slagd gone!" he gasped at his companions' puzzled looks.

"See, I say! I say, slagd only sleeping. I say, he not dead. Now what we do?" Glabella despaired.

"We go," Uhoh said. "Now. We go to Town. We stay here too long."

"Now?" Lumpo moaned as he rubbed his belly.

"Now," Uhoh said. He pulled Lumpo's bag from its hiding place in the corner and threw it at him.

"Get food, much as you can carry," he ordered.

Lumpo looked at his bag. "Me need bigger sack," he muttered as he stuffed apples into it.

In minutes, they were ready. Their bags were packed with food, and Lumpo had indeed found a large canvas sack, which he filled in Nalvarre's forbidden root cellar. He slung it over his back, looking very much like a small soot-begrimed Yulefather with his bag of toys. When everyone was ready, Uhoh pushed the table away from the door. Millisant rose and hobbled to his side.

"What we do with her?" Glabella asked.

Uhoh looked into the eyes of the hound, and a deep regret brought tears to his eyes. If he took her, she might not survive the journey, but he truly didn't wish to leave her behind. She'd saved his life twice now, and unlike most gully dwarves, Uhoh did know the meaning of thankfulness. At last, and with much sadness, he made up his mind.

───

183

"Millisant stay here. We lock door. Nalvarre come home tomorrow and take care of her. He good man, good innkeeper," he said.

It truly broke Uhoh's heart to have to push Millisant back and shut the door on her. She pawed and whined, not understanding, but her injuries prevented her from bulling her way past the gully dwarves. By standing on Lumpo's shoulders, Glabella was able to work the latch that locked the door. That done, they gathered their bags and, without a word, set out.

Millisant's howls followed them down the mountainside.

*   *   *   *   *

Nalvarre stumbled from the valley forest near daybreak, but weary as he was, he didn't stop. Fear drove him onward. He feared not for himself but for the gully dwarves he'd left on the mountainside. Clearly they were involved in something much more sinister than he first suspected. The manner of Lord Gunthar's death chimed too closely with the way Uhoh's Papa had met his end. Whatever the dwarves' involvement, they were in danger, and he'd left them unprotected.

As a priest of Chislev, Nalvarre's life's work had been to protect and preserve the creatures and the woodlands of Krynn. When he was still a young priest, he'd been given the guardianship of a lovely forest hidden away in a quiet corner of Solamnia, near the city of Kalaman. During the siege of Kalaman, the Knights of Takhisis were spreading their influence all over Ansalon, marking the lands with fire and sword. A band of Knights had come from the south with a party of draconian soldiers. They set up camp in his beautiful woods, and they began to cut the trees to build siege engines for their armies. When they had all they needed, they cut trees apparently for the fun of it. They torched the dead and dry leavings of their works, and these fires soon spread throughout the forest. Nalvarre's home was destroyed, his forest decimated. Even in those days, when he wielded clerical powers, there was little he could do. He moved to a new woodland, but this one also fell to the armies of Takhisis. Each time he moved, it seemed they came to destroy what he loved, until there were no more woods for him to move to. The Knights of Takhisis took control of Qualinost. Nalvarre fled to Sancrist, the very last place on Krynn where he expected to find Knights of Takhisis and their malicious, life-hating draconians, and now, here they were!

Even so, Nalvarre needed a few moments' rest, water, and something to restore his strength. The water was easy enough, for all the lake lay between him and the mountain; it was food he was hard-pressed to find. He hadn't had time to search for food, and he'd already eaten the small ration of bread and honey he brought with him on the journey, but there was nothing to be done. He had to keep going. He felt time was already slipping away from him.

At one point, the path swung near the lake where an outcropping of flat rocks formed the shore. It was an easy place from which to draw water and was often used by such travelers as visited the valley. Nalvarre laid himself out flat on the rocks in the morning sun. Leaning over the edge of the rocks, he drew handfuls of water to his parched lips. He drank first to quench his thirst, then to lessen the edge of his hunger. When he'd drunk his fill, he lay there a while, resting his weary feet and looking at his own reflection in the water.

He didn't like what he saw. He looked weary, haggard, old. His beard was a mess, but he didn't really care about that. The cheeks beneath the beard looked drawn, the lips thin. His hair was shockingly gray. He didn't remember it being that gray, but then again he couldn't remember the last time he saw his own reflection. How many years had it been?

He turned his attention to the reflection of the morning sky. Pillowy white clouds chased each other across the crisp azure of the heavens. Mountains rose all around, with colors of granite and stone, and the grayish-green of the evergreens on the highest slopes. Like some kind of magic spell, the beauty and serenity of the scene relaxed his aching muscles, eased his worried mind. His eyelids grew heavy, began to droop, but it wasn't magic; it was only his exhaustion and his desire for sleep. He fought it off, shaking his head and splashing cold lake water in his face. He blustered and gasped, spraying droplets from his beard. He looked again at his reflection in the water.

"Fool!" he shouted at himself. "To think you almost fell . . ." A spot of movement in the reflection of the sky caught his attention. He rolled onto his back and gazed up.

Like a sparkling droplet of blood against the blue of the sky—high, high above, tiny with distance, flew Pyrothraxus. Nalvarre knew it was Pyrothraxus even though he'd never seen the dragon; it could be no other. He felt all his trepidations and fear rush to a head. The gully dwarves were involved in something more sinister than the death of one unfortunate Aghar. Why else would draconians be hunting them? Why else would Pyrothraxus choose this day to fly over the valley, where he'd never flown before?

"What am I to do? What can I possibly do?" Nalvarre wondered aloud. "I am only one man." A vision of the gully dwarves sitting at his table, their faces smeared with food, rose unbidden to his mind. He knew then what he had to do. He had to draw a line in the sand, for there were no more forests in which to hide. He'd never again sit by and watch what he loved destroyed, using his solitude, one man against many, to excuse his lack of action. All his life he'd adhered to the principles of balance but without really understanding them. Chislev taught the philosophy known as neutrality, a philosophy of balance. Both good and evil must exist in contrast, so that the balance of the world is maintained. Nalvarre had always thought this meant he must never take sides, must treat both equally. Only now did he realize that the importance lay in balance. When evil seems ready to overwhelm the world, good must be assisted to regain the balance. When good threatens to consume all in its fires of righteousness, evil must be given room to breathe and grow.

Now evil threatened to consume Nalvarre's last home. He'd been pushed across half a continent, and there was nowhere else to go. It might not mean much in the grand scheme of things, or it might be the difference between peace returning to the forest and evil sweeping down and destroying his last home, but he had to try to save the gully dwarves. He leaped to his feet and charged off through the bulrushes. The mountain, and home, was still many miles away.

All that day he marched up the mountainside, over the stream, over the bridges he'd crossed only yesterday. He marched late into the afternoon, and as he neared home, his steps quickened despite his weariness. Each step was indeed a toil. The mountain had taken its toll upon his body. He no longer felt his legs, and his lungs ached with the cold. His arms were so tired, he'd have long ago cast aside his staff if he hadn't needed it to hold himself up. All the while, he had to battle his common sense, which seemed to scream, "All this trouble for a bunch of gully dwarves!"

Finally, there was one more bridge to cross, and then a short walk beside the stream. How many times had he walked it before, never realizing how great a distance it truly was? He thought he'd never see the roof of his house again, but as he rounded the bend, there it was, beneath the shade of the beech tree. Everything seemed fine—no signs of violence.

A low and mournful howl chased away the last of his doubts. "Millisant!" he gasped as he broke into a run.

"Uhoh! Glabella! Lumpo!" he shouted as he neared the door. He threw back the latch and opened the door. Millisant came hobbling out and began to sniff the ground around the cottage.

Immediately he noticed the bandages on the hound's front legs. He kneeled beside her and examined them. She'd nearly chewed them off to get to her wounds, knife wounds by all appearances. It didn't make any sense at all. What had happened here?

Millisant seemed determined to sniff out some trail or other, so it was with much difficulty that Nalvarre wrestled her back into the house. The night promised to be cold, so Nalvarre quickly built a fire. Once it was burning brightly, its light illuminated still more mysteries. The house had been ransacked, but not for treasure. Every scrap of food in the house was gone, except the honey pots on the mantle. The flour barrel hadn't been touched, but anything readily edible had been taken. The gully dwarves' personal belongings were also missing. Nalvarre busied himself making dough and rolling it out for bread while pondering the puzzle set before him. Millisant sat at the door and whined.

He ate a frugal supper of bread and honey. It just didn't make any sense. If the gully dwarves had been captured by the draconians, who had bound the wounds of Millisant and locked her up? When he had finished eating, as he began to put away the dishes, the solution finally struck him.

The gully dwarves were alive! They'd escaped. In his joy, Nalvarre strode vigorously around the room, clapping fist to palm in his excitement. Millisant whined.

"Yes, there was some kind of fight. They left you behind because you were hurt, and you wanted to follow them," he said, very serious. "We will follow them, but it is too dark to follow now. In the morning . . ." he yawned as he began to climb to the loft.

"If you and I can't find three gully dwarves, then we've no right to call ourselves dogs," he laughed as he collapsed into his bed.

Soon, snores rattled the rafters. Millisant lay down beside the door with her chin on her paws, her eyes open. She licked her bandages for a while then whined softly to herself well into the night.

Chapter Nineteen

"The North Tower is the tallest tower of Isherwood," Jessica said, her voice echoing in the high drafty hall. "It is called the Roseburg Tower, as it was named for the Knights of the Rose. The best rooms are here. This is where I have my room," she added with a tinge of regret that she couldn't conceal "and where I'm sure you'll want to live as well."

"I'm sure," Alya said with a polite smile.

Jessica stopped beside a low, arched doorway in which was set an ironbound door. "Through this door is the courtyard, if you'd like to see it," she said.

"Of course," Alya said. With a smile, Jessica opened the door and followed her guests outside.

Once the courtyard had been paved with flagstones, but most of these had long since been broken or pushed up by the roots of trees. A small forest filled portions of the courtyard, and those areas not covered by trees were filled with a profusion of weeds, thorny vines, and grasses. Dark green ivy covered every inch of standing stone walls, though Jessica kept it trimmed from the window casings from the habitable areas of the castle. Where parts of the ancient stone curtain wall had fallen into the courtyard, piles of rock provided coverts and dens for all manner of

THE ROSE AND THE SKULL ❧

small animals, from lizards to chipmunks. Alya strolled around the area near the door, stopping to examine a maple sapling pushing its way through the flagstones. Valian Escu stood like a statue of a warrior, sniffing the air, his eyes far away.

Castle Isherwood was a remnant of a past age. Its towers and battlement, its very design, were old-fashioned even before Huma rode to glory astride his silver dragon, ages upon ages ago. Once upon a time, its four square towers rose majestically over the valley, guarding an ancient way-road to the north, a symbol of the strength and wealth of the lord of the keep. Between the towers ran four thick walls, as strong as the stonemasons of the day could build. Halls and storerooms, kitchens and armories had once lined the inner wall, surrounding the great paved court-yard where men-at-arms marched and trained, battling with wooden swords and staves or jousting against the quintayne.

"Most of the castle is in ruin," Jessica apologized. "I tried to fix up things here and there, but I could never make much headway. In the end, I rather grew to prefer it this way."

"It will soon rain," Valian said, abruptly changing the subject.

He seemed able to tell the weather by the smell of the air. All along their journey from Castle uth Wistan, the dark elf had astounded them with his nature lore. Being born an elf of the sylvan forest, he was in tune with his surroundings in a way that, to humans, seemed almost supernatural. He was a mystery to Jessica, strange and ugly with his sharp features and cold manner, yet strangely compelling and attractive too. His physique was unmatched by any man she'd ever known, yet he was neither muscular nor skinny. His every movement bespoke feline grace, his every glance burned like fire, while his tone and his manner were as cold as the glacial blue of his eyes.

———
191

Seeking some way to bring him into a conversation, Jessica said, "The rain fairly pours through the roof here, though the North Tower is dry enough. It's like living in cave. Rather delightful, actually."

"Dwarves live in caves," Valian said as he turned and re-entered the castle. "I'll see to the horses."

"I've learned to ignore him," Alya said, smiling at Jessica's efforts to be friendly. "Elves seem to live on another plane than we do. Mind you, it isn't any higher than ours, only different. They like to think it is higher. They only think a profound mental life makes up for their physical weaknesses. Not that Valian is weak. For an elf, he is almost statuesque."

Jessica nodded. A dark elf was simply any elf who chose to follow a lifestyle not in accordance with traditional elven concepts of morality and goodness. Therefore, he was "cast from the light" of elven society.

"So what did Valian do to be cast out of elven society?" She felt bold enough to ask.

"Oh, he killed another elf," Alya absently remarked as she stared at the darkening sky.

"That's horrible!" Jessica exclaimed. "Why?"

"It does look like rain," Alya said. "What? Oh, it had something to do with class. He is Silvanesti, of course. It seems when he was young, he and an elf maid fell in love and wanted to marry, but she had already been promised to someone else, an elf of some importance, I believe. On the morning of the wedding, as the groom was traveling to the ceremony, Valian confronted him on the trail. They fought, and Valian killed him.

"That's why they banished him. Can you believe that happened before the War of the Lance? He doesn't look any older than you or I, but actually he is older than Lord Gunthar was. Perhaps we should go inside?" Alya suggested as the first drops of rain plopped on the cobblestones.

The two Knights entered together and made their way up the tower stairs to a chamber Jessica called the tapestry room. The walls here were hung with ancient fading tapestries, some of them hanging in shreds, and in the corners of the room stood numerous dusty old racks and frames for the sewing and embroidery of tapestries. A single tall window looked northward toward the wild mountains and the frontier of the Knights' lands. The sky lowered, and rain came down in sheets, hissing against the thick stone walls, while an occasional distant thunderclap rolled and echoed in the empty halls of the castle. Jessica lit several candles and dusted off two chairs near the window.

"So how did Valian come to join the Knights of Takhisis?" Jessica asked after they'd settled into the chairs.

"Well, the elves may have cast him out, but he didn't leave Silvanesti. He lived there for years afterward, stealing moments with his beloved whenever he could. It was a deadly and dangerous game he played, for if he'd been caught, they'd have killed him on the spot. That's the elven moral code for you," Alya said, her feelings getting the better of her for a moment.

"So, as I was saying, he continued to live in the Silvanesti forest, avoiding contact with everyone except his beloved," Alya continued, "but then came the war. The dragonarmies of Takhisis attacked the northern borders of the realms; the elves armed themselves and patrols became more frequent. Valian found it harder and harder to avoid being discovered. He retreated to what was probably the deepest, least explored part of Silvanesti forest. Something happened to him there, something terrible. He refuses even to this day to speak of it, but it is a testament to his will and courage that he survived at all. When Valian was captured by the Green Dragonarmies, his hair was white, just as it is today, and he was ranting like a mad man, claiming visions of the future. The Dark Queen's clerics spirited him away, to probe and question him, and they kept him in a dungeon for many years. Valian claims that in those visions he saw the inevitable creation of the Knights of Takhisis, and that the priests of Takhisis tried to probe his mind for further details. His main concern was the promise granted in the vision that by joining the Knights, he would eventually be reunited with his beloved. So they say that when Lord Ariakan formed the Knights of Takhisis, Valian begged to join. It wasn't until the war that he was finally released from the dungeons and accepted into the Knighthood. The leadership was not yet ready to trust an elf, and only their desperate need for soldiers opened the way for him."

"And was he finally reunited with her?" Jessica asked, enthralled by the story.

Alya nodded. "He was part of a reconnaissance force sent to probe the defenses of Silvanesti. After the War of the Lance, Porthios, son of Solostaran, and Alhana Starbreeze returned with a contingent of elves to reestablish the kingdom of the elves. With them came Valian's beloved, hoping against hope I imagine to find him still there. The Dark Knights wanted Silvanesti for their own purposes. The leaders wanted to test Valian's resolve. If his intentions were to betray the Dark Knights, then they needed to discover it before accepting him into the order. If he were true to the cause, he'd make an excellent scout against his kinsmen, and he was. The elves had laid an ambush for the Knights, but Valian spotted it and helped design a counter ambush. The elven *kirath*, or border guards, were caught, and a bloody battle ensued, but the Knights had the advantage due to Valian's planning. When the last arrow had flown, the Knights were victorious, every elf was slain.

"That's when Valian found her among the elven dead. He later learned from elven prisoners that she'd never married. Believing Valian lost to her forever, she vowed never to marry and dedicated her life to the ways of the warrior, becoming a scout and ranger under the tutelage of Kagonesti elves. So when Porthios and Alhana returned to try to reclaim Silvanost, she volunteered as a border guard," Alya concluded.

"That's horrible!" Jessica exclaimed.

"Isn't it, though," Alya laughed. "It's not at all how a love story should end."

"Why, in heaven's name, is he still a Knight?" Jessica asked.

"I don't know. I imagine it's all he has left. They accepted him, provisionally, after the skirmish, and although he has risen to a position of some leadership, he is still only a provisional Knight. He lost his love, he lost his people, all he has left is his honor and the few friends he has made among us, so I suppose he has nowhere else to go," Alya said.

Jessica shook her head in shocked disbelief. She'd never heard anything so terrible as what she'd just been told. It brought a dreary end to an otherwise pleasant day. The rain beating against the castle walls usually made her feel peaceful and safe, but not now. Wind howled around the towers, and thunder shook dust from the rafters. The old castle mumbled and groaned as though all its ghosts had wakened and were holding conclave in some secret hall. Jessica shuddered with a chill.

"This is quite a storm for Gildember," Alya said, using the Solamnic name for October. "Is this common?"

"Very rare," Jessica answered.

The door to the chamber opened, and Valian stepped into the room. "Our horses are settled in the stable. It seems warm and dry enough, with plenty of feed and hay," he said.

"Waterstone, my retainer, worked very hard this past summer patching the roof," Jessica said.

"Ah yes, your dwarf," Valian said blandly. "I'll retire to my room to await mess call." Without waiting for an answer, he turned and strode away, leaving the door open.

"We don't really have a mess call around here," Jessica apologized.

"Don't worry. When he gets hungry enough, he'll come down," Alya said with a smile.

For a long while, neither of the Knights said anything. They listened to the voices of wind and stone, the wailing of the storm. The thunder abated and drew away, shaking the hills to the south. Alya rose and walked to the window. "It's getting dark out," she commented.

A different pounding echoed from below. Alya stopped. "What's that?"

"Someone at the door," Jessica said, a puzzled look on her brow.

"Visitors?" Alya asked.

"We never have visitors," Jessica answered. The pounding came again. The two hurried from the room and down the long spiral stair to the heavy, double-paneled door at the front entrance. Waterstone was already there ahead of them. They heard him speaking to someone. He seemed to be arguing, for his stony voice rose in pitch.

"No. No, we have none. Good night to you," he said.

"What is it?" Jessica called, but the dwarf didn't answer her.

Instead, he said angrily, "We don't take in vagabonds. Now be on your way. Good night!" He slammed the door and shot the bolt.

"Waterstone, who was that?" Jessica asked.

"No one, no one at all, Lady Jessica," the elderly dwarf answered. "Supper is almost ready. I have a lovely roast goose for you."

"Waterstone, who was at the door? We never have visitors," Jessica demanded.

"Just some raggedy human and his mangy mutt," Waterstone said.

"How could you turn him away in this storm?" Jessica scolded.

"I've seen his type before. Give 'em a hot meal and you never get rid of 'em. Best to send 'em on their way," the dwarf said.

The pounding on the door resumed.

Quickly Jessica stepped in front of Waterstone and opened the door, allowing the stranger to stumble wearily inside. The man was drenched from the storm and dripping pools on the floor. He was followed by a large hound of some sort who looked more even more miserable and bedraggled. Both were limping; the hound had old, wet bandages wrapped around its forelegs.

With a scowl at his mistress and the stranger, the dwarf turned away with a growl.

"Reorx's bones!" he swore.

"A Knight of Takhisis," the stranger said with some surprise. "Then it's true." Everyone suddenly turned away as the hound shook the water from her coat, wetting everyone with a fine spray. Waterstone swore blackly.

Alya then asked, "What is true?"

"But I thought they were lying. Then it must also be true about . . . Papa," he said absently, as though speaking his thoughts aloud. He seemed to realize what he was doing, for his eyes suddenly cleared and he bristled beneath his thick bush of a beard. "Forgive me," he said. "A habit of living alone. My name is Nalvarre Ringbow, former priest of Chislev."

"A priest!" the dwarf exclaimed. "Reorx's black boots!"

"And this poor bedraggled hound is . . ."

"Millisant!" Jessica exclaimed. At the sound of her name, the hound lowered her head and began to wag her tail, slinging water on everyone's shoes. Jessica knelt beside the dog, petting and scratching her behind her wet ears. Millisant replied by licking Jessica's face. "This was one of

Lord Gunthar's favorite dogs. How did she get here? Were you sent by Sir Liam?" she asked Nalvarre.

"Who? No. She was in the company of the three gully dwarves. Did you say she was one of Gunthar's dogs?" he asked.

"I see there is a story to be told here," Alya said, "and you are soaked."

"Oh! I'm so sorry," Jessica said, suddenly remembering her guest. "Please, come in. We'll find you some dry clothes. Waterstone, set another place for supper."

"The goose isn't big enough for five," the dwarf grumbled as he stalked off to the kitchen. "Someone will have to go without, and I bet I know who that unlucky person will be!"

* * * * *

After dinner, the Knights related recent events of Sancrist Isle to Nalvarre, bringing him up to date on the change in the Knighthood and the untimely death of Lord Gunthar. The newcomer seemed particularly interested in the manner of Gunthar's death, asking if they were sure about the facts of the Grand Master's demise. They recounted their mission both to garrison this castle and to pick up the trail of a gully dwarf named Uhoh Ragnap. At the mention of this name, Nalvarre nodded, as though finally convinced of something that he long suspected.

As Waterstone cleared the dishes away, Nalvarre told them his curious tale, how he came home one day to find Uhoh, Glabella, Lumpo, and Millisant firmly entrenched in his house. He told them Uhoh's story of his Papa's death, and everyone agreed that it sounded very much like the circumstances of Gunthar's death. However, Alya pointed out that Uhoh could have heard the story told at the castle before he ran away, and in the usual gully dwarf fashion, imagined himself in an important role.

"Then you agree. He must have been speaking of Lord Gunthar's death, and not the death of his own father," Nalvarre persisted.

"Of course! What's more, everyone knows that Uhoh called him 'Papa.' All the gully dwarves did," Jessica said.

"Where do the draconians fit in?" Nalvarre asked.

"What draconians?" Alya asked. Valian looked up, suddenly interested. Jessica noted with some surprise that he stared hardest at Alya, not Nalvarre.

"I haven't finished the tale. Uhoh said that after Gunthar died, draconians appeared on the scene and tried to kill him. He escaped them, and they've been chasing after him ever since," Nalvarre said.

"Preposterous!" Alya snorted.

"There aren't any draconians on Sancrist," Jessica said in agreement.

Valian, however, said nothing.

"Uhoh insists that draconians are trying to kill him," Nalvarre said, and he related events of the last few days, ending with his discovery of the wounded Millisant and the disappearance of the gully dwarves. "He claims to know a big, important secret."

"What secret?" asked Valian sharply.

"I don't know," Nalvarre had to admit doubtfully.

"Well, did you see any draconians?" Alya asked.

"No, but I did see Pyrothraxus fly over the valley," he said. "It was the same day. A sure portent of evil, I'd say."

Jessica gasped.

"Not only that, but I found a pile of strange dust in front of my door. I didn't see it that night, but in the light of the next day, it was quite obvious. Millisant growled at it," Nalvarre said.

"Dust? Did it have any kind of shape?" Valian asked.

Nalvarre eyed the dark elf. "As a matter of fact, it did.

The wind had disturbed it somewhat, but it had a vague humanoid outline," he said.

To everyone's surprise, Valian pounded the table in anger. "A baaz! Damn!" he shouted.

"Let's not jump to any hasty conclusions, Sir Valian," Alya said softly, but with steel in her voice. She turned to Jessica. "There must be another explanation. I find it quite hard to credit any reason why draconians would be chasing three gully dwarves halfway across Sancrist."

"Why?" Valian asked. "That's exactly what we're doing. And what about that pile of dust? It has to be a baaz draconian. They turn to stone when slain and then to dust. I should know. I had enough of the cowards in my command during the Chaos War."

"I agree with Alya," Jessica said. "There has to be some other explanation. If draconians were roaming all over Sancrist like this, someone would have spotted them by now and raised the alarm."

"Not if they kill anyone who sees them," Valian said. "Not if some of them are sivaks who have the power to assume the form of anyone they kill."

"It just seems so improbable," Jessica said.

"There is only one way to find out. We have to go to this place you talked about," Valian said nodding to Nalvarre. "Town. We have to catch up with Uhoh before the draconians do."

"My thoughts exactly." Nalvarre said. "We can't leave those poor gully dwarves at their mercy."

Valian stared at Alya for long moments. Finally, she nodded. "We'll go to Town," she decided.

Chapter Twenty

No trap, no matter how clever, could be this obvious. A trail of crumbs, rinds, crusts, husks, shells, and cores marked a spoor a blind gully dwarf could follow. Harj thought this statement supremely ironic, considering the quarry of his hunt. Though the quarry had a name, Harj still thought of it only as an "it," an object, a target for his knife when the time came.

That time was fast approaching, he now knew. His tongue flickered excitedly in the air at the thought of the slaying to come. At first, he'd had little enough enthusiasm for this hunt, but with weeks of failure, his anticipation of the kill sharpened. When first he picked up this newest spoor, he'd left a message on the trail—an encoded pattern of sticks in the elven fashion—giving a likely destination. He let the others know the gully dwarves were headed for Town.

So now it was with some surprise that Harj found the trail ended at the blank face of a cliff wall. He searched the surrounding area for some time without finding further signs. He began to suspect that he'd been thwarted once again. They'd obviously backtracked somewhere along the trail, but Harj never suspected gully dwarves could be so clever. Unless he got spectacularly lucky, he'd never find their trail in the dark. With night swiftly approaching, he'd have to wait until the morrow to search it out again. He began to suspect a greater mind at work, for the spoor had obviously been left on purpose for him to follow it to this dead end. Perhaps this was even . . .

"A trap!" he snarled, drawing his dagger as a twig snapped behind him. He spun round, only to see the rugged scrub terrain common to this area, darkened now in the shadow of the mountains. He crouched, ready to fight or flee, his long reptilian tail thrashing angrily behind him. He licked the blade of his dagger to envenom it with his poisonous saliva.

"Ssssso, Harj hasssss losssst the trail already," laughed a voice from the bushes.

Harj angrily sheathed his dagger as a figure robed all in black appeared from behind a boulder. It approached, its robes whispering over the stony trail.

"These are not mere gully dwarves," Harj asserted as he stared at the cliff face. "No gully dwarf is this smart."

"He issss not sssmart," the robed figure hissed as it pushed back its hood, revealing a draconian face. "You overthink him. He issss only a gully dwarf."

"Bozaks know everything," Harj snarled. "If you know so much, why haven't you caught him?"

"That isssss the kapaksss's job. I am here to assissssssst you, not ssssssniff out sssspoor," the bozak draconian lisped.

Harj's mouth writhed into a sneer, revealing long, yellow fangs made for shredding flesh. "Bozaks let the kapaks do the work, then claim all the glory." he said.

"Let ussss not forget we are brotherssss," the bozak warned.

Harj bowed. "All praise to the Old Master who guides us," he said. "His wisdom is without measure."

"Well said, Brother Harj."

"Thank you, Brother Shaeder," Harj replied. "But now what? You said I overthink him . . ."

"You exxpect guile where there issss only ssssssimplicity, even ssssstupidity. He doessss what only an idiot would do, and therefore you never conssssssider other posssssssibilities," Shaeder said.

"Like what?" Harj asked, his impatience with his fellow draconian growing.

"They can't sssscale the cliff. It isss too sssteep," the bozak answered, looking up at the rock wall hanging well out over their heads, "and they didn't go around. So you examined the cliff face for sssecret doorsssss?"

"Not yet, I didn't think . . ." Harj's voice trailed off.

"Didn't think what?"

Harj spun around and quickly scanned the rock wall for any sign of a craftily hidden entrance. In short order, he spotted words carved in very small letters. They read, "Secret entrance. You no see." A little lower down, next to an all too obvious protrusion, were the words "This not latch." With a malicious grin Harj pressed the not-latch and the stone parted, revealing a dark, narrow passage into the cliff.

With a conspiratorial look at the bozak, Harj entered the passage. Shaeder, the bozak, followed close on his tail. The passage, never more than a few feet wide, wound and doubled upon itself endlessly in utter darkness. They didn't need to see to know they were on the right path, for as they walked, they stepped on the litter of rinds and crusts and husks left behind, but they did have to keep low, because the gully dwarves had strolled easily under the edges and overhangs of rock that Harj had a tendency to crash into. After one particularly painful knock on the pate, he thought he was seeing stars until he realized that he was seeing stars. High overhead, through a crack in the roof of the cave, a few stars glimmered in the black sky.

After a few hundred more yards of careful stalking along dry and dusty floors, the roof opened again to the night sky, but now as they progressed, it continued to widen. Soon, they realized they were heading generally north along the floor of a steep canyon. Their pace slowed. Even by starlight, they saw the walls were riddled with caves and hollows. The floor of the canyon, once smooth and flat, became broken and rugged, with slabs of rock tilting this way and that, some rising, some falling, and some dropping off into cracks of blackness into which a pebble might slide and vanish without a sound. One of these slabs ended abruptly at a dizzying precipice of several hundred feet. Harj stopped suddenly at the edge, while Shaeder stumbled into him, almost toppling him over the edge. Harj said nothing. Instead, he stared down and hissed happily to himself.

"There it issss," Shaeder said after he climbed up beside his companion. "Gully dwarf Town."

Several hundred feet below them and about a mile away, on the floor of a scrub valley dotted with small inky water holes, sprawled a multitude of earthen mounds. No lights shone, but here and there a gray tendril of smoke rose against the lighter shade of the valley floor, while a smell of burning mopane wood rose into the air. Even stronger than the wood smoke was the strong, unmistakable odor of gully dwarves—hundreds and hundreds of gully dwarves.

Shaeder pointed at a cut in the rock at the edge of the precipice. "Look, ssstepsss," he hissed. By leaning well out over the edge of the cliff, the two draconians spotted steps cut into the vertical face of rock, providing a rather dangerous but serviceable stair to the floor of the valley. Neither had any desire to try to navigate that narrow stair with their broad wings and long tails, but neither did they need to. The draconians had their own way of descending the cliff. Although not powerful flyers, they were very good at gliding. Given a high enough starting point, they could soar for many minutes, covering great distances.

Harj stepped back to gain a little running room, then launched himself into empty space, unfolding his wings to catch the wind. Shaeder watched him glide outward from the cliff like some huge carrion bird, working his tail like a rudder to steer himself clear of the rock. Shaeder then stripped off his heavy robes, crouched, and leaped over the edge. He unfolded his wings and soared after his companion.

They landed a few hundred yards from the mound nearest the cliff, just beside a little pool of water. The ground was rocky, with more sand than soil, but near the water holes a few hardy plants had managed to leech out enough sustenance to survive. All around the valley tall mountains rose like the jagged walls of a crumbling fortress, effectively shutting off this arid land from the outside world. Desert hares and smaller rodents abounded, as did herds of tough and wiry mountain ponies. The draconians' flight had carried them over one large herd, startling them into a stampede, and even now the ground rumbled with their distant panic. Heavy clouds of dust rose against the stars.

Harj crept over to the pool and dipped his snout into the water to drink. He came up coughing and gagging. Shaeder laughed.

"Alkali," Harj spat. "This land is cursed."

"No wonder the gully dwarvessss took it," Shaeder said. "They can live almossst anywhere, on food that would ssstarve a goat."

"Well, I say we find this one particular gully dwarf and get out of here. I'll slip into one of these mounds and 'question' the inhabitants," Harj said. "Once we know where he is, we'll break in and grab him."

205

"No killing," Shaeder reminded. "The Old Man wantsss Uhoh alive for quessstioning."

"Questioning a gully dwarf? It can't be done!" Harj snarled derisively.

"We have waysss. He'll talk. He'll wish he wasss sssmarter sssso he can tell usss more," Shaeder cackled while rubbing his clawed hands together in anticipation.

"Well, once we've found out where he's hiding, we'll slip in, subdue him, and carry him off before anyone is the wiser," Harj said.

He crouched and started off towards the closest mound of earth, his bozak companion at his side. Together, they crept up to one mound and searched for a door or hole. The mounds seemed made of nothing more than heaped-up sand, gravel, and soil. The carving and writing on some of the stones gave them an appearance of great antiquity. Probably the gully dwarves had burrowed their way into some ancient burial mounds and taken up residence among the bones and artifacts of a forgotten people.

"Maybe there will be some treasure here," Harj whispered greedily. "Perhaps we should stay and explore about that possibility, too."

"Firssst the gully dwarf. You and I can return later for the treasure," Shaeder warned. "Of coursssse, if sssomething along the way catchesss your eye . . ."

They slipped into a cut in the mound, where a narrow wooden door stood in a frame made of thick wooden beams. The wood appeared old and gray, weathered to the point of rotting. Harj pushed his companion aside and approached the door. With a grunt, he kicked it in.

With a groan and a crack of wood, the entire mound collapsed upon itself. Dust and sand billowed outward with a roar, drowning out the screams of those buried alive within. Harj and Shaeder stumbled away, coughing on the thick alkali dust and blinking sand from their eyes. The screams of the trapped gully dwarves quickly faded. Finally able to breath, the draconians stared in awe at the destruction.

Soon they found themselves surrounded by hundreds of gully dwarves who, hearing the noise, had come rushing from their own barrow homes. They ignored the draconians for a few moments while they too stared in fascination at the collapsed mound. This was not a new occurrence. A closer examination of the town would have revealed several other mounds in a similar state. Nevertheless, the gully dwarves seemed awestruck by the event, so much so they didn't even acknowledge the presence of the draconians.

"If they turn on us . . ." Harj hissed.

"Show no fear. We are their masstersss of old," Shaeder answered. "They've not forgotten usss already." He raised his head and gave a long piercing cry, the one given in olden days by draconian slave drivers, which awakened captives to a new day of work.

The gully dwarves shrank in terror at the remembered sound. Despite their huge superiority in numbers, they immediately cowered before the two draconians standing in their midst.

"We have come for the gully dwarf known to you as Uhoh Ragnap," Harj shouted.

"Run away!" an anonymous gully dwarf screamed from the darkness. Instantly, the area erupted in confusion, gully dwarves fleeing every which way, stumbling over each other, colliding in huge pileups, bumping into the draconians. Harj and Shaeder were in very real danger of being crushed in the stampede.

Harj shouted, trying to frighten the creatures into obedience, "We destroyed one barrow; we can destroy another. Hide if you like, we'll bring everything down on top of your miserable heads if you don't deliver Uhoh to us!"

It did no good. In moments, the gully dwarves had vanished. Many they heard blubbering in terror inside the mounds, many more had fled screaming into the desert.

Harj looked at his companion and shrugged his coppery wings. They stalked over to the nearest mound and pounded on the door. It cracked and shivered but didn't collapse.

"Uhoh Ragnap, come out or die!" he shouted.

"Uhoh not here," a sobbing voice answered.

"Deliver Uhoh Ragnap and we'll spare your lives!" he shouted.

"But he not here!" the voice cried.

Harj kicked open the door. Screams of terror burst from the darkness beyond, but the mound remained intact. Shaeder stepped into the doorway. He held forth his clawed hands with fingers spread in a fan shape, the thumbs touching, and he began to mutter in a strange tongue whose words the mind had difficulty grasping. Their result was sudden and violent. A fan-shaped sheet of flame erupted from his clawtips. It flashed into existence only for a moment, but when it had gone, the dry support timbers and rotting door frame burned as though doused with oil.

Shaeder skipped back from the flames, cackling with glee. Soon, a pillar of fire roared from the doorway, while a jet of blue flame hissed from the chimney. The gully dwarves inside screamed pain and terror, their voices rising in pitch until they were finally cut short by a deafening roar. Sheets of flame leaped up from the barrow top. The mound collapsed upon itself thunderously, while a mushrooming cloud of black smoke rose high above the valley.

The other barrows grew suddenly silent. Harj and Shaeder approached the next one. Its door was illuminated by the flames, and they saw that it was slightly open. A small gully dwarf female stood there, eyeing the destruction with her large, tear-filled eyes. Around her neck hung a necklace of gold, from which dangled a ruby pendant as large as a robin's egg. It glowed in the firelight, and the gold sparkled red. Harj sucked in his breath at the sight.

"Gully dwarves wearing gold," he snarled. "We'll soon fix that." He pointed at the jewel-bedecked gully dwarf and shouted, "You there!"

She eyed him without fear. "Yes, you! Come here, you miserable slug," he shouted derisively, trying to intimidate the gully dwarf.

She seemed to hesitate, as though trying to decide whether to run or brave him out. In the end, she approached slowly, warily, as though ready to bolt at any moment. Harj chuckled to himself.

"You are the leader here?" he asked.

She nodded. "Me Highbulp Mommamose I," she squeaked.

"You know Uhoh Ragnap?" Harj asked.

Again, she nodded.

"Bring him to us or we destroy this Town, kill you all," Harj demanded. She looked at him for a moment, and then at his companion.

Shaeder wiggled his fingers at her and said, "Abracadabra."

She jumped, her eyes wide with fear now, then turned and motioned at the door of the barrow where she'd been hiding. There was a scuffling noise and a wail of despair, but then the door opened and three gully dwarves spilled out backward. Several more followed, crying and hurling curses at the three, but upon seeing the draconians, they cowered back, weeping hysterically.

The three gully dwarves dragged a heavy sack before the draconians. They dropped their end, gave one look at the Highbulp, and fled into the night. Something inside the sack thrashed and moaned and struggled.

Harj picked up one end and slit it open with his dagger. He then lifted it, dumping Uhoh out on the ground. Shaeder snatched the gully dwarf up by his collar and shook him violently.

"Be ssstill," he hissed.

"That's him," Harj said to his companion. He bent down and stuck his snout in Uhoh's face. "You ran me quite a race, little worm, but I've got you now," he growled. "The Old Man wants to see you."

Uhoh's legs gave beneath him. He collapsed like an empty sack, his eyes rolling up in his head. The two draconians bent over their victim, taking delight in tormenting the gully dwarf with descriptions of what awaited him. While they were thus occupied, the Highbulp backed toward the door where the other gully dwarves still cringed and sobbed. As she neared them, one female detached herself from the others and crept toward her leader. It was Glabella. Lumpo cowered nearest the door, his eyes frozen with terror.

"Mommamose, how you do this to Uhoh?" Glabella cried as she clawed at the Highbulp's filthy dress.

"Shut up, gulpfunger. Slagd kill all if I not give them Uhoh," she answered.

"But he your son," Glabella wailed. "Uhoh your baby!"

"I got plan. You shut up, watch," Mommamose said. She motioned to one of the other gully dwarves. He crept forward, his eyes on the draconians.

"Give me twig that make thunder," she said.

He nodded and pulled a long leather wallet from some hidden fold in his rags. It had a gold snap and was beaded with seed pearls. He opened it, retrieving a long wand of amber. As thick as a finger at one end, it tapered to a needle point at the other. At the thick end, a tiny sapphire was embedded in the amber. Glabella stared at it in wonder, forgetting for a moment her fear for Uhoh.

"What that?" Glabella asked.

"This twig that make thunder," Mommamose answered. "It big magic, fix slagd good."

"How it work?"

"When I say magic word and touch this pretty blue rock in the end," she said, indicating the sapphire, "it shoot thunderbolt out other end, fry everything wham! just like that."

"What magic word?" Glabella asked.

"I not tell you," the Highbulp said, turning her nose up with disdain. "You only little gulpfunger."

"You there!" Harj snarled.

The Highbulp spun around, hiding the wand behind her back. The draconians had bound Uhoh's hands behind his back but left his legs free. He stared miserably at Glabella, his heart in his eyes. Glabella burst out crying.

"Come here," Harj yelled at the Highbulp.

She approached within a few yards and stopped, still hiding the wand behind her back. Glabella followed her, and the gully dwarf with the leather wallet trailed behind. Despite his fear, it was his wand, and he wanted to see it didn't get broken.

"Come closer, little one," Harj said in honeyed tones. "I'll not hurt you. I want to thank you for delivering this criminal to us."

The Highbulp took another step closer. Harj's long arm shot out, his claws tangling in the chain around her neck. With a sharp jerk, he snatched the jeweled amulet away, breaking the heavy chain and nearly decapitating the Highbulp. At the same time, Shaeder leaped forward and tore the wallet from the other gully dwarf's grasp.

"I'll take thisss," he laughed.

Harj kicked Uhoh and grunted, "Get moving!" meanwhile tucking the amulet into a pouch at his belt.

Shaeder fell in behind them, cackling to himself. The Highbulp rubbed her bruised neck while the other gully dwarf crowded close to her. Glabella crept nearer as well.

Highbulp Mommamose pointed the wand at the backs of the draconians. "Toejam!" she barked. Nothing happened. She tried it again. "Toejam!"

"That not magic word!" the other gully dwarf said.

"I touch blue rock," the Highbulp said. "What wrong with this thing?"

"You got to say magic word," he answered.

"But I say magic word," she said.

He grabbed the sharp end of the wand and tried to pull it away from her. Thus began a struggle, the two gully dwarves spinning round and round on either end of the wand, one yanking one way, one the other. Harj and Shaeder stopped to watch. Uhoh peered between their legs.

"I touch blue stone!" the Highbulp shouted from the melee.

"You not say magic word."

"I say Toejam!"

"Toejam not magic word."

"What magic word?"

"Crackling!"

With a deafening clap of thunder, a blue bolt of lightning streaked into the night sky. Although well over their heads, Harj and Shaeder ducked reflexively, cursing in awe at the sudden display of magic from a lowly gully dwarf.

Harj grabbed Uhoh to prevent his running away and shouted, "A magic wand! Go get it before she uses it again."

Ducking, Shaeder hurried back to the spot, but he found the street empty and not a gully dwarf in sight. A tattered pair of shoes lay on the ground in the center of a small pile of smoking ash. The wand was nowhere to be seen. Still ducking, he scuttled back to his kapak companion.

"Let'sss get out of here," he said without stopping to wait. He vanished in a cloud of dust.

Harj lifted Uhoh and slung him over his back, crouched, and dashed off in a low, almost four-footed run, his wings beating and helping him along. With a low mournful wail from the back of his captor, Uhoh vanished into the night.

Chapter Twenty-One

"Oh no," Nalvarre cried. Millisant barked and whined as she limped back and forth at the edge of the precipice. Jessica hurried forward, followed by Valian and Waterstone. Alya brought up the rear at a casual pace.

"We are too late," Jessica sighed as she stood beside Nalvarre.

A column of black smoke rose above gully dwarf Town. All the plains between the cliff and the distant mountains was covered with small clusters of little black dots wandering aimlessly, like ants whose nest has been ravaged.

"Do you think . . . Pyrothraxus . . ." she stammered.

"The dragon would have destroyed everything," Valian said. "By the signs, I'd say only our two draconians attacked the Town."

The group had followed the trail of the gully dwarves and the draconians, led for the most part by Millisant but helped on occasion by Valian's woodlore. They'd traversed the night-black tunnels, though torches brought by the wise advice of Waterstone saved them many a knock on the head in the passages, and come at last to the canyon and the cliff overlooking the plains and Town.

"Only two draconians against an entire town?" Nalvarre marveled.

"They're gully dwarves," Waterstone said, as though that explained it all. When no one said anything, he added, "Two kender and a sick chicken could take the place."

Alya came up then. "Well, that tears it," she said when she saw the town and the smoke. "All this way for nothing."

"What do you mean? We have to get down there and find out what happened," Jessica said.

"Isn't it obvious? Whoever has been hunting the gully dwarves has got what he wants. We are too late. There's nothing we can do," Alya said.

"The draconians might still be there," Jessica said.

Valian growled like a panther. "I doubt it," he said, "but I would like to find out for sure."

"As would I," Nalvarre said.

"If Uhoh was there, they've already found him and are long gone by now. All you'll find is a dead body, if anything," Alya said. "We've got more important things to do. That includes you, Valian."

"Draconians on Sancrist Isle aren't important to you?" Jessica asked in astonishment.

"Not particularly," Alya said. "What're a few draconians? Why does it matter? Besides, I'm still not convinced that there are any draconians."

"Then you are a fool," Valian said to her.

"I'd watch what I said, Sir Knight. I outrank you," Alya returned. Valian turned away. He looked at Jessica, but in his anger, his eyes seemed to bore straight through her, without even seeing.

"There are steps here," Nalvarre noted. Curious at the discovery, Waterstone looked over the edge of the precipice.

"Uhoh was Gunthar's favorite," Jessica began hesitantly as a thought occurred to her. "We have to at least find out why the draconians were hunting him." Her eyes pleading, she turned to Alya. "And if there's any chance he's still alive, we can't leave him to their mercy."

Alya glowered without saying anything.

"I'm going down there," Nalvarre said.

"Very well," Alya snapped.

Valian eased himself onto the first step, then bent down to examine the stonework. After a few moment, he announced, "These steps weren't cut by gully dwarves. They are much much older than that."

"An elf's opinion of stonework, " the dwarf snorted.

"If you don't believe me," Valian said, "come take a look yourself."

With a dour expression, Waterstone reluctantly examined the steps. He leaned back and scratched his head. "Reorx's bones! I'd be a kender's uncle if I can tell you who did cut these steps. They're as old as these hills."

"Millisant can't go with us," Nalvarre said. "We daren't carry her down these steps. They are very narrow."

"She'll have to stay with Waterstone," Jessica said.

"But I'm coming with you!" he protested.

"I need you to go back to Isherwood and keep an eye on things. You can take Millisant with you," Jessica said. "Take care of her, and make sure her wounds heal."

"Nursemaid to a dog. My grandfather is turning over in his cairn, to think a Waterstone playing nursemaid to a dog," the dwarf scowled.

In the end, it seemed Millisant was no more enthusiastic about being left with the dwarf than he was about being left with her. She whined, howled, and barked when Jessica and Nalvarre left her behind on the cliff. Waterstone watched them out of sight, then gradually led Millisant away from the cliff's edge.

With a wall at one shoulder and a sheer drop at the other, the slippery footing provided by the crumbling steps made things touch and go almost the whole way down. The stair wound along the uneven face of the rock, entering cracks and washes where the action of the infrequent rain had weathered the steps almost completely away. Eventually, everyone reached the base of the cliff, and not without many a sigh of relief. Near the stairs' foot lay the grisly remains of those who'd not been so careful in their climb.

After a brief rest, the four set out across the scrub tablelands toward Town. In his eagerness to discover the fate of his former guests, Nalvarre took the lead in trudging across the dusty plains. The others followed behind, and they were thankful that they didn't have to cross this region during the heat of summer. The late autumn sun seemed like a hot eye glaring down at them, sucking the strength from their limbs and the breath from their lungs. The alkali dust kicked up by their passing feet turned to clay in their mouths and caked around their eyes, giving their faces a ghoulish gray tone except where it cracked around eyes and mouths, showing pink flesh beneath. It chafed beneath chain mail and caused the joints of their armor to creak and stick.

In the heat of midday, they stumbled into Town. A hot rising wind blew dust in swirls and eddies around the mounds to collect like snow in drifts in the lee of ancient stone walls. As they wandered through the empty village, they saw no signs of life other than evidence of a recent and sudden abandonment. They made their way to the still-burning mound, reaching it as the last embers of fire sent thin tendrils of smoke snaking along the wind. Nalvarre stopped to examine a pair of well-worn shoes lying in the middle of a broad way that might have served as a street. Valian and Jessica investigated the surrounding mounds, finding them all strangely empty. Meanwhile, Alya found a nice shady spot beneath an ancient wall and sat down. She pulled off her boots and emptied them of the morning's accumulation of sand and gravel. She checked her wineskin and found it uncomfortably flat. They hadn't filled their skins since the night before, and every water hole they'd passed in this miserable desert was undrinkable.

"We can't stay here long," Alya shouted to Jessica and Valian. "We'll have to head back before we run out of water." Valian nodded and continued his investigation.

Alya leaned back and closed her eyes. The shade provided by the wall was a blessing. She allowed herself a sip of tepid water and held it in her mouth to wet her parched lips and tongue. It wasn't so much the heat in this desert as the thick alkali dust. It sucked the moisture from everything it touched. She swallowed the sip of water, then opened her eyes to check on Valian, Jessica, and the priest.

Standing directly over her were three squat gray ghoulish-looking creatures. They'd appeared as silently as ghosts. They eyed her waterskin with obvious longing, smacking their thick, leathery lips. Alya leaped to her feet and drew her sword, but the three creatures seemed not to notice the weapon. One reached a grubby gray hand tentatively toward the skin dangling from her belt.

"Touch it and you'll draw back a stump," she warned.

"Me Highbulp Mommamose I," the creature croaked. 'This my Town. You pay tax, one drink water."

"If you are the Highbulp, you can get your own water," Alya said.

"Water in well," the Highbulp sighed.

"A well! Where?" Alya demanded.

The Highbulp pointed at the burned-out collapsed mound. Just beside it stood a low circular wall of crumbling blackened stones and a few bits of charred sticks. "Well deep. Fire burn bucket. No reach water now," the

Highbulp croaked. Alya crossed to the well and, shading her eyes, looked over the lip of stone. In the darkness below, she saw a faint glimmer of a reflection, and a cool wet scent wafted up the stone shaft, promising water.

"I don't suppose you have a rope," Alya said as she scratched her head and looked around, trying to figure out some way to get to the water.

The Highbulp nodded and dug into the sack dangling by a strap from her shoulder. In moments, she produced a foot-long piece of rotting cotton twine and handed it to Alya.

"Something a bit longer," she said absently. "Valian! Jessica!" she shouted, seeing the two Knights and the priest exiting a distant mound. Catching sight of the squat creatures beside Alya, they hurried over.

"Have you seen any rope?" Alya called as they neared.

"Is this . . . is one of these Uhoh?" Valian asked. Alya shrugged.

At the sound of that name, the three gully dwarves cringed away from the Knights. They seemed almost ready to forget their thirst and run away.

"We are looking for Uhoh Ragnap," Jessica smiled, trying to calm the gully dwarves' fears. "Have you seen him?"

The smallest of the three dust-coated gully dwarves burst into wails of lamentation. Tears tracked down her face, forming little mudballs, which clung to her cheeks.

"Slagd take Uhoh!" she yammered.

"Slagd?" Alya asked.

"Draconians," Nalvarre said. He knelt beside the weeping gully dwarf. "Glabella? It's me, Nalvarre."

She blinked at him for a moment, sniffling, then threw her arms around his neck and renewed her sobs. The third gully dwarf joined them, adding his tears to the reunion.

"These are the two who were with Uhoh," Nalvarre

explained, having to shout to be heard. He pulled Glabella from his neck and brushed the hair from her face. "Listen to me," he said. "Was Uhoh alive?"

She nodded, her lower lip trembling.

"Where did they take him?" he asked.

Sobbing between words, she said, "They take Uhoh to mountain."

"Which mountain?" Alya said. "The whole area is nothing but mountains. Meanwhile, we need to find a way to get to this water. Did any of you see any ropes or chains?"

"Yes," Valian said.

"Well go and get them, and see if you can scrounge up a bucket with a handle," she ordered.

With a dark look at his commander, the elf stalked away.

"After we've all had a good drink and washed the dust from our faces, we can sit down and find out what really happened here," she added.

"Right!" the Highbulp agreed. Then in an aside to Alya, she whispered, "These gulfungers die of thirst without me and you."

Chapter Twenty-Two

The scent of water drew gully dwarves in from the desert in droves. Nalvarre and Lumpo spent most of the afternoon drawing water from the well and filling every vessel and jug the gully dwarves could scrounge. To the surprise of the Knights, many of these were bowls and chalices of beaten gold and jeweled silver. Like magic, the gully dwarves conjured from the earthen mounds treasures worthy of the finest families of Sancrist or even Palanthas.

As darkness fell, Nalvarre built a bonfire around which the gully dwarves celebrated their deliverance by breaking out cactus beer, a bitter brew concocted by a group of old gammers who chewed up pieces of cactus into a mush, which they then spit into a communal cauldron. Once the cauldron was filled, they let it sit for several days to ferment. With this celebration, the gully dwarves brought out a cauldron that had been fermenting for two days. Soon, everyone had a bowl or cup and was dipping into the roiling pink stew.

Glabella brought Valian a frothy bowl, but he politely declined it, saying he preferred water. She shrugged and flopped beside him, sipping her beer and watching him from the corner of her eye. Timidly, she reached out a hand and touched his long white hair.

"You pretty," she said.

He eyed her with a bit of alarm. "Thank you," he said.

"You nice Knight," she whispered. "Uhoh say Knights bad, but you good Knight."

He leaned his head closer to hers and asked, "And why did Uhoh say Knights are bad?"

" 'Cause that's what Papa say when he die," she whispered.

"I see," the elf said.

"But he wrong. You nice," she cooed.

Across from them, Alya and Jessica sat on either side of the Highbulp. Alya leaned forward and clanged her golden drinking bowl against a rock. "I think it is time that we get the whole story. We've wasted enough time on this trip. I want to know what happened to Uhoh?"

The Highbulp rose unsteadily to her feet. "Highbulp Mommamose I tell you. This way it happen. I born good place, plenty food, I very happy," she began.

Alya sighed in exasperation. "We don't want your whole life story, just what happened to Uhoh last night," she said.

With an impatient wave of her hand, the gully dwarf continued. "I very happy. I grow up happy, I marry happy, I have happy baby. Then I drop happy baby on head. I name him Uhoh."

Glabella clapped. "That my favorite story. Tell it again," she said.

"Later," the Highbulp scowled. "One day things go all wrong. Slagd come, put all us Bulps on big ship, we sail and sail and sail, two days. There many slagd on ship, all kinds. Captain no got wings."

"An aurak," Valian said. "How many slagd were on the ship?"

"Two," she said, holding up five fingers. "Ship bring us here."

"Here?" Jessica asked.

222

"Not here, there," the Highbulp said, pointing north. "How you think ship get here? This desert," she said sarcastically.

"Sorry," Jessica said.

"We get off ship," the Highbulp continued. "Slagd make us help build big castle on mountain by sea. They whip Bulps and put us in dungeon. We no get plenty food. We not happy. I cut stone. All day long I cut stone." She wrung her hands as though in remembrance of the pain.

"When castle done, big no-wing slagd say he Highbulp. Other slagd call him Old Man. They busy, busy all the time then, forget about Bulps. Sometimes we cook, sometimes clean castle. One time thunder hit tower, so we fix it. They forget us most time. We a little happy, but we still not get food."

During this account of the gully dwarves' misery, the look of disgust on Alya's face was slowly replaced by one of curiosity. Finally, she interrupted. "Do you mean to say that there is a draconian stronghold somewhere on this island?"

"Castle Slagd," the Highbulp nodded.

"I never heard of it," Jessica shrugged.

"How long has it been here?" Valian asked.

The Highbulp held up four fingers. "Two years," she answered. "Not more than two."

"This is unbelievable," Alya declared.

"But what happened to Uhoh?" Nalvarre asked.

"I try to tell, but they butt in," the Highbulp said with a frown. "I try to say, I hungry at castle. Those hungry days I look for way out to go find food, and I find way out. So I go find food. Aghar follow me, lots Aghar. I walk this way. We come here. I say I Highbulp now. I Highbulp Mommamose I, and this place Town. We got lots to eat here. Got good lizards, good bugs, good cactus. Good water, good beer. I happy.

"Uhoh sad. He funny 'cause I drop him on head. He not

stay. He take young Aghar and go that way," she said, pointing south. "I tell him you no go. You get in trouble. But he not listen. He never listen to Mommamose." She sniffled and wiped away a motherly tear.

"And he get in trouble, like I say. He come back here, but trouble come too. Slagd come. Slagd burn down mound. They take Uhoh, go that way." She pointed north.

"How many slagd?" Valian asked.

"Two," she answered, holding up two fingers.

"Then there is only one thing to do," Nalvarre declared. "We have to go north to this castle."

"I agree," Jessica said.

"Something must be done. A reconnaissance is needed, even if we can't rescue the gully dwarf," Valian said.

Alya paused, considering as she stared northward. Valian watched her. At last, she said, "I agree. But the most important thing right now is to alert the Knighthood."

Jessica started to protest, but Alya silenced her with a raised hand. "We are dealing with larger considerations than one gully dwarf. The others must be warned of this development so that plans can be made. If there are draconians on this island, we must alert the Knighthood. We can't all rush off blindly without any plan at all." She stood and dusted off her leather trousers.

"One of us should continue north to scout out the castle, while the others return to Castle uth Wistan to warn the Knights," she announced.

Valian stood. "I'll go," he said.

"No, you return with the others," Alya said. "I will head north and do my best to rescue poor Uhoh."

"I do not think this is wise," Valian countered. "I am best suited for tracking the draconians. Why choose to send me back?"

"And what makes you think I intend to turn back?" asked Nalvarre.

"Because," answered Alya, "if what we heard is true, the real danger is yet to come. It is your duty to spread the alarm. Go fast—safeguard each other, and return with reinforcements."

"How will you follow their trail?" Valian asked.

She shot him an angry glance. "I don't need to follow their trail. Mommamose knows the way to the castle, doesn't she? She'll take me there."

"I will?" the Highbulp asked in surprise.

"Valian is in charge now," Alya said as she gathered two extra wineskins from her companions and slung them over her shoulder. "Jessica, you must help convince the Solamnics. I can't imagine what Liam Ehrling and the others would say if Valian and a former priest of Chislev show up with two gully dwarves proclaiming the existence of a previously unknown stronghold of draconians. Stop by Isherwood and pick up Millisant. That—and Nalvarre's firsthand testimony—should do the trick."

"I wish to protest this decision," Valian said.

"Your protest is duly noted. Now give me your rations. You can pick up more food at Isherwood," Alya said. She turned and grabbed the Highbulp by the collar of her dress and pulled her to her feet. "Come along, Mommamose."

Half-leading, half-dragging the Highbulp, she strode into the nighted desert.

Valian watched her until she was well out of sight, then he turned and looked at the puzzled faces of his companions. His lips were an etched line in his stony white face, but his almond-shaped eyes blazed with anger.

"Let's go," he growled.

* * * * *

Not too far away through the pines, the stream roared and fumed in its channel, filling the air with a cold damp mist, which the weak sun did little to dispel. Lady Jessica Vestianstone, Nalvarre Ringbow, and the two gully dwarves Glabella and Lumpo huddled together and shivered, their teeth clacking, while Valian struggled to nurse a spark in the damp clump of tinder in his hand. The others watched intently, as though willing the fire to burn in the stream-soaked tinder.

Finally, however, the elf's skill prevailed, and a small flame rose amongst the grass and shreds of cloth cupped in the palm of his hand. He lowered it quickly to the ground and set small, moderately dry twigs and chunks of pine bark around it, all the while blowing encouragingly at the growing flame. Soon they had a rather weak fire to huddle round, and they held their hands before it, rubbing them together, even though the fire's heat was barely enough to feel. It seemed to encourage them somewhat. Glabella, who'd been snuffling ever since her near-drowning, managed a smile. Lumpo's stomach began to growl.

"That-t-t was s-s-some s-storm last-t-t night," Nalvarre chattered. "I've n-never seen Ish-Isher Creek so sw-swollen and raging."

"Neither have I," Jessica agreed as she clasped her elbows and pulled them tight to her sides. "The ford has always been passable, even in the worst weather. I am sorry."

"It's not your fault," Valian muttered. "I should have known better than to trust it, but we had to get across. We've no time to waste."

"Lucky for us you had us rope together like mountain climbers," Jessica said. "When the streambed slid out from beneath our feet, I thought it would be the end of us all."

"Yes, well, it's over now. As soon as we are dry, we must get to Castle Isherwood," Valian said. "We need horses."

"And food," Lumpo added.

Despite the elf's best efforts, the damp wood burned

coldly and smoked horribly, preventing them from getting near enough to dry their clothes in any kind of timely manner. It took hours for them to warm their stream-chilled bodies and wring the water from their clothes. The gully dwarves looked particularly bedraggled, like drowned rats, and when their raggedy clothes finally did dry, they became so stiff as to be nearly impossible to walk in. There was also something else, some strange almost ethereal quality to their appearance, which none of the others could quite place, until Nalvarre finally put his finger on it.

"They're clean!" he said triumphantly.

Glabella tentatively sniffed Lumpo, then wrenched her face away. "You stink," she said, pinching her nose. "Smell like nothing."

"The air hurts my skin," he complained. "Clean not healthy."

The two set off to find some mudhole to wallow in. The others gathered their things and followed, kicking out the fire before leaving.

A couple of hours' hard marching through the rugged pine forests of Isherwood brought them eventually to a small hill whose top was bare of trees. Across the gold and crimson autumn valley rose another hill likewise bare of trees, but this one was crowned with the crumbling walls and towers of Castle Isherwood. Through the trees on the hill's slope, they saw the trail.

"Come along. We're almost home. There's still much to do," Nalvarre said.

He started off down the hill, while the others followed, but Jessica lingered a moment longer, drinking in the sight. She sighed, glanced at the sky to judge the time of day. Something rising above the far end of the valley caught her eye.

"Look," she pointed. "There's an eagle. I've never seen

an eagle around here before."

Nalvarre squinted curiously at the eagle, while Valian glanced over his shoulder in the direction Jessica was pointing. He froze.

"Get down!" he snarled.

"What?" Jessica asked in astonishment.

"Get down, hide, all of you!" He grabbed the gully dwarves and pulled them behind a boulder. "That's no eagle. It's a dragon."

"What?" she said, confused. "Here?"

Nalvarre, who'd already fallen flat, pulled Jessica down beside him. "Lie still," he whispered. "It's too late to try to hide. He'll spot any movement."

It was a testament to the dragon's size that they mistook it for an eagle, for it was still some distance away. It took an almost unbearable amount of time for it to draw near enough for those without elven eyes to distinguish its features. The batlike wings, spreading impossibly wide, cast a shadow on the valley floor, while the tail trailed behind it, whipping, thrashing the air with a sound not unlike claps of thunder. Its scales, red as fresh blood, glistened in the sunlight.

What each person felt at that moment, watching the dragon glide impossibly slow upon the air, was beyond ordinary mortal fear. It was as though they were looking upon a god descending from the heavens, or more appropriately rising from the Abyss, seeing him in his true, undisguised form. His slow, deliberate flight and his tremendous size made them wonder if it was not his wings, but his indomitable and divine will, that held him aloft. They were horrified by his beauty, yet they could not look away.

"Pyrothraxus," Nalvarre whispered in awe.

As the dragon glided over the towers of Castle Isherwood, he began to drop. He descended upon the hilltop, the wind from his great wings ripping trees up by their roots and blasting them hundreds of feet into the valley. His tremendous bulk settled upon the fragile walls of the castle, crumbling them under his weight, and as he grasped two already ruined towers, his huge and powerful claws crushed them to dust. His tail toppled a third tower. Only the strongest tower remained, the one where Lady Jessica had her rooms.

"No!" she cried as she struggled to rise.

Nalvarre pinned her to the ground with his own body. "You mustn't," he said. "Be still. There is nothing you can do."

They heard horses screaming then, and looking they saw the dragon rip the roof from the stables and fling it aside. He reached inside the stable with two of his massive claws and plucked out a writhing, screaming horse. Tilting back his horned head, he dropped the poor animal into his open jaws, then returned to the stable for another, and then a third.

When all of the Knights' horses were devoured, the dragon turned his attention to the final tower. Again, Jessica began to struggle.

"Waterstone!" she cried.

"The dwarf!" Nalvarre gasped. "I'd forgotten about him."

The dragon's jaws gaped, his throat bulged, white hot liquid fire vomited forth, enveloping the tower. The ancient stones melted like wax, bubbling and popping so loudly that they could be heard even from across the valley. In moments, Jessica's home was little more than a pool of molten rock, the rest of the castle a scattering of stones. She wept, furiously struggling against Nalvarre, until finally she grew exhausted and lay still.

Apparently satisfied, the dragon raised its wings and leaped ponderously into the air. The great wings beat down once again, lifting the beast higher and higher as it swooped out across the valley. Jessica and Nalvarre suddenly became aware of their exposure as the dragon turned their way, but there was nowhere else to go. With nowhere to hide, they cowered together, while Valian and the gully dwarves tried to disappear behind their one, pitifully thin tree.

The dragon passed directly overhead no more than a few feet above treetop level. They felt the heat radiating from his body. A rank odor of sulfur and burning meat gagged them, and a sickly metallic tang of hot gold and steel filled the air.

The dragon banked and circled back toward to the north, the direction from which it had come. Nalvarre released Jessica, but she continued to lie on the cold hilltop, her tear-streaked face turned blankly to the heavens. Valian clambered up beside them.

"Do you think the dwarf . . ." he began.

Nalvarre raised a finger to his lips, glancing knowingly at Jessica. He nodded. The elf bowed his head, his white hair spilling down to hide his face. Below them, still cringing behind their tree, the gully dwarves whimpered pitifully.

"Dragons," Jessica whispered.

No one had the heart to look at her, to see the grief on her face.

"Dragons," she repeated in a husky whisper. Slowly, she rose to her feet.

"Look!" she cried. "Silver dragons!"

Like quicksilver arrows just loosed from a bow, three silver dragons shot up from the valley. Two from the left, one from the right, they rose unerringly toward the receding form of Pyrothraxus. At the last moment, Pyrothraxus saw them and swerved. They crossed just beneath him, screaming, long plumes of white frost arcing from their mouths to strike and freeze his wings. A gout of flame from his nostrils responded to the attack, but too late and much too slowly. The smaller, quickersilver dragons rose above him and met, hanging in the air for a moment, as though conferring, while Pyrothraxus laboriously increased the beat of his wings.

Jessica screamed with joy, a veritable battle cry that surprised the others. She drew her sword and swung it vigorously around and around as she performed some kind of mad dance. Nalvarre and even Valian drew away from her.

"Kill him!" she yelled fiercely to the silver dragons.

In response, the silvers dove as one at the red dragon's head. He pulled it back, and flying hunch-shouldered like an eagle pestered by magpies, made his ponderous way to the north. The silvers continued to dive and bomb his head until all four were out of sight. Jessica kept up her war dance until, with the dragons no longer visible in the darkening sky, she collapsed.

Chapter Twenty-Three

"Do you know where you are?" a voice asked suddenly
from the darkness.

Uhoh nodded, rattling his chains, then remembered that
they probably couldn't see him. "Yes," he said meekly.

"Do you know who I am?" the voice asked, echoing in
the vast emptiness of the chamber where Uhoh lay.

He was chained to a low stone slab by his ankles, wrists,
neck, and waist. Occasionally he felt things scurry across
his legs, but the darkness prevented his seeing them. He'd
been there for days and days, it seemed.

"Me know nothing," Uhoh replied.

A light flared into life, revealing a small balcony with a
dark alcove behind it. A creature stood there, glaring
down at Uhoh with one hideous red eye. It was a draconian, but one twisted and malformed by the magic that created it. One side of its face had eerie, semireptilian,
semihumanoid features, but the other side of the face was
melted like candle wax. In some places, bare bone showed
through the distorted flesh, while in others hideous
growths of bone and horn protruded in fantastic shapes
beneath the skin. The draconian looked like a nightmare
brought to waking life.

"Me know nothing!" Uhoh screamed in terror. He

averted his face and closed tight his eyes, as if that simple act could make the nightmare go away.

"They call me the Old Man," the draconian said. "They call me the Old Man because I am indeed the oldest. I am the firstborn, the first of my kind to crawl forth from the egg, in the days before the magic of our draconic transformation was perfected. The magic was flawed, and so I am flawed, but I survived where my brothers died hideously, their bodies twisted, their minds shattered by their deformity. I am also more perfect than any that have come after me. I am more powerful. I know all things. In fact, I know something about you, Uhoh Ragnap."

"Me not Uhoh Ragnap. You got wrong gully dwarf," Uhoh shouted.

"That's not true," the draconian laughed. "We both know it. Would you deny your own identity to save your miserable skin? But of course you would. You are a gully dwarf."

Uhoh tried to lower his voice and sound dour. "Me not gully dwarf. Me hill dwarf. You doorknob. You got wrong dwarf."

"Come, come. Enough of these foolish games," the draconian said with magnanimous patience. "You are a gully dwarf, and you are the gully dwarf whom my servants have chased halfway across Sancrist Isle. You have led them a merry chase and done me great service. I see they are in need of training."

A door banged open. Uhoh turned his head to see two draconians enter, one bearing a lit torch, the other rolling a cart.

"Not all my servants are hunters—assassins, as humans call them. Some have other skills. These baaz you see before you are quite talented in the arts of torture," he said.

Uhoh looked up. "Why you torture me?" he asked. "Me only a gully dwarf."

233

"Because, dear Uhoh, I want to know what Gunthar said to you before he died. We know he told you something, by the words from your own mouth," the draconian said. The balcony light dimmed. As the draconian continued to speak, the sound of his voice seemed to slowly float down the wall. While the baaz torturers busied themselves setting up their implements, Uhoh eyed these fearfully even though he didn't know their uses. "You were with Lord Gunthar when he died. I am quite certain, shameless thespian that he was, he saved some dire secret to import to you with his last, gargling breath."

"What?" Uhoh said, utterly baffled.

The draconian's twisted face appeared from the shadows as he stepped into the light of the torturers' torch. "What did Gunthar whisper in your ear, you miserable wretch? Don't try to deny it. What did he tell you?"

The door banged open again, and a man dressed in a crisp blue captain's uniform entered the room. He strode to the table, his bootheels clicking on the stone floor. He doffed his tall, plumed hat and bowed.

"Well, General Zen?" the draconian leader asked.

"The ship and its cargo are intact. As we speak, it is being unloaded, and the prisoners removed to dungeon cells," the man said.

"Unfortunate for them that they sailed too close to this shore. You have done well," the draconian said.

"Thank you, Grand Master Iulus," the man said as he bowed again.

"This is an interesting form you wear," Iulus commented, indicating Zen's appearance.

"Ah, yes. The captain was a bit of a dandy," Zen said. "I flew out to the ship as it passed, and in the usual manner, killed a member of the watch, thus taking his form and disposing of his body overboard. I then proceeded to the captain's cabin, where I killed him and took his shape.

Once this was done, it was a simple enough matter to order the helm to steer to the castle's harbor, where our soldiers were waiting. We took them without a fight."

"General Zen, your efficiency is a model to us all. Reward the wyvern watches with a few of the prisoners from the ship. Make sure the master of the dungeons chooses lively ones. The wyverns do so love to play with their supper," Iulus commanded.

"Yes, my master," Zen said, bowing as though to leave.

"Not yet, my friend," Iulus purred. "It can wait. First shed that hideous human form. It's making the baaz nervous."

General Zen stepped back and closed his eyes, folding his arms before his chest. His body began to change shape, his nose lengthening into a snout, his fingers narrowing into claws. His smooth human skin erupted with silver reptilian scales, while from his shoulders and back spread large, powerful wings. In mere moments, he had resumed his natural shape, that of a sivak draconian. Uhoh's mouth fell open.

"Ah, that's better," Zen said in a deep powerful voice. He shook out his wings and stretched like a cat awakening from a nap.

"Now, allow me to introduce to you our long-awaited guest. General Zen, meet Uhoh Ragnap, esquire," Iulus said. The sivak stared down at the prostrate gully dwarf.

"Hello," Uhoh said.

Iulus laughed. "Oh, he is a good sport, don't you think?" he said. "Uhoh was brought in by Harj and that sanctimonious idiot, Shaeder. Harj has once again proved himself valuable in this little affair, but I think Shaeder's blatant disregard for subtlety needs addressing."

"I agree, my lord," Zen said.

"In the meanwhile, Uhoh was just about to impart to me the dire nature of his master's last words. He also needs to tell us who else shares his little secret," Iulus said. "We know that, at the very least, he spoke to that onetime priest of Chislev, Nalvarre Ringbow."

"I blame myself, my lord," General Zen said. "I had him right across the campfire from me. He suspected nothing because I'd take the form of the ranger I'd killed just after dark. If I had known of the priest's involvement, I'd have silenced him then."

"I know, my friend. I don't blame you," Iulus said. He turned and knelt beside the gully dwarf, his reptilian snout almost in Uhoh's ear. "Torture is so messy," he hissed, "but we have to be sure you are telling the truth. Now tell me, what was Gunthar's last shuddering whisper that fateful afternoon?"

"What afternoon?" Uhoh asked.

"Don't play stupid with me. You know which afternoon," the draconian Grand Master snarled.

"Yes," Uhoh squeaked.

"What did he say?"

"The book . . . Kalabash . . . in bell room," Uhoh began.

"Stop blabbering, you fool! You are only making it worse for yourself," Iulus warned, pointing one long, goldish claw at the terrified gully dwarf.

"Tell him Liam tell no one," Uhoh continued.

"Master, this is useless," Zen said. "Just kill him and be done with it. That way, no matter what the secret, he can never tell it to another soul."

"But if Gunthar suspected anything, said as much to this creature before he died," Iulus said with a disdainful gesture at Uhoh, "then he might have told others. Our plans could be thwarted. What this gully dwarf tells will help us decide whether we can proceed with caution or confidence."

"I see, my master," Zen said, his voice betraying a shade of uncertainty.

"It is fruitless to resist. We have ways, painful ways of making you talk," Iulus said as he returned his monocular gaze upon Uhoh.

"I talk already. I go now?" Uhoh asked.

Suddenly, Iulus chuckled. Rising to his full seven-foot height, he motioned to the baaz torturers. "I must say, he is a good sport. Don't go too hard on him, but make sure he isn't hiding anything," he ordered.

Turning, he took Zen by the arm and led the sivak from the torture chamber. As the door closed, a shrill scream shattered the night.

* * * * *

Aurak Grand Master of Assassins Iulus set down his silver goblet and gripped the edge of the table with his clawed hands. His one good eye rolled up in his head.

"This wine is superb!" he groaned in ecstasy. "Zen, you really have outdone yourself with tonight's catch."

"It is quite good," Zen agreed, though not with the emotion displayed by his master.

Iulus picked up the goblet in one clawed hand and swirled its contents thoughtfully. Human servants wearing iron collars scurried about the chamber, lighting tapers, trimming wicks, and clearing away the plates from supper. The Grand Master tossed back the remainder in his glass, all the while eyeing the sivak. General Zen merely toyed with his cup, sipping lightly and infrequently.

"Something bothering you, my friend?" Iulus asked. "Would you like a little music with your wine?"

Without waiting for an answer, he turned in his chair and lifted a bronze cap from a metal tube protruding from the wall. Faint echoes of tortured screams welled from the tube.

"No, my master," Zen sighed.

"Is your cup dirty? I'll have the dishwasher flogged," Iulus said.

"The wine is fine," Zen said. "That's the problem. We drink the finest wines of Palanthas while our warriors have to content themselves with watered ale or whatever they can brew themselves. It doesn't seem right. I remember the days when you and I ate boot leather and hobgoblins just to keep alive. That's what made us what we are today—hard living. It made us strong."

Iulus nodded in agreement.

"Do you remember when we pillaged Qué-shu and burned Solace to the ground?" Zen asked. "Do you remember how we laughed at how fat those lands were, and how much they deserved destroying. That is what I fear, that now we are grown fat and deserve destroying. This unsettling affair with the gully dwarf only justifies my fears."

"The gully dwarf is nothing. We'll soon learn what we need from him, then we can mop up those he told and be done with it," Iulus said.

"But the Knights . . ." Zen protested.

"Soon the Knights of Solamnia will not be a concern. Matters are coming to a head there. The Knights are finished, and they don't even know it," Iulus said.

A servant entered the room and approached the Grand Master. He knelt beside the table and whispered something that Zen was unable to hear.

Iulus nodded, then looked up at Zen. "Speaking of Knights, we have a visitor." The servant hurried away.

After a few moments, the door reopened and an armored Knight entered the room. The Knight wore a full helm with the visor pulled down hiding the face.

"What is the word?" Iulus asked.

"Pyrothraxus has retreated to Mount Nevermind," the Knight answered in a voice muffled by the helm.

"What?" Iulus screeched in surprise. The twisted, mal-formed half of his face turned scarlet. "Was Isherwood destroyed and the Knights there killed?"

"Isherwood is no more, but the dragon retreated with-out ascertaining that the Knights and the priest of Chislev were inside," the Knight said.

Iulus slammed his clawed fist on the table, cracking the heavy oaken plank down its full length. "A flight of red dragons would have served better," he cursed. "At least we can control them."

"Pyrothraxus won't allow reds onto the island," Zen said.

"Fool, don't you think I know that?" the Grand Master snarled.

Zen scowled at the rebuff, but said nothing. Meanwhile, Iulus seemed to regain control of his emotions.

"Well, it is of no concern," Iulus said. "Even if they escape, they'll never make it to Castle uth Wistan before the council. Liam has agreed to an open vote for the suc-cession. Once Lady Mirielle is in command, the Knights of Solamnia will be finished."

"They'll demand someone be sent to rescue the gully dwarf," the helmed Knight said. "He can still cause prob-lems. It were best if he is killed now."

"I think you overestimate the importance of our little friend," Iulus said. "When we find out his secret, then we'll dispose of him immediately. Meanwhile, with Pyrothraxus threatening their border, they'd never risk sending a contingent just to rescue a gully dwarf."

"Very well," the Knight said. "Oh, by the way, I've brought you a little present."

"Really? And what, pray tell, is that?" Iulus asked.

The Knight removed her helm and shook out her dark hair. "Something called a highbulp, the fugitive gully dwarf slave," she said. "Her name is Mommamose. She would already be dead, and I wouldn't be so inconvenienced, if it wasn't for the incompetence of your soldiers."

"Really, something must be done about Shaeder," Zen said as he motioned the Knight to have a seat at the table.

"Bring another bottle of that excellent wine," Iulus ordered one of the servants.

"Bring two," Alya said with a laugh as she tossed her dragon helm in the corner.

Chapter Twenty-Four

A knock on the door startled Liam from his reverie. He'd been nodding off, dreaming of things that could have been, while atop his desk, Gunthar's desk, the old man's manuscript lay just as he had left it in disgust some three weeks earlier. He'd spent nearly every day since the reading of the will in Gunthar's study, supposedly editing the Revised Measure into some kind of workable order. Instead he'd spent most of that time looking out the window, examining the paintings on the wall, picking at his fingernails, or simply dozing. He couldn't bring himself to sit down at the desk and try to organize Gunthar's life's work, his parting gift to the Knighthood, the work for which he'd be remembered throughout the ages. For Gunthar's Measure frightened Liam as no mortal enemy ever had. He'd faced dragons in battle, thousands of feet above the ground, but this task he'd set himself, to edit the Measure, paralyzed him with its enormity.

The first third was not only legible, it was perfect, the work of a brilliant mind. Gunthar had begun this section of the Revised Measure not long after the War of the Lance. Strict and mindless adherence to the Measure had very nearly destroyed the Knights during the War of the Lance, so Lord Gunthar made it his life's goal to revise it into a fluid document of broad all-encompassing guidelines, from which a Knight could draw inspiration for any particular situation. He'd worked on it carefully and diligently during the years between the War of the Lance and the Chaos War.

However, the death of his last surviving son during the Chaos War wrought a change in Gunthar's mind. Where his previous work had been clear and concise, the newer writings were little more than outlines and incomplete ideas. It needed expansion and elaboration, although it was not wholly corrupted. After the death of his wife, Gunthar's work on the Measure deteriorated. He began to ramble, mixing his thoughts on his work with thoughts of the past and musings upon everyday life. He filled pages and pages just doodling, with maybe an idea about ceremony hastily scrawled at the bottom of the paper. There were unfinished letters to his wife written on the same pages as directions for various types of battle, and he repeated himself endlessly. After just a cursory glance through these disappointing pages, Liam found eleven variations of instructions for sentry placement in mountainous terrain. At that point, he threw the Revised Measure down in disgust and hadn't looked at it since.

Tomorrow, Liam had told himself. I'll begin tomorrow. What's one more day? I need to get my thoughts together before I begin.

Preoccupied with the Measure, Liam had reluctantly handed over temporary leadership of the Knights to Tohr Malen, and he was forced to admit that the Dark Knight handled things admirably. His quick command and powerful personality had already won over many of the Knights of Solamnia. With his charisma and magnetism, it seemed all too easy for them to forget that once Tohr had dedicated his life to the cause of evil. While Liam sank into depression, Tohr Malen was forging the Knights

of Sancrist Isle into a powerful well-organized body of
warriors. He was breathing new life and energy into men
and women who'd become jaded with inactivity. Liam
felt his authority, his control, slipping away.

That's why he'd called the Grand Chapter, to force a
vote before Tohr Malen won everyone over to his side.

The knock on the door awakened Liam to the reality
that he must now go down and face the assemblage. He
rose slowly to his feet, while the page pounded impatiently on the door. Liam settled his sword in its baldric
and ran a nervous hand through his graying locks, then
strode to the door and opened it.

The page bowed. "Forgive me, my lord. The Chapter is
ready," he said.

Liam took a deep breath, then nodded. The page led the
way down the hall. Liam fell in behind and walked with
his head proud, his eyes level, as though walking out to
what might likely be his last battle.

They arrived before a low arched doorway just as the
midday bell was being rung, sounding a changing of the
watch. "How appropriate," Liam muttered. The page
opened the door and stepped back. Liam ducked and
passed through.

It brought him to a small antechamber, where several
other Knights of renown were waiting. There was Lord
High Clerist Meredith Turningdale smiling at him sympa-
thetically, and Lord High Warrior Quintayne Fogorner
purposefully avoiding his eyes. So Quintayne has already
gone over, Liam thought.

The strange and aloof Thorn Knight Trevalyn Kesper
brooded in the corner, while Tohr Malen anxiously paced
the tiny confines of the chamber. As Liam entered, Tohr
smiled and approached him, his hand extended.

"I just want to say, Sir Liam, that no matter how the vote
goes, I do not consider you my adversary. In fact, I hope

that we can one day be friends," Tohr said as he earnestly shook Liam's hand.

"As do I," Liam responded politely, "and I shall put aside my personal feelings and abide by the lawful decision of this Chapter."

A tall door in the opposite wall from the entrance opened with a creak. Sir Ellinghad Beauseant stuck his head inside the antechamber and whispered, "My lords and ladies, we are ready."

Liam nodded, indicating his readiness. Sir Ellinghad then looked at Lord Tohr for confirmation. And Ellinghad as well, Liam noted with some sadness. How many others? he wondered. Tohr nodded.

Ellinghad stepped back. "Gentlemen, ladies, Honorable Knights of Sancrist Isle," he said in a loud and forceful voice. "All rise for the Lord High Justice Liam Ehrling, Lord Tohr Malen, Lord Trevalyn Kesper," he announced as each presiding Lord Knight entered the chapel.

It was the same place where they'd held Gunthar's funeral, but before the altar they'd set up a table and six chairs. In the center of the table stood a clay pot filled with small circular tiles. Most were white, though a single black tile peeked through the top. The five leaders of the Knights took their seats behind the table, facing the congregation, which was made up of every available Knight in the area. The sixth seat at the table remained empty, and it was only then that Liam noticed the representative of the Knights of the Lily was not present. He looked around, but no one proposed to fill the vacant chair.

The Lord Knights entered last, like jurors in a trial. Once everyone was seated, Liam rose and asked, "Where is Lady Alya Starblade for the Knights of the Lily?"

"We have a report that she will arrive within the hour," Tohr said. "In the meanwhile, I believe we can proceed with the introductions."

"Yes, well . . ." Liam mumbled. He cleared his throat. "Honorable Knights of Sancrist Isle, I declare this Grand Chapter open," he said in a disinterested monotone while he arranged some papers on the table before him.

"As you know, this is the first Grand Chapter of the Sancrist Knights, so I will attempt to explain the changes in rules, some of which you may already be familiar with." Liam droned on for some time, while the gathered Knights shifted restlessly in their seats.

At last, Liam said, "So if there is no news or announcements, we can begin with the real reason for this Chapter. We are gathered here today to elect the first Grand Master of the Knights of Sancrist Isle. Now, since we cannot yet proceed according to the Measure as laid down by Lord Gunthar, I and my fellow Knights have agreed to a procedure that we believe is fair to all concerned. Are there any objections?"

He waited, but when no one offered any arguments, he continued. "First, nominations for the office shall be accepted."

Lady Meredith rose. "I nominate Sir Liam Ehrling," she said with a defiant tone.

"Thank you, Lady Meredith," Liam said. "Is there a second?" He turned to Quintayne, but the leader of the Knights of the Crown only stared straight ahead, his face a blank page.

Someone from the audience shouted, "I second!"

"The nomination is seconded," Liam said, a little shaken by the desertion of onetime stalwarts. "Any other nominations?"

"I nominate in absence Lady Mirielle Abrena," Lord Tohr said.

"And I second it," Trevalyn barked before Liam was able to respond.

"Lady Mirielle Abrena nominated and seconded," Liam

said with a frown. "Are there any other nominations?"

The chapel remained as silent.

"I declare the nominations closed, " Liam said. "Now the vote shall be held in the following manner. Each member of the presiding council of six Knights shall cast one vote. Lots shall then be drawn by those Knights in attendance, choosing six additional voters. Should a tie be the result of the first vote, a seventh lot shall then be drawn to determine the final and deciding vote.

"But since the Lady Alya Starblade is not yet arrived, I think perhaps a recess in is order," Liam finished.

"We may as well go ahead and draw the six lots," Tohr offered.

"That's a good idea," Liam reluctantly agreed. He gestured to the front row of Knights. "Everyone come up here and file by the table. When you reach the center, turn your head to the side and draw a single tile from the pot. We rely upon your honor not to look at the tiles as you draw them. Only those who have drawn black tiles shall cast a vote."

The first row of Knights rose from their seats and solemnly filed into the center aisle. One by one, they passed before the table, each stopping and drawing his or her tile from the pot. Some hid the color of the tile they'd drawn, some displayed theirs either with relief or dismay. At last, all the tiles were drawn from the pot, and the last Knight returned to his seat. Still Alya had not come.

Tohr rose from his seat and cleared his throat. "I received information this morning that a Knight was riding hard from Castle Isherwood, and that she is expected here at any moment. Until that time, I believe we ought to go ahead. If the decision comes down to her vote, then we can always await her arrival."

Liam considered for a moment. "I agree that it is better to proceed," he said. "There is but one more matter. As a nominee, I am not allowed to vote, but I have the right to choose someone else to cast a proxy."

Liam looked round the room. He was about to play his best card. He hoped the trust he was about to place in someone would sway that person's vote, and by the display of trust so sway the votes of others. "I choose Sir Ellinghad Beauseant," he declared.

"Liam!" Meredith whispered. "Ellinghad has privately expressed to me his admiration for Lady Mirielle."

"Sir Ellinghad is a man of great personal honor. I trust him to make the right choice," Liam answered in a voice loud enough for everyone to hear.

Ellinghad bowed solemnly in appreciation.

"Knights with black tiles, arise!" Ellinghad commanded.

Six Knights, randomly scattered throughout the chapel, rose to their feet. Liam noted with a glimmer of hope that only one was a Knight of Takhisis.

"Sir Trevalyn Kesper, how do you vote?" Liam asked.

"I vote for Lady Mirielle, of course," the Gray Robe laughed.

"Lady Mirielle," Tohr said.

Meredith stood to cast her vote. "Sir Liam Ehrling!"

Quintayne remained seated and refused to look at his fellow Knights. "Lady Mirielle," he said.

Now the six Knights who had drawn lots cast their votes.

"Sir Liam Ehrling," said the first, a Knight of the Rose.

Following the Lord of his Order, a Knight of the Crown voted, "Lady Mirielle."

"Lady Mirielle."

Again "Lady Mirielle." Liam's face fell as he watched his Knights vote against him.

"Sir Liam Ehrling."

To everyone's surprise, the sole Knight of Takhisis had

cast his vote in favor of Sir Liam. A murmur went around the room. Liam counted the votes and sighed. He looked up mournfully at Sir Ellinghad.

Ellinghad had also counted the votes, and as he turned to face the table, beads of sweat broke out on his proud forehead. "I vote for Lady Mirielle," he said. "I am sorry, my lord."

Liam nodded and smiled weakly.

"Well, it seems we don't need the vote of Lady Alya after all," Lord Tohr said.

"It seems so," Liam agreed with a sigh.

He waved to a page, indicating that the white and black tiles should be collected and returned to the clay pot. The room remained quiet, although the outcome of the vote had never really been in doubt. During the weeks since the funeral, both veterans and Knights newly in spurs had been won over by Tohr's command. His tales of the deeds of Knights serving under Lady Mirielle had stirred their Solamnic hearts, one and all. They saw not dark days ahead under the leadership of a onetime servant of evil, but a glorious future under the command of a brilliant military mind. No longer would they bide their time. Once the forces had been consolidated, Tohr had promised, there'd be war, war against the alien dragons from across the sea, war against Pyrothraxus and his kind. Few resisted such visions.

Still, most realized that, with this vote, the Knights of Solamnia were truly finished. The end had come too quickly, too easily. There should have been more pomp and ceremony. Instead, the meeting came to an abrupt and unceremonious end when Tohr stood up and said with a barely suppressed smile, "Well, I guess that's it, then."

"When Lady Alya arrives, have her brought to me immediately," Tohr said to Ellinghad. Glad to be given the opportunity to leave, the room, Ellinghad bowed and turned to go.

Just then the doors at the back of the hall swung open and a dusty, road-weary Knight strode into the chapel. "Lady Alya will not be coming," he announced.

Chapter Twenty-Five

The Knight stopped before the table and removed his helm.

"Sir Valian!" Tohr said with some surprise. "I thought you'd be in Xenos by now, inspecting our fortifications there. I sent a messenger to alert you of these proceedings."

"I never made it to Xenos," Valian said. "Pyrothraxus has crossed the border and attacked Isherwood!" he announced.

The chapel erupted with shouting. Sir Liam arose and pounded the butt of his dagger on the table until the excitement quieted. "Sir Knight, please explain yourself. When did this happen?" he asked.

"Two . . . no, three days ago, I think. I've ridden hard, the days have blurred," the dark elf said. "We were already headed this way when the messenger met us on the road with news of the Grand Chapter. When I heard that, I took the freshest horse and rode as fast I could. But I don't imagine the others will be far behind."

"Why didn't Alya come?" Tohr asked.

"She was not with us. She has gone north to scout the draconian stronghold," Valian said. Again, the room erupted with shouting. Liam pounded the table with his dagger, but Tohr didn't wait for the others to quieten.

He shouted, "Draconians! Explain yourself. Who is with you?"

"A former priest of Chislev, two gully dwarves, one of Gunthar's boar hounds, a hill dwarf, and Lady Jessica," Valian answered.

"This is very strange indeed. " said Liam, "Perhaps you should begin at the beginning,"

Valian stood before the assembled Knights and unwound the tale of the last few days. He told them of Nalvarre Ringbow and what his story revealed, that Uhoh claimed draconians had been involved in Gunthar's death. At this point, the gathered Knights erupted again, some angry at the accusation, some furious that they were asked to credit the secondhand tales of a gully dwarf. Tohr ordered the chapel cleared, despite the strenuous objections of those evicted. Angry murmuring continued in the halls outside for some time afterward.

Meanwhile, inside, without noisy interruption, Valian continued his tale. "We followed the trail of the gully dwarves," he explained. "Soon I noticed another set of tracks overlying those of the gully dwarves. These tracks were draconian, kapak draconian I'm almost certain."

"How can you be sure?" Quintayne asked, but Valian ignored him.

"As we neared a cliff," the elf continued, "a second set of draconian tracks joined the first; these appeared to be a bozak magic user. We followed them to a cliff, where a secret door of unknown origin or construction, as our hill dwarf companion assured us, led into a passage that seemed likely to lead through. In any case, all the tracks led this way, so we followed.

"At the other side, we found a gully dwarf village. It lies in a great basin in the mountains, cut off from the outside world. Even rain does not often find its way in there, for the land was parched. As soon as we saw the place, we knew the draconians had been there before us, for some of the dwellings were destroyed and the gully dwarves scattered. That is where we met two of Uhoh's companions; they had accompanied him when he fled from here after Gunthar's death. They confirmed what the priest of Chislev had already told us.

"We also met the leader of the gully dwarves. She knew of a draconian stronghold. It lies somewhere on the north coast of Sancrist. As soon as Lady Alya heard of this, she ordered us to return and warn you, while she continued alone to scout the stronghold," Valian said.

"That seems an odd decision," Liam commented. "As you are an elf, I think you'd make a better scout than she."

"Lady Alya knows how to handle herself," Tohr said. "If she thought Valian was needed here, she'd not hesitate to take the more dangerous assignment."

Liam nodded, but he didn't seem convinced. "In any case, you still haven't told us about Pyrothraxus," he said to Valian.

"Yes, well, we returned as ordered, despite my own objection to Alya's orders," Valian said. Tohr's eyebrows rose in surprise at this admission. Valian continued, "We marched with all speed to Isherwood, but the distance is too great to cross in a single day. We camped for the night, and all throughout the night storms crashed on the mountain peaks surrounding the valley. They sounded like giants battling; the sky was lit up like day. We had little enough shelter. The next morning we found our path blocked by a stream, which had been transformed by the rains into a raging river. We spent all that day trying to find a crossing, and that delay probably saved our lives."

"How fortunate," Trevalyn commented.

"And how do you know it was Pyrothraxus?" Quintayne

asked. "Have you ever seen this dragon before?"

"No, but I have seen many red dragons in my time. This dragon was was larger. His wings seemed to stretch from horizon to horizon, covering the whole sky and darkening the sun. And when he breathed . . ." the elf shuddered. "Such destruction I have never before witnessed. The entire North Tower melted like a candle, with molten stone running like wax down its sides. He then turned his attention on the stable, where horses screamed in terror of the flames. He tore off the roof and plucked out our horses like candies, devouring them whole."

Valian staggered, gripping the table to steady himself. "Forgive me," he whispered.

"You are exhausted," Meredith said. "We will send for food and wine. You need to rest."

"In a moment," he said. "I must complete the tale. As we watched from some distance away, the dragon leveled the castle. What he did not crush, he incinerated with his fiery breath.

"Lady Jessica was shattered, for she truly loved the castle like a home, and she hated to see it destroyed. When we descended to the desert basin where the gully dwarves lived, we'd sent Jessica's retainer, a hill dwarf, and Gunthar's boar hound back to the castle to await our return. Jessica feared they'd been killed by the dragon, either buried under tons of rubble or consumed by the dragon's fire. So it was to our great surprise that the dwarf appeared, burned and bruised but alive, and Millisant was with him. They'd escaped through a bolt hole just as the dragon burned the castle to the ground.

"With the castle destroyed, the dragon seemed content to leave. He beat his great wings, sending sparks and hot ash swirling through the forest. Then, from the south, we saw . . ."

Liam rose from his chair and held up one hand silencing the elf.

"You are weary, Sir Valian. Tell us quickly what happened after you left the castle, so that we may reach some kind of decision," Liam said. A few of the other Knights shot him questioning glances, but he ignored them.

Valian shrugged and continued. "We walked until we found a village. The people there gave us horses. Although they hadn't seen the dragon, they had sensed approaching danger, and many had already left, heading south away from the lands of Pyrothraxus. We passed many on the road. As we neared Castle uth Wistan, we learned of the vote taking place today, so I rode ahead as quickly as possible. Even so, my horse was once more accustomed to pulling a plow than fast riding. I think Jessica and the others will arrive before nightfall."

With that said, Valian staggered to the empty chair beside Trevalyn and sank into it. He rested his head on his arms. The Thorn Knight eyed him with ill-concealed contempt. Meanwhile, everyone seemed to ponder what they'd just been told. Quintayne stared out the window, his round face wrinkled with thought. Meredith looked from one to another, as though searching the Knights' faces for some clues. Liam fiddled with the pommel of his dagger, his brows knit, while Tohr leaned back in his chair and stared at the ceiling. Trevalyn Kesper yawned.

Finally, Meredith broke the silence. "It seems obvious to me, there is but one thing to do. We must go north. If we do nothing else, we must rescue that poor gully dwarf."

"I doubt very seriously if he is even alive by now," Quintayne muttered.

"It doesn't matter!"

"You two aren't seeing the real threat here," Tohr said in impatience. "You Solamnics would sit at the knife edge of disaster and argue the color of the sky."

"Excuse me?" Meredith said in surprise. "We Solamnics?"

254

"You heard me," he growled. For the first time since they'd met him, his facade had crumbled. He stood, his fists clenched at his sides. "The real danger is not the draconian stronghold, if it even exists."

At these words, Valian's head lifted from his arms. He eyed his leader curiously.

Tohr continued, "The real danger is Pyrothraxus. If he catches us without leadership, we might as well swing open the doors of this castle and invite him inside."

"Pyrothraxus is no threat to Castle uth Wistan, not yet," Liam interjected.

"How can you say that?" Tohr shouted. "Are you an even bigger fool than . . ." He paused, swallowing his words.

"Pyrothraxus didn't cross the border for a random attack. His destruction of Isherwood had a specific purpose, to stop Valian and his group. I imagine he thought they were at the castle and his attack would catch them inside, but he didn't know about the storm and their delay," Liam said. "When he is ready to confront us, he'll come here, yes, and strike at the heart of the Knighthood. So why is he threatening the unimportant border outposts?"

"Who can read the minds of these new dragons?" Tohr argued. "After all, he did assault Mount Nevermind without warning. We can't assume this is anything but the precursor to a full-scale onslaught, perhaps with the backing of a full draconian army. Have you thought of that possibility?"

"The draconians! It always comes back to the draconians," Meredith said. "If they are such a formidable army, why go to all the trouble of assassinating Lord Gunthar, and then scurrying around to hide that fact? Why hunt a poor stupid gully dwarf all over Sancrist? It doesn't make any sense to me."

"Nor to me. It's all the more reason to take firm control of this Knighthood here. Otherwise we are in confusion and vulnerable to attack," Tohr said.

Valian spoke up at this point. "Did I hear you say Lady Mirielle has been elected the new Grand Master?" he asked.

"Well, not officially. Lady Alya is still to vote for the Knights of the Lily, but it's a mere formality only," Quintayne said. "She already has enough votes."

"But until her vote is taken, no official proclamation can be made. Someone could still reverse his preference. Sir Valian is the next ranking member of the Order of the Lily; he could vote in her stead and bring closure to this matter," Tohr said.

Valian shook his head uncertainly, his elvish nature preventing a hasty decision. "I need more time to consider," he said. "I did not expect to cast such a momentous vote. I haven't thought my decision through."

"What is there to think through?" Tohr growled. "Your vote is meaningless, a mere formality."

"Then it won't matter if I take a day to think about it. I need time to consider," Valian returned. Though his voice remained calm, his eyes were flashing.

"You have twenty-four hours," Liam said. "We cannot wait much longer than that, whether or not Tohr is right about Pyrothraxus. We must call a general council at Whitestone to announce the decision."

Everyone rose to leave. A door opened and a page entered, awaiting a command. "No decision has been made," said Tohr. "Sir Valian is to cast the last vote tomorrow at Whitestone Glade. Spread the word."

The page turned to go, but Liam stopped him with an additional order. "When Lady Jessica and her group arrive, have her brought immediately to my chambers. Allow the others to refresh themselves, and tell the grooms that a dog and two gully dwarves will need dinner tonight." The page nodded and scurried away.

The Knights prepared to leave. With a final look at Tohr, Valian stalked away. As he passed, Tohr whispered, "Don't be a fool." Valian said nothing in return.

Chapter Twenty-Six

In the dark of the Sancrist night, Dalian Escu walked the battlements of Castle uth Wistan. He wasn't on watch, and a good thing too. An army of goblins could have stormed the wall without his even noticing. His mind was elsewhere, walking in the dreamland forests of his elven childhood. In Silvanesti he'd been born, and there he'd died, when they banished him from the light. From that moment forward, no elf on Krynn was allowed to speak to him or even acknowledge his existence. His parents spoke of him as though he were already dead.

In Storm's Keep, the birthplace of the Knights of Takhisis, he'd been reborn. With the Knights of Takhisis, he found the family to which he so desperately needed to belong. Even so, they'd never completely accepted him. Now it seemed all he'd worked toward had been a lie, a carefully concealed deception. Where was the vaunted honor of the Knights of Takhisis? It lay in some draconian dungeon, wrapped in the vestige of a gully dwarf.

What had first alerted him? Had it in fact been with the surprising willingness of the leadership of the Knights to attempt a union with the Knights of Solamnia, their most bitter enemies? Or had it come later, at Isherwood, when Alya displayed a strange stubbornness to accept the existence of draconians on Sancrist Isle? Or was it some strange coincidence, by which Pyrothraxus chose to attack Isherwood, breaking the uneasy and undeclared peace?

Then there was Lord Tohr, displaying the same incomprehensible unwillingness to accept the fact of the existence of the draconian stronghold, and his pressure to conclude the vote to determine the leadership of the combined Knighthood. Sir Liam had been right. There was no real threat from Pyrothraxus; the dragon had been sent to destroy Jessica, the priest, and himself.

While he pondered these matters, Valian circled the entirety of the battlements, crossing over the gate by its postern walk. He passed above the stable yard, where Uhoh had lived, and he passed the place where Gunthar and Liam met on the battlements that first night, so long ago it seemed. He continued, his head bowed, his hands clasped behind his back.

A familiar voice brought him up short. He found himself very near the rooms of Lord Tohr. By the torchlight from the courtyard, he saw that a window was open to the chill night air, but dark drapes prevented any light from escaping. He heard Tohr's voice.

"Are you certain it will work?" Tohr was asking someone.

Valian stepped closer to the window to better hear.

"Of course, my lord. The potion was created before the Chaos War. Rest assured, once its magic has surrounded you, no human on Krynn can resist your charms. They will wish only to please you," a voice that was Trevalyn's answered.

Without warning Valian pushed aside the curtain and stepped into the room. "And how does it work on elves?" he asked. The Thorn Knight almost fell over himself in his surprise, but Lord Tohr's face remained calm, almost as though he'd been expecting Valian. He held in his scarred hand a tiny glass phial filled with a red liquid.

"I am glad you are here, Valian," he said in a pleasant voice as he placed the phial on the desk before him. "I've been meaning to talk to you, to bring you up to date on our situation here."

"If I were planning to usurp the Solamnics in their own castle, I'd at least have the sense to shut the window," Valian sneered.

"An oversight," Tohr said. "Very careless. Trevalyn, please close the window, won't you, so we don't have any more unexpected guests."

The Thorn Knight stepped behind the curtain and closed the window with a snap. He returned to Tohr's side, his hands folded in the sleeves of his gray robe.

"This has been the plan all along," Valian said.

"Actually, no. We fully expected Liam to be elected Grand Master. That's why Lady Mirielle didn't come herself. We thought it would take years for all our plans to develop, when we could place the scepter into the hands of one of our own. But now?" he shrugged. "His own men were surprisingly easy to win over. All I can say is, he took his chances. He lost in a fair vote."

"You're leaving out Gunthar's murder," Valian snarled. "Now we take through assassination and duplicity what we could not win in battle. Why wasn't I told?"

"You know the answer to that question. This is a political world, my friend," Tohr said. "Heroes don't ride silver dragons to glory anymore. They wade through the trenches of words, taking what they can and counting every small victory no matter how it is won."

"Even victories without honor?" Valian asked.

"The honor will come later," Tohr explained. "Be realistic, Valian. The Knights of Solamnia are dying. They've never learned the great lesson Lord Ariakan recognized from the start. Warriors need to fight wars. In peace, the Solamnics have destroyed themselves.We could defeat them in battle, but at what cost? How many lives do we save, by defeating them in this manner?

"I hate to disappoint you, my lord, but you have not won yet," Valian said. "I know your secret now."

Tohr smiled threateningly. "If you really wanted to thwart our plans, you wouldn't make the mistake of announcing yourself here, tonight."

"I offer you a way out, an honorable way. Ask for another vote, and this time exclude Lady Mirielle's name from nomination. Gunthar was right. We'd be better off working together instead of against each other," Valian urged. "We'd be stronger, greater, nobler."

"And what about our queen? What about Takhisis?" Trevalyn hissed.

"Takhisis is dead," Valian snapped. "She died that day at the High Clerist's Tower, when Lord Ariakan called her name, to no avail."

"She didn't die. She only retreated from the fury of Chaos. She will return," Trevalyn said vehemently.

"It doesn't matter. We can't wait for her to return," Valian said. "The best thing we can do right now is unite both knighthoods."

"My friend, for an elf, you really are naive," Tohr laughed. "What was Gunthar's dream but a way to absorb us into the Knights of Solamnia without having to defeat us in battle. It was Gunthar who sent the letter to Lady Mirielle, Gunthar who proposed we join our two orders into one. Granted, we had already placed draconians on the island in the hopes of gaining a foothold here. We also sent them to negotiate with Pyrothraxus, or else we'd have had to fight him as well as the Solamnics. As we've learned with the sinking of *Donkaren*, treaties with the dragon are tenuous at best.

"Gunthar's letter came as a complete surprise to us. Haven't you realized that that is where Gunthar's genius lay? He'd have been the first Grand Master of the combined order and could have directed it as he wished. As an order, the Knights of Takhisis would have vanished, while the Knights of Solamnia lived on under a new name. All we did was turn the tables on his plan."

"Not yet," Valian countered. "It won't work. I shall expose you."

"You don't realize the precariousness of your position," Tohr said.

"My position has always been precarious," Valian said.

"You fancy yourself a hero, going to save the Knighthood from itself, like Sturm Brightblade?" Tohr barked mockingly. His voice grew sinister as his features drew into a snarl. "Dead men make poor heroes."

Reacting suddenly and swiftly, Valian drew his sword before Tohr could call for help. He leveled it at his master's heart, ready to strike the death blow.

Tohr froze. Trevalyn stood at his side, trembling either with fear or anger. Tohr tried to calm himself to speak, but it did little good. When he spoke, his voice quavered with fear. "You'd not kill an unarmed man?" he asked.

"Where is your sword?" Valian growled through clenched teeth.

"I don't need a sword," Tohr answered. "I have a Thorn!"

With that, he seized Trevalyn by the sleeve and flung him at the dark elf. The gray-robed Knight shrieked in surprise as Valian's sword slid between his ribs.

"It is bad luck . . . to kill . . . a mage," Trevalyn gasped as he clung to the sword. Blood flecked his lips and poured from his breast, staining his gray robes to black.

Valian, momentarily thrown, yanked free his sword. Trevalyn fell at his feet. "You have no more magic," he said to the corpse, "and I never liked you anyway."

He turned to pursue Tohr but found the Knight of Skulls already outside the door, shouting for his guard. With a

THE ROSE AND THE SKULL ❧

snarl of rage, Valian slashed aside the curtain and burst out
the window, escaping to the battlement just as three
Knights erupted into the room, swords drawn.

*　*　*　*　*

Liam's candle had burned down to a stub no bigger than
his big toe. Gunthar's papers lay before him on the desk,
and still he had not begun. Despite the Knighthood's pressing need for some kind of direction and order, he couldn't
bring himself to begin the task. Was it fear of failure, his
own failure, or was it fear of having to announce that Gunthar's Revised Measure was a failure? Could he bring himself to admit that possibility before everyone?

There were so many other things to consider right now.
There was his failure at the vote of succession, and the news
brought by Valian Escu of the draconian stronghold. During
his interview later that evening with Jessica Vestianstone,
she'd confirmed everything Valian said, even adding to what
he'd been told. She'd expanded on the part of the tale concerning the priest, Nalvarre Ringbow. She told Liam of Nalvarre's encounter in the forest with a creature able to take the
form of anyone it killed and of the attack on his house while
he was away. She described the injuries to the hound Millisant. When she mentioned it, he seemed to remember some
talk among the grooms that one of the hounds had not
returned from the hunt, but at the time he'd paid it no mind.
Jessica had broken down in tears when describing the
destruction of Isherwood. She'd wept for it as though
mourning the passing of an old and very dear friend.

Liam sympathized, though it was not in his nature to
show sympathy. All the old ways and old places were passing away, without anything to take their place: the gods, the
Knighthood, even magic. As much as he distrusted magic,
Liam was forced to admit the world was a better place with

it than without. There were no true heroes in the new age, and those left over from the last age were proving to be straw, powerless scarecrows of their former selves, gully dwarves living off the leavings of a glorious world destined never to return.

Liam took a deep breath and steeled himself. He lit a new candle from the old one and set it on the desk, then reached for the top sheet of the stack of manuscripts closest to him.

He went page by page, marking out with his pen the passages irrelevant to the whole of the work. Outside his room, darkwatch came and went, and his pen continued to scratch. Sometimes he laughed at what he read, sometimes he shook his head with sorrow, but on into the night he worked, forgetting his supper, forgetting sleep, forgetting everything but the work before him. Rising late, the new white moon shone through his window. He stopped briefly to open a new bottle of ink.

Liam reached for the next page and spread it on the desk, his pen poised above it, when a scrap of paper fluttered from the top of the stack and landed upside down before him. He flipped it over and read,

Abandon this foolish notion and leave this land, or you and all your Knights will suffer the consequences.

Liam sat back in his chair and read it again. He held the paper up to the candlelight and saw that it appeared torn from a book. The watermark was of Betterman's, a bindery in Kalaman.

Before he had a chance to ponder the note, there came a reluctant knock at his door. Still holding the note, he cautiously approached the door, listening for sounds. When he heard none, he asked through the door "What do you want?"

"Milord, forgive me, but there is a man here who

demands to see you," answered the captain of the guard from the hall outside.

"At this hour?" Liam asked. His instincts were aroused since hearing the priest's tale of dopplegangers or sivak draconians murdering people and taking their shape. "Who is he?"

"He is the priest who arrived with Lady Jessica this afternoon," the captain said. "I told him you were very busy, but he insisted."

"Tell him I'll see him in the morning," Liam said.

Another voice answered, shouting, "I must see Sir Liam!"

"Sir Liam will see you in the morning. Now you must go!" the captain warned.

"I have news of Gunthar's death. I have been to the crypt!" the man said. Sounds of a struggle began.

Liam gasped and jumped to the door, angrily snatching it open. "Bring him here," he hissed. "And be quiet about it. You'll wake the entire castle."

The captain, a tall powerfully built Ergothian, dragged Nalvarre Ringbow into the room and unceremoniously dumped him on the floor. "You can go," Liam said, waving the warrior to the door. "Tell no one," he added.

With a baffled expression, the captain of the guard closed the door behind him. Nalvarre rose to his feet, brushed back his hair and turned to face Sir Liam.

"What is this about visiting the crypt?" Liam asked as he moved behind the heavy oaken desk, placing it between the wild man and himself. At the same time, he used the desk to conceal the dagger in his hand. "That is a holy place forbidden to all but the initiated."

Nalvarre cleared his throat. "You have been told that I spent some time with a gully dwarf named Uhoh Ragnap, and that he claimed to be present at the time of Gunthar's death," Nalvarre said.

Liam nodded impatiently.

Nalvarre continued, "Uhoh did a remarkable job of imitating the manner in which Lord Gunthar died. And he mentioned several other things, about the dog Garr for instance, that made me suspicious as to the cause of Lord Gunthar's death."

"The cause of Lord Gunthar's has already been determined by Trevalyn Kesper. He said that . . ." Liam's voice trailed off as he raised an eyebrow.

"Ah, now you begin to see why I was in the crypt," Nalvarre said. He stepped forward and reached into his pocket.

Reacting swiftly, Liam stepped back, his dagger poised to strike. Nalvarre halted, his hand half out of his pocket.

"I have no weapon," he said. "Look." He inched the scrap of paper between his fingers out enough for Liam to see. "It's only a bit of paper."

Liam lowered his weapon.

Nalvarre breathed a sigh of relief and carefully unfolded the paper. "I took these from the wound on Gunthar's thigh," he explained as he laid the paper on the desk.

"You did not desecrate the body!" Liam said in alarm.

"No, of course not,"' Nalvarre laughed nervously. "I found them right on the surface of the wound."

Cautiously, Liam leaned forward to look. Several tiny amber beads lay in a crease of the otherwise blank scrap of paper.

"Before I came to Sancrist, I learned from the elves of Qualinesti of a poison sometimes used by draconians to envenom their arrows," Nalvarre said.

"Poison?" Liam exclaimed.

"When dried, if hardens into amber-like nodules. It only dissolves in one substance—blood. No other liquids have an effect upon it," Nalvarre said.

"How can you prove what you are saying?" Liam asked.

"I have come here to test the poison," Nalvarre said, "so that you may see with your own eyes. If you will pass me that bottle of brandy, we can begin."

Warily Liam took a bottle from the table behind him and handed it to the priest. Nalvarre removed the cork and tipped the bottle until a little brandy spilled out into his cupped palm. Then, dipping his finger into the liquid, he shook a drop onto one of the amber beads. The drop splattered on the paper, staining it, but the bead remained unchanged.

"Now, if you would be so kind," Nalvarre said, holding out his hand.

Liam looked at it without understanding.

"With your dagger," the priest said as he wiggled his fingers.

Liam took Nalvarre's hand and held it firmly in his own. Reversing the dagger, he pricked the priest's thumb. Nalvarre jerked, and a drop of blood welled from the tiny wound.

Careful not to let the wound touch the bead, Nalvarre squeezed his thumb above the paper. A drop of blood swelled, dangling for what seemed an eternity, before finally falling. It splattered on the paper next to the brandy stain.

As the blood soaked into the paper, the amber beads began to shrink, then disappeared as they dissolved in the blood.

Liam's fist slammed on the desk, sending stacks of papers sliding to the floor. "They did poison him!" he snarled.

"That's why the draconians hunted the gully dwarf so relentlessly, because he knew Gunthar's secret," Nalvarre said.

"What secret?" Liam asked, the blood rising in his face.

"Something Gunthar whispered to the gully dwarf just before he died. As it was told me, 'the book . . . Kalaman . . . Liam . . . in bell room . . . tell him . . . tell no one else.' I think it might have something to do with the Revised Measure."

"Perhaps," Liam pondered this surprising information hopefully. If Gunthar had finished the Measure and hidden it somewhere, it would certainly be welcome news. But where? In the bell room? There wasn't a bell room in Castle uth Wistan.

Perhaps in Kalaman? Kalaman!

His eyes shot to the note in his hand, to the watermark on it, from Kalaman. The book he'd given Gunthar several years ago, a book which was kept not in the bell room, but in Belle's room, the former bedchamber of Gunthar's lady-wife. The room now occupied by . . . .

"I want Lord Tohr brought to me this instant!" Liam shouted as he stalked to the door. He jerked it open.

Liam stepped back from the open door, finding Lady Jessica already there, her arm raised as though about to knock. Her mouth gaped open.

"Lady Jessica!" Liam shouted. "What are you doing here? Excuse me please. Guards!" he shouted, then stepped back again in surprise. "You!"

Valian, held firmly by two Knights of the Sword, struggled as though to escape.

"Sir Valian came to my room and asked me to be brought to you," Jessica tried to explain. "He said it was important."

"I'll say it is," Liam said as the captain of the guard appeared at the door. "Captain, hold this elf. Don't try to escape, Valian."

"I came here to warn you," Valian shouted as the captain entered the room with drawn sword, "not to . . . escape."

"Warn us of what?" Liam asked.

"That all along Lord Tohr has schemed to take control of the Knights of Sancrist Isle," Valian said, "and that he had Gunthar killed. I don't know how."

"It was poison," Nalvarre said.

"I suspected as much," Valian said.

The captain of the guard stood in the center of the room, looking in confusion from one person to the next.

"Lord Gunthar was poisoned?" the captain of the guard asked.

At that moment, a guard appeared at the open door. He glanced around the room for a moment, as though looking for someone in particular. His eyes lighted on the captain.

"Captain, Sir Liam, Trevalyn Kesper has been found dead in the chambers of Lord Tohr Malen," he said.

"That was my doing," Valian said.

"And what of Lord Tohr?" Liam asked.

"He is not in his room. All the other Knights of Takhisis are missing as well. The watch is having trouble finding many of our own Knights as well. Perhaps the others . . ."

They turned at the sound of horns from the courtyard. Footsteps pounded in the hall. Liam raced across the room and threw open the window. An arrow thudded into the heavy curtain beside his head.

Outside, men shouted Solamnic challenges, and metal clashed against metal. Axes rang like hammers on shields, and men cried out in pain. Fires flared up, lighting all the sky.

Liam turned, a tear in his eye. "Brother against brother," he groaned. "What have we come to?"

Chapter Twenty-Seven

Despite the Cataclysm, which shook the land to its foundations, and the Chaos War, which shook the world to its core, robbing it of both its gods and its magic, the Whitestone Glade had endured virtually unchanged, a strange and magical place. The monolithic pale white stone and the meadow surrounding it had been held a blessed sanctuary by the people of this land. No matter the weather, in winter as well as in summer, the weary found rest there, the tormented peace.

For the Knights of Solamnia, the Whitestone Glade was their most sacred place. Legend stated that Vinus Solamnus had received his celestial vision of an order of honorable Knights at Whitestone Glade and that the gods themselves had sanctified it. Certainly some of the most important decisions concerning the fate of Krynn had been made here. It was here during the War of the Lance that a dragon orb was destroyed and the dragonlance was revealed, thus directing the course of the war from certain disaster to eventual victory. When the power of the dragonlance was demonstrated, the stone itself was split to its core. There were some who mourned its defacement in such a vulgar and melodramatic display, but the magic of the Whitestone had not been harmed. It bore its wound

like a proud old soldier, with dignity. A few even claimed
it was more beautiful than before.

It was natural that the survivors gathered there, as the
moon shone down, filling up the glade as though with
silver water. In the distance through the trees, numerous
fires burned a deep golden red. It would have been a magical sight, with a sylvan loveliness, were it not for the
knowledge that each pillar of smoke and each merry flame
was a house, or a barn full of the summer's harvest. Slowly,
singly or in weary pairs, Knights straggled into the glade
and collapsed near the Whitestone, where a group of
Knights had gathered around a bonfire. One or two stood
guard, but there seemed little need for a watch any longer.

"They are gone," Valian commented as he bandaged his
wounded arm. Blood ran from a cut on his brow, and his
armor was rent in a half-dozen places. "I imagine they're
half way to Xenos by now."

Liam rose and stood quietly for a moment near the
Whitestone, weighing his thoughts. Everyone looked at
him expectantly, even the dark elf. Lady Meredith sat in
the grass with most of her battered armor strewn about
her, a bloody sword lay across her knees. Ellinghad
Beauseant stood at the edge of the firelight, warily keeping watch in the night. With a towel and a bowl of watered
wine, Lady Jessica cleaned a ghastly slash to the ear of the
Lord High Warrior, Sir Quintayne. Nalvarre assisted her,
directing her efforts with his bandaged hands. He'd
fought at the stables, protecting the horses, wielding a
quarterstaff with deadly purpose, but staves against
swords is rarely a fair contest, and the wounds he sported
on hands, head, and chest bore this out.

Compared to the skirmish in the stables, the fighting in
the courtyard had been horrendous, bloody, a tragedy in
the annals of the Knighthood. No clear lines were drawn.
Knights of Takhisis had fought alongside Knights of

Solamnia, but against other Knights of Takhisis and Solamnia. Lord Tohr, wielding the terrible magic of Nightbringer, the black mace once owned by Dragonhighlord Verminaard, wreaked havoc among those opposing him. The heaviest fighting had taken place at the postern gate, as the forces under Liam tried to prevent the forces of Tohr from escaping. There Valian had proved himself, winning Liam's ultimate trust by capturing Nightbringer and bringing the trophy from the battle. Nightbringer, and its owner's right hand, now lay in the grass near the fire. Thus wounded, Lord Tohr had fled into the night.

Unfortunately, most of the Knights loyal to Tohr escaped with him. Liam's forces pursued them into the forest, where the Dark Knights and their allies set torch to barn, cottage, and crib. Over half the castle's garrison had been lost this night and for nothing. Nothing was resolved. Many had died fighting, but many, many more fled, joining Lord Tohr and his promises of glory. Quite a number of these were blooded Knights — a terrible blow to the Solamnic ranks — while those few who'd come over from the Knights of Takhisis didn't even begin to replace the Solamnics lost in the battle, much less those who'd gone over to Lord Tohr.

To say that the battle resolved nothing was perhaps not entirely true. It had concluded the question of who would lead the Knights of Sancrist Isle—no one. Gunthar's dream of a single united order had died, and the Knights of Solamnia were reborn from the ashes (a little worse for wear, it was true).

Quintayne impatiently brushed aside Lady Jessica's hesitant ministrations and pointed at Tohr's hand, lying on the grass. "There's your coat of arms," he said, laughing, to Valian. "Severed hand and mace on a field of red."

Valian stared back at him with his cold, blue eyes until Quintayne's laughter nervously subsided. "I hardly think this is the time for morbid jokes," he whispered.

"Quite true, Valian. Now is the time for hard decisions," Liam said, staring up at the waning moon. "What shall be our next move? As Valian said, Tohr and his allies will be fortified within Xenos before the next night falls. They are probably dispatching wyvern couriers for reinforcements this very moment. They'll want to strengthen their position and hold it, and with Pyrothraxus guarding their rear, they could very well succeed. Should we pursue and try to catch them?"

"We'd never find them. They are scattered throughout the forest, I'd imagine, following a hundred different trails to Xenos," Valian said. "Such a hunt would be fruitless and only serve their needs by causing us to waste valuable time."

"Let's not forget that we ourselves gave the Knights of Takhisis the citadel at Xenos, and now the people there will suffer for it," Ellinghad said from the edge of the shadows.

"And what do you suggest we do?" Quintayne asked.

"It's obvious what we need to do," Ellinghad said. "Raise the alarm, muster our forces from all over the island. Lay siege to Xenos as soon as possible and drive out the Knights of Takhisis before they have time to prepare."

"Xenos was our gathering point should anything go wrong," Valian said. "Lord Tohr had it provisioned to withstand a siege of many weeks, long enough for reinforcements to arrive from Ansalon. There are secreted several wyverns in the cellar; they are ready to carry messages at a moment's notice. As you can see, they are already prepared."

"Then we have no time to lose!" Ellinghad urged.

"Have you forgotten about poor Uhoh?" Jessica cried. Quintayne snorted derisively.

"I believe Jessica has a point, " Lady Meredith said. "We

cannot leave the draconian stronghold in a position to molest our lines of supply. They are sure to send agents to wreak havoc among the civilian population. The draconians might even attempt to strike here, at the heart of the Knighthood."

"That's not my point at all," Jessica argued. "My point is that Uhoh is trapped in that awful place because of what he knew about Lord Gunthar's death. As soon as the draconians learn what has happened here, they'll kill him for sure."

"What's the point of rescuing him?" demanded Quintayne.

Nalvarre leaped to his feet, his face a scarlet color beneath his beard. "The point is, if not for that gully dwarf, you'd be handing over control of this Knighthood to the Knights of Takhisis tomorrow morning, right here in this very place, and willingly!" A cool white hand reached up and touched his arm. He seemed to start, then glanced down at Lady Jessica. The color slowly drained from his face. "I'm sorry," he said to the Knights, "but I do not think you should forget the noble service Uhoh Ragnap has performed for you."

"Yet Lady Meredith is correct. The draconian stronghold is a threat to us," Liam said.

"Not so grave a threat as the Knights at Xenos," Ellinghad said.

"That is what we have to decide," Liam said. "Do we lay siege to Xenos before the Knights of Takhisis can bring in reinforcements, or do we first go after Uhoh and attack the draconians?"

"Let's not forget about Pyrothraxus," Valian said. "There is some arrangement between the draconians and the dragon. After all, he did attack Isherwood in an attempt stop us from bringing the gully dwarf's tale to light."

"Quite right," Liam said. "Quite important."

Everyone grew silent as the leader of the Knights of

Solamnia considered his options. Liam paced slowly before the sacred stone, his brows knit, his hands clasped behind his back. The air in the glade stirred with a fresh breeze from the north, sending shreds of smoke swirling like wraiths across the open meadow. Minutes crept by. The Whitestone brooded over the scene like a pale giant, his face turned to gaze at the heavens and the pale white moon coursing overhead.

Suddenly, Liam stopped and knelt beside the Whitestone. He ran his fingers through the grass at its base, being careful not to actually touch the sacred stone. With a small smile, he plucked something from the grass and stood up. By this time everyone was watching him. He turned his face to the moon.

"He missed a piece," he said to the sky and laughed.

He held out what he had found in the grass for all to see. It glinted in the moonlight. "Do you know what this is?" he asked. No one answered.

"It is a piece of a dragon orb," Liam said. "The dragon orb shattered here at the Council of Whitestone almost forty years ago. The elves and the Knights of Solamnia were at the brink of war over the orb, while the armies of darkness were sweeping across Krynn. A very dear friend of Lord Gunthar's was at that council, and it was he who saw what needed to be done, and he did it.

"He smashed the orb that day, destroying the prize for which the Knights and elves would have fought each other, much as we did here tonight." Liam paused, looking back toward Castle uth Wistan. "After he had smashed the orb, he said rather bravely, 'We kender know we should be fighting dragons, not each other.' With the prize no longer tempting them, the Knights of Solamnia and the elves turned their attention to winning the war against the armies of Takhisis.

"That hero's name was Tasslehoff, and he was only a

small person, not very important to anybody except his nearest friends."

Liam thought for a bit, staring but without seeing the tiny crystal shard lying in the palm of his hand. "Kender aren't the only small people in this world," he said. "There are also the gully dwarves, a race that seems even less important than kender in the grand scheme of things.

"I will tell you one more story, and then I'll shut up. I know I am boring you with all this history, but we humans forget our history all too easily. And I do have a point to make," Liam said.

"This is the story as Gunthar told it to me. He learned it from Sturm Brightblade.

"It was during the War of the Lance. A group of heroes had been sent to the fortress of Pax Tharkas to divert the dragonarmies from their attack on Qualinesti. Inside the fortress, the group became separated. Tasslehoff Burrfoot and the wizard we know as Fizban were alone, and they discovered that a certain helpless, and to all appearances worthless, gully dwarf had been doomed to feed a dragon, quite literally, as he was fated to be the dragon's supper. Now the wise thing for Tasslehoff and Fizban would have been to find their way back to the others to help organize the resistance against the dragonarmies. They chose instead to rescue the gully dwarf. Why? Not because it was the wise thing to do. In fact, it was foolish, and it almost cost them their lives. What they didn't know, and what the other heroes didn't know, was that the group's plan had been discovered and a trap laid to capture them all. It was Tasslehoff and Fizban's foolish quest to rescue a gully dwarf that disrupted those plans and eventually led to the mission's success.

"They rescued Sestun, not because it was wise or militarily sound. They did it because it was the right thing to do."

Liam grew quiet then, looking in turn at each of the

gathered Knights. He cleared his throat, his voice little more than a whisper. "We'll give them time to barricade themselves inside the fortifications at Xenos, and then we'll lay siege to the place. However, the wyvern riders from Xenos will never reach Ansalon alive."

"How can you be so sure?" Quintayne asked.

"The silver dragons. They guard the island ceaselessly. Now that we are openly at war they'll not allow anything to escape."

"We saw them at Castle Isherwood. When they came Pyrothraxus fled. So that means it will be days before the Knights at Xenos realize their messengers haven't gotten through," Valian said excitedly.

"Correct," Liam answered.

"That gives us time to plan, time to coordinate our assault," Quintayne said.

"And time to deal with the draconians," Meredith added with a grin.

"And rescue the gully dwarf," Liam added. "He is, after all, a hero. If he were human, we'd not hesitate to rescue him."

Lady Meredith rose and crossed the grass between the fire and the Whitestone to stand beside Liam. "That's right, Liam," she said, her voice choked with emotion. "You are absolutely right."

"But what about Pyrothraxus?" Valian asked.

"Pyrothraxus has retreated to his lair at Mount Nevermind. The silver dragons assure me that he will remain there for some time. It seems they surprised him at Isherwood and gave him a lesson he will long remember," Liam said.

"How do you know all this?" Quintayne asked.

"Since the War of the Lance, the master of Castle uth Wistan has ways of contacting the silver dragons. When I became Lord High Justice, Lord Gunthar showed me many of them. I have been in contact with them this night. Some of them were here tonight, during the fighting, though I doubt any of you recognized them, and more were watching." His eyes strayed to the starry heavens.

"If not for the silver dragons, Pyrothraxus would have long ago driven us from Sancrist," Liam continued, whispering. "We owe them more than anyone knows. It was through Lord Gunthar's careful diplomacy that so many have stayed here on Sancrist, guarding the heart of the Knighthood, while their fellow dragons retreated to their lairs in the Dragon Isles, abandoning humanity to the new dragons from across the sea."

"As long as they are holed up in Xenos, the Knights of Takhisis are harmless." Quintayne agreed, "Meanwhile, let's deal with Castle Slagd, the draconian fortress."

Chapter Twenty-Eight

"It will not be easy," Liam said. "These draconians are not the normal sort. They've somehow managed to keep their stronghold a secret for at least two years, possibly more."

While he spoke, a servant poured brandies and served them to the other Knights in the library. It was late, only a few hours before dawn. The Knights had left White-stone Glade in order to make hasty preparations for their next move.

Liam continued, "According to the gully dwarves, whom I had the pleasure of interviewing after the Grand Chapter . . ." The other Knights laughed. ". . . the draconians are led by someone called The Old Man. He is some sort of master of assassins, by my guess an aurak draconian, the most powerful kind. They are magic users, so that makes him doubly dangerous. The gully dwarves also assured me that there are not more than two draconians in the place, but we all know what that means. We must decide the best way to approach this problem, whether we should assault the castle in force, or send a small rescue party to find the gully dwarf and escape with him."

After much debate, it was decided that a small rescue party would work best. Even if Liam could spare the Knights to make up a large force, he had no way of getting them to the draconian castle. In any case, an assault would only serve to get the poor gully dwarf killed.

Instead, Liam chose a party of seven Knights to send on the rescue mission: Lady Jessica Vestianstone, Lady Meredith, the gully dwarf Glabella, two young Knights of the Crown, Ladies Michelle and Gabrielle. Sir Ellinghad also begged to go along, to attone for his voting against Sir Liam.

Liam finally chose Sir Valian. His wilderness skills would go far toward getting the group close to the fortress. "Besides," Liam added, "I believe Sir Valian has a score to settle with someone there."

"Indeed I do," Valian said into his glass. He drained its contents in one gulp.

* * * * *

When they had all gone, some to snatch a few precious hours of rest before dawn came fresh and rosy fingered, Liam paused with his back resting against the door and took a deep breath. This is it, he said to himself. Paladine, I pray I've made the right decision. I think it's what Gunthar would have done. No, I am sure of it. Now, only one more thing to do. He walked to the fireplace and ran his fingertips along the edge of the mantle. As though searching for something, his fingers played across the surface of the wood, feeling each bump and groove. With a muted click, a false brick on the hearth swung open, revealing a small compartment behind it. Liam reached inside and withdrew a tiny silver bell. He rang it vigorously, but it made no sound, and he returned it to its secret compartment.

Satisfied, he walked to the window and opened it. A brisk autumn air entered the room, bringing with it smells of smoke from the fires still raging in some parts of the forest. Liam breathed deeply of it, feeling it course through his body, as he stood in the open window and watched the night sky.

Among the stars gleaming overhead, one in particular caught his attention, one that seemed to move occasionally, though to a casual observer it would seem nothing more than a trick of the clouds racing overhead. As he watched, the star detached itself from the firmament and descended toward the castle. The closer it came, the less like a star it seemed, and more like some object of polished silver, which reflected the light of the fires burning here and there in the forest. As it dropped into the shadow of the trees, it disappeared. A few moments later, a human figure detached itself from the shadows of the battlements and approached Liam.

"Greetings, Lord Ehrling," the shadow whispered. A silver-haired man with elven features stepped into the light spilling from Liam's window. He was wrapped entirely in dark heavy robes, but his sapphire eyes glimmered like a low fire in the shadow of his cowl. A few strands of long silver hair spilled from the hood and onto his shoulders. "You rang the bell that only our ears can hear. I came."

"I need your help," Liam said. "I need the help of all the silver dragons on Sancrist. I am sending a small group of knights to the north end of the island. . . ."

Chapter Twenty-Nine

"Come. We go now," Glabella hissed. "This way." She pointed at a narrow overhang of rock, under which the shadows seemed especially deep and dark, bespeaking the probability of a cave. Castle Slagd brooded above them like some great carrion bird or crag-faced gargoyle, hunched and watchful. Its black walls rose in impossibly slender towers not unlike fangs, from which fantastic minarets hung, suspended as though by magic. The stormy sea crashed thunderously below.

The rocks where the Knights huddled were slick with sea spray and rain, and the Knights themselves were all but soaked. Jessica's short brown locks clung to her face as she looked up at the castle above them, and she wondered how they'd ever get inside.

Glabella stomped her foot in impatience. Valian snarled at her, "We can't go anywhere until our weapons are free."

He pointed at the half-dozen stone draconians lying among the rocks at their feet, the Knights' swords protruding from their petrified bodies. They'd surprised the patrol of baaz guards and given urgent battle, among the boulders beside the sea, until no enemies remained alive. Jessica tended a cut on Lady Meredith's brow, and Valian's cloven shield lay in the sand, but this was all the damage they suffered.

Like all baaz draconians, when slain their bodies turned instantly to stone, trapping the weapons of their enemies. Only Lady Meredith had withdrawn hers in time. She wiped it clean of the black draconian blood and returned it to its sheath, but the others were forced to wait until the stone bodies turned to ash and released their swords. Sir Ellinghad had gone up the shelf of rock to keep watch for other patrols.

The silver dragons had deposited them at a sandy cove about three miles away, and for the last few hours, they'd scrambled across that hard, broken landscape to reach this point by the sea, where Glabella said the secret entrance lay. Now the only thing to do was wait and try to keep as dry as possible.

A storm such as few had ever witnessed was lashing the rugged coast. Huge waves pounded the rocky shoreline, tossing spray and foam hundreds of yards inland. Icy rain blown by gale winds stabbed like daggers at exposed skin, making the Knights thankful for their armor. Glabella enjoyed no such protection. Only the thick mat of her hair, which shed water like an otter's skin, protected her face from the storm's worst.

Earlier that morning, in the bleak darkness, they'd exited Castle uth Wistan with their packs, weapons, and supplies, and found three silver dragons waiting in the courtyard.

The three dragons had agreed to transport the group over the wild mountainous north of Sancrist Isle, to a place near the draconian castle, but they wouldn't be playing a part in any assault. Once the Knights were safely on the ground, the silver dragons were to return to keep watch on Pyrothraxus.

Sir Liam stood on the battlements and watched them rise into the air. The wind from their wings whipped his long Solamnic mustaches and stung his eyes to tears. He raised his hand in farewell. When they were no longer visible against the night sky, he paced the battlements, deep in thought, until sunrise.

Dawn rose in a glut of scarlet and crimson, promising a storm before the day was done. The mountains of Sancrist loomed before them jagged, wild, and merciless. Few but gnomes lived there anymore since the coming of Pyrothraxus, and so there was no one to see the three silver dragons passing, higher even than the clouds racing before the storm.

As fast as the dragons flew, the storm flew faster, and it crashed ashore before they reached the citadel of the draconians. As the lead dragon sighted Castle Slagd, a fork of lightning split the formation, forcing two of the dragons to veer left. For a few terrifying moments, they vanished into the black clouds, then they reappeared and all three glided along the shore until they spotted a sheltered cove, offering a place to land out of the wind.

The dragons had deposited them on the sand and hurried away before the full fury of the storm struck. The Knights set out, climbing a rocky slope, until at its summit, they saw the draconian castle in the distance, starkly illumined by a flash of lightning.

Now rain continued mercilessly as they huddled behind boulders, waiting for the dead draconians to turn to ash and free their trapped weapons. Thunder shook the skies and lightning leaped from the mountain tops, while the rising sea surged around their feet, washing the draconian bodies. It seemed possible that their weapons would be lost, but then one sword toppled over as the stone crumbled, then another and another, and the Knights waded out to retrieve them before the surf washed them away.

Finally, everyone was ready. Ellinghad descended from his watch, reporting no movement within sight. Glabella pointed up the hill at the cave, and wordlessly they climbed to it. They entered cautiously, with Valian in the lead, as his elvish eyes gave him the advantage in the dark. Glabella stalked beside him, one hand in her bag, ready to wield the mighty magics she promised were at her disposal. The others lit torches and followed.

* * * * *

Grand Master Iulus drummed his claws impatiently on the arm of his golden throne. The throne was a recent acquisition, taken from a minotaur galley sailing from the landless west. The minotaurs had died to the last bull without revealing the source of the throne or the place from whence they'd sailed, but to Iulus it didn't really matter. He wasn't an explorer or even an adventurer. He was a Grand Master of assassins, and so that meant he was an opportunist. The throne was an opportunity he could not resist.

To General Zen, however, the throne was a symbol of degeneration. He looked upon it with disgust, seeing his Grand Master slouching there like some filthy hobgoblin king, his mind filled with greed and petty desires.

"So, our little friend still won't talk, eh?" Iulus said. "We shall have to do something about that."

"My lord, I believe we are wasting our time with the miserable creature. It is obvious that he has told us everything. We should kill him and be done with it, as Lady Alya suggests," Zen said.

"Your job is not to think," Iulus purred dangerously, "nor to listen to the councils of humans, no matter how pretty. This gully dwarf knows more than he is telling."

"But he is only a gully dwarf," Zen protested.

Iulus rose from his throne. "Do you dare disagree with me?" he snarled. His twisted, malformed draconian face grew livid, the exposed veins and muscles pulsed, almost seeming to glow. "Who do you think you are? I am the master here. I trained you in the arts of assassination. I trained all of you. Without me, you'd still be a mercenary licking the boots of every hobgoblin chieftain with two more pennies than his rival."

The sivak general growled but held his tongue. "Forgive me, my lord," he said, bowing.

"Bring the gully dwarf here, and bring that self-proclaimed Highbulp, Mommamose. Perhaps young Uhoh would respond better if his dear old mother were under the lash," Iulus directed.

"Yes, my master," Zen said. He bowed and prepared to leave.

"Oh, and inform Lady Alya. I think she might enjoy this," Iulus laughed. "Tell her that if Uhoh refuses to talk this time, we'll kill him, but first we'll let him watch Mommamose die. That should pique her interest."

General Zen bowed once more, turned, and stalked from the chamber.

After he had gone, Iulus stared thoughtfully at the door. He whispered to himself, "And I think, once this is done, that I shall teach you the final lesson of assassination, my old friend."

* * * * *

"It all comes of trusting a gully dwarf," Ellinghad snarled as he plucked a draconian arrow from his chain mail and tossed it aside. Pausing a moment to gauge the time between the blows that rained against the door, he threw back the bolt and jerked it open, slashing out with his sword and felling a draconian raising a mallet. Ellinghad then slammed the door shut and dropped the bolt back in place just as a dozen or so arrows struck the other side, sending splinters flying.

Beside him, Valian ground his teeth and nodded in agreement as he bound his wrist. He'd been pinked by a draconian sword, and he only hoped the blade wasn't poisoned. Lady Michelle hadn't been so lucky. She lay a few feet away, her eyes glazing, a poisoned arrow still lodged in her shoulder.

"This way is no good," Meredith shouted. She and Jessica pressed their bodies against another door. It shook under a storm of blows.

There was a third exit from the kitchen, but in their urgency to hold the first two against the draconians, no one had yet had the opportunity to investigate it. In any case, it seemed their mission was near failure. They'd already lost Lady Gabrielle in the initial encounter, and now Lady Michelle was dying as well. With draconians attacking from two quarters, they could not hold out for long.

It all came from trusting a gully dwarf. They'd wandered in the dark for hours, it seemed, taking one wrong route after another in the endless caverns that honeycombed the mountain. They'd not seen one door or stair indicating habitation of any sort, and they would have doubted the existence of the castle entirely had they not seen it with their own eyes, perched atop the mountain two thousand feet above the sea. Occasionally they stumbled across the bones of a long-dead fish or the bleached white shell of a crab, in some of the darker, wetter caverns, where the air was stale as though it had indeed been there since the Cataclysm. Strands of glowing algae still clung to the walls, giving off a weird phosphorescence. Once, they stumbled into a rank and fetid pool of sea water, though by their best guess they were by then many hundreds of feet above the sea. The pool stretched away into echoing darkness, bespeaking great size and depth, and the Knights shuddered to think what ancient monsters of the sea might still be lurking in its depths.

Despite Glabella's misdirections, they nonetheless climbed steadily upward. The sounds of the crashing sea had steadily diminished, and at the far end of one cavern, they came upon narrow stairs delved into the wall. The stairs followed a fault in the stone, past narrow outcroppings of rock that forced the Knights to squeeze by. At one of these places, Valian found a bronze-colored draconian scale wedged in a crack in the wall. He showed it to the others, proof-positive that they were on the right track.

The stair eventually led to an iron door. The Knights had climbed to it, exhausted and out of breath, finding it curiously unguarded. Lady Meredith called a rest, while Sir Valian cautiously opened the door and peered inside. He reported an empty torchlit corridor beyond.

Glabella, now confident of where she was, led them through a maze of dark and twisting corridors. They passed doors and passages all along the way, but she strode forward with such assurance, they'd trusted they were being guided to the dungeons where Uhoh was sure to be kept, if he was still alive.

At last, she brought them to another iron door, lit by only a single smoky torch. It looked exactly like the entrance to a dungeon should look, huge and forbidding, with its ironwork rusted and hanging with dank growths of moss. Upon opening it, they found themselves thrust into the middle of a draconian barracks, with several dozen of the evil creatures caught by surprise, staring back at them. From then on, it was a fighting retreat, and with each moment that slipped by, the hope of rescuing Uhoh dwindled. They began to doubt their own chances for survival.

Valian had been stabbed, causing him to drop his weapon, and Lady Gabrielle sacrificed herself to pull him to safety. She was cut down from behind by draconian swords. As they reached the kitchen, the draconians brought up archers. The Knights had managed to shut the doors, but not quickly enough to save Lady Michelle.

Meredith shouted to Glabella, "We need a way out! Check out that other door."

The gully dwarf was paralyzed with fear. She cowered on the floor under a table, unable to move.

"I can't abide the thought that I am going to die here, for nothing," Ellinghad shouted. "This was a fool's mission."

"Look out!" Valian shouted as the third door swung open. Jessica prepared for the worst, while Glabella screamed.

A gully dwarf wearing a tall white hat entered the room carrying a pottery bowl nearly as big as himself, white gruel caked in his beard. At sight of the Knights spinning round with swords drawn, faces set to meet their death, the gully dwarf dropped the bowl of porridge, turned, and fled the way he'd come.

"Follow him!" Meredith shouted triumphantly. "Go, all of you. Run. I'll hold this door. The rest of you go. Jessica, don't forget Glabella."

"I'll not leave you," Ellinghad said. Valian sprinted through the open door. Jessica followed him, the gully dwarf tucked under her arm.

"You will," Meredith answered. "I'll hold them at this door for a moment, then follow you."

With a final look of mute protest, Ellinghad Beauseant, Knight of the Sword, dashed after his companions.

Meredith stepped away from the door, drawing her sword. In moments, the wooden planks cracked. The door burst inward, and draconians poured into the room. Lady Meredith backed into the door. The draconians licked their swords and advanced.

A shout from the corridor brought them up short. They backed away angrily, making way for the entrance of a huge silver draconian. He was heavily armored and stood a good foot taller than his fellows. He strode into the kitchen, a long, wickedly curved blade in his clawed fist. Seeing only Lady Meredith before him, he laughed.

"The Lord High Clerist!" he said with apparent delight. "My name is Zen. I wanted you to know that before you die."

She answered him with the Knight's salute to an enemy. Then, with a battle cry surprising for her small stature, she charged, her sword lancing the air before her, her red hair flying.

* * * * *

Valian slipped for perhaps the thirtieth time in the refuse and offal that littered the halls. It seemed more like the dark and dirty alleys of some ancient city than the halls of a castle only a few years old, but he was, after all, in the gully dwarf quarter.

He'd chased the surprised cook for a few hundred yards before losing both the gully dwarf and himself in the maze of twisting passages. The halls of this castle followed no recognizable pattern, and their strangeness and nightmarish quality reminded him of something. The memory fled whenever he tried to grasp it. He tried to backtrack to the kitchen, but the way only seemed to lead him deeper into the heart of a stinking nightmare.

Hoots and howls echoed through the corridors, and gibberish like the ravings of madmen. The walls narrowed and became more uneven in their spacing, until above him they meshed together, overarching the way like the branches of trees. Occasionally, some warm wet hole opened to the right or left, but as Valian stopped and looked into these, trying to decide his way, he felt eyes staring back at him from the darkness, eyes hungry and at the same time frightened. As his elven eyes grew adjusted to the darkness, he saw the warm, red outlines of their bodies, sitting in huddled groups, shifting nervously.

With a shock of horror, Valian remembered. Those days and nights and weeks of terror in the twisted and ancient depths of Silvanesti, years ago now. He'd fought his way through, avoiding legions of dragonarmies and patrols of elves, to a place where he knew no one ever ventured anymore. He'd hoped to find some lost or forgotten enclave of elves, some memory of the beauty he'd once belonged to, if only to stand at their fringes unseen, or to die there.

At last, he'd found them. Hope lifted Valian's heart at the sight of the village through the trees. The war didn't seem to have reached this place. Here no one was preparing for battle or escape. He'd approached slowly, warily, for despite everything, he still bore the stigma of being cast from the light. If seen, these elves still had the right to kill him.

Some tickling of danger warned him as he'd neared the village, but he'd ignored it, so anxious was he to find contact with his race. As he drew closer, he saw that the elves of the village walked with hunched shoulders and bent backs, and their arms seemed unusually long. No elvish voice was raised in song, only brutish grunts and snarls sounded from their throats. When one turned, as though sensing Valian's presence in the trees, Valian nearly cried out in horror at the sight of the twisted, malformed elf. Long fangs thrust up from his bottom jaw like the tusks of a boar, and his almond-shaped eyes glowed red with hate. His hair, once smooth and silken, bristled like fur.

Valian was so stricken with anguish that day, he'd been unable to move, unable to resist, as they gathered round him, grunting, snarling, drooling and touching him with their horrid claws. They grabbed him and lifted him and carried him triumphantly into the village. They brought him to an altar, where wood was piled, wood soaked with tar and oil, and they tied him to the altar, all the while dancing around his prone body. Valian had felt himself outside his own body, as though looking down on the scene from some point high above. He watched them bring torches and light the wood of his pyre, and he watched the flames lick around his body, consume his hair, caress his limbs, sear his flesh.

He hadn't died. Valian awoke on the forest floor, with the ancient and crumbling stone buildings of his dream village all around him. The village had long been abandoned and forgotten, and the forest had reclaimed it, and Valian awoke with a vision of things to come. As he stood and his hair fell about his face, it was white as ash, burned by the fires of his nightmare.

Now, apish hands reached out to touch his body, caress his flesh. Small creatures crowded around him, grunting, snarling like ghouls over a fresh grave. Terror awakened in him, but he was able to move, able to respond. Valian lashed out, and the apes leaped screaming back to their dark lairs. Valian fled; he knew not where.

Chapter Thirty

"Where is Dalian?" Ellinghad shouted as he skidded to a stop beside Jessica. Behind them, Lady Meredith's war cry echoed down the hall. The ring and crash of steel upon steel followed.

"I don't know," Jessica answered. "By the time I got here, he was gone."

"He's betrayed us," Ellinghad snarled. "Either that or he's run off to save his own miserable hide, the coward."

"I can't believe either," Jessica said. "We've just lost him. He'll be back."

Jessica bent down beside the gully dwarf. Glabella's eye were as round and white as goose eggs. "Which way to the dungeons?" Jessica asked her. "Which way to Uhoh?"

Glabella's mouth worked, but no sound came out. "Think, Glabella, think!" Jessica shouted.

The gully dwarf only closed tight her eyes and shook her head.

Suddenly, the battle at the end of the hall grew quiet. Then footsteps pounded, running. Ellinghad poised, his blade ready. Meredith appeared, bleeding from a dozen wounds. She staggered into them and collapsed, almost falling on Glabella.

"Lady Meredith!" Jessica exclaimed.

"What happened?" Ellinghad asked.

"I managed to close the door. There was a key. It won't hold them for long," she gasped. As though to confirm this, a thundering boom echoed from the direction of the kitchen as the draconians began to hammer down the door.

"Which way now?" Meredith asked as Jessica bound the more severe of her wounds. "Which way did the elf go?"

"We don't know. I think he's abandoned us," Ellinghad said.

"Damn him," Meredith cursed. "We should have known better than to trust an elf."

Jessica looked at the leader of the Sword Knights in surprise. Never before had Lady Meredith shown racial prejudices. Perhaps it was the stress of her wounds and the imminent danger.

"What about the gully dwarf? Does she know the way?" Meredith asked. Jessica helped her to her feet.

"I don't think so," Ellinghad said.

Meredith roughly grabbed Glabella by the collar of her dress. "Which way?" she snarled. "Tell us now. No more games."

Glabella only stared in wide mouthed terror. Suddenly, she lashed out, sinking her teeth into the thumb of the Knight. With a scream of pain, Meredith dropped the gully dwarf.

As soon as she hit the floor, Glabella raced away, screaming, "Slagd! Slagd!"

"Glabella!" Jessica shouted as she started after her.

"Wait. Let her go. She's no use to us," Meredith said. "Let's just pick a direction and go."

Without waiting for the others, she stalked away, choosing the opposite way in which the gully dwarf had headed.

"We came here to rescue one gully dwarf." Jessica muttered. "Shall we leave another behind?"

Behind them, the kitchen door crashed open, and draconians poured into the hall. Ellinghad ducked as a draconian arrow whistled past his head.

Jessica and Ellinghad hurried after their designated leader.

Lady Meredith chose a path which seemed to always take them around a corner just before the draconian archers loosed their arrows. A half-dozen times or more, scores of arrows buzzed angrily though space they had just vacated, or shattered against a wall where they had been standing only moments before. The Knights ran, even though fleeing the enemy was against everything they believed in. All those rules seemed silly now. The only thing to do was to save themselves long enough to save Uhoh.

After making yet another hair's breadth escape, they found themselves in a hall which ended in a door. There was no other outlet. Meredith tried the door and breathed a sigh of relief when it swung open on oiled hinges.

"Through here!" she shouted, as draconians appeared once more at the end of the hall.

Jessica and Ellinghad ducked through the door, and Meredith slammed it shut just as the draconians released their missiles. Meredith threw home a heavy iron bolt. Arrows hammered against the door like hailstones on a slate roof.

"That ought to hold them for a while," Meredith said with a laugh.

"For all the good it will do us," Ellinghad said in response.

They found themselves in a wide, circular chamber whose ceiling was lost in shadows above. In the center of the room stood a low stone slab draped with chains.

Opposite the door and dozens of feet above the floor, a narrow balcony jutted from the wall. Heavy curtains concealed the back of the balcony, but torches set in sconces to either side illuminated a short figure draped in dark robes. As the Knights stared up, the figure began to clap, slowly, in mockery of applause.

"Well done," the figure laughed. "Is this the best the Knights could send?"

"Alya!" Ellinghad shouted. "Come down here and find out for yourself."

She threw back the cowl of her robe and shook out her dark hair. "Now I ask you, would that be an honorable fight, Sir Knight? Two against one?" she said.

"Three against one," Jessica said.

"Yes," Alya laughed, "but I think the true odds are more like two against two, isn't that right, General Zen?"

"That's right, Lady Alya," Meredith answered in a deep voice.

Ellinghad and Jessica spun round and watched in horror as their leader threw back the bolt on the door and swung it open. Draconians poured into the chamber, snarling in anticipation.

"Lady Meredith!" Jessica cried.

"At these odds," Alya continued, "I think you might prefer to surrender."

Ellinghad laughed. "I'll never surrender," he said. "Death first."

"Lady Jessica?" Alya asked, a note of concern creeping into her voice.

Jessica swallowed the dry lump in her throat. "Death," she croaked.

"Well, we can't always have our own way," Alya said. "Grand Master Iulus wants you alive, and so alive you must be taken." She clapped her hands.

The draconians nearest the door parted, making way for

a figure robed in black. He strode into the room and looked up at the balcony as though awaiting an order. Ellinghad and Jessica turned to face this newcomer.

"Shaeder, I believe you have an opportunity to redeem yourself," Alya said.

The figure walked toward the Knights.

"Get behind me," Ellinghad whispered to Jessica. "When he casts his spell, you come round and attack him before he can recover."

As the bozak mage lifted his voice in chant, Ellinghad gave the Knight's salute to an enemy, then started his war cry. Before he could do anything, however, his mouth filled with some sticky substance, which also clung to his eyes and covered his limbs. Magical webs engulfed both Knights, binding them completely.

* * * * *

Valian started from a sleep, with something clutching his leg like a shackle. He lay in a pile of ash, and as he kicked himself free, he realized that the "shackle" was Glabella. The gully dwarf moaned in her sleep and tightened her grip on his ankle.

"Wake up," he hissed. "Glabella, wake up!"

Her eyes flew open, and for a moment she seemed not to realize where she was. She sank her teeth into the calf of his leg. He cried out in pain. With one mighty kick, he sent her sliding through the muck.

They lay in some side hall. A door some distance down the hall stood ajar, allowing a little light to spill out. Valian rose, staggering, feeling the bump on his head for the first time. His right shoulder and side were also sore. Obviously, in his fear-crazed flight, he'd slammed into a wall and knocked himself out. As he swayed to his feet, groaning in pain, Glabella came crawling back to him.

DRAGONLANCE

"I sorry," she whimpered.

"Don't worry about it," he said. "How did you find me?"

"I ask other Aghar. They see where you go," she answered.

"And the others? The other Knights? What about them?" he asked.

"I no like other Knights now. I like you best. We stay here," she said as she cuddled up to his leg.

Gently, he pried her loose. "Glabella, listen to me. We have to find them. We have to find Uhoh and get out of here. What happened to them?"

"Red hair lady is slagd now," Glabella answered.

"Lady Meredith?"

Glabella nodded. "She not Knight anymore, she slagd."

"A sivak," Valian murmured in horror.

"They go with her," Glabella said. "Aghar say they caught. But not Glabella. I find pretty Knight. We live here forever." Again she wrapped her arms around his thigh.

Again, he worked himself free, managing to keep her at arm's length. "We have to find them. Do you know where they have been taken?"

"No," she said stubbornly.

At a sound from behind them, Valian spun. An armored figure stood there, peering into the darkness.

"Valian?" the figure called. "Is that you?"

Glabella hissed. Valian turned, pushing the gully dwarf behind him. She clung to his legs.

"Lady Meredith," he answered smoothly.

"Thank the heavens I found you!" Meredith said. "Come on. We've found Uhoh."

"Where are the others?" Valian asked as he inched toward the Knight. Glabella's leghold threatened to trip him.

Meredith saw the gully dwarf as Valian neared the light.

"Ah, I see you've found Glabella as well. Good, very good," she said.

As Valian emerged into the light, Meredith stepped back and laughed. "Shoo, you stink," she laughed, holding her nose.

He smiled weakly and shrugged. "Lead the way," he said.

Meredith nodded and turned. In a flash, Valian's arm locked around her throat and a dagger pricked her flesh between the plates of her armor.

"Valian, what are you doing?" she croaked.

"Shhh, no more tricks, sivak," he hissed into her ear.

"Sivak? Have you gone mad?" Meredith exclaimed.

"Don't play me for a fool," Valian said. "If you want, we can wait here until you are no longer able to hold this shape, then we'll see what happens."

"By that time, your friends will be dead," Zen's voice answered from Meredith lips.

"That's why you are going to lead me to them, now," Valian said. He increased the pressure, strangling the draconian. "And don't try to change shape, or I'll spill your kidneys on this floor."

"Go ahead," the sivak grunted. "You know what will happen if you kill me?"

"I know ways to kill you safely and slowly, draconian. So unless you care to experience them, you will show me the way." Valian released his hold, freeing the sivak. He drew his sword and used its point to shove Lady Meredith forward.

"Come on, Glabella," he said.

* * * * *

At the far end of a hall stood a magnificent throne of solid gold, more fabulous than any treasure Jessica had ever seen. On it sat a creature from the darkest nightmare imaginable. It was draconian, but only partially. Its twisted face reminded the knight of pictures glimpsed in a book long ago, of the creatures supposed to inhabit the Abyss. His visage filled her with such fear and loathing that she could barely stand to look at him. He laughed as she turned her face away.

To her surprise, a very miserable looking gully dwarf lay beside her. He seemed only half-conscious. No cords bound him and he wore only a dirty loincloth. She almost burst out in tears at the sight of him. His little body was bruised and battered, his skin burned, his hair and beard singed to ash in places. Droplets of sweat spattered his forehead, and he was tossing in some fevered dream.

"Uhoh," she moaned.

"Gulpfunger!"

Jessica turned to find Mommamose also had been brought in and set beside Sir Ellinghad. The draconians were cutting the last of the webbing from his mouth. He gagged violently, which made them laugh with delight.

Despite being bound hand and foot, Mommamose managed to lunge at one of the draconians, trying to wield a gully dwarf's favorite weapon—her teeth. The kapak leaped back to avoid those flashing yellow incisors, then brought his mailed fist crashing down on her head. She slumped to the floor.

A door slammed as Lady Alya stalked into the room. She paced before the throne of Iulus, cracking her knuckles in impatience. Finally, Iulus spoke, gesturing to a pillow on the floor beside his throne. "Lady Alya, please relax and take a seat," he said in honeyed tones.

"I can't relax," she snapped. "Hasn't it occurred to you that if they have sent Knights here, then they must know of our whereabouts!"

"If they know so much then, why bother to try to rescue a gully dwarf?" Iulus crooned. "Perhaps they do not yet know how Gunthar died. If they did, the gully dwarf would be useless to them."

"Maybe useless to you, but not to us," Jessica spat.

"See there," Alya said scornfully. "I told you so. They have come because it is the right thing to do." She moved quickly to stand before Jessica. "You know everything, don't you? You're here purely for the sake of honor, aren't you?"

"I am only following orders," Jessica answered defiantly.

With a scream of rage Alya cuffed her with an iron gauntlet. Jessica crumpled to the floor.

"Lady Alya!" Iulus said.

Ellinghad spat the last of the magical webbing from his mouth. "If I were free, I'd make you regret that," he growled.

"Is that so?" she smiled as she brought her knee smashing into his stomach. He gasped and fell to the floor.

"Lady Alya!" Iulus shouted. "Restrain yourself."

"What does it matter? They'll be dead shortly," she said sulkily as she crossed to the throne and flopped onto a pillow.

"The gully dwarves, yes, but these two are much too valuable to be killed right away," Iulus said. "They'll bring a fine ransom, even though I regret not being able to keep the female for my own purposes."

"No ransom!" Alya exclaimed. "They are to be executed at once! They are too dangerous." She climbed to her feet and addressed one of the draconian guards. "Where is General Zen? He should be back with Valian by now."

"This is my domain, Lady Alya," Iulus snarled. "I don't take orders from the Knights of Takhisis. You are my guest, and these are my prisoners. I'll do with them as I like."

"You should listen to her, my master," said a voice from the doorway. "She is right. You have grown too greedy with all this talk of 'ransom.'"

Alya spun to find Lady Meredith standing in the doorway. "Zen! Where is Valian? Didn't you find him?"

Zen edged into the room, arms raised in surrender. Behind him, the dark elf warily crept, his sword poised to strike.

"I am right here, Lady Alya Starblade," he sneered.

Glabella peered around the doorpost. When she saw Uhoh lying on the floor, a whimper escaped her lips.

"Valian, my old friend," Alya smiled. "I was very surprised to learn you were part of this . . . rabble. I thought you were above this sort of thing."

"I came here for one thing, my lady," Valian said.

"And that is?" she asked as she edged toward the throne.

"Justice. You and Tohr have disgraced the Knights of Takhisis with your dishonorable schemes. I missed my chance at Tohr, but I shall not let you escape so easily." With a snarl, he shoved the sivak to the wall and charged his former leader.

General Zen caught himself before his head smashed into the stone wall. He rose and turned, shaking off the human form of Lady Meredith, just as Valian and Alya's swords clashed. He stood back and solemnly watched developments. Grand Master Iulus, it seemed, was also content to wait and see how things turned out, a hideous grin on his wizened, reptilian face.

The battle between the Knights of Takhisis seesawed back and forth before the throne. Alya gave way before Valian's superior strength, then counterattacked, putting him on his heels. As the fight grew close to the bound prisoners, Jessica gathered her wits and found Glabella near at hand.

"Glabella," she whispered.

The gully dwarf turned, her filthy face streaked with tears.

"See if you can reach my dagger. Cut our bonds," Jessica said.

"Hurry, Glabella!" Ellinghad whispered.

Hesitantly, with a glance at the Grand Master of the draconians, she crept to Jessica's side and felt for the dagger. With a smile, she freed it from the webs and began to cut away at the sticky cords binding Jessica's arms.

She didn't get far before a huge silver claw grasped Glabella by the arm and snatched her into the air. Zen wrenched the dagger from her fist, then tossed her aside. He looked down at the helpless Knights, then glanced up at his master. Iulus, greedy for the sight of blood, still watched the battle.

Jessica, sensing the sivak's next move, closed her eyes. "Make it quick and merciful," she whispered.

"My last act as a Knight of Solamnia," answered Lady Meredith's voice.

Jessica's eyes flew open, but it was still the sivak, hovering over her. Only, something was different, something about the eyes. There was no mistaking: They were the soft blue eyes of Lady Meredith Turningdale.

The sivak smiled, showing his fangs, and lifted Sir Ellinghad to his feet. With one swooping move, he cut the webs from the Knight's arms. Ellinghad struggled free and drew his sword.

"Zen!" Iulus shouted, noticing them at last.

"You have grown soft, my master," Zen said. "Let's see how you fare against a real opponent."

He rolled Jessica over and cut loose her bonds, then dropped the dagger beside her.

"Fare thee well, Lady Knight," he said in Meredith's voice, then the look of her old comrade was gone. Cold black orbs stared back at her.

Zen turned and strode from the room, motioning for the guards to follow him. Reluctantly, they obeyed.

* * * * *

Alya and Valian circled each other, seeking some weakness, some mistake, probing, feinting. Valian was slowly growing weary, while Alya wasn't even breathing hard. Blood seeped through Valian's bandages and onto his sword hand, making the hilt slippery and hard to hold.

Out of the corner of his eye, Valian saw Ellinghad streak past. That one moment of distraction was all Alya needed. Lunging quickly, she caught Valian's blade, then with a deft flip, sent it spinning through the air.

He stepped back, his arms raised.

"Justice is what you make of it, my old friend," Alya said as she raised her sword above her head.

* * * * *

Ellinghad drew his sword and kissed the hilt. Across from him, the Grand Master of draconian assassins sat in his golden throne, eyeing the Knight with contempt. Ellinghad shouted, "For Gunthar!" and charged. Iulus sat unmoving, but his chest swelled as though preparing for the blow.

All of a sudden, his head shot forward and his mouth gaped open, and a cloud of noxious gas poured forth. Ellinghad charged into it, unmindful, but the fumes robbed his legs of their strength. He stumbled and fell, his sword slipping from his grasp. He couldn't breath. He gagged. A shadow loomed above him. He looked up, blinking through the haze of his own tears. Iulus leered down at him, pointed and spoke a single word. Magical energy burst against his skull.

* * * * *

Jessica's only thought was to pull Uhoh to safety. The other Knights could take care of themselves. It was her job to rescue the gully dwarves.

Grabbing Uhoh by his arms, she dragged him to the door, then returned for Mommamose, only to find Glabella had already freed the Highbulp. The two were huddled over something and arguing. Mommamose clutched a thin wand of amber, which Glabella tugged at from one end.

"It mine!" Mommamose snarled.

"I find it at Town. I bring it here. It mine," Glabella responded.

It was at that moment that the aurak breathed forth his cloud of poison gas, felling Ellinghad. As Jessica and the two gully dwarves watched in fascinated horror, Ellinghad clawed at his throat for breath, while the cloud spread across the floor towards them. The draconian stood and spoke a word of magic, calling forth a burst of energy from his palms, which struck Ellinghad.

No!" Jessica screamed as Iulus calmly resumed his seat in his golden throne.

The gully dwarves resumed their squabble. "I say magic word."

"No I say magic word."

And then a rare event occurred. Glabella said, "I hold magic stick, you say magic word."

"Okay," Mommamose said.

Glabella stood and pointed the wand at the Grand Master. Mommamose touched the sapphire at its base. The one good eye of Iulus grew wide.

"Crackling!" Mommamose shouted.

* * * * *

Alya staggered, the sword still poised above her head, as thunder rocked the chamber. Though momentarily stunned, Valian recovered more quickly, and in one fluid motion, he drew his dagger, ducked under Alya's blow, and brought his fist up into her chest. She toppled to the floor, a dagger protruding from her heart.

* * * * *

The force of the magic knocked Mommamose and Glabella to the floor; Jessica grabbed onto something. A lightning bolt struck the heavy throne, lifting it up and sending it crashing partially through the back wall. With Iulus wedged in it, the throne hung precariously, suspended two thousand feet above the raging sea. Rain slashed through the opening in the wall.

Meanwhile, Iulus had begun a horrible transformation. Like other draconians, an aurak underwent a series of changes after death. Usually they were immolated with green flames and entered a killing frenzy. Iulus, though he raged and frothed, remained firmly stuck. The lightning bolt had melded his flesh to the gold throne, trapping him. The throne rocked with his struggles.

Jessica started from her trance when Valian touched her arm.

"Come on," he urged.

"The gully dwarves," she cried, tearing from his grasp. She rushed to Glabella's side and lifted her to her feet.

"That some magic," the gully dwarf said thickly as she rubbed her head.

Mommamose had already regained her feet. She was pointing at something, her face frozen. Jessica spun around, sickened by what she saw. She turned away.

Ellinghad had staggered upright, but he was no longer a man. He was a thing somehow clinging to life. His face and head had been blasted by the draconian's magic, his lungs destroyed by the poison gas. He clawed at the air , then turned blindly toward the tortured screams of the Grand Master.

Ellinghad lunged toward the dying draconian. A weird sound erupted from him, low and hysterical, bespeaking the madness of pain he was suffering. He stumbled into the chair, felt burning flesh beneath his fingers, and found the throat of the draconian. The green flames consumed him, but still he kept choking Iulus.

There was a tremendous crack, and the throne, the Grand Master, and the Knight vanished. Where they'd been, rain poured in, soaking the floor and raising steam from the flagstones. A cold wind blew into the room, blowing out all the candles.

In the darkness, Jessica felt a cool hand. "Let's get out of here," Valian said.

Chapter Thirty-One

The halls of the castle at Xenos were decorated with boughs of evergreen. Everywhere one looked, there were arrangements of bright scarlet crystals carved in the likeness of kingfisher feathers and tiny golden crowns. Red winter roses filled vases, and logs burned in every fireplace, spreading light and cheer to every room and chamber. The Knights as they walked their watches on the cold snowy battlements were served steaming mugs of nog or warm mulled wine. Many wore roses in their belts and wreaths of holly around their helms, all to celebrate the festivities. For tomorrow was Yule, and a fine Yule it promised to be. Not for many a year had the people felt such a sense of hope and gladness.

However, despite the foot-thick covering of freshly fallen snow, evidence of recent events offered a stark reminder of how dearly this Yuletide was bought. Here was a wall battered to rubble, there the charred skeleton of a building. In the courtyard, masons were busy erecting a pedestal for a monument. The names of many, including Quintayne, would be inscribed there. Never would the siege of Xenos be forgotten.

Even so, in the chapel of the castle, they remembered a different occasion, a Yule tragedy long past. Tomorrow was the anniversary of the Cataclysm, so the Knights commemorated the event by raising the chant of the thirteen days, of the time when the gods sent warnings of disasters to come, warnings ignored at the time.

As the service ended and the Knights filed out of the chapel, Sir Liam Ehrling found a young lady still sitting in a quiet corner. He approached her quietly, smiling.

"Lady Jessica," he said.

She looked up, her face pale. "So much pain," she whispered, her voice choked with emotion.

"The Cataclysm?" he asked. "Yes, it was a dark time, but hope renews. Evil turns upon itself, good redeems its own."

"I sometimes wonder why we fight. It seems, no matter what we do, nothing changes," Jessica said.

"That is exactly why we fight," Liam said.

"My Lord Ehrling, I have made a difficult decision. I wish to leave the Knighthood," Jessica whispered. "I want to serve Lady Crysania."

"That is a noble desire, Lady Jessica, but I cannot grant your request. I need you here," Liam said.

"You need me?" she asked, blinking up at him. "Why?"

"I will tell you, if you will accompany me to my chamber. I believe Sir Valian is waiting for us there," Liam said.

"Valian?" Jessica asked as she rose.

"Yes, I've asked him to share a midnight toast with us," Liam said as they walked from the chapel. Two Knights shut the doors behind them, bowing as Sir Liam passed.

When they reached the door to Liam's private study, it opened and Seamus Gavin stuck his red wizened face into the hall. Seeing Liam, his eyes widened.

"Ah, there you are! Seems I'm not the late one this time," said Gunthar's old friend from Palanthas.

Jessica and Liam entered the study and found a fire blazing on the hearth. Sir Valian sat near it, absently rolling a pewter mug between the palms of his hands as he stared into the flames. On a side table, a crystal decanter half-filled with pale yellow wine gleamed in a bowl.

Liam poured four glasses and passed them to those gathered. Seamus, his lap full of various papers and documents, accepted his with a smile. Without moving from his chair, the dark elf took the glass offered him and returned his gaze to the fire.

Liam walked behind his desk. It lay bare, the only thing on it a single bound volume as thick as a man's wrist. He looked at it and placed his fingertips on its cover.

"Here is the Revised Measure," he said. "I regret that Ellinghad and Meredith—" he choked, then sighed "—and Quintayne, who succumbed to the wounds he suffered here at Xenos will not be here for the unveiling. I wanted you three to know something. I trust in your judgment to keep it a secret. In his last days, torn by grief and worry for the future of the Knighthood, Lord Gunthar's mind threatened to leave him. The burden was almost too great for him. His work on the Measure suffered greatly as a result.

"This past month, I've labored long and hard to finalize his work, and I have done it, I think. The Measure is complete. My one desire is that no one else know of my, let us say, collaboration. This is Lord Gunthar's last accomplishment, his Revised Measure, not mine."

Valian nodded. "Yes, milord." Jessica also nodded, although she didn't understand why she was being trusted with this secret, especially since Liam knew her desire to leave the Knighthood.

"You know, of course, that you can trust to my discretion," Seamus said.

Liam walked to the fireplace and turned to face the dark elf.

"Sir Valian, I want to extend to you an invitation, to join the Knights of Solamnia. Your honor and your courage are beyond question. As for your past deeds, that is something you and your maker will have to deal with, when that time comes," Liam said.

"Lord Ehrling, you know as well as I do, that if you accept me into your Knighthood, you will lose the support of the elven nations. I am a dark elf, and nothing can change that," Valian said. He blinked, then turned his gaze to the fire. "I won't destroy the delicate alliance between the Knighthood and the elves. One person's feelings cannot outweigh the common good."

Liam sighed. "I thought you'd refuse, but I wanted to make the gesture."

"Thank you, sir. Your offer touches my heart," Valian softly answered.

A knock on the door interrupted them. It opened and a Knight stuck his head in the door. "He is here," he said.

"Send him in," Liam said.

The door opened wider, and Uhoh strode into the chamber. He looked about in some confusion at those gathered. For the most part, his wounds had healed, leaving no obvious scars, but something about him was different. There was an air of caution about him and even a haunted look.

"Uhoh Ragnap, I want you to meet your legal counsel, Seamus Gavin of Palanthas," Liam said.

Uhoh turned to the elderly man, staring curiously at him. Seamus shifted uncomfortably, spilling a few papers from his lap.

"Ahem . . . Yes. Master Uhoh. How do you do? I've waited a long time to meet you."

"Hello," Uhoh said.

Seamus turned to Liam. "Well?"

Liam looked at the ceiling, as if seeking guidance from the heavens. "Go ahead, Master Uhoh. Seamus has something to tell you about Papa Gunthar," he sighed.

Seamus smiled and nodded appreciatively to Liam.

"Master Uhoh, Lord Gunthar made you one of his rightful heirs."

Uhoh's face sank. Tears sprang to his eyes. "Papa," he sniffled."Papa gave me hair?"

"He has made you master of Castle Kalstan," the barrister added, " You are Uhoh Ragnap uth Kalstan now."

"Under one condition," Liam interrupted.

"What's that?" Seamus asked.

"That Lady Jessica serve as his seneschal, liaison between the new lord of my family castle and the Knights of Solamnia," Liam said.

"Lady Jessica?" Seamus asked. "Do you accept?"

"Yes," she whispered.

"So, Master Uhoh Ragnap uth Kalstan, as Lord of Castle Kalstan and honored guest of the people of Xenos and all the Knights of Solamnia, what is your first desire? Would you like a feast for all your gully dwarf friends?" Seamus asked. "How about a nice big bed?"

* * * * *

Uhoh set his candle on the floor. The echoes of the door still reverberated down the empty stairs and low dusty hall. He climbed atop the crate which Jessica had brought for him to stand on, and steeling himself, looked down.

Hesitantly, he touched Gunthar's hand. "Poor Papa," he cried as he buried his face in the old man's beard.

THE SOULFORGE
MARGARET WEIS

The long-awaited prequel to the bestselling Chronicles Trilogy by the author who brought Raistlin to life!

Raistlin Majere is six years old when he is introduced to the archmage who enrolls him in a school for the study of magic. There the gifted and talented but tormented boy comes to see magic as his salvation. Mages in the magical Tower of High Sorcery watch him in secret, for they see shadows darkening over Raistlin even as the same shadows lengthen over all Ansalon.

Finally, Raistlin draws near his goal of becoming a wizard. But first he must take the Test in the Tower of High Sorcery—or die trying.

THE CHRONICLES TRILOGY
MARGARET WEIS AND
TRACY HICKMAN

Fifteen years after publication and with more than three million copies in print, the story of the world-wide best-selling trilogy is as compelling as ever. Dragons have returned to Krynn with a vengeance. An unlikely band of heroes embarks on a perilous quest for the legendary DRAGONLANCE!

DRAGONS OF SUMMER FLAME
MARGARET WEIS AND TRACY HICKMAN

The best-selling conclusion to the stories told in the Chronicles and Legends Trilogies. The War of the Lance is long over. The seasons come and go. The pendulum of the world swings. Now it is summer. A hot, parched summer such as no one on Krynn has ever known before.

Distraught by a grievous loss, the young mage Palin Majere seeks to enter the Abyss in search of his lost uncle, the infamous archmage Raistlin.

The Dark Queen has found new champions. Devoted followers, loyal to the death, the Knights of Takhisis follow the Vision to victory. A dark paladin, Steel Brightblade, rides to attack the High Clerist's Tower, the fortress his father died defending.

On a small island, the mysterious Irda capture an ancient artifact and use it to ensure their own safety. Usha, child of the Irda, arrives in Palanthas claiming that she is Raistlin's daughter.

The summer will be deadly. Perhaps it will be the last summer Ansalon will ever know.

THE CHAOS WAR
MARGARET WEIS AND DON PERRIN

This series brings to life the background stories and events of the conflagration known as The Chaos War, as told in the *New York Times* best-selling novel *Dragons of Summer Flame*.

THE DOOM BRIGADE
MARGARET WEIS AND DON PERRIN

An intrepid group of draconian engineers must unite with the dwarves, their despised enemies, when the Chaos WAr erupts.

THE LAST THANE
DOUGLAS NILES

The Choas War rages across the surface of Ansalon, but what's going on deep under the mountains in the kingdom of Thorbardin? Anarchy, betrayal, and bloodshed.

JUNE 1998

TEARS OF THE NIGHT SKY
LINDA P. BAKER

A quest of Paladine becomes a test of faith for Crysania, the blind cleric. She is aided by a magical tiger-companion, who is beholden to the mysterious dark elf wizard Dalamar.

OCTOBER 1998

BRIDGES OF TIME

This series will bridge the stories in the thirty-year time span between the Classic and Fifth Age DRAGONLANCE novels.

SPIRIT OF THE WIND
CHRIS PIERSON

Riverwind, the fabled plainsman, answers the call for heroes and aids the kender in their struggle against the great red dragon Malystryx.

JULY 1998

LEGACY OF STEEL
MARY H. HERBERT

Five years after the Chaos War, Sara Dunstan, an outcast knight of Takhisis, risks a dangerous journey to Neraka and confirms rumors that the Dark Knights are reorganizing. Escaping from Neraka, she goes to the Tomb of the Last Heroes where she mourns for her fallen adopted son, Steel. In the tomb, the image of Steel appears before her to give her a message that will haunt her memory forever.

NOVEMBER 1998